Broken

Broken

Angela B. Chrysler

Copyright (C) 2015 Angela B. Chrysler
Layout design and Copyright (C) 2017 Creativia
Published 2017 by Creativia
ISBN: 978-1977723048
Cover art by Indigo Forest Designs
Edited by Mia Darien

Broken is a work of creative nonfiction. All events, opinions, and views are that of Angela B. Chrysler and are portrayed through subjective perspective based on the memory of Ms. Chrysler. While all the events are true, names, places, characteristics, and relationships have been altered and/or changed to protect the identity and privacy of the people involved. Some characters have been combined into one. Others have been divided into two, while some have been dramatized to better suit the story. The events themselves remained unaltered to the best of the author's memory. The dialogue was composed to create the essence of conversations in an effort to recreate the scene and mood best to the author's memory, and is not to be taken as verbatim quotes.

All rights reserved. No part of this book may be reproduced or transmitted in any form or by any means, electronic or mechanical, including photocopying, recording, or by any information storage and retrieval system, without the author's permission.

This one is for me because it has to be...

...and for Tribble, who shared and endured much of the same hell alongside me.

Preface

The events revealed in *Broken* are based on a true story—my story—and are shown exactly as I remember them best to my ability. Writing *Broken* was one of the hardest things for me to write and began as a very personal experience. In one week, I wrote 56,000 words. In the second week, I revised *Broken* and finished the manuscript at 96,000 words. Over the next two weeks, I edited *Broken* as my beta-reader provided feedback. Within those two weeks, I relived every event all over again.

I am writing to you, dear reader, because there are a few things I wish to say.

All mental healing begins with awareness. *Broken* was written as the events shown in Part Five occurred. I had decided to do what I've always talked about doing: accept my loneliness instead of fighting it and become a hermit. With this decision came one simple question: Am I sure this is what I want? To determine this answer, I wrote *Broken*.

As you will see, I needed to remember. I needed to make myself aware. I needed answers that were dependent on a change of perspective. Perspective. That is what this is really about. Perspective. The only way I could gain the perspective I needed was to write *Broken*. This was all about being honest with myself and coming to terms with what I am.

I wrote this not to berate those who wronged me, to wallow in self-pity, or to help others. I wrote this for me. I wrote this to understand why I was what I had become and to decide if I had to accept loneliness. *Broken* is simply my journal that I wrote for me. The more I wrote, the more I became aware of how absolutely broken I am. Through my writing, I captured my state of mind and the severity of my mental conditions. I wrote this for me. I chose to publish it for you.

By the time I finished *Broken*, I realized three basic truths:

1. My children were being affected by my mental conditions.
2. It was time to be honest with myself.
3. Many others could benefit from this reading experience.

This third truth is what led me to make a very conscious decision. *Broken* is raw.

This manuscript has seen one revision, one carefully selected beta reader, and one authorial edit. My editor put Broken through two professional edits. That is it.

Normally, I would subject a book to multiple revisions, more than three dozen edits, and a dozen beta readers before even allowing my editor to see this, let alone you, dear reader. This revision/editing process is gruesome and mandatory. However, my perspective and mental awareness changed so quickly after writing *Broken* that, to edit this manuscript or pass it on to several beta-readers, would be to lose the honesty that I had captured. It is imperative, that I not change a thing.

I did not review *Broken* for story, flow, or characterization because I truly believe the more I revised and edited this manuscript, the more I would lose what I needed to present here. Near the end of my first and only authorial edit, I caught myself applying changes that I soon realized altered the psychological meaning. Those changes could complicate the process needed for diagnoses and my own awareness. More importantly, those changes could have allowed me to slip back into denial. I removed the additions made, finished that only edit, then cut myself off from this manuscript. I repeat for emphasis. I cut myself off from the manuscript. If the reading is rough, I ask that you forgive me.

The topics covered in *Broken* are difficult for some people. I portray a number of sensitive subject matters including animal abuse, torture, graphic rape scenes, violence, strong language, and drug references. I do not sugar coat any of this. Rape, torture, and abuse are true horrors people live through. No dramatization was needed for this part, and I do not believe in softening the truth. *Broken* is brutal, ugly, and honest. It was not written for shock factor. It was written only for me.

If you are victim of sexual abuse, I strongly encourage you to speak to a therapist before reading this book. Not doing so could prematurely awaken memories you may not be ready for. The results could be disastrous.

As always, I thank you for your support.

Warmest wishes and may the kindest of words always find you.
Angela B. Chrysler

*Sink into my mind with me.
I will show you what I see.*

You are my sunshine.
My only sunshine.
You make me happy when skies are gray.
You'll never know, dear, how much I love you.
Please don't take—

Who Am I?

When I was 15 years old, I began studying philosophy: Theology, Logic and formal argument, Socratic Method, Psychology, Karl Jung, a complete history of, and Existentialism. While Logic became the backbone of my existence and Theology ends off prejudice (Yes. I studied Theology of all things, to end prejudice), nothing quite helped me identify who I am like Existentialism: the study of why we exist.

I'm not doing this for you. I have too much Ayn Rand in me to ever write for others. I'm doing this for me. Because, for the first time in twenty years, I don't know who I am anymore. And I can't find me.

I was recently challenged with the question, "why do I exist". I like to think I put up a hell of an argument, though he may disagree. In all honesty, it's a question I haven't stopped thinking about since. I knew the answer once.

I exist to conquer Death. Death has it in for me and I for Him. We never quite learned how to get along. I think He's determined to take me. I, on the other hand, have different plans. So I run from Him. I hide. We're waiting it out to see who wins.

But, I live knowing He will win and some day He will defeat me. For me, there is no after life. There is no second chance. It's why I live life to the fullest now. It's why I smile and laugh and love and live as deeply as I know how because this... this is all we have. Every choice I make is with this in mind that this life right here, right now, is all I've got. And I could never live with myself if I squandered this. Yes. This mind set has shaped my morals and ethics, but that is for another time.

It isn't fear of Death that keeps me running, certainly not fear of the End. It is simply fear of being forgotten. I am terrified I won't be remembered. For if we are not remembered, what lives have we truly lived? I can't help but think about this. This fear drives me in every choice I make. So many people like to say their children are their legacy, but how many of us can recall the names of our Great Great-grandparents?

Let's face it. Your legacy will forget you. And in three generations, they won't even know that their dislike for mixing foods came from you, which came from a long line of grandfather's who didn't like mixing their peas with carrots (I mean really why would you do that!? Green and orange don't mix!) or that their incessant impulse to lie stems from a multi-generation legacy they never knew. I have dedicated my life to the truth to compensate for the generation of Liars I have stemmed from. If there is one truth I am certain of in me, I do not lie. There's been enough falsified records throughout human history. I refuse to contribute to that.

We strive to record our history books so that we will know where we came from and so we can learn from our past. *laughs* We never learn. I have studied more than six thousand years of human history. All I see is the human race making the same damn mistakes over and over again.

1. Rule – You don't burn the books
2. Rule – You don't destroy the art work

Hopefully, we will try to remember that when next we imperialize a nation. After six thousand years, you'd think we'd learn that lesson.

So back to my point. Why do I exist? I don't live to preserve the human race or contribute to our culture. I don't exist to please a deity who may or may not approve of my choices so that I may have a chance at an afterlife or a happy ending. I exist to be remembered. I write so that I may be remembered. I wish to say to the world, "I am someone worth remembering because I am. And what about me is worth remembering? Well, that's my story now, isn't it?

Prologue

I opened the red door of my cottage and peered through the crack into the early morning and at the stranger who approached my door. My home was out of the way of everything. Those who came to visit had to make an effort, and almost no one made the effort. I liked it that way.

"Miss Lundy?" the stranger said nervously. "Miss Elizabeth Lundy?"

Like a sniper staring through the scope of a rifle, I assessed the youth, determined the level of threat he posed, and punched out the stats in my head: Male. Twenty-two years. Five-five. One twenty pounds. Thin arms. Wide shoulders, straight back. If he worked out, he could turn more than a few heads. Pity he didn't bother.

He smiled a bright smile that exposed a decent set of teeth. Everything about his composure exuded relief and elation once he saw that I hadn't slammed the door in his face.

"Good morning," he said and it truly was. The sun bathed the deep greens of the forest and hills despite the white clouds that streaked the Irish sky. The stream that cut through the land behind him caught the light and glistened like crystal glass. The rains would be here by evening, but for now, it was a very good morning.

He was American. New England. His hair was sandy, short, and brushed back. Eyes were hazel and clear. Skin, pasty pale. Not the fair Irish pale I had grown used to seeing, but an unhealthy sickly complexion one can only get from living in an office too long. Desk jockey, I concluded. Pencil pusher. Virgin. I could take him. I could teach him a few things. I would break him.

"Dia Duit," I answered softly and waited for an explanation.

"Miss Lundy. I'm William D. Shaw from the university." He nervously shuffled his bag then freed and extended a long, slender hand. His fingers were strong, almost pianist quality and I felt my blood rise when I slid my hand into his. Strong shake. Confident. Not feeble or limp. I imagined his hands on me. Sliding up my neck, through my hair. If he knew what he was doing, that was. He didn't look like he would. He was shaking, but doing a decent job keeping it together all things considered.

"We spoke on the phone," he said. "Well... we didn't speak on the phone so much as I left you a voice message. I... May I come in?"

I released his hand and noted the warmth. His blood pressure was high, but no sweat. That was a plus.

I pulled my cell from my pock and woke the phone. Yep. There was the message I didn't want to listen to yesterday. I hated checking my voicemail. I associate it with matters of importance and nothing ever was. Such a pain. I also hated guests, change, interruptions, and the feeling I got when someone came to my door. Anxiety, terror, then the arousal. I wanted him to leave and afterward I would indulge in a bit of fantasy. The anxiety always won and I rushed them out the door. I never invited them in. Never asked them to sit down. They were not welcome. They needed to know that. But I had promised myself I would do better. I had felt myself regressing again. Two months was too long to go without contact. Even I knew this. I could invite him in or don my coat and go out. I felt sick at the thought of a crowded room.

"Yes. Come in," I said and pushed the door open, giving him room enough to enter my domicile while granting myself the space for my own comfort.

Mine was a small domicile with one floor, perfect for just me. Aged rich planks made up the wood floor and whitewashed stone formed the walls, which were dressed in moss, roses, and ivy on the outside. The old kitchen that greeted guests, if ever I had any, extended into an eatery that turned a sharp corner around the only bathroom and into a quaint living room I had converted into a greenhouse years ago.

Aside from a plain but comfortable sage couch, a rocking chair where a faux fur blanket hung on the back, and a bookshelf containing my most prized possessions, the room was dripping in plants. Floor plants, hanging plants, and floral potted things all strategically positioned to bask in the morning light that poured in through the giant bay window where my tabby cat, Cookie, spent her days watching the birds. That room gave the same feel as an old forest. I loved reading in that room. A Steinway electric piano graced the corner and provided a gracious view of the forest outside when I played. My bedroom was accessible only through the green room.

Mr. Shaw stepped into the small part of my kitchen reserved for dining. He studied the converted living room/greenhouse across from the dining table. Cookie flipped her long, plush tail and stared at the birds through the large bay window where the morning sun seeped in.

He appeared surprised at the simple accommodations and inhaled the scent of Irish stew simmering on the stove. Directly left of the red door was the only fireplace I used to dry the air on the dampest of days and coldest of nights.

"What can I do you for, Mr. Shaw?" I asked.

"Thank you, Miss. Lundy, for seeing me," he said. "Please, call me William."

I gave him a disapproving stare.

"I was wondering if you would be willing to do an interview with me? I'm a big fan. Longtime fan, actually, and your work with the Druid Series was astounding. Ian was..."

I said nothing, unimpressed with his compliment, but forced a smile. I was still too annoyed at the interruption.

"I've been following you for quite some time and... well, nothing is known about you," he said. "Nothing, really. It's all so limited."

He saw I wasn't impressed and was eager for him to get to the point.

"Right," he said. "So I was wondering if you would be willing to do an interview..."

The tension was unbearable. I watched the way he rubbed his thumb on the strap of his back pack.

He was still rambling when I zoned back in and hadn't heard a word he had said. I took great delight in watching him squirm. Maybe if he was as anxious as I, he would get the hint and leave.

"My dear Mr. Shaw," I said and raised my chin so that he could see the sunlight graze my neck. "Please, speak plainly," I said softly.

I felt myself doing it again. Already my defenses were up. If I could coerce him into thinking about sex, I would be safer. I needed to calm down. He was no threat. I had already assessed that. Good God, I missed my swords.

"Beggin' your pardon ma'am?"

I watched him glance at the slender lines of my neck. It was working. He would calm down soon enough.

"There is something else you wish to ask me," I gently declared. I watched him relax and I smiled. I knew the light gleamed in my eye and I tipped my head ever so slightly. I had this routine mastered. "Instead of winding your nerves into all sorts of knots, please just ask what you will of me."

I could feel the smooth coercion in my voice, the way my words rolled off my tongue and soothed him like a charmed snake heeding the words of a succubus. He inhaled and I waited patiently.

"I had hoped to wait until later to ask this, you being a recluse and all. I..." He nervously glanced away. "I wish to do a full biography on you."

The room fell quiet. The boy was holding his breath as if afraid my answer hinged on whether or not he breathed in the next two minutes. I toyed with the idea of delaying an answer for ten minutes just to watch him squirm.

After three minutes, I put him out of his misery. "You wish to write a biography."

"Yes, ma'am."

"About me?"

"Yes."

"So..." I grinned. I could see his jaw line twitch. He still hadn't breathed. "...you've come to descend into the bowels of my psyche, have you?" I took up the coffee pot and poured myself a cup. "And what is it you think you'll find there, Mr. Shaw?"

"Uh..."

I added a tea-spoon of sugar and opened the fridge.

"Why a biography?" I clarified.

"Well, you've been strangely quiet about your life," he said. "Your past. Almost no one knows anything about you prior to your thirties. People want to know. I know some who have started a pool that you've killed someone. They think you're a serial killer hiding from the law."

I leaned out of the fridge, arching my brow. I permitted a smirk.

"It's the eyes," he said. "They..."

He caught the look, my posture. Nothing he was saying impressed me and he knew it. For a moment, there was a hungry flash in his eye and surprising even me, he dumped his bag to the floor.

"Miss Lundy..." He took a step and I straightened my back, my hand went up and before he knew it, I was holding a knife to his throat. He didn't move.

"Miss Lundy?"

I blinked and realized he hadn't moved. There was no knife. There was only me and him in my kitchen. The fridge door was wide open. The coffee creamer in my hand. The look in his eyes was enough to know I had my boundaries and he was on them.

I knew where I was. It had been too long. I blinked back the image and tried to clear my head. I had to remember which world I was in. I put the creamer back in the fridge and reached for the Baileys I kept with my whiskeys and wines on the top of the fridge instead.

"This isn't just about your books, Miss Lundy," he said. "This is about you, the author. People want to know about you, the woman behind the books, and you've told us precious little."

"That was no accident," I said, pouring two shots into my coffee. "Do you want coffee?"

"Please. Black."

My invitation for coffee was enough to urge him to slide off his coat and drop it on the back of the chair nearest the door.

I let the silence settle between us while I poured a second cup then walked to the table beside my guest. I set the coffees down and extended a hand, directing him to sit.

"So," I sighed, taking my seat as he scrambled eagerly to take his. "You wish to write my biography."

"Yes, ma'am," he said. "People want to know who you are. What you are. What made you write the books that you write. They wish to know your schooling, your loves, your struggles. What challenges in your life made you what you are. They want to know your lows, your highs. They want to know..." He sighed. "They want to know what struggles shaped you to write the macabre you portray in your books."

I clutched my coffee. I felt sick. The challenges in my life? I held my cup steady against my shaking hands. I didn't trust myself to move. I knew what he asked. The poor whelp didn't. My hands went white.

"Get out," I said darkly.

William stared at me stupidly, and I felt the anger surge. He didn't move. Nor did I.

Perhaps I needed to tell my story, to talk, to not be alone. I knew where I was. If I were alone right now I would descend into the bowels of my mind and, this time, I wasn't certain I could come back. There was less and less reason for me to.

I heard William shuffle and take up his bag from the floor. I thought of Jacob and Isaiah. I thought of my Raven. Oh, how much I missed Raven. So much. So... so much.

Don't think about that.

I took a sip of my coffee and felt the tears burn, but that well had dried up long ago. I heard William take up his coat. He opened the door and just like that, I didn't want him to go.

"You think this is some love story?" I said.

He stopped at the door.

"The life I've lived, you think it's something to admire, to aspire to? You think I hoard romanticism within my silence?"

He watched me with a look, uncertain if he had offended me or not.

"You hope to hear a fairy tale, Mr. Shaw, a "Hemingway-lost-love" story, but what you will get is a nightmare."

He closed the door.

"There are those whose lives are hell," I said. "Hell barely begins to explain what I have lived. The books I wrote were buried beneath the endless screams. Most days, I can not write or think or breathe over the screaming in my head."

William dumped his bag to the floor. This time, he remained at the door.

"You let me into your home," he said. "You agreed to hear me out. You invited me in and poured me coffee. Part of you wants this story told."

And he wasn't wrong. I did want this story told. I did want to release this poison inside of me. Something longed to put it out there. I ached to be heard. I had tried so many times before. I had written the outlines, drawn up the plans. I knew exactly what parts to tell. I knew which parts needed to be heard. But it felt selfish. It felt wrong.

A part of me ached to do this in the chance that someone, anyone, would hear me, just once. Oh, how I longed to be heard just once. Perhaps that was why I always spoke my mind. I was tired of not being heard.

I gazed at the man-boy in front of me. The fire in his eye confirmed his determination.

"It feels selfish," I said. "Talking about myself like this."

"I'm asking you to do this," he said. "I want to know."

"I don't want to," I said.

Something in the boy told him to hold his tongue. Now was the time to listen. For that, I was grateful.

"I want to bury this inside me," I said. "You must understand. There is a part of me that always longs for death. There are days, it hurts too much. I can not get angry. I can never be angry. I won't allow it. I'm afraid of what I will do if ever I get angry."

He stared with that look I've seen so many times. The look everyone gets when they hear pure honesty. People don't hear it often. The inner-most thoughts of our psyche. Those are the words we keep secret.

Not I.

I gazed out the south windows across the table. The hills were green and calm as if they had suffered and weathered and aged over a lifetime of ancient wars. And endured it all, they did. Today, nothing more could bother them. Nothing mattered anymore. Endurance teaches us one thing, if nothing else: to savor the calm after a storm. To savor the lives of those who survived.

Hadn't I savored long enough? Perhaps it was time to reflect.

"Twenty-four hours," I said.

He blinked as if stunned I had agreed.

I took up my coffee, grateful I had added the double shot. This morning, today, I would need it.

"I'll give you until dawn. Whatever you ask of me, I'll answer. Whatever you wish, I'll consent."

He blinked again, this time relief, shock. He didn't smile.

He dropped his coat, slid off his shoes and placed them properly beside the door, toes pointing away from the wall. He grabbed his bag and, in a rush, dropped a notebook and pens on the table.

He pulled out a recorder, checked its batteries, and positioned it between us. I waited until he was settled in before beginning.

"How is your tolerance for swearing, Mr. Shaw?"

"Uh... fine, I guess," he answered.

"If I am to tell this, then I am telling this the only way I know how," I said sternly.

He nodded attentively.

"At times, I will be vulgar, crass, and uncouth. I will be graphic and blunt and honest. Understand that if I attempt to censor myself, then there is a chance—a good chance—I will not finish this. So I ask again, Mr. Shaw, can you handle vile and vulgar?"

He nodded. I knew I made him nervous.

Good. He needed to be. "Let's start," I said.

He settled into the chair and positioned his pen, eager for the lesson.

"I have a fear of relationships," I began. "When I love, I love easy, deep, hard, strong, and long. But I can not marry. I can not live with anyone. I can not accept gifts from anyone or let anyone close enough for intimacy. If we do this..." William looked up from his paper, suddenly aware that I was addressing him directly. "...you are not to touch me," I said. "You are not to comfort me. You are not to approach me."

He stared at me, not sure why I was saying this. But I knew. I had given this disclaimer so many times before. This was the best way.

"Know my intentions now. Know what I am, so when I flirt and smile and play with you, you'll know exactly what my intentions are. We will never be more than friends. If we have sex, it will be nothing more than just sex," I said.

"I will cry afterward and you are to let me. If you touch me, I will attack you. I will want to kill you."

He looked stupidly at me now. But when we got into it and I threw myself at him, if I broke and lunged at him, he'd know why. He'd need to know why.

"Do not love me. You can not have me. You can not keep me or wife me. I can not be owned or possessed. I will stray. I always stray. If you get close, there will be a day when I will push you away only to pull you close to me to push you away again.

"Do not love me. I will love you hard and long and deep, but to keep you safe from me, I will destroy what little is left between us. I will reject you. Let me save you the time and trouble. Do not love me. You have been warned."

* * *

I can feel it in me, right now. My hands shake, my breathing is erratic. Fear.

In most people, it provokes a response to run. At times, it evolves, and encourages most to fight. In me, arousal sets in. Right now, I'm scared, but I don't want to fight. I want to lay you down and fuck you. Cold, hard, meaningless sex.

I will ravage you so quickly that you will have no idea what to do with it. That is my plan and I know exactly how you will respond. You'll throw your arms up and let me devour you because I move so fast you won't have time to keep up. After the shock wears off, you'll give in and respond. Your mind will be blank and I'll do things to you that you can not imagine.

It will all be about you. I will fuck you and taste you. This isn't love. This isn't sex. This is fear. I will make you cum and then I will run. That is what I was trained to do.

Broken

My brain is programmed this way. My body is conditioned this way. Fear is my trigger. This is what I am. Fear. This is what I have become. This is my defense. You asked for my story. I will tell you exactly how I came to be like this.

Think of how often we fear. How often we experience it every day. Fear is the core human emotion. We are prey. Prey move on fear, live on fear, they think on fear. Fear makes mothers kill to save babies. It makes men into warriors. It turns hate into prejudice. It turns Hitlers into leaders. Fear is the primary emotion programmed into the center of our brain to command each and every choice to keep us alive long enough to breed. Fear of death spawns religions. Fear of the unknown spawns philosophy. Fear of repercussions spawns lies. Fear of isolation spawns love.

But I don't hate. I don't fight. Not anymore. I don't lie. My fear converts to lust. The stronger the fear, the more I pursue. Its honed in me. My body has grown around it, shaped it until I drip sex in my smile, in my eyes, in my posture, in my words. I control the flux in my voice to provoke the most sensual of images from you. Every word I speak is with the intent to relax you, to woo you, to draw you in, to make you love me, so I can weaken you, kill you, and run.

That is what I am.

Even now, I want to fuck you hard. Because I'm scared. I want to pull off my skin with lust and devour you. That is how scared I am. And if I don't...

* * *

I pinched the bridge of my nose. I wanted to cry. I wrung my hand on knee. The desire to lunge across the table and fuck William—Mr. Shaw—right then was unbearable.

"Are you okay?" he asked.

I looked up and allowed him to look right through me. I know how my eyes appear to others: honest and completely open. Haunting is what I've been told. My smile forever glows in my eyes and I know it. Too many men have told me this. I'm lethal. Everything about me, I unknowingly developed to attract and seduce a male. I mastered seduction, but there is venom in my blood. It drips from my thorns.

I watched William's eyes dilate. I watched his breathing increase, his neck flush red. I made him feel things, think things all with a glance. I had this mastered. If I smiled right then he would think I desired him. They always think I want them. I was already working on him. I did it the moment I spoke my words. I had a way with words. It was just one more bit of poison I used to seduce.

"I don't exactly wear my heart on my sleeve," I said. "I wear my soul in my eyes. Everything in my life primed me for the next event good or bad. Every event left me in the mental state I needed to be in to enter and maintain the next stage. If something had altered at any point along the way, then maybe I stood a chance. But it didn't. One train wreck prepared me for the next train wreck, which only prepared me for the next train wreck until I had inevitably become what I am before you.

"The hard part is watching men—good men, decent men—fall for me over and over again. The hard part is not knowing how to shut this off. The hardest part is not being afraid."

"When life itself seems lunatic, who knows where madness lies? Perhaps to be too practical is madness. To surrender dreams — this may be madness. Too much sanity

Broken

may be madness — and maddest of all: to see life as it is, and not as it should be!"- Don Quixote

Part One: Classical Conditioning

Chapter 1

I guess the best place to start is the beginning. I'm not going to drone on about every tedious event of every year. I'm going to be honest. I remember very little from the first eight years of my life.

I was born in New York. I remember the staircase where my older brother, Charles, and I threw little parachute men off the banister while my father watched the news with his back to us. I remember the toy I played with in the driveway that belonged to my neighbors. I remember the walk we took down the road in the stroller, and my sister's bedroom: a large closet painted pink. I remember my mother crying over a load of ruined clothes because she had washed a black crayon with the laundry. The dryer had melted wax all over the machine and the clothes. That day taught me never to wash children's clothes without checking the pockets first. I think I was four.

Her mother was there. It was the only time I ever saw her mother leave the dump of a trailer where she festered. My mother was Irish and had a sliver of Egyptian in her. O'Lundy and Flannigan were the family names. I don't know much about her family. In fact, I know almost nothing. My mother was—and is—a chronic liar. Don't get me wrong, I love my mother. But I don't believe a word that has ever left her mouth.

My mother was beautiful, but insecure, and she boosted her lack of confidence with boasting and bragging. Every story was embellished. Every truth, exaggerated. The rule with my mother is simple. Believe nothing. My mother was, to say the least, messed up. From my earliest memories, the signs were there.

Her punishments were random, unpredictable, and, at times, unusually cruel. My half-brother, Shaun, would receive the brunt of those fits and, more times than not, she humiliated him to such a degree that it left him scarred. Most of the time, she exercised the classic discipline from the early 19th century. Bend over and hold the chair while I spank you with a belt. She was the mother who literally washed our mouths out with a bar of laundry soap. I grew up with my mother threatening to spoon feed us castor oil. I think we were the only children in the school who knew what castor oil was.

But it wasn't the punishments she doled out that groomed my siblings and I into what we would become. It was the constant, dedicated lack of support and complete absence of physical touch. My mother made sure we were clean, cared for, and beautiful. My brothers had suits. My sister and I were dressed as porcelain dolls with curls, petticoats, pinafores, and saddle shoes. I don't remember a single hug. Ever. What little I remember in way of affection was too boldly overshadowed by her rage, her anger, her screaming, her reprimands.

My father was a by-the-book kind of guy. According to his religion, he was to go to work and bring home the bacon while the wife cooked, cleaned, and mothered children. The only time my father stepped in was when we deserved an extra hard spanking. We went to church on Sundays, Saturdays, and Wednesdays. Yes, we were well-behaved children. Yes, we were manicured into perfect ladies and gentlemen. My mother would have it no other way at any cost.

I remember very little of my father from those days. I remember when I was four, we were camping and a recent spanking had left a bruise on my leg. My father never spanked me or my sister ever again after that. I remember that camping trip well, though. We went to one of the many state parks, and oh... we swam beneath the falls. I loved the forests in New York. The water and gorges... the trails. More on that in a moment. I could talk for hours on the forests of New York.

A few years later, we moved to a larger house that I have no memory of, then, when I turned eight, we moved into the ranch. Town was an isolated village with a population of one thousand and was fifteen minutes away. We had two traffic lights. We lived on a dirt road and the ranch-styled house sat in a clearing. I remember that day very well. Not the house, but the forest, endless stretches of woodland area that went on for days behind the house. All around me were hills and mountains covered in endless forest.

Barefoot, I would run to the trees and play. For hours I would explore the Wood.

The forest was old. So very old. You could tell there were places where no man had walked in centuries, if ever. There was a peace there. A refined, ancient peace preserved from society, electricity, and people. Electricity is loud. Did you know? When we had power outages, the peace from the forest would seep in and blanket the house in perfect, beautiful silence.

Those were my happiest of days.

One hundred years ago, there had been a road that cut through the wood. An old wagon trail still remained. Moss and grass had grown over it, streams flowed across it, shaping it into an old path through the wood. I always strayed from the path. I would climb into those woods and find little newts, the beautiful little red ones with black spots. They're endangered. I would love them, carefully pick them up, pat their tiny heads, and return them to their streams and beds of moss. I visited them often. I knew they were precious. I miss them.

I remember little from that time. Only the forest. I remember when the screaming got loud, I would run barefoot into the wood and find my newts. I named the trees and followed the streams to the gorge. Oh, how I loved the gorge.

If you've ever seen central New York, you'll know it's all hillside. Everything is at a constant forty-five to sixty-five degree slope. Houses and farms were built on the occasional slot of not-so flat land. The wagon trail in the wood was on a rare layout of farmable land flanked by sheer drop offs, massive slopes, and plummeting gorges. This was my playground and oh, did I use it.

I had this one spot in the forest mastered where I could jump on the leaves, slide for three feet, snag a branch and slingshot myself around and bolt, hopping and sliding, surfing the hills on leaf litter into the gorge. I would end my dance on a jump into the shallow streams with my skirts hiked up to my thighs. That was my home. That was where I wanted to be more than any place in the world.

The stream continued down to the river below. The Tioughnioga (Tee-off-nee-o-ga) River. Some summers we would swim in that river. It was so, so beautiful. The streams that trickled down the mountains cut through the shale and earth, leaving behind massive walls of slate and stone that cradled streams and waterfalls. One stream formed the Gorge.

The Gorge had walls nearly thirty feet high. I would climb them in my skirts, stand at the ledge, and gaze down at the deer with their fawn. Up there with the wind and the trees, I found me. I could slip so easily into the elements and feel them move through me. It felt like I could really fly and wanted, so badly, to jump, to try. Self-preservation and Darwin said otherwise. I could see the rows of waterfalls and, upon, my descent, I would strip off my dress and swim naked in the pools of cool, clear water. I crossed rivers and streams hopping bare-foot from stone to stone.

There, in my glen, I was home. That is the only happiness I remember.

* * *

Life on the ranch was quite the opposite. Life in the ranch was hell. Together, my parents had four children: Charles, myself, Marie, and Eugene. The year we moved into the ranch, our half-brother, Shaun, moved in. Shaun was my father's son from his first marriage and my mum hated him.

My mum was a screamer. The screaming was relentless. There was always noise. If we fell and got scraped my mother screamed and coldly reassured us that we were fine, as if she was annoyed that we bled at all. There was no hug. No kiss. No contact.

At night, we watched TV. My sister sat snuggled into my father's lap while I sat on the floor as far from everyone as

I could. No one touched me. I was fine with that. I don't think I would have known what to do with it if they did.

I remember seeing Marie, her thumb in her mouth, her head resting on my father's shoulder. I remember wishing. I wanted it. I pined. So I hated. I never said anything. "Children should be seen and not heard" was verbally beaten into us. You didn't speak. You didn't ask. You didn't talk. I turned my thoughts back to the TV.

TV.

That was a memory I had. The TV was precious and when it was on, we were not to speak to our father, and it was on from the moment he came home from work to the moment we sat down to dinner to the time we went to bed. The TV was more important than us. My father loved it more than me. It was one of the first lessons I learned and I learned this lesson well. I detested the TV. It was a fifth sibling who absorbed all my father's love and attention. I was jealous. I loathed it.

Dinner was the only time we had with our father. Again, we were not to speak, but my father did. Every meal, he made his rounds. He'd start with my half-brother, Shaun, and would spend fifteen minutes telling him how worthless he was, how selfish and miserable he was. He moved on to Charles and repeated the lecture. Then it was my turn.

I would slip food in my mouth and I'd hear the words.

"You're selfish, ungrateful, and spoiled."

I'd swallow.

"You only think of yourself."

I spooned food into my mouth flanked by tears.

"You don't spend any time with the family."

It hurt to swallow. My stomach tightened. I lost my appetite and I stopped eating.

"You only ever think of yourself."

He went onto my sister. She was five at the time. Eugene was two. He got skipped.

The next night, the routine repeated itself. My father would drive in.

"Go to your rooms," my mother would say. "You know your father doesn't want to see you."

We scattered, knowing we would be scolded if seen.

I'd steal a peek. He kissed my mother and, after changing out of his work clothes, he turned on the TV and watched. My mother called and we'd sit in silence at the dinner table while my father made his rounds again.

"You're selfish and spoiled."

I'd spoon food into my mouth.

"You care only for yourself and shut everyone out."

I'd swallow and the tears would fall.

"You're ungrateful and spoiled."

My stomach would clamp and I wouldn't eat.

"You're useless and rotten and spoiled."

His words became a recording that plays in my head to this day every time I try to eat.

Chapter 2

I don't believe my father is a bad man. I think he is a very good man who had no idea how to parent children. I think he did his best. I think he did love us with all his heart.

Do not misunderstand me. If he was to ask me today if I know he loves me, I would say, 'yes.' But a part of me will never believe it. Growing up, I had never seen it. I still don't see it. I think he loves me today because I am a parent and I believe all parents love their children. Okay, not all. Some parents are that horrible, but I think my father simply didn't know how to parent. I think he was clueless, confused, and, at times, completely unaware of the problem. He did his best. He still had no idea what I am. I don't think he ever will.

I remember one movie we watched that made my father tear up.

"I do not know how to love. Please teach me," the actor said.

I watched my father choke up.

"I feel that way," he said.

My father is not good with words. I think it meant a lot for him to finally hear those words. I imagine he had needed to hear them for a long time. I'll say it again, I think my father did his best. I think my father tried. I think my father didn't have a fucking clue back then.

As a mother, I understand and appreciate that conflict, to not know how to love the way a parent should, to be flying blind and have no idea if what you are saying to your children every day is crippling them. As a child, all I saw were the monsters.

In my early life, I had one friend, one solace that wasn't the forest. I had my black short-haired cat with white patches on her feet. Patches. She was old and sweet and would run off into the Wood for days at a time.

Before the situation in the house turned too abysmal, Shaun and I would wander into the forest. He had his stick as all little boys must. As we walked, he hacked the flowers. I hated that. If it was beautiful, Shaun destroyed it. That should have been the first clue that there was a problem.

"Don't do that," I'd say.

"Why?" He'd hack at a patch with his stick. "They're just flowers."

"They're beautiful and we're in their home. Stop killing them."

"They're just flowers." He'd hack down another patch.

We arrived at the tree house we had started that summer and never finished. The ladder was gray and had begun to crack under the hot of summer and cold of winter. The floorboards no longer sustained our weight. We hadn't been to the tree house in months.

"See this," Shaun said, tapping a pile of stones beside the tree. "Know what this is?"

"A marker," I said. There were a lot of them around there like you see here, in Ireland. This one was small. Very small.

"No," he said. "You don't know what this is."

He had a tone that jeered my ignorance. Not friendly or informative at all. Simply boastful. 'I know something you don't know,' he passively said with his smile.

"So what!" I said and he hacked at another flower. "I don't care."

"You will." He hacked at another flower.

"I know what it is!" I said, though I didn't. I didn't care. I was too annoyed at his smugness.

"No, you don't know," he said. He hacked at another flower.

"I don't care!" I stomped off.

"You will!" He hacked at another flower.

"Shut up! I don't care!"

"It's Patches' grave."

I turned and he stood there smiling at me, proud of his power trip.

"You're lying," I said.

"Nope. She's dead." He hacked at another flower.

"You're lying!" I screamed and stomped off, blinded by tears.

"What's wrong now, Elizabeth?" my mother screamed through the kitchen window.

"Shaun says Patches is dead!" I cried.

"She is."

I looked up at my mother's cold face in the window. The annoyance on her face added to the pain of being excluded on top of the pain of losing my friend.

"Why didn't you tell me?" I asked.

"We didn't want to upset you," she said as if she was telling me my clothes were in the dryer. She was gone, back to her dishes without so much as a hug or encouraging word.

Sobbing, I slumped to the front of the house and dropped into the porch swing. There, I cried and let the hurt wash through me. I cried for an hour, loud and long. And no one ever came.

* * *

After Patches' death, my half-brother developed a new hobby. He collected critters. While I ran to the Wood to escape the screaming, and embrace and nurture my isolation, Shaun diverted his attention to the wildlife.

He gathered up frogs and snakes and stones. One by one, he would throw them into the kiddie pool out back and, one at a time, would pull them out, set them on the back porch, and stone them to death.

My sister and I would scream and cry. "Let them go!"

He'd laugh and I'd watch him smash its hind leg. It would try to hop away on a foot that wasn't there. He'd laugh again and throw another rock. Its stomach would split and it tried to escape, but its skin and blood glued it to the hot porch. Shaun laughed while we screamed for it. He'd smash all its limbs, it's back, and it's belly. And when it was done breathing, he would pick up the remains and throw them at us.

We'd scream and he'd take up a snake.

"What are you doing?" my mother shouted, annoyed by our sobbing.

"Shaun is killing them!"

"So what!" she screamed. "Boys will be boys! Get away from him if it bothers you!"

Get away? And leave the poor victims to suffer their fate? Alone?

A stone smashed the snake's tail. It slithered, leaving behind a trail of blood while making its escape. It made it further than the frog before Shaun stomped it, holding it in place with his foot. Another stone to its back. Blood and guts oozed and my sister and I cried.

"Let it go! Leave it alone!"

Shaun laughed and threw another rock, smashing its body until it was dead. When he was done, he threw the mangled remains at us.

We couldn't leave. We couldn't leave them there alone to their demise. We wanted to help them. But he was too strong to stop. My mother stopped occasionally to tell us to leave Shaun be.

"Boys will be boys! Leave him alone!"

One by one, we watched him mutilate the bodies. We watched the frogs suffer then die. He started to see how long he could keep them alive. He took up the snakes and spun them over his head then slammed their little bodies to the ground. He beat them and broke them and when it was done, he threw the pieces at us.

* * *

I glanced at William across the kitchen table. He massaged his temple with his thumb. When he saw I had paused, he furrowed his brow in question.

"Where was your father in all of this?" he said.

"My father felt this was normal for siblings. He often boasted his own battles with his younger brothers."

"Yeah. Brothers. Not sisters." William's tone dripped with objection. "If I treated my sisters like I did my brother, my father would have whooped me."

I smiled at William's innocence.

"I think my father passed off Shaun's behavior as normal because if he didn't, he would have to own up to his own behavior.

"Shaun was obstinate, determined, and knew exactly what he wanted. He still does. And when there was something he didn't want to do, Shaun made sure he didn't do it. Homework was a constant battle. Every night, Shaun brought homework home. Every night my mother screamed at him to do it until my father stepped in.

"One night, my father stepped in and I watched him pin my step-brother to the floor. He took up the board he used to spank us and he beat my step-brother. Shaun squirmed and it struck his back. Shaun screamed and he raised a hand to us. 'Help me, please!' he screamed. 'Please! Help!' Mum, Marie, Charles, and I just watched while my father beat him. No one raised a hand. We just stood there and cried for him. No one dared stand against my father."

I felt William's eyes on me. Remembering revived an old hurt I had packed away and I crunched my brow in pain. I wanted to cry, but couldn't. The hurt was too old, too stale. I sighed and went on.

"My father knew there were problems with the family. He did try to fix them, but I think he wasn't sure how. He loved the idea of family vacations and made an effort to implement them. Every summer, we drove down to North Carolina and stayed at a cabin on a lake. The trips did work at first. For one week, we were able to put our lives on hold."

I fell back into the memory.

* * *

Most of our trips were filled with day long trips to the sea. I do remember once my mother touched me. I was eight and got caught in a rip tide. The undercurrent in the wave knocked my feet out from under me, but I was small. I went right under the water. As I tried to stand, another undercurrent swept my butt out from under me. I needed air, but I couldn't stand. I felt the ocean carry me. Each time I found the ground beneath me, another rip tide knocked it out from my hands.

I swallowed salt water and thrashed. I could not stand. My mother took my arm and hoisted me up. My head broke the surface and I gasped. I wouldn't go back to the ocean again. Not until I was old enough to keep my own body above water.

That same trip was accompanied with the worst ride home imaginable. We were on the highway heading back to New York in the station wagon. We had been on the road for about three hours when I found a handful of clear spiders crawling up my shin.

I brushed them off and found more on my calf. I brushed those off and found nearly a dozen on my other leg. By the time I wiped them off, my arm was covered and they were making their way to my neck. I screamed and slapped them away, but they crawled too fast.

"What's wrong, Elizabeth!" my mother shouted.

I brushed my leg again and more replaced them.

"There are spiders on me!" I screamed.

"So smash it!" my mother screamed back. Always the one to scream and not console.

I swiped at my arm and more came.

"I can't get them off!" I said. "Pull over!"

"Smash it!" my father said.

I screamed and rubbed them off my neck. I slapped them off my face. "There are hundreds!"

"Stop screaming!" my mother said.

"Pull over!" I screamed.

"We can't pull over!" my mother said. "We're on the highway!"

And so I sat, screaming and slapping the spiders away from my legs, my neck, my arms, my chest, and my face.

I won't lie. I have no idea how long I was in the back of that car. If I were to guess, I would say an hour. I know that isn't true. It felt like an hour. Felt like a day. It may have been ten... fifteen minutes. It may have been twenty. Regardless, I spent that time arguing with my parents to pull over, who were annoyed that I had inconvenienced them at all.

They slowed down and stopped the car along the side of the road. I was still slapping baby spiders off my body. I could feel them everywhere. My parents huffed and sighed while they opened the back seat of the wagon and pulled a shaking eight year old out of the blankets. I couldn't stop shaking. I couldn't get them off. My mother complained under her breath while she shook the spider nest from the blankets.

Five minutes later, and with a mouthful of complaints about how I overdramatized the situation, my mother shoved me back in the car with the blankets. No hug. No reassurance. No comfort. No sympathy. Just an earful of how much I had troubled them. I climbed back into the wagon sobbing and shaking without a single word of solace.

* * *

"This is all in your eighth year?" William asked, looking up from his writing.

I nodded. "Yes. I was eight. Comfort, compassion, and love were foreign to me. And I didn't question their lack of sympathy either. Already, I had come to expect nothing from them or anyone."

William skimmed over his list.

"Locked in a car with spiders, your only friend dead, which you aren't even told about, and then subjected to... how long did he torture the frogs and snakes?"

"That time?" I asked. "At least two hours."

"That time?"

"He mutilated all animals he came across," I said. "In the driveway, in the forest, in the yard. He had a turtle once. The poor thing. He took a rock and smashed its shell. He beat it into powder. It was so beautiful until Shaun got ahold of it. He caught a baby rabbit once. Rabbits scream, did you know? He picked it up by the ears. That sound... that sound... "

I burst into tears.

To this day, I can't hear that sound in my head without sobbing. I threw my hands to my head and rocked, squeezing my head, willing the screams to stop. I could hear it all over again. The sharp staccato of shrieking. A frequency that ripped the fabric of sound like the violin score of Psycho. I hugged myself to stop the shaking.

When I looked up, I saw William staring at me in horror. Poor virgin boy. He had no idea what he was in for.

"I begged my mother to release it," I said, still rocking. "Shaun wanted its feet. He was talking about cutting off its feet. It was the only good thing my mother ever did. While we were at school, she released it. Shaun was pissed."

I looked at the window. The morning sun was high and now poured in through the south window, streaking the table and my empty cup.

"I don't want to talk about it... I don't... "

I stood from the table and took up my cup and his. A moment later, I was rinsing the mugs and pouring ourselves two fresh cups.

"Tell me more about the dinners," William said, in an effort to change the subject while I added the Irish cream. "You said his words play back like a record every time you eat?"

"Every time," I said, setting the cups back on the table and sitting myself back down. "I don't eat. I hate food. I loathe it. It's a constant reminder that my father hates me. I don't eat breakfast. I don't eat lunch. I have to wait until starvation cramps my stomach before I can try to eat. If I'm stressed at all or someone yells at me while I'm hungry, my appetite immediately vanishes no matter how hungry I am. If I force myself to eat, I get sick. The longest I've gone without food is one week."

"One week without food," William repeated. He looked my petite frame over, but asked no questions.

"I survive on coffee," I said.

He returned to his notes. "Well, you are a writer," he sighed. "How did your siblings take to your father's dinner lectures?"

"Marie was so young, I don't think she even remembers. She quickly found a place in my father's heart. She was sweet and kind. A genuine daddy's girl. While I... wasn't. I think I am a mama's girl, but my mum didn't hold me or touch me. I really don't know what I am.

"My father dumped on Shaun and I, and only Shaun my lot. He developed a similar problem to mine. He was as smart as I, but stronger. Bolder too at that time. I was still too shy and obedient. I hadn't been broken yet. Shaun took up his plate and ate alone in his room. Stirred up a whole lot of hell with my father, but... he escaped for a short time anyway, while I endured it. At one point, Shaun stopped eating completely."

"How long did this go on for?" William asked.

"I don't know when it started. It's something that, in my mind, was always there. I think it was there before I was eight, but I'm speculating. I truly don't know. It ended when Charles stopped eating with us. He was seventeen. I was sixteen. And we stopped holding family dinners." I nodded, remembering more details as I spoke. "Yes. It stopped when our family dinners stopped. Charles refused to eat with us and if he did eat, he ate alone. I hadn't realized he had stopped eating completely until he was twenty and had collapsed in his room. Up to that point, he had accused me of being anorexic."

I caressed the handle of my mug, but could not raise the cup to drink.

"In truth, I think he was. He purposely wore clothes two sizes too big. He had a huge winter coat he wore all summer to hide his condition, and by convincing my father that I was anorexic, it took the attention off of him. I was enraged. My father insisted I was anorexic when I wasn't, all because my brother said I was. I ate, just not very much or often. And I never, never threw up my food. Nor did I ever think I was ugly or overweight.

"But when Charles fell..." I shook my head and stared at my full cup of coffee. "I was nineteen. By then, I had my own phone. Charles called me. I yelled at him for bothering me, but he cut me off to say he was paralyzed.

"I went downstairs to find an ninety pound skeleton laying on the floor. I woke my father who followed me downstairs and he fed Charles orange juice through a straw. Three glasses and thirty minutes later, my father picked my brother up off the floor. Charles had no muscle. That is when I realized... The mental nightmare he must have lived through...

My chest clamped and I burst. I cried right then for my brother in front of William.

"The whole time," I sobbed. "He was hurting as much as I... the whole time. He was just as torn up and dying on the inside as I had been. No matter what was being done to me, seeing him like that, I understood just how much hell he had endured. I knew because I too had endured it, and I understood. The hate, the hurt, the longing to be loved and never finding it. He had been as alone and as hurt as I all that time. And if we had just... if I had known, then maybe we could have shared our hell and maybe... just maybe... it wouldn't have been as bad as it was."

I cried, and William moved to stand from the table.

"Don't touch me!" I screamed, and he froze.

"You must not touch me," I said between sobs.

"I was going to get you a tissue," he said.

"No." I shook my head. "No pity. No comfort. No tissues."

He stared at me. I knew the look he was giving me. I didn't have to see. The look that reminds me how different I am. How broken I am. I had to explain. There would be more crying and he would have to know.

"Don't you see?" I said. I rocked myself and sobbed. I was so cold, and I held myself to shut out the chill that wasn't there. "I've never seen comfort. I don't know what it is. I wouldn't know what to do with it if..." The words caught in my throat. I had to explain. He had to know. "If you tried to soothe me, to comfort me, even so much as say, 'I'm sorry,' it would confuse me."

The look on his face confirmed my suspicion. He didn't understand. He couldn't understand. But I had to try. He had to know.

"Your efforts to comfort me would only evoke more fear. I would panic and I would see you as danger. Don't you get it?"

The shock in his eyes made me desperate.

"The only physical contact I've ever known is pain. For the first twenty years of my life, all human contact hurt me. There never was anything else! Approach me and I will run. And if I can't... I will sleep with you. I would let you hug me. I would bury my face into your neck and slide my mouth over your skin. I would kiss you."

I felt it. Already, I ached to have sex, to seduce, sate, sedate, and run. I was shaking with want to fuck him.

"I would grind you," I said. "And when you react, I would ravage you. I would view your attempt to comfort me as a threat and I would respond as if at war. I would seduce you to protect me."

William slowly sat back down.

"Do not approach me," I said. "Do not come near me. I say again, you can not comfort me."

Stunned, William watched as I held myself and rocked.

Chapter 3

I stood staring out the window an hour later. William sat waiting as I took in a deep breath. The sun still bathed the green land in gold, but black clouds had rolled in from the Irish sea.

"How often do you have breakdowns like that?" he asked.

I watched the wind rustle the trees, paying no mind to his question before answering.

"Not often," I said. "I can feel the anxiety long before I get to that point and know how to end the conversation or steer it off topic without others knowing. Most of the time, I don't talk about myself. And people don't ask. I never talk about myself. So long as the topic stays off my past, I'm good."

With a sigh, I left the window and returned to the table. There, I settled myself back down in my chair.

"When I talk about this," I said. "When I exhume these memories, there is no avoidance or curtailing the topic. The anxiety will arise. It's why I warned you."

He peered down at his notes. He looked uncertain of what to say if he should say anything at all.

"Ready to continue?" I asked.

He nodded.

* * *

The next two years passed with a steady amount of problems with my half-brother. Shaun proceeded to torture the snakes and frogs and any other wildlife he could get his hands on. Six months after Patches died, we adopted two cats.

The cats were a whole other nightmare for me. For the first fifteen years of my life, they were the only physical contact I would have. For the first twenty two years of my life, they were the only pleasurable contact I would have. If I cried, I held a cat. If I was lonely, I held a cat. I virtually grew up without any human contact. It was so absent that I didn't even know it was missing. I thought the lack of physical touch was normal and I wouldn't question it or even notice it until I was well into my second marriage with three children.

The cats had their rabies shots, but the distemper shots and any spaying and neutering were considered financial luxuries we couldn't afford. Nearly every kitten that was born into that house contracted distemper. Mucus builds up in their sinus cavity and respiratory system until the kitten suffocates on their own discharge. My cat would bear kittens and, one by one, I watched them die. More kittens were born and I watched them die too.

When I found them, I couldn't leave them. After all that they had done for me, holding them until they took their last breath was the least I could do for them. Alone, I grieved, and alone, I cried. Death and I became very close acquaintances.

Dinners continued as expected. I was carefully taught that I was selfish and worthless. By the time I associated food with rejection, my father added another layer to my value.

Back then, my father was a penny counter. Every speck of food, every drop of milk consumed launched a breakdown of how much we cost him. The financial expense didn't end there. Every Christmas, every birthday, every article of clothing, everything we needed—school supplies and toiletries—was tallied up and the breakdown thrown back at us. By my fifteenth birthday, I had concluded that I was worth one dollar.

My half-brother had developed an odd sense of humor at the expense of others. Within those two years, he threw the cat down the stairs. She landed on me and shredded my back. He blew ground pepper in my eyes. He insisted he was trying to make me sneeze. Maybe he was, but Shaun was apathetic and held himself above the law. If it was an honest mistake, there was too much in question to believe him. My mother reinforced Shaun's behavior with her incessant reassurance that "boys will be boys." And so life went on until the thirteenth day of September in 1990. I was ten years old.

The phone had rung at six o'clock that morning. I remember laying there thinking how odd it was to hear the phone ring so early. It was raining so I lay awake and listened to the rain. Seven o'clock came and went. We should have been up an hour ago. That morning, my mother did not come in to wake us. I climbed out of bed and made my way down the hall. She was in the kitchen crying. The school bus would be there soon.

"What's wrong?" Charles asked.

My mother said nothing.

Eugene, Shaun, and Marie entered the kitchen. We stood there around my mother and waited.

"Mum," I said. "What's wrong?"

She sniffled and quietly sobbed into a tissue. After several moments where we all stood about pondering, she spoke.

"There's been an accident," she managed to say.

A sick feeling came over me. Something bad had happened and we stood waiting for the news.

"Last night..." My mother gulped down a mouthful of tears. "Your uncle was driving home from church when they were hit head-on by a semi-truck."

* * *

I stared at my folded hands resting on the kitchen table.

"Why stop there?" William said. "What happened?"

I shook my head.

"I can not do this justice. That story belongs to my aunt and she needs to be the one to tell it."

I stood and cleared the mugs from the table. When that was done, I took up a dish cloth and absentmindedly wiped down the counter.

"My aunt has a strength in her that I have seen in no other," I said and threw the rag in the sink. "She wasn't in that car accident... because she was home with her son. My aunt buried three of her children and her husband while nursing her one week-old."

William stared as I shook my head.

"I have no right to tell her story," I said. I could feel another wave of tears building and I shoved them back down. "The grief and the hurt I felt was a fraction of the loss she suffered. I will not go on for hours reliving the agony and the grief of my loss when hers far outstrips mine."

I sighed and ran my hands over my face before continuing.

"You need to know, aside from the cats, that this was my first real introduction to death. You need to know that we spent the next year in Pennsylvania. The lone survivor of that accident was my nine-year old cousin, Hannah."

I sighed and, settling myself back at the table, threw my head back, and gazed out the window at the black clouds.

"Hannah walked away with brain damage and a broken leg that would never grow again. Her mind had been reset. She had to relearn how to walk, how to talk, how to read, how to write, all at age nine. Today, she has a child of her own and to look at her, to talk to her... you can't tell she ever had to start life over.

"My mother told me that the adults—my aunt, my grandparents, nurses, and doctors—hoped my exposure to Hannah would help her recovery because she and I had been close. This came from my mother. I don't know if it's true. I do know that I spent the next year at Hannah's bedside."

William scribbled his notes while I thought back to that year.

"Some things are harder to remember than others," I muttered. William looked up from his notes. "But that year, some memories are very clear."

I sighed and turned my attention to William.

"I do not wish to overshadow my aunt's suffering with my own," I said. "So I will be brief. I walked away from my tenth year detesting the taste of Death's bitter hand and I suffered it alone. After my mother told us that my cousins and uncle had died, my siblings and I stood in the kitchen and cried. Not one hug was exchanged among us. Not. One."

Chapter 4

Until the Accident, my mother had run a strict Baptist home. We had been dedicated church goers and attended a Christian private school through the church. To help pay for our schooling, my family spent Saturdays working in the church. We set up and took down tables, chairs, and faux walls. My mother vacuumed, we cleaned, my father mopped. We were a family of janitors working on Saturdays to pay for our education, attending the church on Sundays and Wednesdays, and attending the school from Monday through Friday.

I said school. It wasn't a school. It was a one-room school house that accumulated children from second to fifth grade in one room and sixth to twelfth grade in another room. Kindergarten and first grade were paired up in a separate room.

The "teachers" were a handful of women ranging from thirty to sixty years old—widows or old maids—members of the congregation who volunteered for the position to get themselves out of the house. The work books were a Christian based magazine-like book that required a full day of independent reading and fill in the blank. No teacher, no lecture, no science, and no socialization. It was a homeschooling program for Christians that taught me to read to find answers.

I learned like this until I was twelve years old. The Bible was our primary text book and the only "real" book I was allowed was the allegorical classic *Pilgrim's Progress* by John Bunyan. I must have read that book fourteen times. I adore Classical Literature like none other. Looking back, it is no wonder I devoured that book like I did. We had other books in the classroom. Children's Christian literature and nothing more. I hated them. After reading *Pilgrim's Progress*, the children's books bored me. Within the church, the rule with books was simple: if God was not mentioned, it was not allowed. I should have asked about Dante or Milton. If only I had known they existed.

At home, my mother listened only to Christian radio and traditional Irish folk, mostly the Clancy Brothers. She collected Bibles and had a few children's books... again, Christian Literature.

She splurged once and bought a dozen classics by Reader's Digest, which Mum thought were pure gold. When I saw that we owned *Little Women* and *Tom Sawyer*, I tried to read them. I stopped once I learned that "Reader's Digest" meant "abridged."

You don't chop the genitalia off a Michelangelo. You don't burn a Rembrandt. You don't cut the words out of Dickens, Dumas, or Hugo. Needless to say, I refuse to read abridged classics.

* * *

"You attended a school house?" William asked, peering up from his notes.

"Yes," I answered. "In very much the same style as practiced in the nineteenth century."

"And all you did was read?" he asked.

"Independent reading," I said. "Sit down-silent read. That is how I learned. That system engrained what would become the center of my existence. Everything that I am, everything that I would become, I learned from that one-room-school-house. I learned my most priceless lesson of all from that place. I learned how to teach myself.

"I need no teachers, no classrooms, no lectures, no people. I only need a book. Eventually, I learned how to get sources. Later, I would learn how to determine good sources from bad. When I got my hands on the internet..." I shook my head, smiling. "A mountain of gold had been dumped into my lap and I would need no people ever again. Hand me a book and I could do anything. That school didn't teach me how to read. It taught me how to teach myself. Ironically, it isolated me further.

"If you think about it, every opportunity I may have had to be socially exposed was systematically removed from my early life. The church was terrified of sex and had one steadfast rule above all others: all physical contact was strictly banned. I remember in jest, one day, I pretended to dance with one of my girlfriends. We were reprimanded and broken up as if we had started dry humping each other right there in the auditorium. The look of horror on the deacon's face..."

"What did you do?" William asked.

I shrugged.

"We mimicked ball room dancing."

There was a moment. William and I exchanged glances and together we laughed, just laughed at the sheer idiocy of that situation.

We calmed down after a moment and I continued with a smile on my face.

"I'm sure the other students were getting physical attention from their parents and siblings so the 'no touching' rule had little to no effect on them. Even my own siblings had something in their lives that drastically altered their experience from mine. Every night, my sister, Marie, snuggled with my father on the couch. My brothers would go on to have relationships that didn't abuse them. Now that I think about, Charles went through a stage where he clung to everyone for hugs. He couldn't see one of our aunts without hanging on them. I didn't see it until now. He was starved for physical contact.

"Around this time, my father brought home a rare treat. Someone at the church had thrown out an encyclopedia set. I don't know why my father wanted it. Perhaps because it was a two thousand dollar set he was getting for free, but he brought those books home and I devoured them.

"I read every article on religion, mythology, Rome, Greece, Europe, philosophy, art and the artists, music and the musicians, and Ireland. Oh, how I fell in love with Ireland. I saw pictures of her... She reminded me so much of the forest in New York. I could look out my bedroom window and see such similarities. The rivers and streams I played in, I saw gazing back at me through pictures of Eire."

William gazed at me over his notes. "If you saw so much of Ireland in the mountains and forests of New York, then why did you leave New York?"

"The people," I said. "New Yorkers are New Yorkers. The Irish are the Irish. And the culture, this culture is only found in Ireland. If ever there is still magic in this world, it is in Ireland. She calls to me and I listen. I can't help but love her. Even the lilt in their brogue is like music."

I sighed and knew a shameless smile spanned my face.

"I don't know how long ago my family sailed to the States, but through the blood line, my Irish roots carried over to me. I grew up forever homesick for a land I had never seen. I felt out of place in the States, a black sheep that never quite belonged anywhere. I ached for the land of my ancestors and didn't even know it. When I found Ireland, I found something that felt so right. I found where I belong.

"My mother was Irish and on occasion would trade up her stale, synthesized music for Irish folk. Oh, but to be carried away on the strings of the fiddle and the winds of the flute while dancing away on a gig of my own making. I lived for those moments of Irish folk and dance. I breathed freely when I heard *Danny Boy* and *Lannigan's Ball*. I named my son for *Danny Boy*. When Ireland called, I answered. Every time.

"My mother would smile and dance. It was the rare occasion when she was happy and exclaim with such pride, 'we're Irish'."

I gazed down at my hands.

"My mum," I said. "She played the piano every day for hours. I think on those rare occasions when my mother danced—through the piano playing and the Irish music—she could forget what had happened to her. I think for a short moment, despite all that she had become, Mum could remember who she was and found herself again. In a way, Ireland gave me back my mum as she was meant to be.

"Watching her for the next five years was like watching a time bomb slowly count down to its own demise and we didn't know it."

Tears swelled up and I wiped them away before they could fall.

"I'm sorry," I said. "I don't mean to cry over this."

"What happened to your mother?" William asked.

I paused in thought while I recalled the years of data I had collected. Some of which required phone calls to distant relatives.

"All I have are my own hypotheses based on evidence I accrued over the years. My mother grew up in a chain of foster homes. This I confirmed with three of her family members. The following is information I gathered from my own observation.

"She had a severe fear of closed doors. She removed the bathroom door from her private bath. When I went around the house closing the doors, something I did often, my mother would panic. She would scream like a bean si and go around opening them again. She refused to close her own door even to get dressed.

"My mother never touched, never comforted, never consoled. She never spoke of her problems, her father, or her past. If questioned about her youth, she would slip into a catatonic state and stay there hours after the questions ended. I met her father once and on that day, she pulled my sister and I aside and said, 'under no circumstances are you to be alone with that man. Ever.' I never saw him again. I do not know his name.

"To this day she is a chronic liar who flies into a tirade at the mere mention of a therapist. I was the child who got to walk in and see my parents having sex. I remember the blank look on my mother's face as if she was battling back a lifetime of nightmares, willing for it to be over. What do you think happened to my mother?"

I watched William nod quietly, and I knew he was drawing the same conclusions that I had years ago.

"Despite everything my mother did, I am the only one of her children who has forgiven her. I am the only one who understood her reasons. I am the only one to really know the extent of her mental problems."

"The year after the Accident, family politics picked up and, through the lines of gossip and my mother, information not meant for children, was provided. My late uncle had been a minister of his own church. With his death and that of his children, it was believed among the congregation that he had sinned, and the Accident was punishment from God. Seeing as how this information came from my mother, I strongly question the truth of it. Nevertheless, this was the reason we were given as to why my parents switched us to the public school the following year.

"In fall of '91, I began sixth grade. I will be the first to tell you, I was sheltered when it came to sex, music, and the world. The only physical contact I can recall by age eleven was my ass being groped by a boy."

"Groped?" William said.

I nodded.

"I was eight or nine. I was on the bus and one of the boys about five years older than me grabbed my ass. I was mortified and sat there listening to the girl next to him giggle that he had grabbed my ass. Eh. I would get used to it."

"Used to it?"

I raised a darkened stare to William.

"Yes," I said. "Used to it.

"The males I have been around help themselves when they see something they like. Ass, breasts, legs, thighs, doesn't matter. Dating five minutes... first kiss... doesn't matter. If they like it, they'll grab it. If they want it, they take it from you. If they had plans to rape me, they didn't hold back the details. Going into a bar is a nightmare in itself. Drunk men don't hold back. In a crowded room, they could grab a feel and slip away without being seen. I was often mortified, humiliated, violated, and would get used to it.

"Walking into the public school was like stepping from a sanctuary into the gates of hell. As a mother, I see the appeal of a Christian home. I had never heard a swear word in my life up until then. I had never heard anything sexual, and I certainly had never been around anyone who would show such disregard to others.

"In the Christian school, people were polite. Manners began and ended every sentence, and we were oblivious to our sexual development. It was something that lurked behind the walls of innocence and our parents had safely secured it there. Nothing had prepared me for the filth and vulgarity of the public school.

"Looking back, I can honestly say I experienced a severe culture shock. Girls openly spoke of sex. I watched twelve year old girls grope males who did their best to block the grab while both laughed at their game. There was a collection of trees on the playground where children learned they could indulge during recess. Within the first week, I was asked if I was a virgin. Aside from the Virgin Mary, I had never heard such a word and certainly had no idea what it meant. When I said yes, they laughed at me. When I said no, they guffawed and giggled like a gaggle of lascivious snakes basking in the filth of Babylon's whores."

I looked at William.

"There may be some venom in that statement," I said. He laughed. "You think?"

"I was scared and lost, new and alone. I hated them all. The males were different. Very different. They looked at me like I was an exotic jewel. They made me feel like an exotic jewel. Where the girls were vindictive and cruel, the boys were sweet and kind. They approached me with caution as if they knew I preferred the quiet and gentle touch.

"I remember my first kiss so well. I said nothing. I did nothing. I froze up and waited for the moment to pass. I hated it. Loathed it. He treated me well, moved in, massaged the breasts I had just started developing. He felt me up, sliding his hands over every part of me. I said nothing. I shut down as my mother did, and I let him have his way with me.

"He approached me as if I was a wild horse. He didn't speak my language, but knew if he moved too quickly, he would spook me and I would run. After three days, he knew I wasn't happy. He tried talking to me. I didn't dare speak. I couldn't open up. I simply had no idea what to do with human contact. I knew I didn't want it and that I hated it. I dreaded when he was around. Up until then, the only physical contact I had was my cat and the ass grab. I had no idea what to do with his eager affections.

"I do remember the moments between our one-sided make-out sessions, where I reveled in his absence. Those moments filled me with such relief. It felt good being independent and I loved it. Space. That was something familiar to me. That was something I could understand. Before my first kiss, I prized my solitude and had learned to associate safety and security in isolation.

"We broke it off after three days. He understood through a series of questions and my mute head nods that I wasn't okay with the relationship.

"The situation at home was moving from bad to worse. Shaun had moved on from the frogs and snakes to the cats. He would pull their tails and bite their ears. I would come running and do my best to take the cats from his grip without hurting them. He'd hold them, bite the ends of their tails. When they screamed, he'd hold them tighter and slapped them if they scratched him.

"One day, I walked into the kitchen to find my cat with a sandwich bag around her head. His hands were clamped around her neck to hold the bag in place. Her tongue was out. She was panting while he sat there, slowly watching her suffocate. I ripped the plastic from her head and as she ran, he called me a bitch and chased her down.

But I was changing. I was starting to fight back.

Chapter 5

I gazed out the window. Storm clouds blocked the afternoon sun. A gray shadow had fallen over the forest and the wind had picked up.

"Suddenly so quiet?" William asked and a smile pulled my mouth.

"As miserable as sixth grade was, it was the year I met Isaiah," I said.

"Isaiah?" William whispered and I listened to him take up his bag from the floor and shuffle through the contents.

"Yes," I said before he could find one of my books and pull it from his bag to check the dedication. "That Isaiah. Sweet Isaiah. I remember no other in sixth grade as I remembered Isaiah. He was shy and quiet. He said not a word. His eyes were warm and, thinking back, the day I saw him watching me from across the room, I think that was the moment he fell in love with me."

I sighed and abandoned the memory.

"You want something to eat?" I asked.

William stretched his arms and checked his watch. "I could eat."

"Of course you could." I made my way to the stove and took off the lid then dished some stew into a bowl.

"What is that?" he asked.

"Irish stew," I said, ladling out a bowl. "I was raised on it."

I set the bowl in front of him and pulled out a loaf of peasant bread, slid him a bowl of butter, and pulled down a clean mug.

"You're not eating," he observed.

"Not when I talk of this, I won't."

He stared into his stew.

"Eat," I said. "I'm too stressed to eat. If I try, I'll feel sick and throw up."

He hesitated, but finally wolfed it down as I poured myself a fresh cup of coffee with Baileys.

His bowl was empty when he spoke again. "So, up to this point you had no comfort. No human contact."

"I had already adapted to living without touch of any kind," I said. "Don't get me wrong. I wanted it. I could feel myself wanting it. But I wasn't getting it. If I wanted physical contact, I sought out my cats. I fought a daily war for my cats. I would come home from school and, at once, go to war.

"I remember the walk from the bus to the front door. It felt like I was walking from a bunker into the jungles of Vietnam armed with nothing but my determination and good will. My mission was simple. Save the cats. I collected them before Shaun could get to them. He'd hunt one down and torture it. I would come to its rescue and he would fight with me.

"There was one fight, I wish I could remember the subject. We wrestled, and it landed me a black eye."

"He hit you?"

I chuckled. "He punched me."

William looked stunned.

"Oh, yes." I nodded. "Yes, he hit me. Would not be the last time either. My face swelled and before Mum and Dad could get home, I had a shiner that fit my face like a mask."

"What did your parents do?" he asked.

"Nothing," I said, "I lied and said I fell down the stairs."

"You lied?" William straightened himself in the chair. "For him? And they bought it?"

"Yes."

"Why did you protect him?"

"Protect him?" I scoffed. "I didn't protect him." I rolled my eyes and nodded. "Okay, I protected him. I was scared for him. We kept the ruse going for two weeks. When my aunt asked who hit me, I told her the truth. My mother scolded me for lying."

"And Shaun?"

"What about him?" I asked.

"Did he get in trouble for hitting you?"

"Oh, no," I said. "He was a boy. That's what boys do. That's what my mother said. I learned the lesson well."

"That's what boys do?" William repeated my mother's words back to me.

"Yes. 'Boys will be boys,' she said. Every man has his breaking point. Every man will hit a woman if he's pushed hard enough. Even you. You just need to know where it is. No. Shaun was never punished for hitting me. He was allowed to. I got more of a reaction out of the boys at school than I did my parents. I went to school the next day with a shiner, and those boys, who saw that someone had smashed their exotic jewel, bombarded me.

'Who hit you?'

'My step-brother.' I referred to him as a step-brother to classmates because most had never heard of a half-sibling before. I didn't feel like explaining it either.

'Your step-brother hit you? What'd your parents do?'

'Nothing?'

'Your step-brother hit you and your parents did nothing? If I hit my sister, my parents would beat my ass.'

'Hey, who hit you?'

'My step-brother?'

'Your step-brother did this to you?'

"I wanted to die," I said to William. "I was mortified. I was confused. Why was it such a big deal?"

"Because men don't hit girls," William said.

"They do in my world," I said. "It's what they do."

"No! They don't!"

I flinched at William's raised voice and started stupidly across the table. Like so many before him, he was adamant. And, as always, I couldn't believe him.

"Every man hits," I said. "Every man has his breaking point. Some just have a higher breaking point than others. I prayed every day that I wouldn't find it. I still do."

William seemed to calm himself down and he returned to his paper.

"That event brought Isaiah and I close," I said. "It opened us up. I'm not sure if he sought out my friendship to protect me... I think he did. I think he saw what my half-brother did and he felt he could protect me if he were closer.

"Isaiah provoked me. Purposely pushed my buttons. I was quiet, soft spoken, and shy. I was small. Still am."

"How tall are you?" William asked.

"Four-eleven."

"And weigh what? Fifty pounds?"

I smiled. "One fifteen to one twenty depending on the day. I stopped growing that year. I had a passion inside of me and I think Isaiah saw that it was suppressed. He probed and picked my brain. Selected a plethora of topics until he zeroed in on the one that would ignite my spirit and did."

"What did he say?" William asked.

"He said women were weak." I sighed. "After my black eye..."

I shook my head, feeling the anger rise.

* * *

After my black eye, things changed. Shaun too had learned an invaluable lesson: he could beat me without repercussion. My half-brother stopped torturing the cats and came after me. He was careful to never hit my face again, but everything else was fair game. He'd come to my room to beat me. Some days he would get a punch, maybe two, in before I closed the door on him. He started wearing shoes all the time. I would slam the door as he dropped his foot in the way. Eventually, I stopped opening the door. And he started picking the lock.

Weak? Those beatings aroused a strength in me that I would embrace. There was Isaiah standing over me, smiling, telling me that women were weak, while every day I was single-handedly fighting a man's war.

"You're weak!" he said. "Your bodies were designed to have babies and so nature softened them and made them pliable because you couldn't handle it."

I had a point to prove.

I slapped him.

Hard.

The five foot eleven mass of Isaiah fell back. The room went silent. I could see my handprint on his left cheek. It burned. Oh, I knew it burned. Tell me I was weak.

He straightened his spine, threw back his shoulders. I threw out my chest and raised my face, bracing for the slap back. Daring him, wanting him to hit me.

Hit me. I thought. *Hit me. I'll show you how weak I am.*

He stared at me.

Hit me. Hit me... or kiss me. Oh, please kiss me.

You could cut the sexual tension in that room with a blunt blade.

No one in that room breathed. Eyes shifted from him to me to him. We all waited, not sure if he would hit me or kiss me.

He stepped in, took a deep breath and said, "You're lucky you're a girl."

That slap ignited a series of electrical charges that would not stop until we had sex. That slap became immortalized in our class and was talked about until Graduation Day in '98.

"Hey, remember when Beth hit Isaiah in sixth grade?"
"Epic!"

That slap launched the hopes and dreams of every pubescent female in school.

"Are you guys going out?"
"No."

Every year, since the Slap of '91, someone asked us that question. And we purposely did nothing just to piss them off.

* * *

I listened to William's sweet chuckle.

"I have very few simple stories to tell. When I have one, I share it." I smiled and watched the strand of hair fall over his eyes. I had an urge to brush it back.

"You have a warm laugh, did you know?" He stopped chuckling at once and blushed. "It's wonderful to listen to."

He looked down at his papers.

I sighed and looked to the window.

"Why do you do that?" he asked.

"Do what?"

"Why do you say things like that?"

I shrugged. "My words come easily, but they are sincere."

"Is that more of your sex charm?" he asked.

"Partly," I said. "I hate how hard it is for people to offer a compliment while most are quick to offend and trash talk. Gossiping comes too easy for most. But when compliments are extended, people blush and cower. I know too many who are eager to hear an insult where there isn't one intended and slow to accept a compliment. We are too hesitant to be kind and are too careless with our insults. I hope to change that about this world. And I do my part to change that."

I sighed and looked back to the forest through the window.

"I love you. You're beautiful. You're kind. I like you. These are things we should never hesitate to say."

"I love you," William repeated. "You don't think those words should be reserved for... appropriate occasions?"

"No," I said. "Life is too short to waste on hesitation. Be brave. Be bold. Be blunt. Be kind."

I stood and took up his empty bowl from the table and William took up his bag and pulled out a fresh supply of paper then settled back in again. I set it in the sink and rested my hands on the counter. I bowed my head and waited.

"You alright?" William asked.

I didn't move. I knew what part of the story was to come next. I needed a moment.

Are you? I heard Ian say and I looked to the six foot two Nordic prince standing to the right of me in my kitchen. His longsword was unsheathed. The point on the ground. His palms rested lazily on the pommel.

"Must you be in every book I write?" I asked him.

Ian shrugged and flashed that smile he always gave me. *Only a little.*

"Elizabeth?" William said.

Ian nodded toward William still seated at the table. *He's worried about you.*

"With good reason," I answered. "I'm standing here talking to an elven prince in my kitchen. Somehow, you keep forgetting that you are a figment of my imagination."

He smiled. *I know that.*

I swooned and he knew that too.

"Do you?" I asked him.

You know that, Ian said.

"Do I?"

He doesn't know that.

"Elizabeth?"

Go on, Ian said. *He's waiting.*

"Miss Lundy?" I heard William's chair scrape the floor.

"Yes, William," I said, straightening my back and turning to him with a smile.

I saw him glance behind me to where Ian still stood, and I watched William gaze at the empty void that was Ian.

Outside, the rain had started to fall.

Part Two: Descending the Psychedelic

Chapter 6

The beatings at home continued. When Shaun couldn't get to me, he went for my cats. I had taken to barricading myself in my room. I never came out. Every time I left my room I was mocked and ridiculed, threatened, or downright beaten.

That year, my father accommodated a request I made. He built a cat door for my room. The cat door allowed the cats to pass in and out of my room via the closet without my ever having to open my door. It meant my cats could run from my half-brother and escape without my having to risk a beating myself. I kept a cat box in my room with food and water at all times. The cats quickly learned that my room was safe. They weren't the only ones. I also learned that lesson well.

"Open the damn door!" Shaun shouted and punched the door. I was throwing all my weight against the other side.

"Open the goddamn fucking door!"

He kicked the door and fought, his hand on the knob. I held it tight. If he turned the knob before I could get it locked, he'd be in.

I searched my room for a barricade. My dresser. I could move my dresser, but first I needed to lock the door.

His fists beat the door and I braced myself against the impact. The moment his hand released the handle, I could turn the lock, but one of us had to give first. One of us had to be faster than the other.

He kicked the door and I lost my grip, re-secured my hold, and waited. Another punch to the door then another. My palms were sweating. My hands were slipping. I couldn't stop shaking, but I had to keep myself together. I couldn't fall apart, not until the door was locked and barricaded.

"Open the goddamn fucking door, bitch!"

He punched the door with both fists.

Click.

I turned the lock in place and released the knob.

He rattled the handle. I wasted no time. He could pick that lock once he had a knife from the kitchen.

I got behind my dresser and shoved. I shoved with all my might and moved it the two feet in front of the door. He would pick the lock, but the barricade was all I needed to keep him from opening the door. He kicked and screamed on the other side.

There was a moment of silence, then he was back. Within seconds he had the door unlocked. He turned the knob and the door hit my dresser.

"I'm going to fucking kill you!" he screamed. "I'll fucking kill you!"

I ran to the other end of my room as far from him as I could go. I considered jumping out my window and running, but then, I would have to go back through the house to get in. And I had just barricaded the door. No. I had to stay in the room and listen.

He rattled the knob. He punched and kicked the door. He screamed.

"I'm going to fucking kill you!"

I slipped under my desk and hugged my knees to my chest. His screaming continued as he slammed the door into my dresser. Shaking, I huddled under the desk. I couldn't stop shaking.

"I'll fucking kill you!" he said. "I'll kill you!"

I rocked and held my knees. I sobbed quietly. If he heard me, he would mock me. I held my head, wishing the screaming would stop. I wanted to die and wished for death.

"You fucking bitch!" Shaun screamed. "Goddamn—Open the fucking door!"

A spider was there in the corner of my desk. I jumped and every inch of my body trembled while I weighed my options. Stay with the arachnid or risk my half-brother. I sobbed and screamed into my knees while the spider crawled onto my hand.

"I'll fucking kill you!"

The spider inched its way back to me. I couldn't leave my room. I couldn't get away. I rocked and screamed in my knees. I bit my knees and tried to breathe. The spider wouldn't hurt me, but my half-brother would kill me. Regardless, it crawled up my arm and my body went still. I stopped shaking and slipped into the depths of my mind where everything was silent.

The tunnel was dark and deep. I fell, sliding on the walls of black glass. My foot touched down on the charcoal gray floor and I stood in the room where silence is born. The room was barren save for a set of black doors. Here, wherever I was, I was safe. I was calm. Here, there was peace.

I approached the doors and turned the knob. A happy light greeted me. A breeze grazed my legs and I stepped into a room composed of white marble and light. The doors behind me closed.

Two cat statues carved out of black onyx flanked the door. To my right and in front of me, a fountain of water fell from the ceiling into a pool large enough to bathe in. To my left, a bed made over in Egyptian silk welcomed me if I wished to sleep. Another fresh breeze rolled over the floor and up my legs, drawing my attention directly ahead to an archway trimmed in gossamer. Sunlight poured into the room.

I shifted my weight and saw beyond the light. A vast marble balcony opened up to a forest of green. I could smell the fresh scent of water falling just like in my gorge. I could smell the fresh earth and the life in the grass and the trees. I could hear the birds sing, the thunder of waterfalls, and the soft mews of cats.

I looked to the bed and saw my cats. Some were on the floor gnawing a ball of string. Others had curled up in the pillows sleeping. They were safe. Here, wherever I was, everyone was safe.

I walked out to the balcony and gazed over the forest. It was wild and old. A giant waterfall roared as it tumbled over a cliff into a ravine overgrown with the edge of the forest. The waterfall had formed a vast pool of water as black as it was deep.

I pulled myself up onto the marble banister and found my center. Just like my gorge in the glen, I let the winds blow through me. I drew in a deep breath and, releasing the last of my worries, I jumped.

I flew the forty feet down, and when I hit the water, the cold slid over me like a soft blanket. Beneath the water, I wallowed and washed away the fear, the screams, and the bruises. Here, I had no pain, no danger. Here, wherever here was, I was alone, completely alone and safe. It was here that I found my peace.

I swam for a moment or an hour—time did not exist there—before finding a shallow ledge. I pulled myself from the water, combed my hair back with my fingers, and raised my face to the sun. It was a warm day, and when a gentle wind blew, it felt good, not uncomfortable as one would expect. I breathed deep the summer breeze and I smiled.

From where I stood, I could see a trail that led up and away from the pool. The trail beckoned me and I followed while singing a random ditty of my own composing.

I wandered the forest for hours, soaking in the warm sun and the bird songs. If day passed slow here, or at all, I did not sense it. I followed the trail, then wandered about on my own, paying no mind to much of anything until I found a shallow stream that flowed through the wood. I walked the stream, splashed across the water while giggling, and meandered about on the bank. The day wore on and the clouds moved in. The winds picked up with a cold bite. The chill was a refreshing change. After a few moments, I had adapted to the cold and welcomed it. I took in every sight, every sound and delighted in the wood where I was safe.

I followed the stream until the forest thinned and entered a small clearing where wild grasses grew. There, I found a small cottage. It looked centuries old and was built of whitewash stone. I could see the pile of wood and the rusted axes where a farmer or huntsman perhaps had left it. I could see a chimney that once burned with the warmth of a fire. As if frozen in time, I could see where laughter came to this cottage and ended, and now the forest had grown up and around it encasing the domicile in a preserved state where it waited to be found by me.

I approached the cottage and located the red door beneath ivy and moss that had grown up over the handle. I turned the knob, pushed open the door, and stepped into the darkness where all at once, the world went away and I was back in my room beneath my desk.

* * *

I blinked and stared at the underside of my desk.

The spider, the screaming, and my half-brother were gone. My room was dark. I crawled out from under my desk and, still on my hands and knees, poked my head around the desk just enough to see the window. Night had fallen hours ago. Within that time, no one had noticed. No one had come. No one had cared.

My dresser was still in front of my door where I had left it. My legs were stiff. My face was raw from the stale tears dried to my face. My kitten mewed beside me. I picked her up from the floor, crawled back under my desk where I pulled her into my lap, and quietly sobbed myself to sleep.

Chapter 7

Summers were an endless nightmare I suffered while awake. Nights were filled with broken dreams that woke me, more times than not, to fits of crying. Once, only once, my mother came to me.

"What are you doing up?" She squinted at me through sleep.

"I had a nightmare," I said. "Your arms were cut off and Dad was trying to take us kids and run from you. You tried to keep up. You fell in the parking lot, but you had no arms to break your fall. There was blood everywhere."

"Shut up and go to sleep," she snarled, slapped my light off, and went back to bed.

I sobbed alone in the dark.

I often had nightmares of my mum. I must have seen her killed one hundred times. When I woke, I cried into my pillow. I would sneak into her room while she slept and stand over her where I would cry. She never woke up. I was careful to never wake her again and didn't. I would touch her to make sure she still breathed, finish my cry, then go back to bed.

When September returned, I eagerly ran back to school. School meant no Shaun—well, less Shaun. At school, I was safe. I had Isaiah and things to help occupy my mind from everything happening at home.

On that first day of high school, seventh grade, my English teacher worked well to relax us and lighten our nerves. She was kooky and zany and eccentric and, that day, she had brought in her CD player. She was exercising a fair amount of silliness when she exclaimed, "Oh! I just got my new soundtrack! So excited."

She pressed play and posed like she was singing an opera.

"What is it?" a student asked.

"*The Phantom of the Opera*," she said. "Have you heard it?"

A head nod.

"Have you heard it?" she asked another student.

A head nod.

"Have you heard it?" she asked me and I shook my head. I had never heard of it, let alone heard it.

She crossed the classroom and slipped the head phones over my ears.

Oh, the sound.

Music zapped my soul to life. The violins flowed, their melodies plunged through me and awakened my cold, deadened heart killed by the fear and hate that I had come to know.

Notes from the cellos warmed me and pushed my blood to my heart. The oboes, flutes, and clarinets breathed a life into me like the gods breathed life into Man. I found the rhythm and my heart obeyed. The strings pulled and played me like a marionette and I danced and bent to their will. The music called and I followed. I descended and I fell with each diminuendo, and when the music rebounded in a crescendo, it carried me with it, high above the timpani, the cymbals, and the—

It was gone.

I fell back into the classroom. Idle chatter came back to me, and I gasped, desperate for the sound to revive me once again. My teacher had returned her headphones to her own ears and I hung there mid-orgasm, unfulfilled, unsated, needing something I couldn't possibly get anywhere else.

"What was that?" I asked, swallowing back another gasp.

"*The Phantom of the Opera*," she said.

I did what I only knew how. I went to the library, located Gaston Leroux's *The Phantom of the Opera* and read my very first real book.

* * *

If ever there was a day that changed me, it would be that day.

The words of Leroux pulled me in like nothing I had ever known. I slipped into his world with such ease. Within moments I was there on the steps of the opera house. I was there in the dressing rooms and at the lake. I could touch and burn my fingers on the candles.

It was a macabre Beauty and the Beast set to music. My sweet, my dearest, my life, my love, the bane of my existence. My music, sweet music that gave me air to breathe, strength to stand, and the will to try. My music that, within that moment, became the very essence of my existence.

As I poured over the words of Leroux, I found a music there, a rhythm of its own.

The book ended too soon and when I closed the final page of that first book, those three precious words moved me with such feeling... I was too stunned to cry.

"Erik is dead."

To the books I ran, to the books to learn everything there ever was to learn.

From Leroux, I learned of Paris and Marc Chagall. I wasted no time returning to my encyclopedia set—for I had claimed them as my own—and I learned. I learned of musicals and operas. And wherever *The Phantom of the Opera* was, *Les Miserables* was sure to follow.

Back to the library, I found Victor Hugo. *Les Miserables* was nearly fifteen hundred pages. I was only allowed to take a book out for three weeks. There was no way I could finish *Les Miserables* in three weeks.

When I was just shy of fourteen, I approached my father.

"Dad."

"Hm."

"I want a book."

* * *

I don't know how or why we were ever in that bookstore that day. We didn't go into bookstores. I think my mother wanted to look up something. It was two days before my fourteenth birthday. Screw selfishness. I was doing it.

I held the book to my chest, cradling it as if it was my first born child.

"Dad. Please may I have this book?"

He sighed and stared at the book like I was holding a pile of shit.

"I don't know. It's a book."

"It's my birthday. You can count it as a birthday present. Please. You don't have to give me anything else. Just this. Please."

He made a face that confirmed he thought Victor Hugo was a waste of money.

"Please, Dad. Please. You can skip my Christmas. I don't care. I want this book."

At the end, after an hour of begging and negotiations, an hour of holding the book to my heart, unsure if I would be leaving it behind, my father consented and I had *Les Miserables*.

* * *

The Irish rains picked up outside until the sharp plink of droplets punctuated the silence. William stared in silence, watching.

"I need a Guinness," I said.

I pushed myself up from the table and glanced out the window. I watched the rain strike the glass. The earthen gloom that enveloped the land confirmed that the sun had started to set beyond the black cloud cover. I flipped on the kitchen light and grabbed a beer out of the case resting on the floor.

"You want anything?" I asked. "I have Guinness, Smithwicks, Harp..."

"I can do a whiskey if you have it."

I gazed at him in question. He didn't look like a man who could hold down Irish whiskey.

"Please," he added.

"I have Jameson, Black Bush..."

"Jameson. Neat."

I grabbed the bottle of Jameson from the top of the fridge, an opener from the drawer, and a glass.

"Help yourself," I said quietly and passed him the glass and the bottle.

I opened the Guinness and poured the thick beer drown my throat, taking in the sweet drink. If Ireland had a flavor, it would be Guinness. Liquid Ireland.

"I had taken piano when I was four," I said. "I played until I was five then quit when frustration set in because my five-year-old hands couldn't stretch the octave. At twelve, as soon as I heard the music, I asked to return to piano lessons.

"My mother played. There was no question. It was the only luxury I was allowed. I picked up right where I left off with a passion that allowed me to escape into the rhythmic realm of music. I took up chorus that year as well and began vocal lessons through the school. I wasted no time composing and writing melodies and compositions. I had more staff paper than anything else and it was all over my room, splayed out around my cats on the floor, and tucked into every crevice.

"Over the next eight years, music was the frequency I rode on to carry me through my darkest days."

I gulped down another three mouthfuls and rolled the beer around in my mouth while I fought back images, so many memories in my mind.

I rubbed the bottle on my brow.

Too much was coming back to me. Too much, I was remembering. I saw the darkness. I saw the room... the shadows... the figures shaped like wraiths. I watched William sip the whiskey. I gazed out the window and stared into the Irish hills. I knew what was to come next.

Chapter 8

That year I met Elena, who would be my only girlfriend through high school. I had her and Isaiah. Isaiah brought a smile to my face every morning. Elena helped bring me into the world of music and ballet, classical music, composition, dance, literature. Oh! And theater. I was banned from ballet. My parents insisted that dance was the gateway to sin, sex, and corruption. In secret, Elena taught me and I learned. There were mornings I woke and slipped her toe shoes on first thing. Before my feet ever touched the ground, I was in toe. I do miss wearing toe shoes.

Up to this point, my father had started telling me more than just that I was selfish. He also made it clear that I was beautiful, that I was too smart to be a girl, and that I should have been a boy. I began dressing like boys, loving boys, idolizing boys. I wanted to be like them, then maybe... maybe my father would like me. Father would berate me and openly say he feared me while telling me how wonderful Marie was. And she was. She truly was wonderful. Marie was everything I could have been.

My half-brother proceeded to beat me. I had stopped eating almost completely. Most nights, I listened to Shaun scream from the other side of the door.

"I'm going to kill you! I'm going to fucking kill you!"

You can hear that only so many times before you believe it. During those times, I slipped into my worlds. The more I read, the more worlds came to me. I added a subterranean lake that was illogically bathed in moonlight to my list. Those worlds—that lake, the room with the onyx cats, and Ireland—they all became very real to me. Much more real than the life I lived where a monster threatened to kill me on the other side of the door.

Doors.

Doors were my savior and my bane.

Shaun to torturing my cats when he failed to get the response out of me and it worked every time. Nothing could draw me from my room, save for my cats and an irrational need to rescue them from his perverse monstrosities. I was afraid to leave them and lived forever afraid for them. The only thing that provided me solace were the felines he made scream on the other side of my door.

My nightmares were frequent and vivid. I dreamt of such dark things. Wrapped in a giant spider web while spiders feasted on me. War. So many dreams of war. I was in a fox hole with grenades and guns. Dismembered bodies, mutilated corpses surrounded me. Dolls with melted faces and marionettes. I'm terrified of marionettes. And of puppets.

Even now I feel the rising sick and I'm swallowing back mouthfuls of vomit. I was only eight, and those pictures... those images... forever seared in my head. Every time I remember, I want to vomit.

There was one woman, one vile woman, who I will not forget. She was the monitor of my second to fifth grade Christian class room. She was a monster who lived her life resenting all others because she was unmarried and alone. Okay, I'm not going to lie. This woman looked, acted, and sounded like Harry Potter's Dolores Umbridge. I kid you not. I knew a Dolores Umbridge.

She was determined to shove every bit of Christian goodness down our throats. And she did it by every means she knew how. With that damn smile of hers and her batting of the eye-lashes on her plump face.

She loved showing us Christian Horror movies. Yes. There is such a genre. But there was one that makes me sick to this day. The movie was white, pure white. The walls, the rooms, the sets, the scenes, all white. And there were these teenagers who weren't Christian. In contrast, they were dirty and black. Not the beautiful black you see at night, but a cold, cruel gray black like green-gray fermenting bodies. The main character loathed this Christian puppet show that aired every night so he and his friends rallied up and sought out the studio.

The perfect white studio was black that night when they broke in and trashed the place. I am still so sick from this. I watched the teen shred the dolls. The ugly black streaked their faces as they dumped paint across the white walls, broke everything in the room, ripped the eyes off the dolls, and... I don't know why it makes me sick. I don't know why it... Later, you see the boy beaten by his father with a stick. Everything was either stark white or ugly black. To this day, I'm terrified of dolls and puppets. I don't even know if this is relevant, but it felt right to mention just now.

Stringed marionettes and cold porcelain faces. The Death Men and their steel room with no doors. Blue light, moon light forever fills that steel room. It is dark and wide. The ceiling, I can not see. It's so cold and there are no doors. Only figures, tall men dressed in cloaks like wraiths. They surround me and fill every inch of that room. They will hurt me, but I can not run. I can not escape.

They peer down ever closer, and I want to run, but I can't. And just as they reach for me, they are gone and I'm alone in that room.

It's empty. And I'm on my knees, curled up, naked, and cold in the blue moon light. I'm alone. The room, the Death Men, the eternal ceiling with light pouring in... it all scares me. The only way out is up, but I can not reach and I can not run.

But what I hate most of all is that the Death Men come and go and change. Like lights flickering on and off, the Death Men are there, suffocating me in that room, and then they're gone. They're back again, then gone. Sometimes they are there as men of average height dressed as Death. Sometimes, they are three times taller than that of a man. So tall, you can not see me kneeling at their feet. I'm lost in the thick of their black robes. Then they flicker, the scene changes, and they are normal. It flickers again and they're tall. It's an inconsistent and rapid change, and the change is what scares me.

There are no doors. I can not get out. I am alone in that room with the Death Men.

And I can not get out.

* * *

My half-brother was messed up. As early as three, Shaun stole things and my mother would laugh and say how cute she thought it was. When I was in third grade, Shaun was found with a large stash of trinkets and things he stole from our classmates.

As punishment, the Umbridge woman did what any sensible Christian did: she stood him in front of the entire class, announced his sin, and made him give back every item he stole and apologize. Humiliation galore. I watched Shaun hold back the tears and hand each item back. It took him two hours to complete the task.

I think the punishment scarred my half-brother far deeper than anyone realizes. I think the level of humiliation turned Shaun to resentment. And I don't blame him one bit. I'm all for teaching a lesson and holding a person responsible. I also believe humiliation can be over done. I believe there is a point where humiliation stops teaching the correct lesson and turns to scars instead. That day, the Umbridge woman and my parents took his humiliation to a whole other level.

It was after this incident that the Umbridge woman verbally came after me. She hated me and was adamant that I was "just like my half-brother." I hate those words. My half-brother was three years older, which means teachers met him first then greeted me with, "Do you want to be like your brother?" I hated it when they called him my brother. My brothers, Charles and Eugene, were my brothers and were nothing like Shaun. I hated him being lumped in the same group as them. I inherited a lot of Shaun's teachers. The Umbridge woman was the first, only she was already convinced that I was just like Shaun.

By the time I was eight, my eyesight was bad. We were in charge of grading our own papers with score key keepers. One day, I misaligned my answers with the answer key and was marking wrong answers right and right answers wrong.

Just as I marked a wrong answer right, Umbridge looked over my shoulder and pointed at the page.

"That was wrong! You're lying!" she screamed. She took me by the arm and dragged me down the hall to an empty room. I remember her grip on my arm. It hurt so much. Her sausage fingers clamped my little nine-year-old arm and she shoved me into that room at the end of the hall.

For thirty minutes, she told me exactly what she thought of me. How selfish I was. How vile. How ungrateful I was and how I was just like Shaun. She called me a liar and a cheater and spoiled. She told me my mother was right to call me a liar. That if I didn't change, I would be just as vile as my half-brother.

I stood there fuzzying up my eyes... I can control how unfocused my eyes get. That day, I unfocused them so much that I couldn't recognize the blob of fuzz in front of me.

I hated her. I loathed her. To this day, I detest her.

* * *

I took to staying up as late into the night as I could to avoid the nightmares and the Death Men. I hated sleep. I couldn't eat without remembering how selfish I was... how unwanted I was. I learned to take very little. I learned to want nothing more. I learned something else during those nights. When all the world slept, a new silence settled into the forest.

With candle in hand and dressed in gowns of gossamer, I would slip out into the night and dance to the sound of silence. Barefoot, I would spin then lay in the cool grass in a strip of moonlight. I would lie there all night and gaze up at the stars, so silent, so clear there in the wood, and so, so far away.

I lived between worlds. The war, my reality, my hell and this world in the forest of fantasy. And I'm stuck. I can't go back. I forever toggle between two worlds and one is ever so much more real to me than yours.

At night, beneath the moon, I didn't need my worlds to escape. I only needed to open my eyes and see the world as it was. Quiet and calm and at peace, just as I still see it. I escaped through my music and wrote poetry to ease the pain... and letters. I poured so much of my heart into the letters I wrote to Erik, who I could see so easily on the other side. I still have them. Every letter I ever wrote him. During those times, when the world was dark, Erik became more real to me than anything else. He was quiet. He listened. He held me in the silence. He played his violin for me. And he loved me.

When I cried, I closed my eyes and felt him envelope me. Only Erik and the cats ever came. No matter how long and loud I cried, my parents, no one ever came. I was fourteen. I was alone and all I wanted was for someone to love me.

Chapter 9

The memories melted away and I slipped back into my kitchen.

The overhead light above the table threw a pale orange over the eatery and kitchen. The rains had dampened the air and a chill was starting to creep in, but I didn't care. I savored the damp Irish air brought in by the rains.

I gazed at William, who sat listening with his pencil pressed to his lips. For now, he seemed content to be warmed by the whiskey.

"If it gets too damp for you, let me know and I'll start the fire going," I said.

"I'm good," he answered.

We sat in silence listening to the rains bombard the earth. The ache to run out and dance with them was overwhelming. I found their rhythm and tapped my foot instead.

"At this time, I met Elena's boyfriend, Piss-ant," I said.

William looked up from his notes.

"Piss-ant?"

"That's right," I said decisively. "It's what I've called him since I was fifteen. It suits him. I'm calling him Piss-ant."

William gave an 'okay-it's-your-story' look and returned to his notes.

"Piss-ant," he said. "Is that one word or two?"

"Let's hyphenate it," I said and listened to the soothing scratch of his pencil on the page. The scratching stopped as William took up his glass of whiskey.

"I hate this part of my life," I said and watched William snort the Jameson through his nose.

"Sorry," I said.

He coughed, hacked, and composed himself. I handed him a napkin and watched him wipe the tears from his eyes. He blew the whiskey out his nose.

"Sorry," he apologized for the noise, and coughed. "This!" he exclaimed in the tissue. "This is the part you decide to hate? Not the spiders or the beatings or the torture, but this?"

I shrugged.

"Of all the moments in my life, Piss-ant was truly my fault," I said.

"What happened with Piss-ant?" he asked.

I inhaled and prepared to drop the guillotine on my own neck.

"He was my best friend's boyfriend. He was my first heartbreak and I spent three years pining for the Piss-ant that he was."

William coughed again into his whiskey.

"I hate love triangles," I said. "And all the shit that goes with them, so we're skipping this part."

William made a face that confirmed he looked rather displeased with the idea of skipping this part.

"Fine." I sighed. "I'll summarize. Let's try to keep this at two hundred words or less, shall we? I loved Piss-ant, who dated Elena for three years. I could have gotten over Piss-ant if he hadn't toyed with me like he did."

"Toyed with you?"

"Yes. He flirted, touched me, toyed with me, fingered me. To stroke his own ego, he would make out with Elena in front of me just to watch me writhe with jealousy. He'd flirt with me and I swooned. Elena got pissed. He blamed me and shoved me away. I withdrew, he felt bad, pulled me closer to cheer me up, and we repeated the process... for three years. Eventually, Piss-ant and I slept together. He and Elena broke up. Piss-ant was with me for one month and then he cheated on me. We continued to sleep with each other until I woke up one day and decided I was worth more than him. Never spoke to him again."

William scratched his whiskers with the back of his pencil.

"If he's so irrelevant, why bring him up?" he asked.

"Because everything that happened next happened because of Piss-ant."

* * *

Elena and Piss-ant felt bad for me. To cheer me up, Piss-ant decided the best thing for me was a distraction. That distraction was his neighbor and best friend: Joe.

They arranged a meeting and after school, Elena and I headed over to the library. I was repulsed. Joe was your classic scoundrel. He was a red-haired, white trash redneck whose only aspiration was to be a thug on the streets of New York.

I smiled, was polite, shook his hand, daydreamed about washing my hand, and left. But I was no fool. The look in his eye... his smile. Within those few minutes, Joe had become infatuated with me. He didn't hide it. He gazed at me like a lost puppy.

The next day, he called me. Piss-ant had supplied him with my phone number.

Again, I was kind, I smiled, minded my manners, accommodated the conversation, and hung up the phone feeling like I wanted to shower. He made it clear his intentions, his desires. He liked me. He didn't hold back. He threw himself at me. It repulsed me. He was sweet... kind of... in his own way. But he tried too hard to force something that wasn't there.

He pleaded with me to give him a shot. He threw himself at my feet and implored that I try. He was adamant that if I tried to love him, I would. He reminded me so much of myself and how I felt for Piss-ant.

For Joe, I felt only pity. Nothing else. Pure pity. I knew, too well, the hurt he felt. What it was like wanting someone who didn't want you. I agreed and so began the three year yo-yo. I broke up with him after three days.

I didn't love him. I made that clear. Three days later, after hearing him cry and beg, I agreed to give him one more chance. We lasted a week. I broke up with him again. It just didn't feel right. He cried and sobbed, insisting that I hadn't given him enough time. I tried again. We made it two weeks.

I didn't love him. I couldn't be more clear, more honest. We continued this cycle for a year. He felt dirty and my gut feeling screamed danger while my heart pined for Piss-ant.

* * *

All my free time went to music. Between classes, in the mornings, during study halls.

At home, I walked through the door and entered a battle field. The mission? Rescue the cats. Shaun caught on and would race me. God help my cats if he got to them before I did. I took them up and ran to my room with them. Sometimes I made it. Sometimes, I didn't. Sometimes they escaped and I didn't.

But the moment I passed over the threshold of my room, the rest of the world vanished. Stepping into my room was literally like stepping into a book. I didn't see a bedroom. I saw my fantasy world melting the reality off my bedroom walls and Erik was always there waiting for me. The war vanished and just like that I was in Ireland or at the lake. There was a peace there and no evil could ever find me. So long as I didn't sleep, the Death Men couldn't hurt me.

I dodged Joe's phone calls and I ached for Piss-ant. I turned to Erik where we lost each other in music. He loved me. He held me. He hugged me. He kissed me. When I was older, he would make sweet love to me.

Outside, on the other side of my world, out there, my half-brother would bang on my door.

"I'm going to fucking kill you! You're fucking dead!"

One day, after three years, my half-brother broke in.

Chapter 10

My parents had left to go grocery shopping and they left Marie with us. I don't know what they were thinking. My parents knew the beatings Shaun gave me. I was fifteen. He was sixteen. I lived in my room. By then, I had learned to never open the door. No matter who was on the other side, all conversations were conducted through my door. I only left my room to use the bathroom and even then, I had to execute a carefully laid out plan. It was a necessary risk. Fortunately, I didn't eat or drink very much.

My parents and half-brother mocked me. They ridiculed me when they heard me talking to Erik. They mocked me when I left my room. My mother was just like my half-brother in that regard. I would build up the nerve to leave my room and attempt to socialize and would be greeted with jeering remarks from my mother and half-brother.

"Well, look who emerged from her cave."

Without a word, I turned right around and withdrew back to my room. When they heard me crying, my mother openly scolded me.

"You deserve it," my parents said. "You provoke him. Boys will be boys."

Got it. Males beat on women. Lesson received loud and clear, and Shaun kept on beating me and my cats.

Marie had never seen Shaun like this. She had never known about the daily nightmare I lived. I learned to hide my problems well. Shaun got in that day and he came at me.

Marie stood crying as Shaun shoved me against the wall and slammed his fist into my head. My head hit the wall and bounced back into his fist. He punched my head back into the wall, but it only ricocheted back. Again and again, he punched me and my head bounced between the wall and his fist seven... eight times... over and over until I fell. He hit me and I took it.

I heard Marie screaming. She was watching. I can handle the pain. I can take the hits. But Marie...

The pain fired off shots of heat then the sensation of warm blood seeping down my face followed. More fire and the hits kept coming and Marie kept screaming.

Then all at once, I stopped feeling it, and there was no pain.

It was like I slipped into Ireland right there under his fist. I felt him touch me, but there was no pain. With the pain gone, I could feel the strength to stand, to move. I was elated that he couldn't hurt me despite beating me with his fist. It permitted me to feel anger. I couldn't help but feel the victor. I was elated. Through my strands of hair, I looked up at him as he pounded me with his fist and I smiled.

He looked horror-struck and paused. Marie stole that moment to pull at his back. I saw her crying for my sake.

"Leave her alone! Don't kill her!" Marie shrieked.

Shaun forgot about me and turned his rage to Marie.

No!

He grabbed her hair, and a craze sank in me. It made me an animal and I saw black.

I can take the hits. I can take the beatings and the abuse and the torture. I can handle the war. Not her. Not Marie. I stood. I stood like he had never touched me, like I had never been beaten down.

Shaun fisted his hand into Marie's hair and she screamed. That's all I needed to hear. As he dragged her through my room by her hair, I grabbed the scissors from my desk and I lunged. I stabbed him and drove the blade into his shoulder. He could beat me. I could take it. No one touches my sister. Not Marie.

Yelping, he released her and stumbled. He hauled off and punched me. I dropped the scissors and fell. I didn't feel it, but I lost my balance and hit the floor. When I looked up again, he had Marie by the hair and had dragged her out of my room.

He closed my door and was gone.

I heard her screams. I listened to Shaun slam her door closed, and then silence. I had to make sure he wouldn't harm her and if I moved, he may just go after her to rile me just like he did my cats. I had no idea what he would do to her. I had no doubt he would kill me.

I slowly opened my door and peered into the hall.

Shaun was gone.

Marie opened her door and looked at me. She was frail and shaking. She looked so small. She had never known fear like this. She was only eleven and this was my world, my reality. How I would give anything for her to have never seen it.

"Elizabeth?" Marie whispered through sobs.

I signaled and she ran to me and held me.

"Come on," I said and led her to our parents' room and the phone.

I dialed my grandparents' number too late.

"Oh, isn't this sweet," Shaun said, standing over us. He grabbed us both by the hair, pulled us to our feet, and dragged us out of the room with the two of us screaming.

"Leave her alone!" I said.

He ignored me and shoved me into my room then closed my door between us. I threw it open in time to see him shove Marie her back into her room.

I heard the basement door close. There was a knock at the front door, and the three of us froze.

Our parents were home with Eugene and there was a cop at the door.

* * *

I stood there while Shaun pulled his shirt over his shoulder and showed where I had stabbed him.

"She did that to me," he whined at the cop.

"He beat me!" I said. "And he gra—"

"Do you realize what you could have done?" my mother said, shooting her venom at me.

I held my tongue. My father shouted. The cop agreed and so began the forty-five minute lecture about the consequences of first degree murder.

I looked at Marie for support. For her to say anything. I would not be believed. In five years, I had not been believed. But she was there. I finally had a witness. Someone who saw into my hell. She saw what he did to me. She said it herself. *Don't kill her.*

Marie stood there, shaking from the adrenaline, hugging herself, and sobbing while Shaun trashed my name.

Yes. I know the shaking and the cold, I thought. *The adrenaline dumped into your system prepares you to fight him or run. When the effects wear off you'll be cold then exhausted. You'll sleep well tonight. I know the effects of adrenaline well.*

The officer was done and now it was my mother's turn to lecture. She scolded me and lashed out at me. She screamed. Never mind the five years of threats. The torture, the abuse. I looked at my mother, my father, the police officer. I looked at Marie who never should have seen. She was staring at the floor, shaking. I looked at my half-brother, suppressing a smug smile.

No one believed me. No one was with me. No one knew my hell. I was alone. Got it. Lesson learned. This was my war and it was me against the world.

Chapter 11

"Joe said he'd pay twenty dollars if it meant you would fuck him."

I scoffed at Piss-ant on the other end of the phone and stared out my window. It was a dark summer night. If there was a moon, I couldn't see it.

Joe's offer was twenty times more than I was worth. My father had started counting every penny he put into me. Every dime. Every dollar. He couldn't give me a gift or hand me food without telling me how much I took from him. How selfish I was. How much my existence cost him. I had decided that I was worth exactly a dollar and if my father had to choose between the dollar and me, he would choose the dollar. TV was far more valuable. I was low on his list. Twenty dollars was high.

I hung up the phone enraged. Piss-ant had flirted and boasted and flounced his attraction then shoved me onto Joe, yet again.

My phone rang. Just long enough for Piss-ant to call Joe and say, 'You're up.'

"Hello," I said. I hadn't bothered to hide the irritation in my tone.

"What's wrong?" It was Joe.

"I just got off the phone with Piss-ant. I'm so pissed at him right now that I could fuck you!"

Silence.

Fuck. I thought. *Of all the people I could have said that to...*

"I can be there in twenty minutes," he said and hung up the receiver.

Fuck!

I gazed at the clock. It was ten. My parents were asleep.

"Great," I scolded myself. "Now I have gotten his hopes up. Bitch move, Beth. Now you're a cock tease."

Oh, no. You're not! A female voice scolded from somewhere deep within my head. *You promised,* she argued. *You deliver!*

I did promise. I didn't want to. Maybe he wouldn't show.

Twenty minutes later, Joe was throwing pebbles at my window.

Right. Not show, my ass, I thought and scolded the voice in my head. Going back on such a proposal was downright selfish of me. I had no choice.

"Be right there," I whispered out my window to Joe. I closed my window, sighed, and slipped into the warm night.

"Where do we go?" he asked.

"Here," I said and went to the only place where I knew to go. The wood.

He followed me into the forest. I don't care. I didn't care. I was angry. Only angry. I didn't want to, but I had promised. If I am nothing, I'm a man of my word. I am not a cock tease. I led him into the forest fueled with my anger.

I had walked that trail so many times before. I knew this place. It was dark. The moonlight couldn't penetrate the canopy, but I knew exactly where we were. I knew each curve, each tree. I knew how much time it would take to get there, but that night I walked the longest hike into the wood.

I had no plans. Just walk to the end of the trail and fuck him. I didn't care. I was too angry to care about anything.

"Here," I said when we arrived at the glen.

"Now what do we do?" He asked the question like he was trying to read radio directions upside down.

I wanted this over with. I am not renowned for holding back or wasting time. I shoved him onto the ground.

I knew it would hurt. Hurt was something I understood. Hurt was something I could handle. Hurt was what I wanted. Maybe if I hurt, I could feel again. Feel something again. And it was no less than I deserved. He had no idea what he was doing. I helped him get his dick out. I laid on the ground, braced myself, and shoved him into me. It hit my vaginal wall.

"It won't go in," he said. He was such an incompetent idiot.

"No," I said. "You'll have to break through it." He really had no idea what he was doing. I had no idea what I was doing and spent that night wondering how I knew any of it myself. I had been sheltered. Sex was an evil, an original sin that was kept from me. But somehow I knew there was a wall he had to break through. Somehow I knew how to proceed.

He slammed into me and stopped fast.

"Again," I instructed him.

"And again," I said.

Annoyed, impatient, and frustrated, I braced myself and timed it. I slammed myself down on him as he thrust, and he ripped me apart. Like a blade, he impaled me. Blood, not cum, flowed, and I told him to move, to fuck me. He did. It felt like he had stabbed me between the legs with a blade then fucked the wound. Warm blood, hot blood covered us. I bit down and bore through the pain while he fucked my injury.

I wanted it. I welcomed it. And I hated. I hurt, but I could feel again. I could feel something again. My legs went numb from the pain, and I pulled him in deeper and harder. I hated that I went numb. I wanted to feel something. I purposely ground harder to sharpen the pain. My pelvis screamed. My vagina burned, and I wanted it, I welcomed him, and I hated them all. I hated Piss-ant and Joe and my half-brother. I hated my father. But most of all, I hated me.

I threw my head back and welcomed the rage with the pain. His cum mingled with my blood, he groaned, and relaxed onto me. My anger was finally subsiding. I hadn't finished. I would never finish. I wasn't aroused. I only hated, but the pain was coming back to me. When he pulled out of me, it felt like a second blade re-slicing the raw wound, and we passed out right there on the forest floor as I silently sobbed in the dark.

***

I woke the next morning stiff, sore, and miserable as if my entire body was hungover. He was on cloud nine. My rage had settled into a sick ball of regret.

Fuck. I don't suppose I can go back from this? I thought. I had problems getting rid of him as it was. I was in deep shit.

He woke and we walked back to my house. Our clothes were covered in blood. There was so much blood and it was everywhere.

We didn't make it five minutes.

"Hey," he said. "Let's go again."

I looked at him. The anger had ebbed and left behind the stale hate. He had no clue how much pain I was in. He paid no mind to the blood that covered us and my initial rage toward Piss-ant had ebbed.

"No," I said. "I don't want to."

Wrong words, Beth.

His eyes turned cold and the Joe that I always had suspected was there, that Joe that I knew lay dormant beneath the sweet smiles, came out loud and clear.

He went cold and gazed at me with such loathing.

"You don't love me," he said and broke down whimpering at me.

I felt guilt. And, for a moment, I attempted to stand my ground.

"I don't want to," I said.

"It's because of Piss-ant!" he argued. "I'll kill him, I'll—"

Kill.

Wrong word to use with me. I heard that word and, as always, I believed it.

"Wait," I said as he punched the trees and swore. Fear gripped me and I cursed my own selfishness. I could feel his anger climb.

He looked at me with false sincerity that ripped my heart out and I tasted the bitter stab of guilt. I knew his pain. I lived it. He turned his eyes gentle and whimpered.

"Please, let me fuck you?" he begged.

Or what? Or you'll kill him if I don't? Or worse. You'll reject me.

I said nothing, but laid back on a rock. I let him do whatever he wanted to me. The pain the first time was nothing to the pain the second day.

I bit my hand to stop the screams.

Chapter 12

"I felt him rip right through me. His body shredded mine and the blood flowed. I buckled against the pain and I welcomed it. It felt like I was being fucked with a knife."

I opened my eyes and saw William. The overhead light still cast a dull orange over my kitchen table. Without a word, I took up a cigarette from my pack of kreteks and I lit it. I breathed deep the sweet taste of clove and inhaled.

I wanted to kill. I wanted my swords. I needed to fight.

William just stared, his mouth open like a dead fish.

I looked at him knowing the cold hate in my eyes and I watched him cringe.

I released another stream of smoke.

William said nothing. He just sat and watched as I smoked.

Sometimes silence is all you can say.

After several long minutes, I smashed out the butt of my cigarette and continued.

* * *

Within the next year, I would become their play thing. Joe and Piss-ant were neighbors. I would head on over to Joe's house, fuck him, share a tent with Joe and Piss-ant, and armed with bows and knives, we slithered around the neighborhood pretending to be spies. With the war I fought at home, this play was a joke to me, but they accepted me. I watched their pissing contests, literal pissing contests, shared their porn, and lived like a boy that year.

And when we were done, they toyed with me. It was all a game to me. They would fondle my breasts and stroke my leg. They would delight in seeing me respond. One would shove a hand down my pants while the other sucked my breast. One finger fucked me while I sucked dick. I hated every moment. I hated myself, and welcomed the war. My parents never knew nor did they care enough to notice my absence. My crying was incessant and, as always, was ignored.

One camp out went as bad as bad could go. Piss-ant and Joe were filthy, and I got sick. A week prior, Piss-ant had dropped his dick in the dirt then fucked me with it. It was like being fucked with sandpaper. Just like sandpaper that grated the tender flesh of my vaginal walls like cheese.

The pain was excruciating. I bore down and took it. Hey. At least I could feel something.

The night of the camp out, the pain from the infection was exceptional. I grabbed some pain meds and swallowed without water. The pills stuck and dissolved in my throat. They burned and, for medical reasons I can not give, I found it difficult to breathe. Very difficult. I had to fight for every breath as if my air passage was shrinking. After an hour, they woke and found me unable to breathe. I had turned blue.

They took turns running to a stream to bring me water. It eased the pain and washed the burn away, but I still couldn't breathe. After nearly two hours, I slipped away.

I opened my eyes to a cold room I had not seen before. Erik was there and, before us, we looked through the wall like a window. I could see Piss-ant and Joe and we watched them nursing me. I saw what I was, what I had become.
"What are you doing?" Erik said.
I looked at him. Erik never spoke.
"You're so much more than this," he said. "So much more than any of this."
I watched Piss-ant feed me stream water.
"You would let them consume you, devour you, destroy you?" His voice washed over me like music. "What is it you want?"
"I want you," I answered. "Just you."
"What have you learned?"
I watched Joe fuddle with my head, tipping it up so that I could drink. Neither had any idea what to do. If I was dying, I would be dead before either bothered to get help. Would a search party find me days later? Would the boys do their best to hide my body and keep their secret?
"To thine own self be true." I whispered the words of Shakespeare aloud. Erik nodded and then he was gone.
I looked at Piss-ant through the window wall and in that moment, as quickly as I had wanted him three years prior, I stopped. Just like that, all at once, I stopped.

When I slipped back into the world, I awoke and was calm. I was resolved and had decided I was done with Piss-ant.

The next day we spoke on the phone. He degraded me, offended me, mocked me. He all but opened my mouth and spit down my throat and then he laughed at my expense.

"Why do you think you can treat me like this?" I said.

"Because I always have." I could hear his grin on the other end of the phone. He was so proud.

"Not anymore," I said and hung up the receiver.

I never spoke to him again.

* * *

"Look, you've never really given me a fair shot." I listened to Joe whine. "We've always been on again, off again for no more than two weeks at the most."

I sighed and rubbed my temples. I didn't care anymore. I didn't want him. I felt stronger, determined. I didn't need him. I didn't need anyone. But he was like a giant leech that drained the blood from me. No matter how much I kicked at him and shooed him away, he wouldn't leave.

"What do you want, Joe?"

"I want a fair shot." He wasn't asking.

"And how long is fair to you?"

"Six months," he commanded.

Six months, I thought. *Six months and then we would be over.*

"Six months and I'll never bother you again," he promised.

Six more months of this sniveling, whimpering hell...

"Fine," I said, "You have your six months."

That six months became a year.

Chapter 13

I sighed and slapped my hands down on the kitchen table.

"I need a break," I said and stood. William put down his pen.

"How were your grades in school?" he asked as I made my way to the living room.

"Terrible," I said. "Just a moment."

I grabbed the heavy fur blanket from the back of an old rocking chair and returned to the kitchen table, pulling it over my shoulders. "I was too busy fighting the war in the jungles of southern China to think about school. I used music to escape. Music to feel something aside from the hate, and spent most of my time in the other worlds when I wasn't being used as Joe's play thing.

"Already I had learned to shut down and control my emotions. I remember the day Piss-ant cheated on me... I slipped into one of my worlds where I stayed for three hours. I know it was three hours because when I came back, my cousin had told me how long I had laid on her bed, staring at the wall, not blinking. When I came to,

I was smiling and joking as if the world was right. Her boyfriend was there. I took off my pants and sat on the bed in my thigh length shirt and panties. I just wanted to be comfortable. I didn't think anything of it. The girl in charge of watching us came in and screamed at me.

"I put my clothes back on... I remember feeling very little. No. I felt nothing. Nothing. By the time I started that six month stretch with Joe, my emotions had been sealed. There was very little outside of joy that I permitted myself to feel. Jealousy, anger, hate, rage, fear, sorrow, grief... these were weak emotions to me. These were emotions I couldn't afford to feel. I did my best to seal them away and bury them."

William removed the pencil tip from his mouth. "Where were Isaiah and Elena in all of this?"

"Isaiah was there, always watching, always silent, always smiling, always supportive. And always nothing more," I said. "Elena and I hung out between classes. Now and then I would escape the hell and enter the nirvana that was her home. I couldn't leave my own home often or for very long because leaving meant I left my cats at the mercy of Shaun. My cats were the only reason why I didn't try to run away again."

"Again?" William asked.

I nodded. There was so much to say, I worried about getting all the points in there. I decided to fit them in where I could while I was still talking.

"When I was eight, I packed my bags and left in the dead of winter. I made it to the farm house five miles down the road when I called my parents. I was yelled at, scolded, and openly ridiculed for leaving. My mother wanted to know why I left, and I refused to tell her it was because I felt unloved and unwanted. I refused to open up or talk to them. I would only be mocked, scolded, and ridiculed."

I sighed and let my head fall onto the back of the chair.

"My mother was the kind of person who denied any emotion, any belief, any truth if she didn't agree with it. She had already made it clear there was no love or empathy in her heart. 'Children should be seen and not heard.' I loathe that proverb. I was raised on it. So I said nothing. She was unsatisfied with my silence.

"When I said nothing, she made up a lie and insisted that was the reason for my runaway. I think she was embarrassed that she had a runaway for a daughter. She then told everyone in the family her lie and everyone believed her. Everyone laughed and my mother was their leader. To this day, my siblings believe her lie over my truth. It is so old that they have no idea they were fooled by her lie."

William creased his brow in question. "What was her lie?"

I stared across the table, not bothering to hide my contempt.

"I have lived in the shadow of that lie since I was eight. My mother would present my one-time attempted runaway to the family as an amusing anecdote at reunions. My siblings soon followed her example. To this day, they bring it up and laugh at my expense.

"I will tell you how I was raped and beaten. I will tell you how fucked up and psychotic I am. I will tell you any truth you wish to know. I will not tell you her lies. I tried to run away once. I never ran away again. My cats needed me to protect them."

* * *

The first three months of "officially" dating Joe were spent with our parents practicing the child exchange. My mother dropped me off at Joe's house. Joe's father, Jake, dropped Joe off at the ranch. Joe and I would go to my room and fuck.

Jake. Jake was a light in the dark for me. Joe had spoken of me often to his father. I remember the very day I met Jake. I had walked to Joe's house and Jake came home from work. I was fifteen. Jake looked miserable. I love Jake, but I won't lie. Jake was miserable then. He had no girlfriend, no wife, paid an insane amount of child support that left him impoverished, and worked a day job that sucked the life from him.

"This is Beth," Joe said.

Jake gazed at me as if he had just shot up with a dose of exhaustion and misery.

"Okay..." he said.

Joe rattled off something neither Jake or I listened to when the light suddenly turned on in Jake's eyes.

"Wait!" he said. "This is Beth?"

"Yeah," Joe said.

"*The* Elizabeth?" Jake said.

"Yes!"

"Oh, girl!" he said to me. "You and I, we're going to have a talk right now."

Right there, Jake sat me down on the couch in the living room and, for the next five hours, he talked to me about drugs, sex, and rock and roll, everything a parent should have said to me. Within five minutes into the conversation, I was enamored with the man who would become like a father to me.

* * *

By mid-summer, Joe and I fell into the routine of weekly visits, sometimes up to three times a week. Jake dropped

Joe off and left or my mum dropped me off at Joe's and left. One day, Jake dropped Joe off like any other. Joe and I went to my room and fucked. When we were done, we emerged to find our parents sitting on the porch talking. Jake had never left. Joe and I hung out, had sex again, went back a few hours later. Our parents were still talking.

For the next two weeks, my mother was more than eager to drive me to Joe's house at every chance she had. At his place, Joe and I went upstairs, had sex, and when we came back down stairs, my mother was still there. One afternoon, we came downstairs and found my mother buttoning her shirt. Jake had the widest grin on his face.

Soon after, my mother was asking if I wanted to go to Joe's even on days Joe and I hadn't made any plans. I'd consent. My would mother drive us over and leave for a walk with Jake.

After a couple weeks of this, my mother pulled me aside.

"Don't tell your father."

Right. Don't tell my father. Cause he's on my side when Shaun beats me. Right. Neither was she for that matter. I wasn't involved. I had no sides. No one was on my side. I was on no one's side and I sought to do no one any favors. I stayed out of it.

After a month of this, Mum drove me into town to drop me off at Joe's when we spotted Jake's truck outside the local diner.

"Is that their truck?" Mum asked.

"It is," I said.

She pulled over, parked the car, and we went in. I sat beside Joe while my Mum slid down beside Jake. While my mum and I waited for them to finish their dinner, my father showed up at the table. Apparently, my mother was in the middle of groping Jake.

My father lashed out, confronted her right there. When she didn't give him the answers he wanted, he looked at me.

"And you knew about this?" he asked. He looked at me with such hate.

I threw my hands up. "I'm staying out of this."

I loathed him for dragging a child into it. I detested them both for shouldering me with such crap.

If my father hated me before, it was nothing compared to how he looked at me that day. Later, my father would go on to tell me he blamed me for his marriage falling apart. My father reserved a special hate for me after that day.

He looked back at my mother. They argued. I wanted to shrivel up and die. I tuned out their argument, but zoned back in to hear the end of it.

"If you're going to do this then get out," my father said to Mum. "Come to the house, get your shit, and get out."

My father never swore. I watched him leave the diner. Jake threw down his dinner and the race began.

They called Joe's uncles and, within thirty minutes Jake and my mother showed up at the ranch with two pick-up trucks. To Joe, it was a looter's party. He and his uncles cleared everything out. Stripped the place clean. My father sat on the back porch, facing the forest while they ransacked the house. I stole a quick glance at the shell of a man too broken to care if they left anything. They took cookware, movies, everything along with all of my mother's possessions and a good portion of my father's things. Last, but not least, my mother grabbed Eugene and Marie and ordered them to pack their bags. Sobbing, my siblings collected their things without so much as an explanation from my mother. Charles went out and sat with my father. They shared a pack of cigarettes.

For my mother, the event meant she was running off with her lover and riding out into the sunset. For Joe and Jake, their girlfriends were moving in with them. For my father, his life, everything he had worked for, was stripped from him. For Shaun, I think he was thrilled for the break up. My mother was the woman who took his father from him and his own mother. For Charles, he witnessed my mother rip the still beating heart from my father. For Eugene and Marie, they were uprooted, ripped from their home, taken from their father, shipped off to a house they had never seen, and sent to live with strangers.

For me, the experience was like no other. I stripped my room, collected my cats, and welcomed the end of my war. I was leaving Shaun, the daily threats, the beatings. My cats were leaving the daily torture sessions they lived with and the abuse. I was taking them to a place where they would never be hurt again. I could not run fast enough.

I slung my guns over my shoulder, sheathed my swords, took up my cats, loaded my bow, and donned my fatigues and war paint for the last time.

For me, I was getting the hell out of Vietnam.

That first night, I lay in a bed in the upstairs room next to Joe's. I could hear Marie and Eugene crying downstairs, loud and long all night. My mother slept soundly next to Jake in her room. As usual, she ignored the cries.

My heart hurt for my siblings. They didn't understand. They didn't know. They were children. They couldn't possibly understand what was going on. Marie was thirteen years old. Eugene was eight.

* * *

"How old were you?" William asked as I nursed a small flame within the fireplace. The dampness in the air had finally pushed me to start a fire.

"I was sixteen," I said after a moment and strategically layered the peat logs onto the tinder and growing fire. "Charles had just turned eighteen."

"And he stayed with your dad?"

"My father," I said. "Yes."

The fire took off and I pulled my blanket around my shoulders.

"Why did Charles stay?" William asked.

I sighed remembering the years of events I had reviewed with my siblings.

"My brother had an unusual experience with my mother," I said. I stared into the fire and watched the flames lick the air. "About two months before all this went down, he found her sleeping with another man."

"You mean Jake," William asked.

"Not Jake," I said.

"Wait." I heard William scoot his chair. "Your mother was sleeping with Jake, your father, and—"

"A third man," I said. "Yes... at the same time."

William scoffed in disbelief, leaving me to continue.

"That day, Charles went off, smoked a pack of cigarettes, and when he got back, he confronted her. My mother denied everything. As I said, if she didn't like it, she denied it."

"What happened?" William asked.

"I don't know the details," I said, settling myself back to the table. "I was too busy surviving the jungle to pay attention to the opposing sides of the war. What little I know, my father told me about.

"My father went through the courts and got Eugene and Marie back almost right away. I think they stayed with

Jake and my mum for a total of two nights... maybe. My father sought out counseling for himself and my siblings."

"What about you?" William asked.

I threw my head back and laughed. William stared intently at me.

"I went to counseling," I said, still chuckling. "I fucked with them."

"You fucked with them?"

"I wasn't stupid," I said. "I slipped in and out of worlds that weren't there. I wrote letters to fictitious characters. I was passing into catatonic states more times than not. It required a concerted amount of effort to keep myself here in this world. I was a runaway. I tried to slit my wrists. I was clinical, and I knew how to hide my condition.

"My father wasn't wrong. I was smart. I had read up on psychology in my encyclopedia set. I knew the words they would use, the signs they looked for. I knew everything they would ask me and why. I danced with them and played their game. I smiled and dished it back. They were charmed, delighted. I walked away a clean bill of health."

"Why didn't you let them help you?" William asked, no longer the interviewer before me, but a concerned friend. I saw worry, concern, in his eyes and I felt anger. "They could have helped you," he said.

"Helped me?" I scoffed and felt the venom flow from me. "And I thought I was delusional."

He paid no mind to my passive-aggressive wit.

"There are clinics, medicines—"

"I told them what my half-brother did to me," I said. "When I was thirteen and my half-brother was beating me, my parents shoved me into therapy to 'fix' me. When I told them what my half-brother did to me, my mother lied her ass off to protect Shaun. My mother danced her dance and gave her finest performance. She convinced the therapist that I was a chronic liar. I was punished by my parents and the therapist threw out my testament. They believed my mother over me!

"Two years later, I told the school therapist about the hell I lived! About the abuse. Help me? She called the police, who threatened to arrest me for statutory rape because I was a year older than Joe! The officer said if I got pregnant, he would personally arrest me!

"When my father felt I was crazy because I was fifteen and liked opera, oh, he got me help alright. He had me see a third therapist. Asked if they could fix me, to get the opera out of me. He sent me home with a clean bill of health. Help me? They don't help. Therapists don't help! They didn't!"

"They could," William insisted.

"They had the chance in their hands. I told them every horror I had lived. And they branded me a liar and threw it out! They threatened to charge me with rape! They saw nothing wrong with me! I trust no one! Least of all therapists! No one can help me!"

"This is different," William said.

"Do you want to hear this story or not?"

Chapter 14

I smiled to hide the hell I lived. I smiled to hide the darkness. On the surface, I smiled and grinned and laughed. I had mastered my emotions. What emotions I feel, I allow. No one suspected my wars. Living with Joe was better than living with Shaun. I was happy. My cats weren't abused. I no longer needed my subterranean lake or Erik. The war was over.

It was supposed to be.

Joe loved playing with my body. Loved tormenting it. Loved control. What I didn't know, was that the cold hate left in his heart from when his mother beat and abandoned him, left him loathing women. He hated women. He sought to punish each and every one of them. He loved giving them pain. He started with me.

He asked things of me and I said yes because if I said no, he threatened to return me to my father's house. In my mind, Joe threatened to send me back to war. It was selfish of me to say no. I felt guilt for saying no. I never said no. So I said yes, always yes to avoid that war.

The first of his requests were simple.
"Let me tie you to the bed."
I said yes.
"Let me bleed you. Let me bite you."
I said yes.

He handcuffed me down and he bit me. He bit my nipples. He bit my breasts and I'd scream and he'd smile in the dark.

"Let me slide ice on you." Only he'd hold it there and he'd freeze me. Joe loved hearing me scream. He eventually stopped asking altogether.

He put my nose in his mouth and he'd blow. He'd blow so hard my brain burned and I screamed and he'd laugh. Oh, he loved hearing me scream. It was one of his favorite games. He bit my vagina. He bit my clit. He'd freeze my skin then bite me. He dug at me and clawed my skin. He fucked me until I bled. There was never any lubricant. He tore at me and left me cuffed to the bed.

When he was bored with hearing me scream in bed, he made me scream in my head. He'd turn the lights off and make me watch horror movies. He was convinced they would scare me, and I would cling to him for comfort.

Stupid fuck. I don't need comfort. I don't hug humans for comfort. I don't touch. In the dark, I watched movies that scarred me. I walked away terrified of aliens and horror. One more fear. One more condition. At that point, none of it mattered.

During the day, I walked away from the bedroom smiling and pretending everything was alright. I killed the emotion. I deadened myself to feeling anything. My cats were safe. There was no war. So I was good. All was good.

At night, Joe smoked his marijuana and painted pictures on his walls. I laid there subjected to his experiments while I studied the psychedelic glues and he bled me, tasting of ash and weed. He bit me and drank my blood. His fingers would rip me. He didn't ask. He no longer cared if I consented or not. Chained to his bed, he stripped everything from me, including my voice.

He grew colder. The control grew worse. And it wasn't enough. It was never enough. I was his own personal sex doll and I was mute.

He had friends over and he saw the way they looked at me. Physically, back then, I was gorgeous. Green hate consumed him and so he took to locking me in my room.

"Get the fuck in that room and don't come out."

I sat down on my bed and I cried.

He'd come in when he was stoned. He would fuck me and leave me.

Once, I said no. Once, I found my voice long enough to say, "No." It was the only time. It would be the last time I ever said no again.

He pouted and did the one thing I could not stand. He rejected me. He called me selfish. He shunned me and ignored me. What little love I had, he took from me. I fell to his feet.

"I'm sorry. You can fuck me. I'm sorry. Please don't hate me."

I begged for an hour. I unfastened his pants and I sucked him. I did anything to keep him from rejecting me. I can't live with rejection.

It took so much to earn back his love. When I did, he fucked me and left me. He used me. He fucked me. He left me every time. I lay on my bed naked with fresh semen running down my leg and he was already out the door, leaving me there alone to cry. I cried. The voice in my head screamed. Erik was gone, and the lake.

There were days I tried to emerge from that room.

"Get the fuck back in your room!" he would say.

"I'm sorry," I answered and obeyed. Hey. At least I was out of the war. At least my cats were safe.

The sex was cold. It always hurt. He'd slam me down, fuck me, and leave me to bleed. I fell asleep crying every night, left alone to listen to the screams in my head.

* * *

I stood in that room. That steel room, cold and dark. There were no doors.

Every night, I dreamed of rape. Every night I dreamed of being chained down. I felt them on me. Men with no faces. Sometimes one, sometimes many. They would use me and pass me around. I didn't say no, but I didn't want it. They would leave me and I'd be in that room, naked and cold and the Death Men would find me. I couldn't get out. I couldn't get out.

* * *

I knew William was watching me, but only barely.

I stared at the kitchen table and saw nothing while I rocked in my chair, hugging myself. I pulled my blanket close to me.

Hey. Elizabeth, Ian said. *You're slipping again.*

I ignored Ian. I didn't feel like his jokes right now. All I saw was the girl on the floor in that room, swaying and rocking and naked.

"I'm sorry," I said to her. "I'm sorry... so sorry."

I swayed in my chair and I muttered:

"Slowly encumbered. Dying out numbered,

Death now I'm vanquished. Broken and battered.

There on the cold, stone floor, I raise my eyes to the storm,

There where the crow doth go, left me to ponder."

"Elizabeth?" I heard William say, but I couldn't answer.

I was in the steel room with no doors. It was dark and empty. She was there, naked on the floor in the dark. She was bent over on her knees, hugging herself and rocking. Black hair fell like sleek strips and still I muttered.

"And the silence, it cuts me. The silence, it gores me, Spilling my blood as the rain falls on me."

He raped me, she whispered.

I quit my rambling and I listened. She rocked.

He raped me and you didn't know, she said.

I gazed at the blue moonlight upon her spine. I could count each vertebrae.

"I'm sorry," I said. "So sorry."

She hugged herself and rocked, paying no mind to my regret.

"I'm so sorry, Angel," I said. Sweet Angel.

She raised her cold, black eyes to me. Her cheeks were sunken in from starvation. Her chains scraped the floor and her wrists, raw from the metal, bled.

You left me in that room with no doors! she screamed. *I couldn't get out! And you left me!*

"You," I said, hearing her voice and knowing. I had heard her voice before. She who told me I was selfish. She who said I was nothing. She who bled the most.

"It was you who lay in that room, naked in the dark," I said. "Forever in the dark, shivering on the floor."

She opened her mouth to scream, but I was already gone. And her screams followed.

I was in Dublin, standing with Ian in a pub. He had a pint of Guinness in hand.

"I dreamed I was fucking Joe," I said over the music and laughter. I was smiling as if I was having a grand old time. The band was playing a jig. ". . . and his dick broke off inside of me. I couldn't get it out. I dreamed I was fucking Joe and they passed me around like a dead doll. Shredded dolls. Broken dolls. Bleeding broken dolls."

"Elizabeth!" I heard William's voice again over the pub noise, but I ignored it.

"Keep with it, lass," I heard Raven say. "I'll listen."

I strained to hear his voice again, but Angel's screams grew louder.

"Raven!" I cried over the jig and the screams. A sudden belt of laughter filled the pub. If Raven answered, I didn't hear.

"She can't hear you, Raven," Ian said, talking to the ceiling of the pub. "She's gone and I'm drinking her Guinness. Sláinte!" Grinning, he raised his glass to the ceiling. "Today, drink Guinness, for tomorrow we vomit from alcohol poisoning," he said and launched into a song of his own composing:

"Drink, drink, drink to the lass.
Drink to the cock you shove up her ass.
Spill not a drop. Drink the last drop.
Drink to the lasses you can't tup."

"Raven," I whispered. The jig finished and there was applause. "Are you there?"

I looked around the Dublin pub.

"Raven?"

No answer. And the room went quiet and changed.

Silence.

The moonlight touched down on the lake and I was there all over again. In the distance within the shadows, I saw him. Erik.

"I see you, Erik," I whispered. "My silent Erik."

He tucked his violin under his chin and he played. His opera cloak moved with him. Drawn once more to the shadows, I followed. And as I stepped, I sang:
"Within my dreams you are there.
With watchful eyes the shadows stare.
Those haunting eyes I know them to be yours."

"Elizabeth!" I felt William's hands on me. I heard him, but I couldn't see anything, but the lake.

"Those summer eyes forever there,
Haunt me, forever stare.
Within your eyes I see the pain I bear."

"Elizabeth!"

"Silently watching me.
Forever haunting me."

"Elizabeth!"
And I saw William. I focused on him for that moment.
"I can't hate them," I said. "Not any of them. But I want to. I want to hate them, and I can't."
Erik was slipping. The subterranean lake was fading and I was back in my kitchen on the floor. William was holding my face in such a way that I had to look in his eyes.
"I can't hate," I said. "I want to hate them. But I can't. I can't—"
I remembered Raven.
"Raven?" I said, looking about the kitchen. "Where—"
Don't let her fuck you, boy, Ian said to the right of me. *Whatever you do, don't let her fuck you.*
William didn't hear and I kissed him. I closed my mouth onto William's and I kissed him. I licked his lip. I tasted

him. And I felt safe. I was safe. He opened his mouth for me and I shifted, pushing my tongue inside of him. He held my face. I felt his fingers curl gently into my hair, and he kissed me, but I wanted it rough. I was safe and exhausted and spent. I fell into his arms and this world slipped away.

* * *

I was back in the room with no doors. Blue light spilled onto the floor and across Angel's spine. She shook, she whimpered, she rocked, swaying to the music in her head. Slowly, she raised her face from the floor.

Crescents blackened her eyes as she peered through strands of hair. The madness had taken her. The madness was her. She shook and held herself against the death that clung to the air.

"It was you," I said. "You who sent me those dreams. All those dreams."

"You wouldn't listen," she said. Her voice was raw from the endless screams. Each word cut her throat and I could hear it bleed.

"And you left me," she said. "You left me here with no doors."

She hugged herself, her arms wrapped tight across her breasts.

"And you left me," she whispered. "You didn't listen. You didn't hear and you left me."

"They're coming back," I said boldly and before she could look at me in horror, the Death Men appeared and it was I, not she, who lay naked and cold and cowering in the dark.

And I could not breathe. I could not—

"Elizabeth?"

I opened my eyes.

I was in my kitchen again. I smelled the simmering stew. I heard my Cookie mew. I felt William's arm holding me up from the floor.

"Maybe we should call it a night," he said.

"No."

I had to get through this.

"Elizabeth—"

"I have to get through this!"

The memories flooded back and I tried to hold in all the pictures and pain. I was drowning and I couldn't hold my head above water. My lip quivered, I shook my head, trying my best to battle it all back. My hands shook, a tear spilled down my face and with it, the last of my strength.

"For six months," I said. "He held me locked in that room! To fuck me! He used me! He left me, abandoned me while I cried. I wished for death! It was supposed to be better! The war was over! It was supposed to be over! There was no one! No end! I'm alone! I was locked in that room for six months! And no one knew!"

William didn't move.

"I'm still there," I sobbed. "Always there. And I can not get out. I can not... I will always be there. I'm locked in that room with no doors."

And right then, after all the hate and the hell and the horror, I broke right there on the floor in front of William and sobbed like a fucking little pansy girl.

* * *

I stared at the bottle of Jameson. I don't know how long I had cried. The rains had stopped, but the wind blew cold. We sat listening to the wind cry like a bean sí.

"What time is it?" I asked.

"Going on two A.M."

I sat at the table, wrapped in my blanket as if the blanket alone would protect me from further harm.

"I can only imagine what I looked like to you," I said. "War worn and beaten, battered and broken." I looked at William. "That really is all I am. Broken."

He stared like so many others. Enamored, in awe, and confused. I shock them. I always seem to shock everyone. I hate it. In the end, he just didn't know what to say. I sighed and looked back at the bottle.

William sat staring down at his notes. I wished I could read him. I wished I could hear the thoughts in his head. I wished that often, to be able to read the thoughts of another. There are little fluxes in their tone, word choices that clue you in to their true feelings, the feelings people are careful to close up from others and hide. I could read tone and word choice too easily. All I had to do was get people talking. My only bane was when they chose to say nothing at all.

"Did he?" William asked.

"Did who?" I asked.

"Did Joe really lock you in a room for six months?"

"It was a metaphorical lock," I said, not looking up. "Did he literally keep me under lock and key? No. He didn't have to. I kept myself in that room. I had such a need for approval that I couldn't handle upsetting him. To take anything away from anyone was selfish. It still is, even if I don't want it. I relived my father's rejection every time I saw the disappointment and the hate in Joe's eyes. I couldn't live knowing someone hated me. I couldn't live with rejection. I still can't."

We sat listening to Ireland breathe.

William returned to his silent musing while I gazed at the bottle and relived the final days of my life with Joe.

"On the seventeenth day of February in the winter of '96, I had fallen about as far as I could go. On that day, I saw just how broken I had become."

I sighed with relief and pride at the memory.

"I had looked at myself in the mirror and saw the shadow that looked back in my eyes. I picked myself up, fueled on the same determination my half-brother saw the day he had beaten me into the ground when I stood against his fist.

"It was there that I found me. I, who could get me out of that nightmare. Not a man. Not a god or a friend. I and I alone. Armed with my strength and determination, I picked myself up off the floor. With a renewed passion in me to fight, I packed my bags, collected my cats, and I left Joe to return to the war."

William looked up from his papers. "You went back?"

I smiled.

"I went back, but I was not the same."

Part Three:
Agent Orange &
Clockwork

Chapter 15

I remember the night before I left. Joe had just gotten a snowmobile. He wanted to take me for a ride. I remember how odd it was to be let outside. I was already packed and had written him a letter explaining why I was leaving.

Over three years, I had attempted to leave Joe more than four dozen times. I did the phone break up, the "tell it to my face" break up, the "in the heat of the argument" break up, and the calm sensible "it's not you it's me" break up. Every break-up line that exists, I had used on him. If texting had existed, I would have tried that too. I hated the idea of a "Dear John" letter, but, given the circumstances, his temper, and my weakness for him, I decided cutting him off cold turkey was the only way to go. After I left there, I had decided to never speak to him again. We simply could not speak without him playing my heart strings like an Irish fiddle.

When I climbed onto the back of the snowmobile, the room and all my worries melted away and I could think clearly. I felt free. I think it was because I knew I was hours away from being released from my prison.

So much went through my mind while we rode through the forest over the snows. I thought of how much I would be leaving behind and I realized I wasn't. I was a thing Joe could have. He saw me as a trinket. A trophy he could keep, and I was strong. He knew that. Which meant, if he was going to keep me, I had to be broken. I remember how dark it was that night. It's funny. I was in that room for six months, but I don't remember seeing the sun once. In my mind, it was perpetual night. I don't know why. I attended school during those six months, but I don't remember a single moment of it. Only that room, laying in the filth and the dark. It was the ugliest of blacks that forever suspends over my memory.

The snowmobile hit a ditch and I bounced in my seat. It felt exhilarating and suddenly I was free. I was glad to be rid of him.

I don't remember anything after that. Not the ride home or my leaving. I do remember crying in the kitchen because I knew I would never kiss him again. Then he yelled at me for crying and I stopped crying right then because it was the first time I hated him.

I loved Joe. I did. Even now, after everything he did to me, I remember his charm, his wit, little things that made me laugh. He could be sweet when he wanted something. He accepted me. That was enough.

I mistook his acceptance as love. I know now it wasn't love. It was obsession. He was obsessed with me. Have you ever noticed how much the word "obsession" looks like "possession"? It's because they are nearly the same.

No. Joe did not love me. But Joe had me. He accepted me. That was all I was worth. You forget. I held my value to that of a dollar bill. And Joe was willing to pay twenty.

In my mind, he loved me twenty more times than my father ever would and I will never believe I'm more than that because my daddy told me so.

* * *

The next day, I was back at my father's house. I showered and felt like I was washing the filth of three years from my body. I scrubbed Joe from my flesh and my hair. I scrubbed every fold and crevice of my body and with it, I restored my sense of self. I was finding me. Developing, honing, and defining a sense of self that would stay with me to the end of my days. It was fresh and young and new, but it was there.

I didn't fear for my cats or myself. I think, after Joe...

If Joe taught me anything, it was to abandon fear. Don't misunderstand me. Beneath the dragon skin I was making for myself, I was very afraid, and fear would go on to rule my life. But by then, being back at the war... perhaps... Yes, that was it. The war was familiar. The war made me comfortable. I was a soldier who had returned home and didn't know anything else, but war. Being back was like returning me to my element and I wasn't afraid of the war anymore. I was afraid of love, of affection, of comfort. I was afraid of relationships where the danger could get close and personal. I was afraid of being touched.

At my father's house, with my half-brother, I could keep the threat at a distance and minimize the damage done. No... I was still afraid. But I was in control.

I showered for two hours. And when I emerged I remember saying, "It felt so good." My father remembers that too.

It was a Saturday. The house was quiet. The sun was shining and the internet was new. It was February '96. I was sixteen and single. For the first time in three years, my heart belonged to no one.

I remember the hissing of the dial up. The grating beeps of the land line being hooked up to a microphone—seriously, what dip shit thought up that idea?—that 'plink' and 'Welcome.' The freeway was open to pedophiles eager to find primed victims at their fingertips.

Three days after I left Joe, I found mine.

* * *

"Primed?" William asked.

"Yes," I said. "It takes a certain type of female to be preyed upon. There's a. . . requirement. My father, my half-brother, and Joe had done their best to prepare me for mine."

I popped the cap of another Guinness and downed half the bottle. I savored the beer while I thought for a moment before continuing.

"I need to prepare you," I said. "I don't know how to tell this part of my story from the victim's point of view. I hate. . . the concept of victim. Victim is one who was attacked, wounded, and never survived. I survived and grew strong from it. I conquered my existence, stood above it, and declared, I will not be taken down nor will you keep me! I am free. I am strong. I am not a victim! But I was hurt. They were the predators. I was preyed upon. I am no victim.

"To get through this next part, I must tell it the only way I know how and that is to reverse roles. To show you the mind of a pedophile as they see it. Maybe, just maybe, if you know how they think, you'll be far better prepared than I was and maybe. . . just maybe, there will be a father who reads this and learns."

Broken

* * *

When selecting your target, you want to move fast.
Online predators have mastered the art of sitting back and scanning a forum for a "target." They look for females who brag and boast: first sign that the target is insecure. Then they move in and feel her out. They ask about her: what she likes, what she hates. Insecure people often and easily talk about themselves when barely coaxed. Within five minutes, a predator can determine if the target is close to her father or not. You absolutely want a female who has daddy issues because if the "pinch and grab" is to work, the predator must segregate the child from the parent as soon as possible. If the female has a good relationship with her father, this can never happen and the predator knows it. The female with a healthy parental relationship will confide in the father they trust and the father will move in to protect.

The pedophile does this all while appearing sincere, genuine, loving, and affectionate. They compliment the target. Tell her things... like how smart or how beautiful she is. While they shower her with praise, they reinforce one message. "I accept you. I approve of you."

In truth, they are literally making notes as to what the target desires, dreams, and wants. They listen and reciprocate. The first three days are crucial for selecting a target. It's all about trust and earning it fast. Time is of the essence.

I walked into that room, opened my stupid fucking mouth and in my few boasts, announced to every pedophile there that I was insecure and had daddy issues. Scott messaged me two minutes later to tell me I was beautiful.

He asked my name with such sweet words. And when I replied, he answered, "Beautiful name for a beautiful woman."

I was sixteen. No one had called me a woman before. I had never heard a bad pick-up line before. At once, I was putty in his hands and he knew it.

I don't remember what we talked about. I remember blushing and smiling a lot. We were there only an hour, and he made me feel more loved than I had ever known in my entire life.

On day one, you want to select a target and study their wants, loves, hates, and weaknesses. Make an agreement to meet next day, same time, same place. This establishes a sense of dependency with the target.

"He came through for me."

"I can count on him."

"He is a man of his word."

These are the feelings you want to leave her with for day two. Always remember that time is of the essence.

I signed off, smiling like a hyena on morphine. I couldn't stop smiling. He had me. Already I was willing to give him anything all because he would accept me. I should be so lucky. I was only worth a dollar, after all.

Day two. Don't be prompt. Be earlier than prompt. Take her by surprise and message her with a compliment before she can even check to see if you are a man of your word. Joke and play with her. Use humor and flattery to give her all the attention she craves and will never get from her father.

The next day I woke and ran to him. The grating, the dial up, the cringing, the beep, the "welcome" of that stupid voice. I ran into that room, threw open the cyber doors, and slammed head first into his words.

"Good morning, beautiful."

And just like that, he had me. I had passed his first test. I would suck his dick. I would lick his shoes. I would build him a shrine where he could throw me down and rape me without my even knowing what he was doing.

He played and laughed. We joked. He teased. He led me around by the few remaining pieces of my heart and I willingly, stupidly followed. I was primed for what he would do next.

Once you've settled your target into a false sense of security, she'll have dropped her guard, which will prepare her for the next step. Shake her up, scare her and you'll have her where you want her. After that, she'll follow you anywhere. Beneath her boasting and bragging lies an untapped fear of rejection and/or abandonment. Play on that. The moment she is drugged on euphoria for feeling like the center of someone's world for a change, tell her you have to go. Do it fast, like ripping off a bandage.

She will cling to you, ask for you to stay. She will beg, implore that you to stay. Act uncertain and say little because you have to go. Give her no hope, no words that can sate her current fears. She must be afraid of losing you. Drive the sense of loss through her. Convince her that the only male who ever made her feel valuable is now leaving.

"That acceptance you looked for your whole life? Yeah, it's walking out the door."

She will beg you to stay and try to propose the same arrangement, which can become too complacent and you could lose the target before you can snag her.

"Meet me here tomorrow?" she'll ask.

"Eh... Don' t know. Maybe. I'm not really on that often," should be your response.

Scarcity enforces her fear of loss and rejection. Use that. Then ask for her number and if she declines, tell her you have to go. Do so suddenly. This will drive home the lesson that if she does not comply, she will be punished. You will need that later. Reinforce that she will lose you if she doesn't comply by replying to all her requests with indifference. Be brief. If she presses again, say nothing. Let her think she already lost you.

She will break because she finally found the acceptance she has needed. She will cave and give you her number. And when you do, reward her with a smile, a few more minutes of your time, another compliment, then leave—fast, while the relief is still dumping adrenaline in her system.

"I have to go."

He said the words so suddenly, so quickly, I felt like he ripped out my heart. I felt like I had done something wrong.

"What? Why?"

"I have an appointment."

Well, he did say he was busy, after all.

"Well, when can I see you again?" I asked.

"Don't know. I'm not on very often."

"Well, can we talk tomorrow?"

"I don't know," he said. "Maybe. I have to go."

"Well, what about tonight?" I was nearly screaming. I couldn't breathe.

"I don't know. I have time to call you if you give me your number, maybe I can find the time."

I felt sick. I wasn't allowed to give out my number.

"I can't," I said.

"I gotta go. Later."

"But when?"
"Don't know." His tone was cold and indifferent. "Bye."
"Wait!"
Silence.
"Please!" I implored.
Silence.
"555-856-1742," I caved.
"Thank you," he replied and just like that, I could breathe again.
"I think I have time to call in the morning," he said.
Suddenly he had time to chat? Yeah. I didn't notice. I was too relieved to see he stayed.
"I'll call you tomorrow," he said.
And just like that, he was gone.
That is how you hook your targets.
Shower with praise and develop a sense of acceptance. Make a request and watch her obey. Punish her with rejection. Reward with approval using gifts and compliments. All of this is impossible if a daughter knows her father loves her, and she isn't needing the acceptance from others.
You want to keep your daughter safe from a pedophile? Make sure she knows you love her. Accept her for what she is and she'll open her heart and tell you everything. A father who nurtures the love of a daughter protects her. Mine didn't.
The phone rang. I looked at the clock. My father was still in bed. It was 7:00. I ran to the phone and answered it before it had a chance to ring again.
"Hello?"
"Hello, Elizabeth?"
"Hi." I grinned like a fool and I remember nothing after that.
He told me how old he was, but it didn't matter. I was already head over heels in love for this forty-five year old

monster. I was sweet sixteen and eating out of the palm of his hand.

Chapter 16

We spoke every day, for hours. We made plans to meet four weeks later: March of 1996. We spent that month speaking of philosophy and music. By then, I could feel and recognize the fear. I was terrified of getting close to anyone. I didn't know what it was, but I knew what I was becoming. I felt it only fair to warn him.

"If you hurt me, I will hurt you. If you hurt me, I will run and I will take you down with me."

My way was simple, I thought. Don't hurt me. He didn't quite see things my way.

I screamed, I ranted. He let me talk. He let me ramble on from my soapbox, declaring my threat. And once I had provided him with all the evidence he needed, he tried, judged, and convicted me all while dropping the gauntlet on my sorry ass.

He became so angry. It was the first time I ever saw him angry. It wouldn't be the last and he punished me by taking the one thing I valued: approval.

"No," he said, "I will not be coming down tomorrow. I will not make myself vulnerable so you can attack me. I am hanging up this phone right now and you will not speak to me again until you apologize."

Click and silence.

I sobbed. My hands shook. I cursed myself for what I had done and my hands trembled as I dialed his number.

"S-Sco—"

"Are you calling to apologize!?"

"N-n-no... I—"

Click.

I swear there was a dagger in my chest and he was holding it there, twisting it. I couldn't see the numbers through my tears.

"S-Sco—"

"Are you calling to apologize?"

"I—"

"Are you calling to apologize."

"No—"

Click.

I couldn't stop crying and hated myself. I loved him and I had hurt him. He said so. I dialed the number. My fingers slid over the tears that soaked the buttons.

"Are you calling to apologize?"

"Yes!" I said before he could hang up again.

He listened. And there was my reward.

"Apologize for what?" he asked.

Yes. He was actually walking me through it.

"For arguing, for threatening you," I said.

"What else?"

"For hurting you."

"And?"

My mind scrambled. I couldn't think. What else had I done?

"Goodbye," he said.
"No, please! For..."
"You don't know what you did?"

I punched my brow trying to remember what I couldn't possibly know. I pulled at my hair and I rocked on my knees while I sobbed.

"I cancelled plans to come up to see you," he said. "I had to rework my entire schedule to make it happen and you pulled this shit!"

"Well, can't you still come up?"

"No."

The word slammed the dagger in my chest a little deeper.

"I can't trust you," he said. "I don't know if you can be trusted ever."

Ever. I could lose him. I held my breath.

"Is there nothing I can do?" I asked.

"I don't know. We'll have to see."

And that is what we did. He rejected me and delayed the trip by two weeks.

That argument was the structure for all of our arguments for the next five years. I would have my say. He would listen like the attorney he was. Collecting data, letting me ramble and dig my own grave until I stopped to sigh with relief from my vent.

He would then ask, "Are you finished?"

"Yes."

"Good, because now, you're going to listen to me."

And his rant would begin. I felt like a murderer on the stand of my own trial and my defense attorney was laying drunk on the floor while the prosecuting attorney ate me alive. I watched my words get chewed up and spit back in my face. I watched my logic get shredded. I was always found guilty. Scolded for hurting him. Scolded for taking from him. For ruining his plans.

"It's no wonder your father doesn't love you. Now I am hanging up and you will not speak to me again until you apologize."

Click.

That cold click. How I would grow to hate more than ever before. Scott would take my hate and refine it until I wallowed in it. Mastered it while I was left to scold myself for having imperfect logic.

Soon, he had me scolding myself. I was playing back his records without his provocation. In his absence, I repeated his lessons.

If only my reasoning was better. If only my argument was more solid. If only...

I was determined to do better. I learned fast how to hold in my vents. How to control the need to talk. I leaned to silence my tongue. I learned self-control like never before.

* * *

Scott arrived at my door six weeks after our initial online meet. The day was planned perfectly. I had played hooky, something I had never done in my life. I had told Elena about Scott and that we were meeting up. She had insisted she call me that day to make sure I was okay.

I wasn't excited about meeting him. I was nervous and scared shitless. He had insisted I would answer the door naked and would be ripping his clothes off in a matter of moments. He was determined I would be naked and wet on the floor of the living room. He made vulgar, tasteless jokes that made me feel filthy. I was terrified. I had learned to fear men well. I wore a white turtle neck tucked into my jeans. I could not have made it more clear how I was feeling.

The doorbell rang. I felt like throwing up. I considered not answering the door. I considered calling my dad and telling him everything, but the relationship between us had taught me to trust no one. No one would help me. No one ever did. I was alone. I had hoped Elena had told someone. I slowly walked to the door, giving her time to call someone. The doorbell rang again. I wanted to throw up.

Women have a sense about themselves. There are certain vibes they can feel. They just know. It's survival instinct we were born with and mine was going off like a bean si on coke. I opened the door and my body clamped. Scott stepped through the door, took me up, and kissed me.

He tasted vile. I hated him. Hated us. Hated me. But he was there and I couldn't go back. He wanted me and that was enough. I should be grateful. He picked me up and carried me to the hall.

"Which one?" he asked and I pointed.

"There."

He took me to my bedroom. My pink sixteen year old bedroom. He stripped off my clothes and he fucked me. Cold and senseless. By then, I was used to shutting down and letting Joe have his way with me. This was just one more. Perhaps if it ended, it would go away. I shouldn't be so selfish.

My body was young. Already it had been shredded from the abuse endured under Joe. Already I had been beaten by my half-brother and loathed by my father. But this. His body was older. Different. I could feel it. If Joe was a two-by-four that slammed into my body and shredded my skin, his was a mac truck that ripped me apart. His fingernails dug. They scraped and cut me until I bled from the inside. Every time. His mouth always dripped cold saliva into mine. He tasted vile and smelled of every sick thing that he was and I—too desperate to be wanted, too starved for the smallest amount of approval—I let him.

He finished and I smiled. I had mastered the masquerade. He shook my hand, laughing, and said, "Hi. I'm Scott."

And I laughed with him. I laughed at his sick joke and I couldn't stop shaking with fear and orgasm.

"Here," he said and I felt something hit my bed. Confused and curious, I looked over my head and gasped.

Books.

More books than I had ever seen in my life. I gasped and crawled to my knees. I couldn't breathe. Books galore. Music books, philosophy books. Math books. Geometry. Opera scores, logic. I sobbed and cradled the books. I hugged them to my naked chest and I cried. I smelled them and touched their spines. I remember how violently my fingers shook. I buried my nose in their pages and wept. Never had I ever held so many books in my life. And they were mine. All my very own. The orgasm still riddled my body. It had barely begun to fade. One orgasm ended, but the euphoria was just beginning.

I had no idea, but the adrenaline from my orgasm, coupled with the euphoria from my books... he was already training my body to respond.

* * *

I got dressed balancing a biography of Glenn Gould between my hands while I pulled on my shirt. Within five minutes, we were downstairs. He sat at my piano. My old, dilapidated un-tuned full upright, and he played.

He took the breathe from me. Music engulfed me as I listened to Rachmaninoff's third piano concerto and my love, my dearest love consumed me. My music filled me and all at once, nothing else mattered. There was music. I would never have believed that such a sound could rise from that old instrument.

He stopped playing and laughed his sick laugh, amused with himself—he would do that often, I would quickly learn—then turned to me.

"Will you teach me?" The words had left me before I had thought them through.

The phone rang. It was Elena.

"Hey," she said on the other line. "How are you?"

"I'm good."

"Is he there? Did he come?" she asked.

"Yes," I said. "He's here."

Scott was licking my neck.

"And... how is he?" I could hear her nerves fraying.

"He's fine," I said. Scott was rubbing my clit under my jeans. "Everything's fine."

"You're okay?"

"Yep," I said and bit my lip.

"Okay," Elena said. "Do you need me to call anyone?"

"Nope. I'm fine," I said.

"Alright. Let me know if you need anything."

Click.

Two hours later, Scott and I were saying goodbye and he was out the door. Quicker than light, I sped to my room and devoured the books splayed on my bed. Grinning, I took up *Sophie's World* by Jostein Gaarder and I read.

Chapter 17

He didn't tell me he was bringing me books. He only did it and made sure he gave me the books before the orgasm had worn off. Literally, while I was still high on euphoric dumps of dopamine and serotonin, he enforced the state of euphoria with giving me the one thing I wanted more than anything in the world: books.

Things proceeded like this for a year. If I obeyed, I was rewarded with his "love," attention, and books. The books were sporadic so as to not allow me to grow accustomed. Never once did I develop an association. He wouldn't let me. He was careful to avoid the fine line between prostitution and award. But in one way or another, he awarded me.

If I disobeyed, he cut all communication off, rejected me, and threatened to take back the books. In times of punishment, he said things like, 'This is why your father doesn't love you.' When I obeyed, he said, 'If your father loved you, he would give you books.' Every word that slipped from his mouth was geared to condition me, to train me.

Broken

A month after our first meeting, Scott came up for my seventeenth birthday. He met my father an—
"*Hold on a minute.*"

***

"Just... hold on," William said, holding up his hand at the kitchen table.
"Yes?" I asked.
"Your father knew you were hanging out with a man who was thirty years older than you when you were only sixteen?"
"Yes."
"And he didn't do anything about it?" William leaned in, stunned as if he hadn't heard right.
"No. He didn't," I said. "Why would he?"
William fell back into his chair. I knew the shock he displayed. I had seen it time and again.
"Should he have?" I asked, feigning naivety.
William dropped his hand to the table in disbelief.
"Well... yes! Jeeze! I don't have a daughter and I'm pissed! I'm pissed for him! And this doesn't bother you?"
I shrugged, milking the indifference.
"I see no reason why it should," I said.
"It should," William said. "He's your father! He had a frickin' predator in his house and he did nothing!"
"And what could he do?" I asked.
"Kill him! Kick his ass! Call the cops! Something!"
"We've already established that I am worth nothing."
"That's bull shit," William said. I raised a brow at his language. He didn't strike me as the type. "You can't believe this now! You know it's wrong and you're okay with it! How can you sit there and be complacent about this?"
"Does my complacency bother you?" I asked.

"Yes!" he said. "It does! I don't understand it at all!"

"And you won't," I said, leaning in. "Any more than I can understand why you would get so upset now."

William stared, unsure of what to say. I could see that clearly enough.

"The only reason why you feel rage and animosity about this is because of the love you were taught as a child," I said. "I promise, you wouldn't think twice about my father's actions if you were raised as I. Normal. Acceptable. These are terms that are defined only by the parameter by which we teach our young. Without your ideal childhood, you would lose any point of reference in which to base your current conclusions.

"Yes, your perfect family, your ideal happy home, is great for those of you who lived something even remote to the ideal childhood. But what about the rest of us? Where does that leave the abused, the neglected, the forgotten, the lost? Where does that leave the outcasts? Remember this when we get to the end of my story and I make my decision."

I stood from the table, and sighed. I stared into the fire place. I had gotten ahead of myself. I forced myself back on track.

"My father made it very clear that I scared him," I said, watching the peat logs burn. "Charles and Shaun knew what Scott was and my brothers wanted our father to press charges. I remember overhearing their conversation. Shaun tried to convince my father to take me to a doctor and have me swabbed for semen while Charles told my father to call the police."

"What did your father say?" William said.

I watched the flames dance in their heat.

"My father told them both to leave it alone."

William was silent. I stayed where I stood by the fire.

"I felt invaded," I said. "Shaun hated me. He made it very clear what I was. For him to suddenly care. For anyone to suddenly care... Shaun didn't spend a day in his life where he gave two shits about me. I couldn't figure out for the life of me why he would start now. I chocked it up to control. I still do."

* * *

The first year with Scott was spent studying. He told me he was a professional pianist, guitarist, and organist... a graduate of Julliard. That claim was often challenged by everyone I met. Was it true? I don't know. At the end of day, the man could play. I mean, he could play. His music lessons were ruthless. He had me utilizing three hours a day of slow piano practice timed to the metronome. Each performance had to be perfect and emotional before I could bump that metronome up two beats. He had me punching out a number of compositions, enough to fill four binders. Two and three point counterpoint—Gregorian chant—followed by four part harmony and chorales, then ballads. That's not including the music history, musical form, opera scores, and reading up on the composers and their styles. Was he a Julliard graduate? I have no idea.

He also claimed to be an attorney. He could wind arguments around me that left my head spinning for days. I have known my share of attorneys. I am no stranger to their verbiage and technique. I learned their logic by living under their mastered manipulation of the written and spoken word to gain a desired affect without breaking rules. The art of linguistic precision. That is what I call it. Knowing what I know now about logic, I have no doubt in my mind Scott was an attorney.

He kept me on a tight leash. I was not allowed to leave the state of New York. Liability, loop hopes. The risk was too great. I was not allowed to question his decisions. I poured over the books he gave me and, per my request, he began teaching me music composition.

I had always been proud of my piano playing. That changed when Scott witnessed my technique. He told me to place my hands on the keyboard and the first thing he had to do was correct my hand position. When he told me to play middle C, I didn't know what he had been talking about. When he told me to modulate to...

"What?" I asked. "Modulate? What the hell is that?"

"Modulate!" he shouted. "Change keys."

"What keys?" I asked.

"What do you mean, what keys?" He gave the most contemptible sigh. "If you're on C and I say modulate to the relative minor, what does that mean?"

"What!" I shrieked.

"The circle of fifths!"

"What the hell is that?"

"What have you been doing for ten years?" he asked.

"Playing," I answered.

"And you've been doing that terribly," he said. "Your instructor never taught you music theory?"

"Music theory?" I asked. I had never heard of such things before. If I had, I would have looked it up in my encyclopedia set.

Scott made a sound like my cat makes when it throws up in the hall.

"Okay." He sighed. "Back to the beginning."

The following month, after the sex and the orgasm, he brought me Harmony by Walter Piston, boasting this was the text book used in Julliard. I began teaching myself immediately.

My lessons came to a screeching halt when Scott realized the holes in my comprehension stemmed from a lack of basic logic. In other words, problem solving. Word problems.

"Let no man who has not studied geometry enter these walls." Scott quoted the words of Plato back to me.

"What's that?" I asked as he threw down the newest book to my collection. Still naked, I curled up and cradled the red composition book.

"Logic. Geometry. Algebra," he said. "The building blocks to refined thinking, which should jumpstart your brain into understanding the music theory."

I could feel my eyes glisten with excitement as I flipped through the pages of algebraic equations, proofs, and angles.

"Get through this," he said. "Finish *Sophie's World.* Then you should be set to go on with music theory and composition. Some study in philosophy couldn't hurt, either."

Sophie's World.

If ever there was a book that shaped me into what I am, it was *Sophie's World.* Who are we? What are we? Why are we? Where did we come from?

I am no plot spoiler. I will not tell you what happens, but the book is designed so that when you make it to the final page, the reader has begun to think logically and you don't even realize you're doing it. It's a great book if you're new to logic and formal argument.

Scott and I tackled and argued Existentialism. He ripped me apart with it and left me godless. All at once, I questioned my center, my existence, my purpose. I didn't know what I was, who I was. I felt myself slipping, uncertain if I was even real and wondered if I wasn't a figment of someone else's imagination. For all we know, that is exactly what we are.

Existentialism forces you to question and change your perspective.

Perspective.

Such a powerful concept. With Existentialism, you stare down this psychedelic kaleidoscope and see how completely insignificant we truly are. Expendable. Without value. Worthless. Exactly what I already believed I was.

Why are we here? We could die tomorrow and the universe would go on. Why live? Why breathe? Why bother? Why be?

Existentialism destroyed my ideals and purpose, everything I believed I knew. God exists because I was there to think Him up. And the day we are all dead to not think of Him and worship Him, He will cease to be, for a god is only as good as the people worshipping it.

How do I know? I don't. I know no more than the atheist declaring there is no god or the Christian insisting there is one. It was all a matter of perspective.

But I wonder. I can't help but wonder. What happened to the gods of the Incas and Aztecs when their civilizations fell? Where are the gods of the Mayans and the Cherokee? Where are the gods of the Greeks and the Romans? The Celts and the Norse? I often wonder if the Hindu gods are next, then the Christians, the Jews, and the Muslims.

What if we're all wrong and it's only a matter of time before all the people are gone and no one is left to worship them? I see hundreds of gods standing in silence without a people. Staring down at an empty Earth. No one to believe. No one to pray. No one to worship. I see them vanishing one by one. Like us, they too will be forgotten. Where will the gods have gone? Will they wander the universe looking for another people to believe in them? Is there a god heaven do you think? Is Christianity just the newest religion destined to be myth?

Is it the people who give a god its power? And what are the people but expendable insects on this world?

I studied Existentialism and wanted to die.

Chapter 18

Scott stepped out of the car and stretched his back. Everything he did—from his speech to his posture—came off as scripted. As if he was a talentless actor-for-hire who couldn't even get a job at a child's birthday party. Everything about him was phony. I felt it from day one, but wouldn't be able to quite put my finger on it until years later.

"I need to stretch my legs, Elizabeth. Walk with me," he bade.

I had turned seventeen and Scott's visits had become more frequent. Twice a week he would drive the three hours from New Jersey. The routine was expected of me now and I had no skill to argue. I followed.

We would walk down the trail into the forest, the same forest where Joe and I had... We would barely make it to the trees before Scott grabbed me and pushed me to my knees.

"Alright," he had said and shoved his dick in my mouth.

He'd turn me around and bend me over, shove me against a tree, or just kiss me with his hard teeth and his cold saliva. I'd close my eyes and brace for the pain that always followed.

He'd finish with me, leaving behind the stench of sick sex, and we would return to the house. He'd shake my father's hand with a phony smile and then we'd leave.

We went to dinner and the movies. The car rides were always hell. Within five minutes, he'd have his dick out and would shove my head into his lap while he drove. If I said no, the reply was always the same.

"I can drive back to New Jersey. And if I have to drive back tonight, you know the back pain I have. What I had to do to get here."

Guilt and rejection. He was a piece of work.

He'd hike up my skirt and finger me while he fucked my mouth. His nails cut me and I bled. It didn't matter anymore. I always bled. I was finally used to the pain and could block it out. I'd suck his dick and hated every moment. I swallowed anyway. Other cars would drive by. I knew they could see. I knew he let them. I knew it got him off. But he accepted me. He would have me. I was worth just a dollar, after all, if I was worth anything at all.

We would arrive at dinner. I always was brought a merlot with filet mignon or beef wellington with French onion soup. Then afterward a movie. The movie was another kind of nightmare.

He always picked one with graphic sex. And every breast shot, every sex scene I would be expected to perform. He'd drag my hand on his dick. He'd shove my head down and I would have to suck him off right there in the theater. Every movie, every time.

The anxiety, the filth... it was a nightmare without an end. No matter how much I told him no, his argument back was always the same and I would take it. I would submit. I would comply or be punished. I couldn't risk losing him. No one else would have me. I wasn't worth anything more than that. I shouldn't be so selfish.

He always returned me late. Dropped me off with leftover Wellington, cum stains, and more filth in me than a used condom on the streets of New York. And it was exactly what I deserved.

*　*　*

"I hate talking about this," I said.

William looked up from his notes, but said nothing.

"It feels normal. It feels indifferent, unimportant. Is this unimportant? I can't tell."

William only looked at me.

"It bothers me that it doesn't bother me," I said. "It should, shouldn't it? When I speak of Joe, I remember the horror, the filth. I can taste the darkness and a part of me curls up on the floor and cries like a wee babe. I can't stop shivering and sobbing. I think of Scott and there is nothing there. I feel nothing. Just emptiness where fear, hate, and anger should be, but there is only nothing. I am hollow. I think this is important. I need to share this. But whenever I speak of it, I think, 'Why am I talking about this? It isn't that bad. What am I complaining about?' Am I boring you?" I asked.

William shook his head. "Not boring, no. Just listening."

"I remember things. Things I need to say. There were others. Insignificant others whose words stayed with me. I remember them now. He was a nineteen year old senior in the school and I was barely fourteen. He was overweight and reminded me of jelly. He was disgusting and wanted me. He had raped so many girls. My cousin being one of them."

* * *

I went to my cousin's house and she was howling upstairs. I could hear her screams. They carried through the house.

"What's wrong with her?" my mum said.

"Oh, she was raped," my aunt replied, but the tone in her voice stayed with me. It was like my cousin annoyed her. Like my aunt wished for my cousin to shut up and end her senseless wailing.

Mostly, I remember the screams.

That rapist, he had an eye for me. He let me know that. I was beautiful then, so very beautiful. Drop dead fucking gorgeous. That's what Piss-ant said. That rapist, I knew he wanted me. He described every detail to me. How he would tear me apart and make me bleed and that I would enjoy it. Every day, he told me everything he wanted to do to me. He described what he would do, how he would rape me. And then I'd go home and dream of those things. I felt him rip my body apart as if I lived inside one of Dali's paintings and my body was cloven in two. There were pieces of me everywhere. In school, I took paths to my classes to ensure I didn't run into him. He never touched me, but the visions he put in my head. The fear...

He evokes far more horror from me than Scott. Maybe I was too numb to the nightmare to feel any of it or care when Scott came along.

I remember the feeling I lived with for years. That horrible, hellish feeling. It started when the rape threats, the groping and molestation started. My beauty developed well into my teens. Males grabbed every chance they got or slid graphic suggestions into conversations. They all made it clear what they wanted with me. What they would do to me. But that feeling... nothing could shake that feeling.

It felt like I was standing naked in front of everyone all the time. Like I was bound to a wall... my legs forced apart with chains, my arms stretched out, exposing my chest... my heart. My hurt. I was vulnerable, filthy, and exposed. They could see me. Everyone could see my secrets if only they looked at me. I wished to be invisible. I wanted to curl up in a corner, tucked away in the dark and die.

At home, I tried. I'd wrap myself in a blanket and rock myself in the corner, my legs pulled into my chest, and I waited for the feeling to end. I waited and wished for my last breath. No matter how many clothes I wore, or blankets I buried myself under, I was still naked for all the world to see. It would take hours to leave, sometimes the day. It came whenever and was unpredictable. And I lived with that feeling every day of my life from twelve to twenty. To this day, I still don't know what it was. Why it came... or why it left me at all.

Shaun still beat me, but he saw the fight in me. The cold hate I carried with me. I was stronger too and had learned how to fight. I think he knew that. We still had the occasional battle that resulted in his fist landing a hit. I took it. But mostly, he resorted to threats. The tension was high. Forever high and constant. I felt like I was living in an unmapped mine field. I was smarter about things too. My door stayed locked at all times. I never opened that door.

"Don't open the door," Angel said. "Not for anyone."

I didn't leave my room for anything. I didn't eat. I feared sleep and learned how to live with only a few hours. My cats stayed in my room with me. They never left.

I still saw Erik and Ireland.

Oh! And Poe. Those years, I found Poe. If ever my soul had sound it would be Puccini. But my heart bled the words of Poe. His words fell off the pages like streaks of blood and black that mirrored my darkest desires. His words reflected my nightmare, my hell, my heart.

To open and read the words of Poe was to find me. There was a shadow growing within. A shadow that writhed like Death. Cold and distant, a kind of wraith-like beauty only found in the macabre. Skeletal dancers dressed in crimson. Cold roses. Dead forests littered in winter's chill and ghosts of girls in gossamer gowns who saw the beauty despite the dreams of death and decay and bodies buried beneath festering filth. A cold beauty, the kind only which death brings.

I read the words of *Lenore*. I mastered his *Annabel Lee*. I poured over the prose of his Raven. I reveled in his Nevermore. His words did so much to define the darkness in me.

In my eighteenth summer, a beam of light opened up and my beloved friend was born.

Of all my friends, no one would come to mean more to me than Tribble. She arrived a ball of poof on the thirteenth day of July in 1998. Her mews were soft and sweet. Her fur was long and softer than silk and so black almost to be tinged with shades of midnight. Her purr came easily. That cat would walk into a room, see me, and purr. But above all else, from the moment she was born, there was never a day that she didn't come running at the sound of my cries. And she would come to me and purr as I cried into her fur every day of her life, right up until the day she died. Tribble was the first to ever love me in this vile world, the first to ever comfort me of her own will.

My half-brother caught on quickly to my fond affections for Tribble. In no time, she bore the brunt of his abuse. Of all my cats, she was hit the most, bitten the most, and beaten the most. The thing with Tribble was this: she never bore claws, hissed, or fought back. Tribble was too gentle, too good, too sweet to ever do anything but love, and she lived to love me. The least I could do was protect her.

The emotional attachment I developed for her was instant and kept me grounded in this world for the next seventeen years right up until her dying day. When Tribble arrived, Erik went away, I stopped slipping into the other realms. With Tribble, I needed nothing.

* * *

"Tribble," William said. "Like *Trouble with Tribbles* from Star Trek?"

I grinned.

"The very same. Tribble looked like a tribble, cooed like a tribble. She even screamed like a tribble when Shaun bit her soft, little ears. Such beautiful ears. Oh and her tail was like a plume of glorious black silk. She had so much fuzz that toe fur flowed from between each toe.

"Elena, Isaiah, and I had somehow collected an entourage of friends. Together, we formed a group of Bohemians. There were eight of us. We were writers, artists, painters, poets, musicians, and philosophers. Every day, for two years—from eleventh to twelfth grade—the eight of us would gather in the art room for three hours and engage in formal argument much like Degas, Monet, and Renoir in Paris. We would debate, ponder, and explore the ins and outs of our existence. We took on the Man and did our best to wreak havoc among the mundane, and Isaiah and I were their leader. We led the group across the roof of the school. I posed for a still life while drawing my own still life and petitioned to be the art subject for a multiple projects.

"Wrap me! Wrap me!" I implored my teacher. "You say we have to wrap something in fabric and twine then draw it. Me! I choose me! Wrap me!"

I was more than eager to volunteer.

"Yes! Let's wrap Elizabeth!"

"Wrap Elizabeth!" they shouted.

I'm very good at rallying up the masses.

"Wrap me!"

I learned to laugh in that room. I learned to rise above my nightmare and see the good. I learned to forget my grief and smile. I learned to love. I clung to those eight so desperately. At home, I clung to Tribble.

Isaiah had drawn a still life entitled, "The Death of the Tribble."

I had no idea what a tribble was, but the Bohemian imbroglio was more than eager to teach me.

When Tribble was born, I named her after Isaiah's still life. For those two brief years, that collection of artists, that wonderful group of people, planted a light of hope inside me. They nourished it and stoked to life and by our senior year, it had grown into a voracious flame.

Chapter 19

April of 1998, I was seventeen years old. My class was preparing for their senior trip. My relationship with my father was as strained as it could get. Scott had free range to do whatever he wanted, wherever he wanted, and did. If I didn't answer the phone, I had hell to pay. If I didn't "check in" at certain assigned intervals, I had hell to pay. If I didn't comply, I was to be punished.

My lessons continued. My math, geometry and algebra were complete. I had worked my way up to proofs and all at once, something clicked. The logic sank in, the numbers, the shapes, the reasoning all made sense. The results carried over into my music. I could see the math in music. I could understand the frequency, and the quality of my work quadrupled. My philosophy, logic, reasoning, and studies expounded and influenced my reading, which I had been grossly behind on.

I devoured books, drank words, studied everything I could get my hands onto. I bounced between music, logic, theology, history, literature, and art. Scott started showing up with the classics. Books most people had read as children, I had not even heard of.

E.B. White. Roald Dahl. Tolkien. Carol. Lewis. These were names most children grew up with. I would not hear of them until I was nearly twenty-three years old. My anger rebounded every time I learned just how much my education had been neglected. In the name of a deity, I was denied truth, education, and the freedom to question. In the name of a deity, I was denied my curiosity. I trusted no teachers. I only ever trusted books and even then, I learned to check, double check, quadruple check the sources. My logic taught me how to identify prejudice.

Prejudice.

If ever there is anything I hate in this world, it is prejudice and biased opinion. I spent the rest of my existence sorting through altered and biased opinion to find truth and fact if it wasn't destroyed by imperialists in the process.

I had made my plans clear to my piano instructor of my plans for music composition and had requested lessons in music theory. Instead of offering assistance or advice, recommending me books, sources, or other teachers, he argued with me and insisted I would hate the music if I learned the theory. I was months from graduation and no one had done anything to help me. No one, except Scott. Scott, on the other hand, made it perfectly clear that I was not ready for college. I was too far behind.

That spring, when my class went to Disney World, I went to Miami with Scott. We walked South Beach. He wined and dined me. Took me to more movies where I was forced to perform in the car, at the theater, at the hotel...

It was at the point where every movie we watched had sex in it. During every movie, I was expected to perform whether I wanted to or not. I will make this very clear. The word 'no' was not an option. When I did put up my usual, "I don't want to," he shoved his dick in my mouth as if I has said nothing at all. After all these years, I was still mute.

Fear. Anger. My body learned to become aroused when I experience these two emotions. But my body also learned to associate fear and anger with other stimuli.

To this day, I can't watch a movie, see a commercial, or be around any sexual media without my body responding. Scott taught me to become aroused like clockwork. It worked. Scott's conditioning also trained me to respond to the anger, the fear, and media. My brain interprets an image or scenario, which releases fear and begins arousal. I remember the rapes, I anticipate them and associate them with the catalyst—the movie—which dumps more fear and leads to more arousal.

The abuse from my half-brother, the rapes from my lovers... I am terrified of men. I am terrified of penis.

* * *

"But you love men," William said. "You aspire to be them."

"Because my daddy told me so," I said. "I should have been a boy. Remember? So I learned men. I studied them."

"When you're around a male then..." William's voice trailed off as he did the math.

"When I am around a male, fear sets in, and I remember the rapes during the movies. I become aroused and remember the fear of being beaten. A sexed male, a sated male, is a safe male. Fear triggers sexual arousal."

"You can't watch TV," William said.

"I can't watch any movie with sex in it. I can't watch cable. I can't watch commercials. I relive every rape every time I watch a movie with sex or nudity. A commercial with sexual innuendo. A magazine picture with a provocative cover—"

"What happens if you go to the store?" The question was rhetorical, but seeing William's face, his mouth agape, unable to process an answer.

"Shock," I said. "I freeze up, slip into the other worlds, grab what I need, and go. I wallow in fear on the drive home and once I'm back in my room, I fall apart—where it's safe to fall apart. If there is a sexually mature male around me...yeah, he has a good time and I spend the rest of the day climbing the walls." William just stared, unable to speak.

"We live in a society that sells sex everywhere," William said when he found his voice again.

"Yes," I said. "We do. Welcome to my nightmare. Do you want a beer?"

I grabbed another two beers from the box and seated myself back at the table while he popped the top off his. I took a mouthful before continuing.

"I've gotten better," I said. "But I'll get into that later. I got back to New York, celebrated my eighteenth birthday and almost immediately found myself in a new kind of hell. I was pregnant."

William choked on his beer.

"You need a moment," I said. "This is a lot."

William ran his hand through his hair and scratched the back of his neck.

"So the pedophile," William said. "He...conditioned you, raped you, impregnated you, manipulated you...and you're just okay with this?"

"Yeah." I whispered the word. I felt it all building. I was buckling.

"Are you?" he asked again and that broke me.

I shook and, dropping my head to my hand, I cried. "Well, not when you put it like that," I said and I cried. I cried for a long while.

"How did you find all this out? Did you have a therapist?"

"I did it myself," I said.

"Yourself?"

"Yes," I sniffed. "The self-evaluation. The encyclopedia sets. I learned very early on that the subconscious buries only what you can't deal with. It's a coping mechanism. So the problem is there, buried beneath memories and layers of forgotten pain. But to cope, we forget. It's to preserve our sanity and our mind. Later, I noticed problems... I noticed I was different and needed to unearth the root of the problem.

"A therapist will talk to you in hopes to get the patient speaking fluently enough that, in the heat of passion, under pressure, controlled pressure, the patience's subconscious will permit clues or outright admissions to the surface. But only in pieces at a time and only ever what the patient is capable of handling at that time. Once it emerges, the patient can address it."

"But you had no therapist," William said.

"My good friend," I said with a grin. "I am a writer. I knew what I needed to do. I shut down my conscious and wrote free form. It took me three years to unearth all of this through discussions with Ian and my writing."

I watched him twitch as if trying to process the idea that I talk to Ian regularly.

"What about the coping, the depression, the healing..." William listed off the risks.

"I am aware of my alternate worlds," I said. "I am aware that I may have bits of my personality organized into neat little packages called Ian, Angel, and Erik. And the psycho addiction I have to my cats. I am aware Ian is standing right there watching me, smirking as he drinks my beer. And I know he's not real—"

Yes, I am.

"—although he thinks he is."

I looked at Ian and he put my bottle of Guinness to his lips with his grin.

Or maybe it is I who am real, Ian said. *I who am the writer and you, my bonny lass... are a figment of my imagination.*

I hadn't thought of that. I paused for a moment and looked at the world and the room around me.

"If I am a figment of your imagination," I said, "then good god, man! Do better by me than this!"

"Elizabeth?"

"Yes, William," I said. He looked at me all weird like.

"P-perhaps we should continue," he said.

"Yes," I agreed. "Let's."

* * *

The pregnancy test stared up at me. I was still naked in the hotel room. Scott had insisted on sex first—always sex first—and then the test. A blue plus stared back at me and all at once I was elated. Hope filled me and died with his next words.

"Well, looks like we'll need to be getting you an abortion."

I felt sick.

"What?"

"We can't keep this," he said. "I was exposed to radiation. The fetus will be born with deformities and brain damage. If it's alive at all."

It didn't make sense. A lot didn't make sense.

"You want to just kill the baby?" I asked.

"It's not a baby," he called from the bedroom.

I wanted to die alright. And just liked that the little bit of hope inside me, vanished.

June of 1998, a month into turning eighteen and a week into being pregnant, all I cared about was getting out of that hell hole my father fondly referred to as "his house."

To not have to live ever again hearing someone tell me he was going to kill me. To never again have to wake up and save Tribble or stay awake to make sure she lived through the night. I would be safe. My cats would be safe. I felt guilty for leaving the dogs to my half-brother. I had half a mind to call officials and report him. But not unless he made a move. I would have to see the dog beaten with the pipe before I could make the call or file a report.

My room was packed, ready to go. Everything I needed was ready. Boxes lined my room. Scott had made it clear that I would be moving the day after graduation. That morning, I got dressed while battling back the fresh wave of morning sickness. I managed to eat something and was thrilled to see I kept it down. An hour later, I climbed out of his car and found my Bohemian friends. Teachers passed out the slinky, cheesy robes along with our boxed hats then helped us with our tassels.

I remember Fred Milton the most from that day. My name was Lundy. His was Milton, which meant I had the honor of sitting next to him all day. I remembered the one month we dated. He wanted sex and dumped me when I was less than eager. That was forever ago.

I played my part. Walked the aisle. Sat down and listened to a bunch of old men speak while I tried not to throw up on my shoes.

"What's with all this old men talking?" Fred said to me.

He didn't whisper. He was loud and that day suddenly decided to articulate. I swear everyone heard him. I know I did. I had to bite my lip not to laugh.

"Sh," I scolded him.

He was well-behaved for all of five minutes.

"Seriously, who are these guys? Do you know these guys?"

"Sh."

He shook his head as if I had disappointed him. "You don't know, do you?"

I spent the entire ceremony shushing and scolding the commentary.

I was awarded cash to help my college funding. Nearly three hundred dollars in cash to help me pursue the arts. I was handed my diploma and followed Fred Milton back to the courtyard where I attempted to pry my hat out from all the bobby pins. I gave up and stripped off the "robes" almost immediately.

The morning sickness had finally subsided.

I found my Isaiah and ran him down.

"We're having a graduation party," I said. "Will you come?"

He met me with a wide grin. "Yes!"

I turned and Scott was there.

"I'm leaving," he called. "I'll see you later."

"What?"

We walked away from the fanfare. "But the party," I said. "The..."

You're driving me to New Jersey in the morning, remember? I didn't dare say to him.

"I have to go," he said. "Something's come up." And he was gone.

I was given very few gifts that day: earrings from my father, hearts with real emeralds in their center, a $2.00 bill from my grandfather, and a hand-carved box from my aunt with a small lock. I took the three hundred dollar award money and stored it in the little box with the lock before running out the door with Isaiah.

Charles had volunteered to drive us around. I have no idea why he was being so accommodating. I think he was—

I have no idea.

Graduation party hopping. We must have hit nearly six graduation parties that day. We hung out, laughed with friends. I never left Isaiah's side all while I had a baby inside of me. But before the end of the night, the nausea returned.

"Isaiah. I need to go," I said.

He looked like I had kicked him in the groin and I swear the destined-to-be-aborted pea inside of me flipped. I fought back another wave of sick.

"I'm sorry," I said.

"Please stay." He was legitimately sad to see me go, but it was all I could do not to throw up on him.

"I can't." I was going to hurl. I was certain.

"Okay." I watched his face fall, but the nausea was bad. Before I could comfort him, I grabbed my brother and headed back to the car. I fought nausea the entire drive home.

Chapter 20

The situation was simple. I wanted the baby. Scott didn't. He insisted he had radiation poisoning and any child of his would be born with radioactive poisoning. God, I wish I was making this shit up! Within a week after graduation, he had me at an abortion clinic.

I begged him. I pleaded with him to let me keep it. He was adamant that it would be born deformed.

He drove me to New Jersey where anti-abortionists shoved papers in my face about preserving life. I wanted to scream, "I agree with you! He's making me do it!"

I went inside.

I was barely eighteen, gorgeous, and fucking smart. Every nurse that greeted me let me know that. I'm not sure why they all insisted on reminding me. I viewed my looks as a curse and the root cause to my problems with males. I hated my looks. In the end, it didn't matter. I was escorted into a room with a bunch of women as miserable looking as I while the nurse described exactly how the doctor would kill my baby. I looked at the faces of the other mothers.

Mothers.

I wasn't sure the stories of the other girls. I didn't know how they came to be there. I just knew that I was forced to be there. I broke. I sobbed. The nurse scolded me for crying.

"None of use woke up wanting to be here today," she said. "No one wanted this. You're being selfish!"

"I'm sorry," I muttered.

"If you don't want to be here, maybe you should talk to the father."

I walked out to the car where he waited. He was on the phone.

"Are they done?" Scott asked.

"Don't make me do this," I said. "I can't do this."

"You have to," he said. "The baby will die. It's deformed."

"I don't want to... please. Don't make me do this."

"Elizabeth. You can't ask this child to be born like this. It's cruel. It isn't fair to you or the baby."

I nodded, but didn't trust myself to speak.

"Okay," he said.

Crying, I walked back in.

The anti-abortionists shoved another pamphlet in my face.

"Abortion is murder," she said as I re-entered the clinic.

"Okay," I said to the nurse. "Let's do this."

* * *

I woke. The sobbing was soft, but it was everywhere. Behind me, around me, beside me. I opened my eyes. It seemed like forever in the time it took to open my eyes. The light slowly found me and sitting at my head, a woman cried softly into a tissue.

"Why are you crying?" I asked. I took her hand. "Please don't cry." I smiled gently. "You'll be alright. Everything will be alright now."

She smiled back and squeezed my hand, still sobbing into her tissue.

"You're okay," I said. "Everything will be okay. You're alright."

"Elizabeth?" A nurse waddled over to me. "You awake, honey?"

I looked around the room where half a dozen women cried into their tissues.

"Why are they crying?" I said and looked to the lady seated at the foot of my bed. She too was crying. "Please don't cry." I took her hand and smiled at her. "You're alright now. Please don't cry."

"Elizabeth, honey," the nurse said. "Can you hear me?"

I looked up at the nurse. "Why are the women crying?"

"It's the meds," she said. "It amplifies whatever feelings they were having before the procedure."

Before the procedure.

I thought back.

Before the procedure, I had been smiling. I had my cry with one of the nurses. Told her why I had to abort the baby. The talk had helped.

"He would have radiation poisoning," I had said.

"Oh." She scrunched up her face like she cared. "You have to abort this, sweetie."

"I know."

I cried and ten minutes later, I was talking to the doctor about kiwi birds.

"You allergic to anything?"

"Yes," I said. "Men, stupidity, and kiwi."

"Kiwi? Like the bird or the fruit?"

"Fruit," I answered. "There is a kiwi bird?"

"Yep," he said. "I want you to count down from ten."

"Ten, nine, ei..." And I was gone. I had fallen asleep feeling relieved. I had my cry. But these women...

They should have been allowed to cry.

I stood and made my rounds, taking the time to hug each one, never mind the fact that I was in a hospital gown and the pad holding all the blood was slipping from between my legs. I had to hug them. Had to comfort...

Over and over, I said, "You'll be okay. Please don't cry. It's alright now."

Each gave me a smile and called me an angel. I smiled, hugged them and squeezed their hands. I think that was the day I decided to smile and compliment. It did so much to ease their hearts. They smiled back and some stopped crying. They called me angel.

With a bag of Chips Ahoy, I was escorted back to a closet and reunited with my clothes. Ten minutes later, I was back in the car with Scott. The entire thing took two hours.

"How can you eat those?" he asked as I buckled myself in.

I looked up with a Chips Ahoy between my lips. He didn't allow me to eat processed foods and I had lived without Chips Ahoy for nearly three years. The nurses had given each of us a bag to help stabilize our blood sugar from the blood loss. I braced for the scolding and ate my cookie. I had an incessant cramp in my stomach. I was exhausted. I wanted to go home.

* * *

"Of all the political views, of all the religious and ethical views, I would never develop an opinion on abortion. I felt I didn't have that right. Not after what I did."

I smiled.

"No. I tasted that lie as I spoke it," I said. "I was afraid for what I would learn about myself if I ever I attempted to form an opinion about abortion. To this day, I don't have one. I won't comment. Do I regret it? Yes. Were there other options? Yes. Did he make me do it? Yes. Not one part of my mind or body wanted to go through with that and I had made it very clear to him that I did not want an abortion."

"But you signed the papers," William said.

"I had no choice."

"He didn't hold a gun to your head."

"No," I agreed. "He didn't. He only held my future in his hands. He was inside my head, holding my heart hostage. I thought I had no choice. And he made sure I believed that."

"If you had it to do over again?" William asked.

I laughed and shook my head.

"If I had it to do over again, I never would have slept with him to begin with," I said. "Women who abort..."

I stopped talking. William wasn't asking. He really didn't seem to sit in judgement of me. This was my own guilt I was dealing with. And it was time I dealt with it.

"Who am I to judge their choices, their life style?" I said. "Who am I to determine if their choices were right or wrong? I would be no different than those women in front of the clinic shoving fliers in my face. They didn't know I didn't want to be there. If they had taken me by the arm and said, 'you have other choices,' then maybe I would have listened to them. But to call me a murderer while I walk to the execution platform... They were one more enemy out to get me that day."

William politely listened and nodded as he let me talk.

"I will say this," I said. "I would never forgive him for the abortion. I would never forget what he took from me. What he did to me. That day, he turned me into something I never wanted to be: a woman who aborts her own child."

Chapter 21

Scott always wore a wedding ring. And when I asked him why, he insisted it was the ring of his dead fiancé and he could not take it off unless it was cut off. I played with that ring while he slept and tried desperately to take it off myself.

It was legitimately stuck on there. But his reasons for wearing it... his dead fiancé... the story never quite sat well with me.

With my turning eighteen, I was finally allowed to go to the City and New Jersey. He had spoken often of his home and of this girl he lived with, Jen. I still don't know who she was. He claims she was the daughter of a friend of his. She may have been his daughter. She was five years younger than me and there was one rule: under no circumstances was she to know about my existence. His reasons for that rule changed every time he reminded me of the rule.

For my eighteenth birthday, he took me to New York. Three hours and two forced blow jobs later, we were pulling up to his house in a small dingy neighborhood in Jersey.

While he fumbled with keys at the door, we were greeted by a cat.

"Hey, Bruno," he said and I snapped at attention.

"Bruno?"

"Yeah. That's Bruno." His keys jingled.

"I thought Bruno was the name of your neighbor's cat at the mansion."

"It is."

"So you have two neighbors with two cats who greet you?" I asked.

He didn't look up.

"Yeah."

"And both are named Bruno?"

He never should have taught me logic.

"Yeah."

He pushed the door open and I looked at Bruno, who also happened to be a Russian Blue just like the "Mansion Bruno" who he had been describing to me for two years. I followed him inside while doing my best to ignore the sudden desire to throw up.

Scott had said he lived in a mansion. For three years, he described this five million dollar palace to me. He said he had a Persian cat named Cassy. He said he had a lot of things and that the house he took me to instead of the mansion wasn't his. He was "house sitting" for a friend and had to live there for two months. Instead of the mansion and the life he had talked about for three years, he took me to a small... well...

It was a dump. Five years of cat hair was caked on all the furniture. The floors were un-swept and warped from water damage. The whole upstairs was a junk closet, cluttered with boxes of papers, clothes, and filth. Donation garages looked cleaner. And all over the place, no matter where I turned, evidence that a wife lived there screamed in my face. Bras hung on the back of chairs. Prescription meds dated only two weeks out for a woman named "Rose" were everywhere. His clothes and hers covered every inch of the floor. Letters, piles of letters and opened junk mail sat on the coffee table, the counter, the piano, and every available surface.

He poured me a glass of wine and went to work on dinner. I chugged the first glass and shuffled through the letters. My blood went cold at a name: Mr. and Mrs. Scott White.

Within thirty minutes, I had drunk the entire bottle of Merlot and I hate Merlot.

* * *

We settled down on the unmade bed and he put in the movie *Airplane*. The cameras scanned the terminal and a man and a woman began talking over the loudspeakers.

I stared at the bottom of my wine glass.

The man and a woman started arguing.

Scott started laughing.

I gripped the glass hard. I wanted to break it while a single line from the movie cut deep a wound that had not even begun to heal.

"*If this is about the abortion—*"

"*You're going to bring that up again.*"

Scott laughed while I felt the words cut me like a blunt blade.

I looked at the DD bra lying on the floor.

The bed shook with his laughter.

"I'm going to get more wine," I slurred.

I hadn't made it twenty minutes into the movie when a breast shot aroused him and my body responded. Like clockwork, my body reacted and he fucked me right there in his wife's bed while I stared at her medication.

I decided to do what any enraged, broken female would do who had been lied to. I tested him.

The next day, I scattered thirty random sticky notes all over his house. Sticky notes tucked away behind sheet music, hidden in the fridge. Random "I love yous" scribbled and scattered on every orifice. I even scratched it into the two-year-old soap scum ring around the tub.

"What is this?" he screamed.

I played naive. "What?"

"This!" I stared at my note of endearment clenched in his fist.

"What?" I smiled innocently. "It's a love note."

"Where are they?"

"They?"

"Are there more?" he asked.

"Yes," I said. *Damn, I wish I could lie.*

"How many?"

"Thirty." *Damn! Lie already!*

"Get them." I swear he was going to punch me. "Now."

"But, I thought they would be sweet." I tried to recover the last of my brilliant plan. "You could find them after I was gone... when you miss me."

"You know Jen visits! I can't have her seeing these!"

And why not? She's not your daughter. She doesn't even live here. She lives at the mansion.

"Okay." I obeyed, rounded up my plan, and scrubbed the "love note" off the tub.

An hour later, I was back in his car heading home, my head shoved onto his dick once more.

Broken

* * *

That summer passed with me buried in my music studies.
"When will you move me down to Jersey?"
"Not now. We have some renovations to be done on the mansion. But soon."
Mansion. I no longer believed that lie.
"It's been a month," I reminded him. "When?"
"Soon."
You'd think I'd quit asking. I never did.
My music education continued. I read up on Copeland and Beethoven, Liszt, and Bernstein. I studied music from Gregorian Chant and Counterpoint. I composed countless compositions in the two part, three part Counterpart.
I studied Bach and Brahms. . . Mozart. I ran into the romantic period and fell hard for Beethoven. I studied his style, his motifs, his life, his music. I studied Liszt to learn more. And then I fell into Puccini with such a passion. . . That man knew me. He knew my heart, what sounds I would need and he wrote them. Nearly a century before I was born, Puccini wrote composition that was only meant for me.
I moved on to Rococo and Baroque, I flourished in ballad writing, folk pieces, and improvisation. Once I had the theory and modulation under my belt, after three years, I could sit at a piano and play the hurt in my heart. I would lose myself in ballad writing. I completed the courses in Harmony and entered the world of Schoenberg and jazz. I studied the augmented seventh and began on the thirteenth.
I studied music history and theory on up to the 1960's when the Beatles made their scene and stopped just before the British Invasion. I was careful to never cross over from

classical music, Bernstein, Copeland, and Philip Glass. Scott's orders.

I toggled my music composition with theology, history, and completed my studies on philosophy. I worked harder than ever on logic. I still had not won a single argument against Scott, but that didn't mean I didn't try.

After the abortion, I started to notice things I hadn't seen before. I knew he was married. I knew he was lying to me. But I couldn't prove any of it. This was important. I had to prove it.

My piano performance was sharp. I had mastered Schumann at concert level. I ate, drank, and slept the slow practice with the metronome. I was working on the Beethoven waltzes while I watched my friends all move away and scatter around the country. Elena left for the larger cities and went on to Europe to study art in the Louvre. And Isaiah...

September came and with it, a dark cold that filled me. There was no bus, no classes. There was simply nothing but a need, and it had one name.

Isaiah.

The urge hit me hard and sudden. I had to speak to him again. I didn't even have his number. I called Elena who had it.

"Elena! Please have Isaiah call me. I need to speak with him." I couldn't say why. I only needed him.

I would have that same conversation with her for six months.

I pined while I wrote my music. I practiced and my ballads turned bitter. A macabre ensconced me and I let it. I had a need. It was simple. Isaiah.

I spoke to Scott. He'd drill me in algebra. I'd read up on music history. I'd place my call in to Elena and beg her to pass my messages on to Isaiah.

I would proceed with logic and philosophy. Winter came and I drew in. Bitterness chilled my heart and I welcomed it. The scars left by the abortion had maimed my heart. My father and Shaun became more vile than ever now that I was no longer in high school.

Tribble was my only solace.

January brought in February's cold and my phone rang. "Hello?"

"Hi. It's Isaiah. You wanted to speak to me."

And all at once, the ice chipped away from my heart and there was life for me again.

We talked all night long. We talked about everything and nothing all while we spoke of that summer, our friendship, school, the staircase where we spent endless hours engaged in a debate we would carry with us to the art room. We listened to the other breathe. We talked about school. We simply relished the other's company.

I swear the sun rose, the dawn spilled in through my window and I heard a rooster crow that morning.

"It's morning," I said.

"It is."

"I often wondered how long we would speak if ever we were given the chance without interruption," I said.

Silence.

"Isaiah?"

"Yes?"

"I love you."

Silence.

"I don't know what to say," he replied after a moment.

I smiled. How could I not?

"Then say nothing and I will say I love you until you do know what to say."

Silence.

"Isaiah."

"Yes?"

"I love you.

That call was cut short when I heard screaming in the background, followed by, "You talked the whole damn night! Get the fuck off the phone!"

"Gotta go," he muttered and click.

Another cold click.

Chapter 22

Isaiah and I wrote to each other, countless letters, silly letters. We would write every day until we had accumulated twenty pages or so then we would mail them and pour over the other's words. Nothing sexual. Never sexual. Just life, our goals, our dreams, our plans. School and money. He signed every letter "Yours" and I hated it. Just once I wanted him to slip up and write "Love." He never did.

April of 1999 came and my father had had enough with the house. "Your mother's house," he had taken to calling it. Every corner and room reminded him too much of my mother. After four years, they still weren't divorced despite Jake and Mum having my baby-sister, Rachelle, who would be turning one that year. We moved across town and I recruited as many of my Bohemian friends as I could find. Only Isaiah showed up.

Isaiah and I never touched. Not once. Never hugged. Never touched. The sexual tension was unbearable. Everyone in school had felt it since the infamous slap of '91. But we reveled in it. I bathed in it. To hold that tension and never sate it, I wallowed in that glorious tension. I told him I loved him and, as always, he answered with thank you. I smiled and said it again. He smiled and said nothing.

That night in my room, I stared up at him. He wouldn't touch me. Instead he gave me a ring. A simple band with wire wrapped around two beads. Even when he handed it to me, our fingers did not touch. I slipped the ring on and held up my hand. He held up his and I placed my palm against his. It was the only time we ever touched.

I spread his fingers and folded my fingers down over his, but he kept his palm open.

"I can't kiss you," he whispered.

"I know that," I said, smiling.

"I need to go to bed now," he said.

The heat that speared me ricocheted off him. Regardless, he stood, bid me goodnight, and left my room. I crawled into bed that night, a smile glued to my face and a ring on my finger.

* * *

Sunlight filled my room. I remembered the night before and slipped into the hall. Isaiah was there at the top of the stairs laying on his makeshift bed of blankets and pillows. I slipped into the room and kneeled down beside him. His hair fell into his face and I reached out and brushed it back. He looked up at me.

"Behave," he whispered and I obeyed.

The stairs creaked and behind me, my father stood. After a mumbled apology, he went back down stairs. But the moment had ended. I would not be kissing Isaiah that day.

We proceeded to write every day, but my deepest secrets, the ones I could not share with Isaiah, I wrote down in a journal.

My nineteenth birthday came and Scott treated me to a weekend in New York. After two blow jobs in the car, he fucked me then took me out on the town. We went to the Met and MOMA. He took me to Lincoln Center and we attended the Mozart concert that spring. We took a boat around Manhattan and Liberty Island. I got sick and threw up. I still can't be on a boat.

By the second day, Scott knew something was up.

"Who's Isaiah?"

My body went cold.

"What?"

"You talk in your sleep," he said.

I talk in my sleep. I always talk in my sleep.

"Who's Isaiah?" he repeated.

I can not lie and so I said nothing.

"Hand it over."

I furrowed my face. "What?"

"Your journal."

I wanted to vomit. Or die. Maybe I could fall on a knife between the bed and the table. I took up my journal and handed it over.

"Sit down," he said to me.

I obeyed and sat on the bed while he turned each page and read aloud the words that had poured from my heart.

Maybe I would die suddenly right there. I wished. I don't remember what he said, but I remember the tone. He stood there over me, screaming. I hadn't touched Isaiah. I only loved him. Was that so wrong?

More screaming. More rage. My body grew wet as it prepared for sex and I hated myself. His tone intensified with the urge to fuck something. The fear shook my body and my juices flowed.

Scott's hand flew across my face. Now that was something I knew. At last, something I could understand. Something I could work with. Something I recognized. I absorbed the burn and took the hit.

I looked back at him, hate welling up in my eyes. I could feel his hand imprinted on the right side of my face. It burned and was reminded me of one simple truth I had long since forgotten. That day I left Joe. It all flooded back and the words of Shakespeare rang back in my head:

"To thine own self be true."

Had I not been?

I suppressed a grin.

"I can no longer be with you," I said. God, my face burned.

He said something. I don't remember. It didn't matter. All that mattered was that he understood this now. It was over. I would not be with a man who hit me. I would not be that woman.

"I can not be with you," I said again.

He insisted I was full of it. He didn't believe me. It didn't matter. I may move in with him. I may marry him. I may fuck him. But I would not stay. I don't stay. I never stay.

We had tickets to three Broadway productions, an off-Broadway show, and a play that weekend. We kept the dates despite the events of that morning. He had insisted on it. I was on my guard. He was notorious for pulling awards when I disobeyed.

After that weekend, he would spend the next month punishing me with guilt.

"After everything I gave you, you did this to me." That was the one lesson he ensured I learned that weekend.

Between that weekend and my father, I would never willingly accept another gift from anyone ever again. Gifts were a unique branch of manipulation used to provoke guilt. I hate receiving gifts. A gift is owed debt and I had a back log.

He taught me another lesson that week.

"Commitment," he said to me. "Commitment."

The word rang through my head like poison. Commitment. And what is that exactly? The bars that hold you in a prison long after you've worn out your welcome? Or something a lover or partner says when the fear of abandonment arises?

Commitment.

I have loved many people. Love is ever changing, evolutionary. Love changes. It grows. It evolves. It's fast and slow. It's warm. It's fire. It's hot. It cools and sometimes, it fades completely while other times it moves like the ebb and flow of a tidal river. Only one thing is ever certain about love. It changes.

Commitment, though... Commitment isn't love. Commitment is dedication. It's something I give to my music, my goals, my dreams. It's something I reserve for myself. Commit to another? Why should I have commitment for a lover? When I love a man, it is out of love for that man that I try not to hurt him, not because of a promise I may not be able to keep. Sometimes I love so much that I want no other. I still don't consider that commitment. I call it love. But love may stay, it may go. I may stop loving him. I am in no position to predict that. People change and they can too easily become something we can't love. Sometimes two people grow together and sometimes they grow apart. Sometimes, you wake up one day and you think, what am I doing? While other days, your love flexes and flows. You grow together. You grow apart. You grow closer. You fall apart. No one can predict love. The only predictable thing about love is that it is too unpredictable to predict.

Commitment is not meant for love. Why would I ever commit myself to something as unpredictable and ever changing as love?

I couldn't say it then. But that day, commitment would take on a whole other meaning I would explore.

"Commitment," he said. "Commitment."

And all I could think of was the music I would write. I could not give up on that. Commitment.

I would show him.

Chapter 23

"He touched me while I was sleeping and I said your name."

I heard Isaiah hold his breath through the phone.

"What happened?" he asked.

"Well... I have a journal where I wrote down everything I've ever wanted to say to you and can't. He read it."

"Ouch," Isaiah said. "And?"

"He hit me."

Silence.

"He... what?"

"He hit me."

I don't remember what Isaiah said after that. I don't remember much else of anything except that summer.

* * *

It was summer of 1999. Isaiah and I were nineteen and I had found grapes my uncle had planted nearly forty years ago in the backyard. I was in the process of digging them up and had invited Isaiah over to help. We spent that morning replanting roses.

We had three roses, bare and covered in thorns. Some new leaves had begun to sprout. The dog had dug them out and ran with them. I rescued them and had intentions to put them back. The roots were undamaged. The dog had been surprisingly gentle with them. Probably didn't like having his mouth punctured with thorns.

After the roses, we moved on to the grapes. We spent hours digging in the dirt, loosening the vines so that we could free them and bind them on a trellis. The clouds were gray that day and spanned the sky, filling it with the energy carried on by the storm. We stood as the wind picked up. We threw back our shoulders and welcomed the warm summer wind that passed over us.

The rains never fell that day, but the clouds sustained that energy. We went inside and attempted to watch a movie. We made it five minutes into Don Juan DeMarco and shut it down. The ever present sexual energy sustained between us was unbearable and Don Juan was not helping the situation. Really, what is it about that movie?

We said our goodbyes. We did not touch. We would not kiss, and once more I watched him leave. He would be heading to Boston soon to attend college. He had finally raised enough money to travel east. Just like that, he was the last of my friends to go.

A letter arrived in the mail a week later. I ripped it open and read:

Hi, Elizabeth.
I just got to Massachusetts and received my student loan. I have enough to pay for the semester, but didn't know I had to buy my own books. The money from my loan doesn't cover the books so I have to find a thrift store and delve into

my savings. No time to write, but wanted to say I made it and will talk to you soon.
  Yours,
  Isaiah

I read his letter. I sat down to scribble out a reply. After fluffing Tribble's tail from my face a few times and giving her a pat in exchange for her purrs, I wrote my response and sent it off. His next reply contained information to exchange log-on information for instant messaging.

* * *

Isaiah: *Hi*

I sat down at my computer with a smile and typed like a giggling school girl.

Elizabeth: *Hi!*
Isaiah: *Just got computer access and internet today.*
Elizabeth: *Yeah!*
Isaiah: *So now we can talk without a phone bill!*
Elizabeth: *Sorry about that, btw.*
Isaiah: *You're fine.*
Elizabeth: *So how are your classes?*
Isaiah: *They're good. I have someone here I want you to meet. Her name is Jade. Hold on...*
Elizabeth: *Hi, Jade.*
Isaiah: *Hi. I'm a friend of Isaiah's. Isaiah is cool.*
Elizabeth: *Yes, he is.*
Isaiah: *We're in some of the same classes. I'm back. So that was Jade. You'd like her.*
Elizabeth: *Ah.*

I chewed on my bottom lip while I thought of something to talk about. The plink came through and I read.

Isaiah: *We hang a lot. She's pretty cool. We've had sex like three times now.*

My smile fell as a sick chill spilled down my throat. Unease balled my gut.
Another plink and I read.

Isaiah: *Probably going to ask her out. What do you think?*

My hands shook and I fought to breathe as I typed the only question I could muster.

Elizabeth: *Do I mean nothing to you?*
Isaiah: *Not really.*

The words were cold and callous. Was that amusement I felt?

Elizabeth: *Why would you say this?*
Isaiah: *'Cuz its true. Whatever we had, didn't really mean anything and you should know. It's over. Has been for a while. I just want you to go away and leave me alone, but you weren't getting the message so...*

I forced my nerves calm. Above all else, I'd honor his wishes. But I had to be certain. I calmly typed my response.

Elizabeth: *Is that what you truly want?*
Isaiah: *Yep!*
Elizabeth: *As you wish.*

I closed the message window and deleted my account. I opened my email. I deleted Isaiah's email address. I opened my phone and deleted his number. Within five minutes, I had obeyed and every contact I had for Isaiah was gone. I crawled into a shallow grave and wished for death there.

* * *

I don't remember much after that. I remember screaming and crying. Curling up into a ball in the corner of my room. I remember dying a slow, painful death, the kind that leaves you hating the world. I was like a worm. I wove myself a cocoon of dragon scales and there I stayed. When I finally emerged, I was a skeletal, hateful thing. I shunned emotion, hated all, and embraced logic. I was cold and callous. I had given up. While the trees withered and died, so did I. I turned my heart to stone that autumn. By winter, I was as miserable as the gray snows of a New York winter.

The only life in me, the only love left in me, was that for Tribble and my music. I poured myself into my compositions. I mastered my logic. But those around me grew hateful of my situation.

My father became vile. My siblings, wretched. I was nearing my twentieth birthday. Had no job, no foreseeable plans to attend college. Scott insisted I wasn't ready for college or good enough to attend any school for that matter. He visited every two weeks. I banged out the blow jobs, let him rape me during his movies. I began to fight back more boldly. I had stopped caring and was becoming brazen. Or I was just too hurt to hold in all the anger any more.

Scott's punishments became more aggressive. His requests, more cruel. He mentioned a group of friends he had. To enter their internal group, they required a female to pass around. Scott proposed the idea as a joke, suggesting how aroused it would probably make me if I was passed around a room with men.

I shot down the idea and he persisted, telling me I was close-minded. He asked me to drop my guard and open up. Encouraged me to embrace a sex life where I didn't hold back. He knew I had from day one. He could feel it. He loathed my hesitation. He talked of golden showers and gags. He proposed I fuck other girls. I simply wouldn't comply. I had become obstinate. Defiant. The only warmth in my heart was reserved for Tribble and I poured myself into the music and the logic.

Friction between my father and I escalated until, at long last, things had gone as far as they could go and broke. My father wanted me to get a job.

"Scott said! Scott said!" My father mocked me. "Get a job!"

"I must focus!" I shouted back Scott's words.

"To do what?" My father said. "You can't make a career out of music! Go to college! Get married! Do something or get out!"

And there it was. I was already packed. I had been packed since '98, living out of boxes, still waiting for Scott to come get me. Still waiting... still hoping...

I called my mother. She and Jake were there within an hour. The day of my twentieth birthday, I and Tribble moved out of my father's house and moved back in with Jake, my mother... and Joe.

* * *

I sat there in the corner of my new room and let the tears fall. I hugged myself against the hateful heart I had carved for myself. I thought of Isaiah.

I remembered the conversation.

Do I mean nothing to you?

Not really.
Why would you say this?
'Cuz its true.

I heard the clock ticking the time away. Tribble rubbed my hand, purring. She licked my fingers.

Is that what you truly want?
Yep!

Something didn't make sense. I gazed at my books still boxed on my bed.
Logic.
I forced my hand to Tribble's head and touched her ears. She climbed into my lap and I picked her up. She relaxed into me like a rag doll and purred happily while I buried my face into her silk fur and cried.
And all at once, it clicked. I raised my face from Tribble.
"It wasn't him," I whispered.
He would never say that. He would never hurt me... he never did. "It wasn't him."
The reality sank in. I scrubbed the tears from my face, scooped up Tribble, and scrambled to my feet. I ran to a box laden with papers and letters.
"It wasn't him," I said. I was certain.
How long had it been? Six months?
I dug through the letters and the papers. And breathed with relief when I found it. A letter. My hands shook as I yanked open the envelope and located the number at the bottom.
"555-847-3822" I dialed the number. My fingers shook.
"Please leave a message after the tone."
"Hello! Hi... Isaiah? This is Elizabeth. I..." I sighed. "I... Please call me. I... 555-856-1742."
I hung up the phone.

Tribble purred and rubbed her face into the corner of the phone.

"I just need to wait is all."

I picked up Tribble and settled onto the floor as Tribble nestled into my lap.

"I just need to wait."

* * *

"*Please leave a message after the tone.*"

"Hi... Isaiah. It's Elizabeth... I..." I sighed. "Please call me. 555-856-1742."

* * *

"*Please leave a message after the tone.*"
I hung up the phone.

* * *

After the first month, I stopped leaving messages.
After the third month, I stopped calling.

I regressed back to my piano and poured three hours a day into music performance. Another four hours in composition. My piano was sharp, precise, exact, and as cold as my heart. My music had gone dead.

It wasn't good enough. My hands were riddled with pain and yet I played. I tore the ligaments in my hands. I could feel the fire enflame my ring and little finger until the burning travelled up my arms. My shoulders ached. My back throbbed. I shredded the tendons and still I played on. I struck the keys through Beethoven, desperate to make the hate and the hurt stop, desperate to feel something... anything through the hate and the cold.

No matter how long I played, no matter how much I tried, the music betrayed me. And the music, it mocked me.

I dropped my hands to the bench. Everything from my shoulders down to my fingers burned. I shook under my tears. Tribble sat like a lady on the bench beside me. Looking up at me, she purred.

Unable to play another note, I gazed at my compositions. Never good enough. Never good enough...

Every breath in, ripped my lungs apart. Every breath out, pulled a knife through me. I stood, closed the lid on the piano, and walked away, turning instead, to my cold stone logic where I didn't have to feel a thing.

* * *

Scott and I were arguing every day now. I spent more time apologizing than anything. I was a slave to my phone, checking in on a regular schedule. His schedule. And God help me if I missed a check in. It was mandatory that I answer to him as needed. He still made the trips from New Jersey twice a month.

He'd pick me up. Fuck my mouth in the car while we drove back to the City and he'd fuck me there. I stopped refusing. I stopped fighting. I stopped everything. He urinated on me once. We argued.

We fought into all hours of the night. I'd present my newest logical argument. He'd let me have my say then rip it apart. When the arguments grew too heated for his liking, he would drive me to the nearest store and threaten to dump me there.

"Call your father! Have him come and get you!" he said.

But my father was gone. We hadn't spoken in more than a year. My life was hell and I was its bitch. Scott would fuck me and dump me. One night, I enraged him so much, he took me by the hair and tried to throw me into the hall of the hotel naked. I managed to get away. Maybe he let me go. I'm still not sure which.

August 2001, I returned home and walked into the latest shit fest.

"I quit my job!" Jake said.

"What?" I asked. I blinked stupidly at my step-father.

"Yep!" He said. "I quit my job and we're moving to Florida!"

I blinked more stupidly. It was all I could do. My mother was smiling.

"That's right!" Mum said. "We're leaving in a month! You're welcome to come with us. You're not bringing your cat."

I looked around the shit hole I lived in. Dirty dishes in the sink. Ragged carpet. They weren't exactly renowned for their financial prowess.

"What about money?" I asked.

"Don't know. Don't care," Jake said with a smile. "The good Lord will take care of us."

They had my three year old sister to take care of.

"And, where will you live in Florida once you get there?"

"We're moving in with my parents," Jake said.

I nodded.

Well. Looks like Scott is out of time.

* * *

"Hi," I said.

"Hi," Scott replied.

"So. . . my parents just announced that they are moving to Florida," I said.

Silence.

"What?" he finally asked.

"Yep. Florida," I said. "The good Lord will take care of them."

"That's so fucking stupid," he said.

I waited.

"How will they get there?" he asked.

"They're driving there on the last dollar they've got and are moving in with his parents."

"Ah."

I held my breath and waited for the words that would finally come. It had been four years.

"Well, looks like you need to find an apartment."

Chapter 24

31 August 2001, I moved into my own place with Tribble. The constant state of euphoria dropped me on cloud nine and sustained me there. I had a job. I had public transport. I had just turned twenty- one—which would have mattered if I hadn't been illegally drinking wine since I was sixteen— and, for the first time in my life, I felt empowered. I felt... I simply felt again. Within the first week, I had located a dance studio down the street from me. I took lessons twice a week, worked forty hours, and volunteered at a local cat shelter where I surrounded myself with four floors of cats.

I had nothing and my pay was taken by all of my rent. I didn't eat and didn't have enough money to buy food. But that was okay because I hated food. I hated eating. And so I didn't. I managed on half a sandwich a day and a small glass of milk. I drank coffee, which fueled my on-the-go lifestyle. In my spare time, I danced. I danced to spite the music I no longer played. Between the dancing and not eating, I dropped down to eighty pounds at four eleven.

I still visited the City two times a month and was due back September of 2001.

***

I felt William stiffen at the mention of that September.
I looked at him from across the table.
"Yes," I said. "You know what happened that September. We all know what happened that September."
I watched his lips tighten.
"How old are you?" I asked.
"Twenty-two."
I smiled and bobbed my head.
"You know where your parents were?"
"My mom was attending morning classes. She was between classes when she heard people around her talking about it. My dad was home sick in bed and watched the whole thing on the news."
I nodded. Someone always has a story to tell about their September 11th. I had yet to tell mine.
"What about you?" he asked.
I stared at the table. I felt the tears swell.
"I was in New York so much over the last few years. She was my home. The time spent away from New York, I was waiting... forever waiting to go back. I feel like my whole life was spent waiting. I waited for Piss-ant. I waited for Scott. I waited for my mother and my father to help me. I waited for Isaiah. I waited for someone to come and pick me up off the floor. To help me. I waited. No one ever came. Not once. It is no wonder I lost all faith in the human race and their gods."
William listened. I could hear him holding his breath.

***

I was supposed to be in New York that day. Scott changed our plans last minute. I was home that day in my new apartment. I had no television. I had a radio. The sun was shining and I was waiting for Scott to get there. He called me around nine to tell me the news. A plane had hit the Trade Towers. He told me to turn on the radio and see if I could get a signal.

I couldn't get reception. I was frustrated. I didn't understand. He stayed on the phone with me, shouting orders into the phone. I fumbled with the radio dial and tried to get reception. Scott relayed the news on his end.

"The towers have been hit. A second plane. A second plane hit the towers!"

"What?" I didn't understand. I couldn't.

I wanted to scream. I was confused.

"I'll be there in a few minutes," he said.

I fumbled with the dials. I didn't understand. I had no pictures. I only had the garbled voice on the other end panicking as he did his best to relay the horror back to me.

Scott came into the apartment. He shoved me out of the way and played with my radio, trying desperately to find a clear signal. He found one just as the towers fell.

The reporter played back the event. The billowing smoke. The first tower fell. People, New Yorkers, my brothers, leapt from the buildings. I didn't understand. How can skyscrapers fall? I stood there shaking, not quite understanding, terrified and so confused with the rest of New York and the world.

The second tower fell. New York was screaming, she was falling apart. Scott looked at me and said, "I have to go back."

"What? You just got here!"

"I know," he said. "But I have to go."

"Where? Into the war zone? We don't know what's going on!"

"I know. Which is why I have to go back."

"Take me with you," I said. "I can help!"

"No, you need to stay here. Come on now. I don't have much time."

I didn't understand.

Much time?

Scott was unzipping his pants. *You can't be serious.*

New York was under fire. People were dying.

I shook my head. "I don't want to. I can—"

Ignoring my protests, he shoved me toward the bedroom. While my head was still spinning, he fucked me. While New Yorkers died—while I cried for my people, my family, my kin—he raped me.

He finished, got dressed, said something—I don't remember what—and left. I heard the front door close and I lay there naked, his semen dripping down my leg. My frail, eighty-pound, dancer-eaten body withering away while New York burned and I cried for them. I laid there all day, unable to move or understand. I just lay there and cried in my room for my fellow man while my city burned.

I woke the next morning. I moved like a corpse. I think everyone did that morning. I left my apartment and stepped into air thick with death. I lived three hours away from the City. Too many of the people where I lived had kin in the City, moved from there only recently, or were there only days before.

I walked the street to my bus and nearly wretched at the morning newspaper. I saw it and went numb. I tried to understand. I couldn't. I got on my bus and found a seat and stared at every face. Every face looked battered with grief for the three thousand who died only yesterday.

I hadn't heard yet about the Pentagon or Flight 93. Each one of us near tears, each one of us looked as if we had just stepped out of a war zone.

I arrived at my job. The lights were still out. I followed my usual routine and made my way to the break room. The TV was on.

I looked up and froze.

There she was in all her elegance and strength, I stared at my city under fire. The people jumping, the smoke rolling... the towers falling. I went white then quiet.

I left the break room and reported to the meeting.

The managers spoke about nothing relevant. None of it mattered. I remember thinking that a lot. I was locked in my own head. I was silent. Confusion battled grief. The images replayed of the day before. Scott raped me. He left me. He denied me the one thing I needed and that was my New York. To see my Old New York. To help her. To be there. To know she was okay. All he could think about was sex.

I tuned into the meeting.

"Due to recent events, I'd like to propose a moment of silence for those lives lost yesterday."

And then there was silence. That silence cut through my sanity and I broke. I crumbled under my tears and everyone there followed me. We held each other. We sobbed and we hugged. Strangers clung to each other, desperate to be rid of the hurt we all shared. And I broke. I didn't know who held me. I had never been held while I cried in my life. Not when my cats died or my cousins.

I looked up and saw Richard, one of the managers, holding me.

"Lily," he said to a coworker. "Can you take her—"

He passed me to Lily. She closed her eyes and held me, tears lined our faces and that morning I shared my grief with another human being.

* * *

"Richard would be my first husband."

William looked up from his paper.

"There are moments where a writer wants to hold onto the secrets and savor them for the shock and awe of the big reveal," I said. "This isn't one of those moments."

He said nothing, but returned his attentive gaze to his notes.

I pressed my knuckles to my mouth.

"I've never gone back," I said.

I felt William's eyes back on me. "Ever?"

I shook my head. "I can't. Not after..." I kept shaking my head. I felt my eyes burn.

"Why not?" he asked.

I forced myself to take a deep breath.

"For fear of what I might see," I guessed. "A different New York? One that I may not know. Or worse, one that may not know me."

William gave a disinterested face and looked back down at his paper.

"I think it's something else," he said.

I dropped my hand to my lap and forced a playful smile.

"Oh, do you?"

I knew I wasn't fooling him. Not this time.

William shrugged. "New Yorkers are strong," he said. "If there is anything 9/11 taught us, it is that New Yorkers—Americans—prevail. Yes, New Yorkers are rude, obstinate, and impatient, but they have a strength, a determination, seen in very few other places in the world. 9/11 wouldn't change that. It would make them stronger. So what is it?" he asked. "Why didn't you go back?"

I made a point of watching my cat in the green room.

"I've never really had the time," I said.

"Bull shit," William said.

I looked at my guest.

"You're a writer," he said. "You keep your own schedule."

"What difference does it make if I go back?" I asked. "It doesn't matter."

"It matters," he insisted. "Why you didn't go back. Now why didn't you go back?"

My head was reeling. I felt my anxiety rise with the words I needed to say. It had been too long.

"Because. . ." I trailed off.

"Why?"

I was still holding it in, the bottled hurt. How could I dare cry about my lot when others were dying? I bit my finger.

"Because. . ."

"Why?"

"Because I should have been there!" I screamed. "I was supposed to be there and I'm sorry! I'm sorry I couldn't do better by them! I'm sorry I couldn't scream louder! Sorry that I wasn't there."

"*Sure,*" Ian said beside me. "*Your people are dying, but you're sorry. Keep your Irish sorrys and stuff 'em.*"

He was mocking me, but I had to make him understand. He had to understand.

"We had made plans to drive up that day!" I said. "I was supposed to be there and I wasn't! We changed our plans last minute and instead of dying with them, he raped me! He fucked me! He left me. . . and people were dying, people were. . . I should have been one of them, but I was too busy—"

"*Too busy what?*" Ian said. "*Being raped?*" He scoffed. "*You deserved to get raped, is that it? Use it to punish you for not being there for New York? Is that why you didn't go back? You don't feel sorry for her. You felt sorry for yourself.*"

Rage distorted my face.

"Now wait just a minute!" I said to Ian. "I do not! I hate pity. I do not accept it, most of all from me. I loved her! I belonged with her! I should have died with her! I should have suffered with her. I got out easy!"

Ian was nodding too politely.

"You did," he said. "*And why shouldn't you? You were only raped, after all, while they were dying. Their suffering far outstrips yours. What right do you have to cry about your hurt? One would hardly think you cared about New York at all.*"

"I do care!"

"What he did to you was nothing compared to what was happening in New York..."

"It was something!"

"*...you were only raped, after all.*"

"I would have been there for her!" I insisted.

"*So why weren't you?*" he asked.

"Because I couldn't get to her!"

"*And why not?*" he pressed.

"Because he raped me!"

There was Ian's victorious smile. I looked to William, who sat looking horrified at me. Then all the hurt swelled up inside of me and I burst into tears.

"He left me!" I shrieked. "New York was burning and he raped me... as the towers fell! People were dying. Children lay dying, and he raped me! He fucked me! He left me! He raped me and I couldn't... I couldn't even save me."

I shook under my grief and I cried right then for New York and the people who lost their fathers and mothers, husbands and wives. I cried for them as I had cried for days on end. But mostly, right then, I cried for me.

Part Four: Waking Pavlov's Dog

Chapter 25

The hot water rolled over my breasts while I inhaled the scent of fresh coffee from the kitchen. I had wanted another Guinness, but William's insistence on coffee sounded too good to argue. It was three in the morning and I was just a little over half done with this. I needed to stay sharp.

I dug the stress and raw tears from my eyes.

"Almost done," I whispered and sighed.

I killed the water, wrung the excess from my hair and enjoyed the steam for a moment before stepping out onto the plush rug. A minute later, I had patted myself dry, towel dried my hair, and had slipped into my most comfortable pair of gray lounge pants and a sage green tank top that slimmed my body.

After brushing my hair with my hands a few times, I exited the bathroom with a billowing cloud of steam that caught William's eye as he poured two cups of coffee.

"Feel better?" he asked.

I nodded and accepted a cup from him.

"Black?" he asked.

I shook my head and grabbed the creamer out of the fridge. "I never drink it black."

Taking a sip from his own cup, he returned to his place at the table. He had already changed out the batteries to the recorder and was stuffing the dead pair into his bag by the time I had added two teaspoons of sugar to my coffee and joined him at the table.

"So," he began. "September 11th. You met Richard and..."

He trailed off, encouraging me to continue where we had left off before my shower.

I sipped the coffee and sank back into my chair, pulling the blanket back into my lap.

"I spoke to Scott the next day," I said. "I complained. Reminded him that, for five years, he had promised to spend Christmas and Thanksgiving with me then never did. With the holidays around the corner, I told him if he wasn't there for Christmas and Thanksgiving, we were done. That year there was no excuse. He assured me would be there and agreed to my terms. I went all out, planned a homemade dinner, bought a fresh turkey... the fixings..."

"He didn't show, did he?" William said.

I shook my head.

"He didn't show," I said. "He had a friend of his call that morning an hour before I was expecting him with an excuse that he was in the hospital. I wasn't surprised and certainly didn't let it get the best of me. I happily ate my first Thanksgiving alone with Tribble."

* * *

By that point, I was impassive to the world. I had learned to expect nothing from anyone and I don't, to this day. No expectation from anyone at all. I think that has worked out well for me. I don't get upset if people don't do what I want them to do because I never expect them to do anything. Unless they are deliberately mean, people don't get to me.

I didn't care that he didn't make it for Thanksgiving. A part of me said, "Okay. There's always Christmas," but I knew he wouldn't show. I didn't even make plans for the solstice. Instead, I dove into my logic. I was putting together an argument that finally, finally would set me free.

I was dancing and still not eating. If I purchased anything but fresh produce, Scott reprimanded me and I had hell to pay. I also hated to cook, so I went without. I still spent most of my spare time volunteering at the cat shelter.

At work, attention for the populace flowed in. My affectionate, sunny, and, how do you say, honest. . . disposition earned me a plethora of male friends all of whom made their own affections very clear. But I had other problems brewing. Despite my smiles and contagious disposition, I was terrified of men. When I felt one draw close, I smiled and flirted as a means to defend. A happy male wouldn't hurt me. An angry male would. A sexually appeased male was safe. And so, I appeased.

They would draw close, I would flirt. They would interpret my defensive maneuver as an invitation—justifiably so—and I would reciprocate accordingly. It didn't take long before they began making their moves and sex was almost inevitably around the corner. Fortunately, the dance I had rehearsed with Isaiah taught me how to keep them dancing without delivery. I failed once before Richard moved in and sent the rest on their way.

On the surface, I smiled while underneath I screamed. And no one was the wiser. Christmas approached, came, and slipped by quietly without a word about the holiday between Scott and I. There had been no visit even discussed and I counted the relationship between Scott and I as over: terminated by the conditions in which we agreed upon in our verbal contract.

But I had one more battle that was closing in. One more fight to win if I was to be rid of him.

***

My phone rang. I didn't answer. For five years, I had been a slave to that phone. Hating every second that I had been chained to it. To this day, I detest answering my phone. I will miss appointments before I answer my phone.

It rang again. I glared at it.

I knew it was him, knew he was waiting on the other end to slander me, reprimand me, and scold me for not answering for the last two days.

I drew in a deep breath, braced for the impact, and answered.

"Hello?"

"Where the fuck have you been?"

Did I really have to answer to him?

"Busy," I said

"Busy?"

And just like that it was my turn. My turn to sit there and listen to him talk. My turn to hear his rants, his judgment, his abuse. My turn to sit and wait with an ever-growing smile as I clicked the final piece of the final argument into place.

I listened to him quote back the same crap my father said. He called me selfish. Called me abusive. Insisted I was obsessed with money, a gold digger, and a taker. The lifetime of abuse had hardened me for this and his insults ricocheted off my smile. He performed from atop his soapbox while I grinned and waited just as he had shown me.

"Well?" he said at last. I heard him huffing, quite winded from his rant.

I shrugged and answered only one thing. One basic lesson I learned all the way back on that first day.

"That is your opinion, isn't it," I replied.

Another round of screams and insults came at me. I smiled, not even listening anymore. It was over. No matter what he said, no matter the argument, I was home free. He could never touch me again.

This time, I laughed... openly laughed in delight at my revelation inside and out. He screamed again, demanding an answer. This time, I had one.

"Everything you say to me, everything you argue, is all a matter of perspective. Every opinion you form, even the facts you cite, they are all subjective and adherent to one basic truth: that the conclusions you have drawn are only true from your perspective. Where you stand, your conclusion may be the case. But from where I stand..." I shook my head, smiling. "From my perspective, your premises are false and therefore, your conclusion is false."

I know he felt his power over me slipping. I was on a roll and didn't dare stop. He tried to argue.

"It doesn't matter what you say," I said. I almost laughed again. "None of it matters because at the end of the day, you can only report on your perspective, and I on mine."

He made a noise like he was trying to interrupt, but I was way ahead of him. I had this. I had the control. Where he was angry and vile, I was calm and relaxed. I flowed through the argument with a cool precision, hardened by the logic he taught me.

"From where I'm standing, none of it matters anymore and I have done nothing wrong," I said. "From my perspective, everything you say to me will forever be in question because we do not share the same perspective. I must make my own decisions, my own assessments from here. Only my perspective matters. No one else's. Only I can gather the premise I need from my point of view. Only I decide for me and your opinion no longer matters."

He tried to throw "commitment" at me and the "music career." He threatened to drive up and take my books, but for the first time in my life, I knew I could get my own.

"To thine own self be true," I said and hung up the phone.

Chapter 26

William blankly stared at me.

"Just like that?" he asked.

I nodded.

"Just like that," I said, smiling, still pleased with myself. "It was such a kick ass argument. One that had earned me my freedom."

"But it's so simple," William said.

I nodded again.

"It is, and still it took me five years to see it. Existentialism, logic, a cool head, everything he had taught me. But that argument had nothing to do with logic or ethics. This had everything to do with control. It had to do with me picking myself up off the floor and fighting. I was under my half-brother's fist all over again. My father was rejecting me all over again. I was chained to Joe's bed all over again. This was me accepting rejection and standing against them all for the sake of me. Was the argument easy? Yes. Simple, in fact. Simple sense that took me five years to master."

I took a moment and finished off my coffee before refreshing our cups.

"Richard and I started a relationship immediately after the verbal contract was breeched by Scott on Christmas day," I said, settling back into my chair.

"But you, you weren't okay," William said. "I mean... You had sex at fifteen. Were abused, raped, and sexually tortured. And you're walking into a new relationship?"

"That's right," I said. "One of the dumbest mistakes of my life. But I didn't know I had a problem. I didn't know I had any issues. I thought I was normal. I was looking for the traditional marriage, the traditional family, with the traditional dream, despite never once having the traditional childhood to prepare me for that. I was a mental mutation chasing cookie cutter dreams designed only for the status quo.

"That decision—leaving a raping pedophile to enter a marriage—taught me one thing: Marriage made the rapes stop."

* * *

The day that Scott read my journal and hit me came to be known as the "Isaiah Incident." For two years, Scott brought up the "Isaiah Incident" in every argument. It sounded like a disease coming from his mouth. When I lost Isaiah, I turned inward where the pain festered.

If there was one lesson I learned from losing Isaiah, it's that life is too short to fuck around. Be brave. Be bold. Be blunt. And I had every intentions, of being just that, and nothing more. If I liked someone, I told them. If I admired someone, I told them. I held nothing back. I did that once and I lost someone very precious to me. Never again.

Mind you, I didn't throw myself at men nor did I flaunt my condition, but if I saw someone who was attractive, I told them. "You look good." And it didn't matter if they were male or female. Though, the males did take my forwardness differently.

I had learned to love smiling. I smiled, made eye contact. I was sincere. I still am. I had no qualms looking someone in the eye, smiling, and saying, "Hi. I like you." It was my way of branding them "friend." It's something I practice to this day. If I love someone, I waste no time in telling them. Life is too short.

The men fell for me often and hard. If they made me laugh, I let them know it. If they made me smile, I told them. I held nothing back. Honesty, pure and simple. Genuine, sincere, kindness and direct honesty. And I found living on my own made it so much easier to laugh out loud and smile. That is what I had become. Laughter. And I had a lot of crying to make up for.

Richard fell for me like a Steinway piano on an Acme set. Like a breath of fresh air, I entered his life smiling and laughing. I looked right into him when he spoke and I said exactly what came to mind. And I dripped sex. Dancing had sculpted my body into an 80-pound solid mass of muscle, and the endorphins, dopamine, and serotonin fueled my permanent state of genuine happiness. Truth is, I was so relieved to be away from Scott that I couldn't help but smile. It became my habit, my MO, I simply fell in love with smiling and laughter, and once I had reason enough to be happy, I couldn't stop.

My break down on September 12th encouraged Richard to seek me out. What began as a kind follow-up turned into a warm friendship very quickly. He learned of my current living conditions and my pedophile. He learned that I was dancing on a diet that consisted primarily of coffee.

He reminded me, if only briefly, of Isaiah and I, still cursing myself for wasting that opportunity, wasted no time pursuing Richard. Once I was certain he would have me, I ran to him. By February 2002, he moved in with me. A month later, I was pregnant with our first daughter, Anne.

* * *

Richard had seen and heard, better than I, what my male co-workers thought of me. In confidence, they disclosed every detail among themselves, away from the feminine ear. He listened to months of fantasies exchanged by more than a dozen males detailing their desires with I as their subject. When Richard moved in, he immediately demanded I quit my job. I required a proper explanation and he obliged. He relayed every detail back to me that was exchanged among the male populace.

"You do something to them," he said. "You're like a drug."

I was hurt. "I don't—"

"You do it to me. It's like you're heroin. You are. You're heroin."

He described a feeling that he had to take care of me. That he adored me and couldn't stay away.

The following day, I quit my job.

Most of my marriage with Richard was uneventful. We spent the first few months enamored, and we dedicated a good portion of those first few months to learn about each other. He was determined to label Scott as a pedophile and encouraged me to do something about it. He wanted me to press charges, get in touch with law officials. I viewed Scott as an ex and believed my childhood and lifestyle were normal. I just wanted to forget. I told Richard about

Isaiah and how I had lost him. We would visit that topic often for the next seven years.

For me, there was no closure. Isaiah didn't dump me, I just lost him and couldn't find him. I was still trying to reach Isaiah. I told Richard this right up front, that I was looking for someone. Richard listened and supported and did his best to comfort me. He offered words to comfort me, he held me while I cried for Isaiah. That was weird, crying in someone's arms. I still... I don't do that well. Richard tried to tell me that Isaiah dumped me and to move on. He tried to empathize, but, without closure, I could not.

Every few months or so, I would try all the numbers again and write to Isaiah. I only ever received message machines and mail marked "return to sender." I missed our friendship. But most of all, I just wanted an answer to my why.

Within those first few months, whether it was the dancing, or my weight, or my constant inability to eat, my system shut down and I came down with a dangerously high fever I could not bring down. I was septic and held a fever of one-hundred-five for nearly ten days. At the end of the ten days, I was exchanging full conversations with Erik and Angel. I'd pop some over-the-counter fever reducers and chug water. My sweat smelled like sewage and I lay there delusional. At the end of the ten days, Richard decided to take me to the ER. We sat there while he lectured me about taking better care of myself.

I was hooked up to an IV, immediately put on antibiotics for twenty-four hours then was sent home with a prescription. Two weeks later, we learned I was pregnant.

* * *

Having a child was like someone had turned on a switch in my body. It whirled and awakened like a machine brought to life for the first time. Every inch of me was built for a reason and all at once, I saw its purpose. Nearly everything about the female body was designed to bear children. Just amazing.

Richard and I were thrilled about my pregnancy. We went through the motions of excited new parents. I spent the pregnancy begging Richard to be in the room with me. He made it clear he wanted to wait in the hallway until Anne had arrived. At the end, my begging had prevailed. I had a C-section and Richard stood in the OR with me.

I was adamant to start breast-feeding as soon as I awakened from surgery. I had no idea what I was doing and screwed up on the latch. Anne was frustrated. Her mouth was small and I was drugged on morphine. I tried again, dulled to the pain signals sent to my brain that told me there was a problem. By the time I had realized there was a problem, the incorrect latch had begun to sever my nipple from my breast.

The lactation consultant corrected the problem and taught me, but the damage was done. For the eight weeks, breast-feeding on that side felt like a small blade was sawing through my nipple. The pain was excruciating and the option for pain meds was almost non-existent.

Three days later, I walked in the front door with my Anne. I had a prescription, but no time to fill it and I was in no condition to drive. The meds given to me at the hospital had nearly run their course and I was feeling the pain of my C-section and my partially severed nipple.

Richard drove Anne and I home, helped me upstairs, kissed me goodbye, and left for work.

The phone rang. Still holding Anne, I answered it.

"Hello?" I managed to scrape out. I was exhausted.
"Hello, Elizabeth?"
I sighed. It was Scott.
"What do you want?"
"I just felt it only fair to warn you. I have filed some paper work reflecting the books and lessons I gave you as gifts, which means you're going to want to speak to an attorney about tax laws because you'll have to pay the taxes on everything. Thought you should kno—"
"I just got home from the hospital," I said. "I just had surgery. I don't give a damn what you do."
I listened to his stupid stuttering.
"Oh. . . I. . . I'm sorry I didn't know. I. . . I'm sorry."
Click.
I grinned, thrilled that he hung up on his own accord. It felt good not giving a damn what he thought.
Thirty minutes later, the meds had fully worn off.
An hour after that, I was incapable of picking up Anne.
Thirty minutes after that, I was unable to walk or stand or move as the pain burrowed its way through my body. With every step, I felt the stitches pull at my cut. My breast burned as if I suffered from mutilation and it was only ten o'clock. I had another seven hours to go before Richard would come home and I could send him for meds. Needless to say, when he walked through the door at the end of the day, I fell apart.

Chapter 27

Seeing me endure such pain with the breast-feeing made Richard crazed with worry. He begged me to stop and to switch Anne to formula feeding. I wouldn't hear of it and endured, but not without reliving the same argument for nearly two months while I felt my nipple being sucked off my body.

I soon associated breast-feeding with anxiety and waves of pain shot through my shoulder. It felt like a knife sliced through my arm and peeled my skin from my body. Anne drank my blood with my milk, which the doctors confirmed was okay, but the lack of support from my husband and the arguments added to the stress and isolated me. I don't think I blame him. Feeding my daughter was literally a mini-torture session I had to relive every two to four hours while my husband watched me cry and bite back the screams.

The experience secured a rift between us that would remain to the end of the marriage. When times got tough, Richard's first reaction was to quit.

I had planned to breast-feed Anne for one year. I was twenty-two and had gone back to dancing, my figure settled down to one hundred ten pounds and I no longer looked like a skeletal dancer made of muscle and bone. But by June 2003, I had another problem arise that landed me in the hospital for nearly five straight weeks.

The antioxidants in black tea and spinach are exceptionally high and, if taken in large doses, can build up mineral deposits that the kidneys form into stones. At this time, I lived off Earl Grey tea and spinach salads.

A crippling pain, six months after Anne was born, earned me a trip to the Emergency Room. I had three stones. One blocked my ureter—the tube that allows urine to travel from your kidney to your bladder. A second stone blocked my bladder, and the third had formed in my kidney. All three were the size of hazel nuts.

Most people pass stones. I required surgeries, lasers, and a urine bag that allowed me to piss like a man for five weeks. It was awesome.

I walked away with a plethora of stories, a gruesome scar on my back—not really that gruesome, but it makes for a great story—and I must be the only woman who understands why it's so fun to write your name in the snow with piss. I was so mad it was June. Every time I used the bathroom, I got to crinkle up sheets of toilet paper and try to pee on them with my bag. It's harder than you think! It was like a water gun fight every time I used the bathroom! How is that not cool?

"Ooh! I have to use the bathroom." Oh, happy day. I cocked my gun. "Lock and load."

The doctors surgically went in through my back and pulled out the stone in my bladder. Then they used mirrors to shoot lasers through my body. I was shot with lasers and lived. They shattered the stones in my ureter and kidney allowing the debris to pass through my system. But the shards could have nicked my ureter, which risked an infection, so they inserted a tube to protect the lining of my ureter. They inserted a catheter via an incision through my back to drain my bladder to a urine bag tied to my leg for five weeks.

The medication I was on turned my breast milk mint green. When I asked the lactation consultant, they advised me to breastfeed no matter what. When I asked my doctors, they pulled me off breast-feeding immediately. Anne was six months old.

I stumbled out of bed the next morning, grabbed my I.V. pole for the hundredth time, and made my way to the bathroom. Wahoo! Target practice!

After five weeks of in and out visits, I was sick of seeing the hospital, though I do miss their delicious turkey sandwiches.

"Come on, Fred," I beckoned the pole.

By that afternoon, he and I were good friends and I made sure everyone who came to visit formally met Fred. He was my first Fred and thereon every inanimate object I loved would be named Fred. My rock is named Fred. My fish are named Fred... all of them. My computer is named Fred.

I climbed back into bed and Richard stormed in.

Throughout my hospital stay, Anne had spent all of her time with my father and his new wife while Richard went to work. Twice, maybe three times a week he stopped in. Every visit was the same.

With his hands shoved in his pockets, he stood at the foot of my bed and scolded me, berating me for getting sick, for not taking care of myself, and for not thinking of him. He called me selfish and weak. He called me a bitch and walked out, leaving me in tears.

I looked at Fred and patted his round steel back then rolled over and cried myself to sleep.

* * *

On the occasion that I was sent home between procedures, the bandages holding my catheter in my back had to be changed. Richard refused to change them and I couldn't reach them. The fourth week in, we made a trip to my grandmother's house and she changed the bandages for me. She sponged the area around the wound and I lay on her bed for an hour while the incision breathed.

It was amazing. For five weeks, I could feel my skin trying to reknit itself over the catheter that repeatedly reopened the wound. My skin wanted to heal. It tried to heal and it would have, had it not been for the hose shoved through my back. There was no pain, whatsoever.

At the end of the five weeks, the doctor removed the catheter from my back. That was an odd sensation, having a two-foot slimy catheter pulled for nearly twenty seconds from my back. The sensation ended and, at last, my skin was free to heal itself.

The catheter in my ureter needed to be removed through my urethra. It was probably two. . . three inches in length. The doctor had to pull it out with a clamp. It aggravated my body so much that I slipped between consciousness and unconsciousness repeatedly for several seconds at a time.

The body shuts down and enters shock to protect itself. Completely painless, but phenomenal experience. At the end of that period, Richard's true colors shone bright. When an emergency struck, the moment anything became difficult, he was first to ridicule, assign blame, and lash out. If the situation continued to be difficult, he would bail.

Unfortunately, life is almost always difficult.

*　*　*

I had wanted my children to be close in age and by the time Anne was eight months old, I was pregnant with Daniel. This was the best Richard and I would be. He was happy, I was doing well, for me, and life was... decent. Four months into my pregnancy with Daniel, Richard lost his job.

As I said, when things got bad, Richard got worse. In 2004, I worked at a children's clothing store where no men were ever employed. When Richard lost his job, I took on a second job at a bookstore. For the first time since 9/11, I was around males.

I still didn't know that I was housing a severe fear of men. Richard was no help. He informed me that I was not allowed to work around any males at the bookstore. Not exactly a request I could submit to my manager.

Arguments began. Money grew tight. I worked more hours. Time with Richard vanished as my work schedule picked up. More arguments ensued. I quit the job per his request. Money grew tighter. The arguments were relentless and my triggers continued as did our fights.

After two months of incessant bickering, Richard found work. I was six months pregnant with our son.

I give no credibility to old wives' tales and such, but there was something that convinced me I was carrying a son. We never even bothered with female names. I just knew there was a boy in me. My fear of men was prominent. My life with Joe and Scott was a muted memory by then, but my life with Shaun... that was something forever on my mind.

The moment I learned I was pregnant again, I had an anxiety that grew every day. I was convinced all boys were like my half-brother. I still am.

Boys will be boys.

Just as a woman was designed to give life, a man was designed to take it away. Every man had his breaking point. Every man would beat a woman if pushed hard enough. It was only a matter of time.

My mother had carefully taught me this. I saw Daniel viciously beating Anne just as Shaun had beat me. I saw me having no idea how to stop it or prevent it. I didn't even know what a son needed from a mother. From what I could see, my brothers had no need for my mother. The only male in my life who had a loving mother was Richard and my father, both of whom lacked the ability to articulate an answer to my question.

I had nine months to get an answer and searched the libraries, desperately hunting for the answer to my question. Problem was I had no idea where to find such an answer.

* * *

"Well, it looks like everything is okay," the ultrasound technician said. "Do you want to know what it is?"

"Yes," I said.

"It's a boy."

I felt the horror curdle my stomach. Richard smiled. Inside, I was screaming. I bit my bottom lip and nodded.

"Congratulations. Here you go," she said and handed me a towel. I wiped the ultrasound slime from my belly.

Ten minutes later, I was walking to the car. Tears blinded me.

"What's wrong?" Richard asked. "You don't want a son?"

"No... I just..." My throat burned and I bit my lip. I was terrified of a son. Terrified of having a son like my half-brother. Images of my son beating me, of me curled up under a desk just as my half-brother had beaten me played back in my head as I crossed the hospital parking lot.

"I don't... know... how to raise a son," I tried to explain. "He'll be like Shaun."

"You're just upset that you want another daughter," he snipped. "Admit it. You hate males."

I cringed at the resentment in Richard's voice and swallowed back the tears. All the way home, I sat in silence, keeping my tears to myself, already scared to death of the male growing inside of me.

* * *

Again, Richard and I argued about the birth of our child. Again, I begged him to stay with me. And again, he argued that he wanted to hang out in the hallway until it was over. The day of the C-section, we went in at six A.M. By lunch time, we had a son. The medications and temporary euphoria of a new mother calmed my nerves. I had asked that my son be brought to me the moment he awoke to be breastfed then promptly fell asleep.

I slept all afternoon and through the night.

I woke the next morning at five A.M. The lights were off. No one had brought my son to me. I was upset and so pulled myself out of bed less than twenty four hours after having my gut cut open. I walked the halls relishing the pain.

In comparison to Anne's birth, this one was a walk in the park. I expected the pain and knew the best way to handle it. The sooner you move, the faster you heal. The ward was silent. All was quiet. No visitors. No lights, I made my way to the nursery and gazed down at my boy.

He was born jaundiced, which is normal. They had him in the bilirubin lights and he had slept the whole night through.

I smiled and gazed at his little fingers. His little hands.

I tried to imagine him beating my daughter and my worries flooded back. It had been nine months, and I still had no answer.

Why did Shaun beat me? I remembered most of the petty arguments that triggered my beatings. Mostly, Shaun had beat me for loving opera, show tunes, and classical music. He had insisted that I listen to modern bands and told me I would be beaten at school for it if I didn't change. He would then proceed to beat me right there for loving my Beethoven and Mozart.

That was why he wanted to kill me. Because... I don't know. Because I was different? Because I loved Bach? And Puccini? So stupid. It was all so stupid.

"Oh my god!" a nurse exclaimed through a whisper. "You're up? How are you up already?"

I smiled.

"Oh, I'm fine," I said. "I can't lay still. Too much energy to sit still."

She came to stand beside me. "What's his name?"

"Daniel." I smiled. "My Danny boy"

"Isn't that an Irish song?"

I grinned.

Ireland.

How long had it been? How much I had missed...

"Yes," I said.

"How did it go?" she asked and I sang.

She joined me at the chorus and I stood and watched my Danny Boy sleep. I welcomed the ease that came over me and, by the song's end, I vowed, no matter what it would take, my Danny would not be like Shaun.

Chapter 28

"I really hate talking about my ex," I muttered to William.

"No, it's fine," he said. "This is your story. Your book."

I stared at my hands in my lap.

"Most women can bitch about their exes for days and not tire from it. I dread becoming one of them. This is the most I've ever spoken of him. If I had my way, he wouldn't even be in the story. He wasn't worth it."

William shifted in his chair.

"But he's part of it," he said. "He's part of you."

I felt sick about that, but William was right.

"Yes. He is," I said. "I could go on about all the petty shit we fought about, but I won't. At the end of the day, there are really only a handful of things you need to know about him. The man detested—refused to seek medical assistance even if it meant risking the health of the children.

"When a pewter block fell on Danicl and split his head open, Richard promptly smeared gobs of super glue onto the wound to avoid a trip to the hospital. When Anne shoved a bead up her nose and we went to the ER, Richard spent the two hours in the waiting room scolding me for being a bad mother. The day my son put something in his mouth and couldn't breathe..."

My hands were already shaking with rage at the memory. I sighed and forced my anger steady.

"Daniel was on his bed examining something. I turned my back and he had popped whatever he had into his mouth. It immediately blocked his air passage. He couldn't breathe. I stood him up, but had no idea what to do. I grabbed the phone and called 911. While I was on the phone giving them my address, Daniel's lips and toes had started to turn blue.

"He fell to the floor and thrashed for air. I hung up and watched my son, not sure at all what I could do. He clawed at his throat. I picked him up, he threw himself back... amid his thrashing and my... whatever the hell it was that I was trying to do, the object shifted and cleared his throat. Daniel lay gasping for air just as Richard walked through the door."

William stared at me with a look that turned my insides out.

"It may have been a minute, maybe two, while I watched my son not breathe," I continued. "It felt like an eternity. While I rubbed Daniel's back, Richard stood over me screaming at me for involving the fire department. By the time the EMT arrived, Richard had formed his own story and told them Daniel was only holding his breath from a tantrum and I..." I scoffed. "I couldn't tell the difference."

"A tantrum," William repeated.

I nodded.

"Daniel was prone to throwing tantrums and holding his breath," I said. "But I'm not stupid. I know the difference. Richard hadn't even been there when it happened. The boy was clawing at his throat, physically digging at it as if trying to will air through his trachea. My son. Couldn't. Breathe. Richard insisted I had been yelling at him again and had triggered one of his tantrums then went on to scold me in front of the firemen for not knowing the difference. For the rest of the night, I endured Richard's slander.

"Now and then, on his days off, Richard would take off to go hunt something. In those times, the house would settle back to a routine and I would clean the house. I wanted nothing more than to spend all my time at work, locked away where I could forget."

"What did you love about him?" William asked.

I smiled.

"I love your thoroughness," I said. "Little makes me more happy than someone who can see both sides of the picture without being prompted. Richard was sweet when the world was right and all was well. Richard wasn't a bad man. He did treat me well." I cringed. "No. That wasn't true. I have a girlfriend, Penelope, who witnessed my marriage on the inside. Nell has made it very clear that Richard verbally abused me and didn't hesitate to publicly slander me. Richard didn't beat me. He didn't rape me."

"Are those your standards?" William asked, grinning.

"Yes, I guess they are," I said, smiling back. "Richard verbally abused me. A lot. But I also verbally abused him."

"You're doing it," William said.

"Doing what?" I asked.

"Defending Richard. Must you always shoulder the blame of others?"

"Yes," I answered. "It would be wrong of me to say I had no blame in this."

"Perhaps," he said. "But this is your story after all. You are allowed to be the hero."

"I am not a hero," I said. "There are no heroes in this story. Only survivors and victims and predators."

I was ready to move on. Too much was said about Richard. Far too much of my time had already been given to him.

"To this day, Richard has no idea why we broke up," I said. "Simply put, I was broken and neither of us knew it. I wouldn't learn it for another ten years. Richard would never learn of my past nor the mental issues that resulted from my life."

"Why did you break up?" William asked.

I sighed while I looked back at the seven years of our marriage.

"I can analyze all the rights and wrongs we did," I said. "Every little fight. Petty shit that went unresolved... symptoms of a much bigger problem. No." I shook my head. "We broke up because Richard kept tripping my triggers."

"Triggers?" William asked.

"Rape victims have triggers," I said. "Anyone suffering from trauma can walk away with triggers. Victims of abuse, war veterans, and rape victims have triggers. Don't fire a gun near a soldier fresh from war. There was one year, my cousin had just returned from Afghanistan a week before New Year's and my sister was fond of noise makers. He didn't handle the celebrations well.

"I had nearly twenty years of triggers—forty-four identifiable triggers—constantly set to go off like a land mine. Completely avoidable if you know what not to do. Richard didn't know about a single one of them. His life style, his likes, his behavior... almost every day, he set off a number of my triggers without even knowing it. By the way, that land mine, that mental massacre in my head, that is one of the reasons why I can't be married. Who, in their right mind, would want to spend a life tip-toeing through a live land mine. Take a wrong step and I'm curled up in a corner muttering insanities to myself."

"But you've gotten better," William said. "You must have. You're working on it at least."

I nodded. "I am now completely aware of most of my triggers and have worked to gain full control over them so if one is tripped, I can disarm it before others even know there's a problem."

"So you can marry," William said.

I sighed. I was hating this conversation.

"I can't guarantee a one hundred percent success rate," I said. "As I said, what male in their right mind would happily take this on? I'm not worth it."

"What kind of triggers?" William asked. I was glad for the change of topic.

"Richard loved movies with sex in them," I said. "Those movies vividly sent me into rape mode every time. The conditioning that Scott programmed into my brain was still there. It still is. My body still becomes aroused and I anticipate the rape to follow. But panic and fear switched to anger so fast back then, that Richard only ever saw the rage. He never knew I was preparing for rape."

"A flashback," William said.

"Kind of... More like Pavlov's dog. The movies prepared me for rape exactly like the bell making the dog salivate. It was a mental program I had been conditioned to respond to. I anticipated the rape to follow just as the dog anticipated its meal. Severe anxiety. Watching those movies was like hitting a massive alarm in my brain that said, 'you will be raped in the next five minutes,' and I went into fight mode.

"Richard triggered my programming almost daily. Shouting is another trigger. It takes me back to my half-brother beating me. Hearing Shaun scream for hours that he would kill me while he tried to break through my door. Movies triggered my fight. Screaming triggers my flight.

"But Richard wouldn't let me fly. When I tried to run, he held me, forced me into the bedroom or the bathroom and barricaded the door with his body. I was mentally back in Joe's room all over again chained to his bed."

"Another trigger," William deduced.

"A trigger within a trigger," I said. "Richard would start the movie. I would expect a rape, panic, and fight. Richard would scream at me in retaliation. I slipped back to my beatings with Shaun and prepared to be hit. When given the chance, I would run. Then Richard would grab my wrists and barricade me in the bathroom or bedroom, triggering a third flashback and I was chained to Joe's bed where Joe bit me, reinforcing my fear of the rapes. This chain reaction took place all within five minutes.

"Was Richard malicious? No. Richard was clueless. So was I. I still had no idea what was wrong with me. I had forgotten... everything."

"How could you forget?" William asked.

"I think my mind went into a kind of shock and suppressed the memories so I could cope, but left behind the symptoms without a way for me to track them back to the problem. How did I go about forgetting? I didn't think about it. I never once, consciously thought about any of it. Angel did. My subconscious did. That's why she was screaming. But I never once made the attempt to consciously remember. I was too busy trying to put it behind me. The problem was I hadn't dealt with it yet. The bigger problem was, all of it—the lack of affection, the rapes, the abuse—to me, it was all normal. I didn't think any of it was a problem to be dealt with."

I watched William's face contort with horror.

"Richard had no idea what my life had been like up to then," I said. "In fact, no one does. Not even those who were there. I smiled on the outside and hid everything from everyone. I was taught to master complete control over my emotions and not deal with them. Richard knew I had "dated" a pedophile, he knew I lost Isaiah, but he didn't understand how I could "date" a pedophile for five years. In fact, I spent most of my marriage defending Scott."

"Defending Scott?" William said. "Why would you ever defend him?"

"Because if I didn't defend him, I would have to blame him," I said. "Instead, I blamed me. It was easier blaming me."

"Why would you blame you for being raped?"

"At that time, I hadn't used the word rape. It was sex and it was the only kind of sex I had known. The kind that was taken without my consent. Besides... if I didn't blame me, then I would be innocent and that would make me a victim. And if I were a victim, then I would have been victimized. If I had been victimized, then I would have a problem. I did not have a problem. I was normal. I had a traditional American life to pursue and a cookie cutter marriage to uphold. There was nothing wrong with me... so long as I blamed me.

"So I blamed me, defended Scott, and denied the most basic truth of my past: that I had never once said 'yes.'

"Rape is always portrayed as black and white in movies. Either you're violently beaten, tied down, stripped, and raped, or you're slipped the date rape drug. You wake up naked and find yourself filled with cold semen.

"But there is another kind of rape, a passive rape—the kind where you never say yes, or you are forced to say yes. Where you oblige and lay down with a psychological gun to your head. Those kind of rapes are another kind of hell. I remember the movie 300. Everyone was angry that she consented and they called her a whore. They saw a wife who betrayed her husband. I saw a woman who was raped.

"Those kind of rapes leave you with all the feeling of rape without taking the label you need to seek help. You love your rapist in those situations. You protect them. You lie for them. It leaves you hating yourself and not the monster who maimed you because you develop denial. The other rapes are so violent, so blatant of a violation, that the rape victim is incapable of slipping into denial. I'm wrong with this. There are other ways to slip into denial with those rapes. It's just not as easy.

"It would take me ten years to call what I had lived through rape."

Chapter 29

Life after Daniel plummeted fast. Richard lost his job soon after finding the last one and he was back to looking. Daniel thankfully slept through most nights and cried little while I increased my hours again at work and returned to the bookstore.

The arguments resumed, picking up right where we left them while I was pregnant. By the third month, Daniel had developed colic. His screams could be timed to the minute. From four P.M. to eleven, every night, Daniel screamed as if someone had cut off his big toe. The predictable screaming added an immediate tension to the already wrought household and my relationship.

Richard still watched his movies. I was now handling postpartum with the chronic state of depression. I was prone to flashbacks on a daily basis while Richard handled it in the only way he knew how: he screamed and locked me in the bathroom.

There, he barricaded the door until I agreed to comply. He insisted I talk to him, open up, and let him in. Just like my father who screamed at my mother while she was comatose. He couldn't get her to open up either.

The problem was, I never knew what to say. I didn't know why the movies bothered me. Why I felt the need to fight then run. I didn't understand why I kept seeing my half-brother standing over me threatening to kill me. Hearing him kick in my door while he shouted, "I'm going to kill you!"

I could hear Tribble screaming as he bit her ears.

While Richard stood over me in the bathroom screaming, I put my hands over my head and rocked. I had fit my body under the sink in the bathroom, curled up in a corner, sandwiched between the U-bend and the tub, and there I tried to forget. Joe was there telling me to get back in my room. He was there, shoving me onto my knees and ripping me apart from behind with his dick.

Daniel wouldn't stop screaming. I rocked and whimpered, not understanding why the movies bothered me. And I couldn't get out.

Tribble nudged my fingers and I pulled her into my lap. She propped her paws onto my shoulder, snuggled my chin, and she purred. I held onto her as if I had just wrestled her from my half-brother's death grip.

There, in the corner, I slipped into the world inside my head. There, where Shaun couldn't find me and no one could touch me, my realm of trees and clear waters enveloped me. I was in the lake alone with my waterfall. I was back at my cottage in the wood. And no one could hurt me. No one could find me and I calmed, my breathing steadied, and I smiled.

I don't know how long I was there. I had missed it so much. I played in the stream outside my reclusive cottage. I lay on the grass. I gazed at the sky.

When I was calm enough to return from my realm, my vision came into focus.

I looked up and there was Richard, arms across his chest, staring down at me, and leaning against the door. He had stopped shouting. Daniel was quiet.

I was back in my bathroom and he watched me with a look in his eye like he had just seen me lick my own blood off a blade.

"Do you have any idea what you are?" Richard asked.

"Excuse you?" I said. How could I not get offended?

"You need help," he grumbled and dropped his arms, opened the door, and at last, allowed me to leave the bathroom.

* * *

"*Please leave a message after the tone.*"

"Hi, this is Elizabeth Lundy. I'm trying to get a hold of Isaiah. Could you have him call me please? My number is 555-786-1742. Thank you."

I hung up the phone.

He needed to know I was married. He needed to know about Anne and Daniel. He needed to know. I needed closure. I missed him so much it hurt.

* * *

"I tried calling Isaiah again today," I said to Richard. He lay on the couch like sea cow.

"Why are you still trying?" he asked.

"I need closure. I never... got closure."

"He dumped you."

"He didn't," I said. "That wasn't him."

"Whatever."

I hated 'whatever.' Passive aggressive 'fuck you' is what that was. I turned to leave him alone on the couch.

"And what are your plans if you ever find him?" he asked.

"We're friends," I said. "I tried calling Elena too."

"You're wasting your time."

Within two years, Richard and I had settled into a routine, a stale, dreadful routine. He would go to work at whatever job he had while I stayed with Anne and Daniel. Richard would come home and I would leave for work. I still had no driver's license. Scott had made it clear that I didn't need one, and Richard made it clear we couldn't afford one. He wouldn't pay for more auto insurance. When I needed to go to work, he drove me or I took the bus.

Richard hated me taking the bus. In all honesty, I hated me taking the bus. It required I walk home at eleven every night through our less than shady neighborhood. My fear of men was worsening and Richard's random comments of, "well, you should fear men," to guarantee my loyalty, only reaffirmed my fears: that males were something to be feared.

But my son was growing older and, by two, my fear of men had developed into absolute terror. I did not leave the house unless I reported to work. At work I was content where the staff were female and most of the shoppers were women and children. When a male entered the vicinity, I entered a war zone. Like a soldier against the Viet Cong, my eyes widened and my senses sharpened. I strategically maneuvered myself around the store, taking a full body count while I made my way to the stock room where I could breathe a sigh of relief.

Once again I had outwitted the Nazi-scum. I congratulated myself. I was one-step away from war paint and an M16, and no one was the wiser. They thought I hated people. I thought I hated people. I said, "I hate people."

I dedicated my life to that stock room, pouring my heart and soul into organizing a giant closet. My memory was sharp and my dedication in everything I did was honed to precision.

We had no computer database to access what inventory we had. They had me. At any one given time, they could ask me what was back there and I could tell them exactly how much of what, what size, and where. I was so exact with my answers that customers doubted my accuracy. Often, my manager had to confirm, "No. If she says it isn't back there, then it isn't back there."

My petite figure allowed me to move in that place with such ease. I would scale the shelves like a trained assassin in Cambodia. With pens and scissors clamped in my teeth, I would kick off my shoes and climb the shelves to the ceiling and toggle the three-foot hall between ladder and shelves. Suspended, ten feet in the air, I organized, hung, unwrapped, and stored more than twenty thousand pieces of clothing.

This was my jungle. This was my realm. Here, away from all others, I was safe. My productivity earned me the adoration of my co-workers, so long as I didn't have to emerge from my cave. So long as I didn't have to speak to others, I was fine. I had no idea at the time, but that stock room did so much to enable my fears. For five years, I used that stock room to hide from my family, my children, my co-workers, my past, the world. I transformed that stock room into a cave and I made it my home. Only there, was I safe. Only there did I live in peace.

* * *

Richard lost another job. Spent three more months looking and finally landed a night job in 2006. Daniel was two and his sweet, complacent behavior vanished the day prior to his second birthday. He took to biting and hitting. Throwing and screaming. If I spanked him, grounded him, or punished him at all, Richard would come after me.

"Don't spank him, he'll hate you and he'll be just like Shaun!"

"He threw a block at me! I have a welt the size of a brick!"

"Well, you pissed him off!"

"He is wrong! He needs to be punished! I'll ground him then!"

The bickering ensued. Meanwhile Daniel went unpunished and uncorrected.

I was strict with my bed times. Seven o' clock and the children were in bed. They'd go down to sleep for me within moments and they settled into a routine. On nights that Richard had off, I couldn't get them to sleep.

By that year, Richard felt like a constant obstacle in everything I did. He had taken to baking a chicken at nine A.M. and would sit on the couch and watch TV while tossing pieces to the children like dogs.

"It's nine A.M. They need to eat breakfast," I would say.

"They are."

Another obstacle. Another conflict, and the arguments kept flying.

Chapter 30

"*Please leave a message after the tone.*"
I hung up the phone. I couldn't breathe.
"Seven years," I breathed.
It wasn't him.
"Seven years." I rubbed the stress from my eyes.
For seven years, my heart had been cold. I thought of Isaiah and pined. I ached to see him again. For seven years, a hand twisted its cold dead fingers around my heart and squeezed the love out of me. For every year that slipped by, it tightened its hold on me. I had grown used to it. For seven years it had been there suffocating me. I couldn't breathe. I couldn't feel... until that day.
I felt my heart writhe in its grip, unable to beat under the strain, and at last, I snapped. Something inside me surrendered and I couldn't keep it in any longer. The phone slipped from my hands. My chest burned, and I wanted to cut my heart out of me. To curl up and die.
I fell to my knees and willed myself dead while I welcomed the pain and begged it to kill me. I curled up on

the floor, tucking my knees to my chest, and I screamed. I cried. The pain was agonizing. It crippled me and I lay there and endured it while the hand twisted out my heart. I screamed and clawed at my face. I pulled my hair.

For the first time since he left, I screamed his name, wishing him back. Wanting him back, regretting so much that I hadn't done. I was as miserable as I had ever been. More miserable than with Joe, who I had escaped after a few months chained to his bed in his room, or imprisoned as a sex slave in mine. More miserable than I had been in my father's house where I could escape through my worlds. More miserable than with Scott who I could forget in between phone calls and visits to New York.

With Richard, there was no escape. No end. No friends. No worlds. No moments of happiness or laughter that broke my miserable existence. I was in a traditional marriage with two children. I had a stable home. I was fed and provided for. There was no war, no struggle, no rapists. I hated every moment of that cookie cutter marriage and not one bit of me knew why. I was alone, and that day I chose to wallow in my misery and lie with her.

Alone is what I was and alone is how I'd die. Alone was a bitch of a bedfellow, cold and merciless. No one was there. I was still locked in the steel room. The Death Men encircled me and there was no door. I held myself. I rocked and screamed as I killed the last part of me. And just like that, the Death Men were gone.

On my hands and knees, I wept in my room, naked in the light with no door and no place to go, and no one in my room, but me.

* * *

"Why didn't you kill yourself?" William asked.

"I wanted to," I said. "I considered— That's a lie. I dwelt on it. Spent most of my life trying to find a way that I could kill myself and succeed. I was terrified I would fail and leave myself handicapped instead. In the end, I was too much of a coward. I had too much of a fear of failure. Oh. My fear of failure. Now that was something I had developed and honed into fine precision. A fear of failure.

"Nothing gained rejection faster than failure. I was terrified of failing. To this day, it is my greatest fear. Greater than my fear of spiders, of men—"

"Of relationships?"

I looked at William in that moment.

"I had convinced myself that I could still earn my father's love and respect if I succeeded," I said, ignoring William's comment. "I still feel that way today. Maybe if I did better, if I were smarter, stronger, kinder, wealthier...

"Every decision I made was based on seeking my father's approval and I was convinced success would earn that. I still do. I'm still holding out for it. I can not fail. Not with loving men, not with improving me, not with living life. I would force my father to love me. To accept me. To approve. I can not risk the failure. I will persevere. I will endure it! I will succeed. I am determined, and I will do it with a Don!"

William arched a brow. "A Don?"

I smiled.

"Distinction," I said. "I watch too much anime."

William stared, studying my face, and I wondered what he thought of me. Right then, I worried if William approved of me.

"Why didn't I kill myself?" I muttered. "I considered the chances of my children finding me, or the poor officers who had to collect and clean up the remains. I weighed it against my despair and believe you me, I had spent many a day wallowing in despair. Do you know what despair is? Really is? It is an emotional state entirely devoid of hope. It isn't loneliness, or self-pity. It is a place beyond hopelessness. A place where you are completely convinced things will never get better and that despair is all you have left.

"I feel no greater sorrow for anyone as I do for those who commit suicide. I know where they are mentally. I know the state of despair for I too have been there many times. It isn't cowardice or selfishness. It is despair. There are those who fight it back their whole lives until one day... you don't see the light."

"But you haven't killed yourself," William said. "You found a way out."

"I did. Every time I raised the blade to my own chest or my wrists, a flicker of hope came back to me like a lifeline. I used it to pull myself out and went on."

"The lifeline," William said. "The hope. What was it? What did you think that stopped you?"

I thought for a moment of all the times I took up a blade or rolled a handful of pills around in the bottle.

"I thought of the finite," I said.

"The finite?"

"The end," I answered. "Suicide would mean I would have to give up the only existence, this existence, I would ever have. I believe in no after life or a second chance. This, what we have here and now, this is all we've got. This is it. This is our only chance to get it right. Live it up or live with regrets. When you die, only what you've done will remain and if it's good enough, it will outlive you. In a way, my disbelief in the afterlife saved my life."

* * *

The next day, I sat down at the computer and browsed online. Putzed a lot. Came upon this contest that piqued my interest. It was a poetry contest. It was free, so on a whim, I pulled out my old poems and submitted one I had written as a child.

I forgot about the contest almost immediately. I browsed some more, cleaned the house, fed the children, and went to bed.

The next day, I received an email telling me I had been selected. I was floored. Stunned, really. My English teacher made it clear I couldn't write, and I hadn't bothered trying since high school. I decided to see what I could do after ten years, and so I put pen to paper and wrote *Diamond-Gold*.

My perfect love who wasn't
Inside me he beset
His lustrous stone of Diamond-Gold,
Which does not suffer rest.
That summer that we claimed,
(That summer I won't name)
He fervently placed Diamond-Gold
Within my hollowed breast.
He came one night with words of love
He seeded there his stone;
The lustrous stone of Diamond-Gold,
Bound with ardent blood.
Each night I laid me down,
His Diamond-Gold would grow,
Until it grew to golden stone.
The weight, it held me down.
Through time I bore that stone.
Through pain that stone did grow,
And with it wanton, burning lust,

From a summer not forgot
Now I know of Diamond-Gold.
Its burdens hard to bear.
It sits as heat inside my breast
Disabling my breath.
For my love—my perfect love,
Forever I will bear
The pain and weight of that stone
Of his Diamond-Gold.

I was amazed at my words. They weren't great. They were better than I had expected. Much better than I thought I could do. I was stunned at how easily they came to me. From that moment on, words engulfed me and everything I was became them.

* * *

Emotions expose you. They make you weak. When someone can see your weakness, you are vulnerable and they can hurt you. Shaun had seen my love for Tribble and used her against me to control me. Piss-ant had used my love for him and aggressively provoked my jealousy to satisfy his own ego. He'd twist jealousy's vile blade into me and spun me about like a yo-yo, amusing himself with the games he could make me perform like a trained dog. My mother saw my tears and scolded me. She mocked me and ridiculed me as a joke before the family like a side show freak. Joe saw my pity and played my guilt against me. And Scott... Scott saw my desperation, my neglect, my need for approval, my fear of rejection. He fashioned up the strings and made me into his marionette. Through conditioning, he made me his doll. I would walk, talk, think, beg, and fuck exactly as he wanted, when he wanted, at will.

That is why I hide my emotions. There hasn't been a single emotion that hasn't been used against me... to control me.

And when at last I escaped, I had emerged the master of my emotions.

Every emotion—love, hate, grief, anger, fear, guilt, doubt, insecurity, jealousy—I identified each one, separated them, and boxed them. And then I buried those emotions within my darkness and I threw a blanket of cold-stone logic on top of it.

On a dime, at any given moment, I can access each and every one of my emotions and I determined exactly how much of each I let out when. That is when Angel started screaming.

When I sat down to write, I tapped my boxes of emotions. I awakened old memories, old pain. I revived my heart and withdrew a cup of hate, a teaspoon of grief, a pound of rage. Through my writing, I began to siphon the pain out of me. It eased the pressure. Angel kept screaming. I wrote, pouring words onto pages. Every word eased my heartache. After a week, I could think. After a month, I could breathe. After six weeks, I knew little else but the written word. I poured over websites, learned everything I could on writing.

I wrote poems. I let my emotions find me, but only a little. I returned to dance and, for the first time in seven years, I danced with the music instead of against it. That year, I decided I wanted nothing else but to be a writer. It consumed me, revived me. It saved me. My lessons and books returned. Everything flooded back to me, except the music.

Broken

In 2006, I announced to Richard that I was pregnant with our third child: Lynn.

Chapter 31

Richard did not want a third child. He had made it very clear that two was his limit. The nightmare that had become our marriage turned worse with the news of my third pregnancy. Money was as tight as always. I returned to the bookstore and increased my hours. While pregnant, I was pulling forty hours a week in the stock room and mothering two children besides. I wasn't slowing down and six months in, I fell off a ladder.

My third pregnancy was different than the other two. First, Richard and I were always fighting. It was habitual now. He disowned Lynn right off. He often accused me of cheating and insisted she belonged to the neighbor. When he saw how upset I was about that accusation, he insisted it had been a joke, but repeated the same line of humor a week later.

Now that I think about it, I think Richard ruined me for humor. His jokes were always made at the expense of others. Usually me. They were hurtful and shallow. He may have been joking about Lynn belonging to the neighbor. To this day, he swears he was. I found no humor in it.

After I fell off the ladder, my pregnancy with Lynn became high risk and I was bleeding. I was sentenced to bed rest for the rest of the pregnancy, which only put more financial strain on the marriage.

Finances were hell. Richard didn't want to pay any of the bills and he left that for me to do. I took care of it, but then he would make purchases assuming I didn't pay bills. I knew how much we had in the accounts because I paid the bills, but not knowing he made additional purchases, I made purchases, and together, we bounced our bank accounts.

For a third time, I begged Richard to stay in the birthing room with me, but this time... this time I didn't care. We agreed to tie my tubes and this required a non-Catholic hospital. My cousin worked at the hospital where Lynn was born. I don't think Richard was even in the room. He may have been. I don't remember. What I remember is my cousin and the needle in my back. I was alone. I was good with alone. I knew what to do with alone.

They laid my head back and the anesthesiologist rested my head in his hand. He brushed the hair from my face and I laid there while the doctor cut and pulled me open for yet a third time. I looked around the room and focused on an item reflected in the stainless steel cupboard of the OR. It took me a moment before I realized I was looking at my own intestines piled next to my body. I gazed in awe at my own guts. After a while, I laid my head back down and relaxed in the hands of the anesthesiologist.

I closed my eyes and smiled as he brushed his fingers over my cheek. I didn't know this person. I have no idea who he was. He spoke to me, called me angel. His words, his voice, his hands cradling my head... Never had I been touched so intimately in all my life.

They lifted Lynn out of me and, for the first time in several months, I could take a deep breath and fully expand my lungs. I gasped with the sudden rush of air... joyous air.

"Are you okay?" he asked me. His voice was like warm rain.

"Yes." I breathed deep, enjoying the delicious air. "I can breathe."

He caressed my face.

I gasped and he brushed my cheek. He ran his fingers through my hair.

"You're okay, angel. You're okay."

I nestled my head into his hand and closed my eyes relishing his hand on my face.

In that brief moment, whoever he was, I loved him. I imagined him kissing my cheek. I imagined him holding me. Grazing his lips over my brow. I imagined it was his daughter they lifted out of me. I wondered what kind of husband he would be. A tear slipped from my eye and he hushed me. He wiped the tear from my eye.

"You're alright. It's okay, angel. Just relax."

And for the first time in my life, I did.

* * *

I pushed the tears from my cheek and turned to William.

"Whoever he was, I loved him swiftly. To this day, when I think of him, I cry. I don't even know his name, his face, only his touch. He was the first to ever touch me like that. His voice... his words. His touch... He stole my heart.

"I was with him for thirty... maybe forty minutes, and he I will love for the rest of my life."

Chapter 32

I had no medication, no therapy, no diagnoses, and no clue that anything was wrong with me. I was a writer. Before that, I was a composer. It was 2007. Medication was a death sentence to the creative mind. The nurses had me fill out a questionnaire and I answered every question honestly. One of the questions asked about violence and suicide. I confessed that, in both instances of my children's birth, I had vivid fantasies about stabbing Anne, Daniel, and Tribble.

I returned home with Lynn and a prescription for Zoloft®.

"Do not stop taking this cold turkey," the doctor said as she scribbled the script. "You must be weaned off it."

"I understand."

"When you think you are ready to come off it, speak to us first. Schedule an appointment. You will need to be weaned off of it. One month down to every other day, then three weeks down to every two days, then two weeks down to every three days. Do not take yourself off cold turkey."

"I understand," I said and took the script. And I did understand. When I was ready to come off the meds, it had to be gradual. I memorized her explanation and took it to the pharmacy to have it filled.

That day, I began taking Zoloft®.

* * *

I slipped into a deadened state. I had a daughter I didn't love. I had a violent son and I didn't care. I had a newborn I couldn't bond with. My pain subsided and with it, I became complacent. The tension between Richard and I vanished. The relationship did not improve. Our marriage was not fixed. I just. . . stopped caring. Angel stopped screaming. My nightmares, all of them, the Death Men in their room, stopped. Everything went silent.

The medication killed the pain along with everything else I cared about, save for boredom.

Turns out, boredom and logic were exactly what I needed to accomplish what I was about to begin.

I had spent my pregnancy pouring myself into my writing. I had taken a course that steered me toward non-fiction writing. I hated non-fiction writing—

Wait. . .

They explained how to build a writing career out of non-fiction articles. But I wanted nothing to do with magazines and articles. I wanted story.

Almost immediately, I began writing my first novel. It was November of 2007 when I started. The process consumed me. I wrote from seven A.M. and stayed up until two A.M. every night. My husband worked nights and slept days. Aside from diaper changes and feedings, I paused only to cook dinner, clean house, read to children, and put them to bed. At seven, I returned to my writing for the next five to seven hours.

I tried returning to work at the store, but Richard made it clear he couldn't watch three children and had me cut my hours back to almost nothing. My book consumed me and my determination replaced the emotions I couldn't feel. I spent my days researching and writing. I poured myself into that story and in May of 2008, I finished the rough draft.

* * *

I listened to the front door close. No different than any other day.

Richard looked at the mess on the floor.

"What did you do today?"

That tone. That same tone that said, 'So I see you sat on your ass again today.'

I hadn't cleaned that day. I had been so close to the end that I worked through and pushed myself to finish.

"I finished my book."

"Great." His voice dripped with sarcasm.

"I opened an account on Facebook," I said.

"When were you planning on washing the dishes?"

If I hadn't been on Zoloft, I would have cared.

It was as if there was a mesh screen enveloping me. I didn't feel. The meds had shut me down, made me complacent. He was shouting and I didn't care.

Why don't I care?

"I've been at work all day..."

I looked at the children's toys, and laundry that had piled up that day.

"...while you're sitting here on the computer..."

The dishes hadn't been done yet.

"... I'm hungry and I doubt you made dinner..."
Why don't I care?
My four year old screamed.
"What happened, Anne?" Richard bellowed.
Tears streaked her little face.
"Daniel bit me again," she cried.
A set of full incisor marks pierced her white skin.
I don't care.
My daughter was crying.
I should care.
My son had bit her.
Why don't I care?
"I think I should stop taking the meds," I slowly said.
"What?" Richard looked up from Anne's arm. Daniel had gone back to playing. Richard hadn't moved to discipline Daniel and neither had I.
"No!" he said. "You're not coming off those meds! This is the most I've been able to live with you! You're staying on them."
The crying and screaming and yelling ensued while I stood in my living room not caring.
You will need to be weaned off slowly. One month down to every other day, then three weeks down to every two days, then two weeks down to every three days.
Do not take yourself off these meds cold turkey.
Richard hated hospitals. He wouldn't take me to the doctor.
Do not take yourself off these meds cold turkey.
I was alone.
It was time to come off the meds.

* * *

Feelings slowly seeped back to me as if I had emerged from a long dark sleep. I remember the very day. After four to six weeks of gradually decreasing my own dosage, I woke and suddenly I saw the sun shining again. I felt the wind. Angel's screaming returned and my boxes of emotions sat, unscathed, where I had left them in the steel room. Only then did I realize how deadened I had been.

By August of 2008, I was subjecting my book to the first run of revisions and had concluded the final stage of my weaning period from the medication. I felt great. Substantial. I wanted to beat my chest and roar. I felt so alive.

I was more active and involved. I was thrilled to be feeling again. That month, Richard came home with an announcement.

"I'm buying a bow."

"What?"

"I want to take up archery hunting so I can get a deer for a change. Maybe with a bow I will have more luck than with a gun."

I knew our finances. We were consistently two weeks behind in everything and currently owed on the rent, the car, and the electric and gas.

"With what money?" I said.

"It will only cost five hundred," he said. "I'm sick of paying bills and never getting anything for me. And I have a bonus check coming so I'm doing it. The expense is wasted unless I get a deer. But, if I get a deer, it will more than make up for the expense we save in meat. You need to know... I'll have to be out there every chance I get."

At the end of the day, it was his money and his choice. I nodded, held onto my worries and said what I've always told every man. "Okay."

By the end of August, the five hundred allotted expense had grown into two thousand. The rent, electric, heat, and car payment were unpaid, but Richard had his compound crossbow, accessories, lessons, hunting license, and was gone.

* * *

"Gone?" William said.
"That's right." I nodded. "For three months."
"Three months?" he asked.
I nodded again.
"Where?"
I shrugged. "I don't know. Hunting, I think. Not sure where. He left in August and didn't come back until November."

William stared in silent awe. I took his lack of response as consent to continue.

"He would wake, take his bow, and go hunting a few hours before he was expected at work and all before the kids were out of bed. After work, he went hunting and was out long after the kids were in bed."

"The kids." William crunched his face in disgust. "What about the kids? I mean... how did they take this?"

"He didn't see them once in those three months," I said. "The children asked in September, wanted to know where their father was. I told them he was hunting... the entire month. In October, they asked the same questions and I answered. They cried and wailed over how much they missed him. I held and hushed them and loathed him for what he was doing to them.

"I never saw him myself, but I didn't miss him. He came home only after I was in bed. Some nights he didn't come home at all. I proceeded to love and harbor my children and by November, the tears and questions stopped. We adapted and settled into a routine as if he had died. He simply wasn't there. He still didn't know I had taken myself off the meds. Every ounce of my spare time went into my book, but for the first time since Richard moved in, I was at peace. I was content to be cloistered away, fearing men, harboring, enabling, and nurturing my issues that I didn't know were there."

William shook his head in disbelief.

I arched my brow in question.

"To be gone from your kids. . . for three months," William said.

I nodded. "For three months."

William made a face reflecting his doubt.

"You don't really think he was hunting, do you?" he asked.

I chuckled. "Are you implying that he was cheating on me?"

"Yes."

I shrugged.

"Don't care. I'm not a jealous lover."

"You were his wife," William said.

"I'm not a jealous lover."

William wasn't believing it.

"There was one day, Richard came home to tell me he almost had an affair," I said. "I didn't care."

"You didn't care?" Williams asked.

"I asked him what I had done wrong. He said I had done nothing wrong and I said okay. I wasn't jealous. I only cared that I hadn't upset him and that he wasn't unhappy with me."

"How. . . "

"One of Piss-ant's favorite games was kissing Elena in front of me. Piss-ant knew I loved him. He knew I was jealous. He would make out with her, his eyes open wide, and watch me writhe with jealousy all for an ego stroking at my expense. I am very familiar with jealousy and it's an emotion I haven't permitted myself to feel in years."

"No jealousy?" William asked.

I shook my head. "None. I've locked it away in a little box."

"How?" he asked. "How can you be okay with your husband sleeping with another woman?"

"Because I don't view my husband as mine," I said. "People aren't possessions. Husbands and wives aren't possessions. They are people. People with choices and with rights to those choices. They are allowed to make mistakes, to love others, to stumble and fall. Jealousy doesn't permit mistakes. It is there to tell us when something threatens our turf. I don't believe people are 'turf.' The fear of loss leads to a desire to possess. That is what jealousy really is. It is the act of saying, 'I want to keep you to myself so that I can't lose you.' I believe this is at the heart of most marriages. Jealousy enables possession."

"But what about loyalty?" William asked. "Aren't you hurt that he betrayed you?"

"Betray me?" I asked. "How did he betray me?"

"He broke his promise to be loyal and faithful..."

I shook my head.

"To have and to hold, from this day forward, for better, for worse, for richer, for poorer, in sickness and in health, until death do us part. Nowhere in those vows is sexual loyalty... or any loyalty, for that matter, mentioned. Besides, I think very little of marriage vows."

"Why?"

"They are the details of a business contract," I said. "Think about it. A promise to love someone forever. You know my views on love and how it changes. That is a piecrust promise. We don't know what the future will be, which is why the divorce rate is so high. People change and marriage doesn't permit that."

"Couples promise to take care of each other in good times and bad," William said.

I waved my hand, dismissing the concept.

"I did that with Tribble, my children, and my dearest of friends. And I do it without the obligation of a promise. Yes, I can choose to walk away any time that I want. I have that freedom and I will keep it, but it is by choice that I stay, which makes my reasons for loving, caring, and giving to one of my friends all that more sincere. I am not bound to those I love. It is simply something that I have chosen. Marriage will actually devalue my actions."

"So marriage has nothing to do with loyalty to you?" he asked.

"Marriage is about possession and ownership," I said. "The unspoken promise that is really made during a marriage is that 'I promise I won't have sex with anyone but you for the rest of my life.' It's about owning another person's sex as if sex were corporeal. That is what most people make marriage about. Couples hold each other to that unspoken promise so that if their partner strays, they have just cause to be more hurt, more vindictive, more aggressive if they change, which marriage leaves no room for."

"Then where does the sex belong if not in a marriage?" William asked.

"Sex is only an extension of romantic love," I argued. "Love is love. Ever changing and constantly in motion, as are people. We've discussed this. We are not stagnant. If I were to love you, for example, there is nothing to say I couldn't love you in a week, in a year, or in five years. None of us will ever know when we will love, for how long, how strong, or with whom. The only constant about love is that it will change. Sometimes it fades. Sometimes it grows and ages like a single malt scotch until it's smooth going down and palatable. And sometimes, the batch goes bad. The only difference between a friend and a lover is the sex, and the sex invariably follows where the heart goes."

"So you're proposing that sex is an extension of love, and if love is forever changing then you stand a high risk of cheating," William said.

"Yes," I said. "So of course the majority of marriages are doomed to failure. Marriage is a gamble and the stakes are high."

"So, you promote infidelity," William said.

"I promote truth," I said. "I'm just trying to figure out why we're pushing so hard for a system that has a fifty percent failure rate and climbing. Everyone is questioning the ethics of man and the decline of religion. I am questioning the system and the philosophy behind the system itself."

William remained silent, pondering my argument for a moment.

"I grew up in a Christian home where I was taught to pursue a cookie cutter marriage," I said. "Many promote this ideal, insisting it's right. But if it's so right, if it's an ideal, then it should work for everyone. But it doesn't. It doesn't work for more than fifty percent of the population and it didn't work for me. There are those who say it can and maybe it can work for some people. I believe that cookie cutter marriage was designed for those few adults who lived the ideal childhood. But where does that leave people like me who can't conform to the ideal and who are told it's what we should want?

"Don't get me wrong, I think that the ideal marriage does work for some people. But pretending I am capable of predicting the future—loving someone twenty years or a lifetime from now—is something I will not do. That kind of marriage has no place for someone like me."

"So you aren't proposing polygamy and debauchery?" William asked, and I grinned.

"Oh, come now," I said. "There's nothing wrong with a little bit of debauchery now and then."

I managed a smile that set him at ease.

"No," I said, shaking my head. "I support the idea of a relationship that works for you. I believe relationships should conform to the participants involved. I think there is too much emphasis on trying to conform the participants to an ideal concept that may or may not work for those participants. I think that is why the divorce rate is so high. Too many people are trying to fit themselves into a relationship that can not work for them."

William nodded. Whatever objections he had, he kept to himself.

"Love, sex, loyalty, commitment, devotion, faithfulness," I said. "These are not corporeal things we possess. They are ideas. Nothing more. And we have forgotten to treat them as such. Do not misunderstand me. These are ideas that I hold very dear to my heart. I believe these things are an important part of friendship and they carry over into marriage, but I think, too often, we confuse the qualities of friendship with marriage and use concepts like loyalty and commitment to possess and control those we love to satisfy our own jealousy."

I shook my head. "Jealousy is the act of saying, 'I won't share you because that somehow takes something from me.' But what if it doesn't?"

William furrowed his brow.

"If we were lovers and I've promised nothing," I said. "If I simply love you, but sleep with another man, what have I taken from you?"

William shrugged. "I'd be hurt."

"You'd be hurt because you're jealous. Take jealousy away. Remove the possession of another. I'm not breaking any promises. And you know my sleeping with another man would take nothing from you. If you had no fear of loss, then what would you have lost if I slept with another man?"

"Nothing... I guess." He still seemed unsure of himself.

I sat back in my chair.

"What about exclusivity?" William asked. He perked my attention. "The feeling of being special."

Now it was I who searched for a rebuttal.

I furrowed my brow.

"You're talking about ego," I said.

He nodded. I thought about it.

"Which isn't jealousy at all," I said. "Ego. Reall—Ego? Is this all about ego then?"

We sat in silence for a moment while we thought. I waved a finger at him.

"See, now ego, I can respect," I said.

"Then you will have lost something," William said. "You would have lost exclusivity."

"Which then enters jealousy into the equation if you value exclusivity," I said.

"Do you?" I looked at William. "Value exclusivity?" he asked.

I stared at the recorder on the table and shook my head.

"I'll have to give this some more thought," I said. "The concept is too *new for me to begin forming a hypothesis."

* * *

In November, at the end of the first week, Richard came home.

I was shocked to see him so suddenly with three weeks of archery season left.

"Why are you here?" I asked.

He looked beaten down and exhausted. He looked worn and ragged.

"I was out there and realized there were a lot of issues here that we needed to take care of and... I felt I should be here fixing them instead."

I stared, too surprised with his answer to say much of anything for a while.

"You're saying you want to finally consider marriage counseling?" I asked.

"No." He scoffed at the idea as usual. "I would sooner get a divorce than go through marriage counseling."

He dropped himself on the couch and went to sleep. I returned to my book.

The next morning was another day, another revision. Richard was already at work. I set the coffee to brew. Anne was at school and I had my cup of coffee. I turned my computer on. Thanksgiving was one week away and my book was... my book was something. I opened Word, logged on to the internet and signed onto Facebook while I waited for my email to load. I took a sip of my coffee.

I heard the plink that told me I had a Facebook message, glanced up, and felt the blood drain from my face. My body had gone cold. Every inch of my skin buzzed like pins and needles and all at once, I couldn't breathe. I stared at the message before me:

Isaiah has requested to be your friend.

Chapter 33

I must have stared at those words for an hour before I could force my fingers to enter a reply. He was there, right before me, but I was terrified if I moved too quickly, I would startle him and he'd be gone again.

Carefully, I selected my words. I read it through several times before pushing "send."

"*How are you?*"

The words were classic, simple, and wreaked of one very specific meaning I meant to convey and knew he would understand. I wasn't simply asking 'how are you?' I was saying, '*Hello, my dearest friend. Why did you ever leave me?*' all while raising the white flag and releasing the doves. The wrong word right now, and he would be gone again.

I pushed send and held my breath.

I didn't have to wait long for an answer, but the next five minutes felt like I had my neck stretched under the guillotine and I was waiting for Isaiah to kill me or free me. I still believed what was said to me ten years ago had not been him. I refused to believe it and now, I finally had my chance to determine if I had been delusional for ten years or if I had been right.

His response came through loud and clear and immediate.

"*Why did you cut me off?*"

Gasping, I smiled. I cupped my hands to my mouth and let the tears flow.

After almost eleven years, I was right. I sat in my chair hugging myself and I sobbed, allowing myself that moment. It was the one question that proved everything I needed and, for the first time in ten years, I knew. I was right.

"It wasn't him," I gasped and sobbed. "It had never been him!"

The tears flowed and I shook in my chair as sweet relief washed over me.

I glanced up at the monitor.

I needed to think. Needed time to think. I was married. I couldn't rush into this without a plan. I was married. I couldn't throw myself at him. I needed to proceed with caution. Whatever Richard asked to see, he would have to be allowed to see. But I needed answers. I needed closure, and from the looks of things—Why did you cut me off?—he also had lived the ten years without answers or closure. This would take some thought.

What I would say... What would I say?

After several moments, I typed the one answer that would buy me the time I needed and keep him here, just a little bit longer, while I got my head together.

"*We need to talk.*"

* * *

Facebook was a treasure that day. With my finding Isaiah, I was inspired to look for the rest of the gang. I found three of them including Elena. In one day, I had located four of the seven, and my Isaiah. I was on cloud nine and then some.

The front door opened and I turned.

Richard looked miserable. I couldn't stop grinning. He took off his coat, dropped it over the arm of the couch, and laid down to take a nap until bedtime as he did every afternoon. He dropped his arm on his face to shield the overhead light from his eyes.

"What did you do today?" he asked in that tone filled with passive aggressive condescension. I didn't care. Not that day.

"I found Elena..."

He grunted.

"...and Isaiah."

I waited.

He looked out from under his arm. The look of horror there stunned me stupid, but it was nothing compared to what he said next.

"Goodbye, Elizabeth."

He would have done better to have slapped me.

"Excuse you?"

He sat up.

"You're leaving me, so—"

"What?"

"Well, you've been looking for him for ten years. You found him. Now you're going to run o—"

"I am not leaving you!" I was panicking. "I never said I was leaving! I said I found my friend!"

Why was I panicking?

"Well, why else would you go looking for ten years if not to fuck him?"

"To find out what happened!" I was getting angry. I was scared. "To get closure! And, he's my friend! He was my best friend!"

"You're leaving me!" he said.

He stood and stomped off to the bedroom. I listened to his swearing while he slammed drawers, kicked the wall, and proceeded with his adult-sized tantrum.

I went to the kitchen and started dinner. Something about his 'goodbye' scared me.

* * *

I lay in bed replaying Richard's words in my head.
Goodbye, Elizabeth.

Richard snored soundly beside me. It was nearing four A.M. and I wasn't sleeping. Not this night.

I was feeling relief. Just relief. Not excitement or lust. Not love or worry. Okay, yes, worry. But relief. Sweet, merciful relief. I had finally found my friend who I had lost only to be greeted with the one word I hated most in the spoken language.

Bye.

I hate the word goodbye and every variant of it. Such an ugly, vile word. It means finality, doom, the end. To me, it meant never again. Bye was the "Nevermore" spoken by Poe's Raven. I hate the word "bye." After ten years, I found my friend and the first thing that dipshit Richard said to me was "bye." The amount of abandonment and loss I felt. I rubbed the tears from my eyes. Nothing could equate to the depth of insecurity I was feeling. I needed reassurance, support, comfort. Instead, I was told the one thing that confirmed I was still alone.

In the end, people always leave you.

I had made it clear to Richard that I had found Isaiah. I had no expectations, no plans, no hopes, or dreams. I didn't even know if Isaiah was the same. Was I the same? I tried to think back to all that had happened to me since summer of '99 and shook my head.

Don't think of that.

The monsters I hadn't faced lurked there still.

I thought of that summer instead and the heartache, the hell I endured. What he must have endured, thinking I had cut him off.

I was married. This limited me in what I could say. He may be married. We couldn't run to each other like I wanted. I looked at Richard sleeping beside me. After ten years I had a lot to say, a lot of things that needed to be said. Could I speak to Isaiah and not tell him what secrets I harbored all those years? More importantly, could I live the rest of my life never speaking those words aloud? Could I live with any more regret?

I felt the weight in my chest clamp down. It was Diamond-Gold all over again. That was the source of my pain: not saying what needed to be said. The words had festered inside of me for ten years. Married or not, there were things I had to say, if only this once.

Once, I made the mistake of not speaking my mind. It was a mistake that lead to the hardest and longest lesson of my life. Life is short. Be brave. Be bold. Be blunt. No regrets.

To thine own self be true.

There was no closure. Things needed to be said. My loyalty, commitment, my marriage... It would survive this. I would not jeopardize it. But there were some things left undone.

I would allow myself this time to say what needed to be said, just this once. And then I would nurture my friendship and proceed to love my husband. That was my plan and I had full intentions of sticking to it.

* * *

"He found you," William sighed across the kitchen table as if he felt my relief.

I was in the green room thumbing through folders and binders on my bookshelf.

"He found me," I said, pulling a tattered file down from the shelf.

"What did you...what did you say?" William asked. "When you told him, what did you do?"

Smiling, I dropped the file onto the table in front of him and raided the coffee pot.

"Why don't you see for yourself," I said, pouring myself a fresh cup.

"What is this?" he asked, taking up the file.

"That?" I asked, watching William untwist the string that bound the folder closed.

"That is every conversation I had with Isaiah in 2008."

William's hands froze on the documents. "You saved them?"

I added my cream and sugar and settled myself back at the table with my cup.

"I had lived almost eleven years without him," I said. "In those eleven years, I collected every letter, every artifact I could find of his. The ring he gave me? Broken and lost. The letters we shared? I gave them all to Isaiah before he left so Scott wouldn't find them. My journal? Isaiah had that too. I was left with nothing when I lost Isaiah, so yes.

I saved every word he and I shared that first time we spoke all those years ago. Knock yourself out."

I watched William pick up the papers from across the table and open them.

"21 November 2008" glared at the top of the first *page.

Elizabeth: *The question you asked me yesterday. Ask me.*

Isaiah: *I'm avoiding this.*

Elizabeth: *I know. We have for nearly eleven years and perhaps that is why this is so difficult. So I am waiting.*

Isaiah: *I love you and always will. I'm sorry. I just couldn't tell you the truth back then. It was cowardly of me because I thought you would be stubborn and not listen. . . and you wouldn't have.*

Elizabeth: *No. I wouldn't have and I'm still waiting for the question.*

Isaiah: *Do you still love me?*

Elizabeth*: Yes.*

Isaiah: *I'm sorry.*

Elizabeth: *Don't say that again. Now. The question. Ask.*

Isaiah: *Why? Why did you cut me off?*

Elizabeth: *What was the last thing you remember? The last time we spoke?*

Isaiah: *You mean yesterday?*

Elizabeth: *No.*

Isaiah: *Or way back?*

Elizabeth: *I mean ten years ago.*

Isaiah: *I've erased part of my memories from that time period. It hurt too much. Sorry.*

Elizabeth: *Please don't apologize. You had started going out with Jade. You had been online chatting with me and you were sharing the keyboard.*

Isaiah: *. . .*

Broken

Elizabeth: *At times, I couldn't tell which of you was which. At one point, you had surrendered the keyboard, I think you left to the kitchen or something and Jade and I chatted. She said some things that... really hurt.*

Isaiah: *I have zero memory of this... What did she say?*

Elizabeth: *I thought... I was convinced for years that it had been you. Now I know it was her. She didn't know what you were to me.*

Isaiah: *Oh, she knew. I didn't hide it.*

Elizabeth: *And she said some things that were cruel. I couldn't... It hurt and I thought it was you... trying to get rid of me. So I left. I was angry and jealous.*

Isaiah: *I never...*

Elizabeth: *I know that now. I was so jealous. There was no closure.*

Isaiah: *It wasn't me.*

Elizabeth: *And then I moved. My mum had no computer.*

Isaiah: *It wasn't me.*

Elizabeth: *I couldn't find you. There was never any closure. It was eating me alive.*

Isaiah: *You never wrote me... I didn't know why.*

Elizabeth: *I did. I wrote to your grandparent's house. The letters came back, undeliverable. I tried for two years to find you. When I found Richard, I had a similar connection with him. I wasn't going to let that go again!*

Isaiah: *Good god has this gone to hell quick. I thought you had blocked me because you found someone else and didn't have the heart to tell me.*

Elizabeth: *I never had answers. I never had closure. It was hell. Diamond gold will do that to you. Richard held me as I cried over you for nearly five years. I meant it when I said he knows. I just never got closure. I never knew.*

Isaiah: *But I didn't... I wouldn't! It wasn't me!*

Elizabeth: *It was such hell and I realized it wasn't fair to Richard. You had promised me twenty years. It was eating me alive. I was trying to "get over you." So I blocked you to help.*

Isaiah: *I... understand.*

Elizabeth: *I wondered if you knew. At the time, I didn't think you would care. It took me a LONG time to strop dreaming about you. Only two years ago... the shadows in my dreams stopped and the diamond gold was... well let's just say it became bearable. The worst part was not knowing. Not having that closure.*

Isaiah: *Well now we both know.*

William set the file on the table.

"What's wrong?" I asked over my cup of coffee.

He politely pushed the file toward me. "This is... this is... private."

I chuckled. "It's all private. Isn't that what you wanted? To know what made me tick?"

William suddenly perked up and looked around my cottage as if seeing something wasn't there for the first time. Like he had visited me many times and only just now noticed a large piece of furniture was gone.

"Where is Isaiah?"

I set my cup to the table and pressed a hand to my mouth, supported by an elbow on the table. My finger tapped my lip while I mustered the nerve to proceed with the conversation.

"He isn't here," I said.

William looked around the room as if to see if I was serious.

"What happened?" he asked.

"My dear friend." I sadly smiled. "I am broken."

Chapter 34

With the air cleared, I resumed my friendship with Isaiah. It was as if the ten years had never happened.

I must clarify this. Isaiah and I adored each other. We were best friends. In high school, the love I felt for him was warm and comforting like I imagined Shaun's love should have been, safe and secure. Now, ten years later, the warmth between Isaiah and I was there as strong as it ever had been.

Since I slapped him in sixth grade, there was an electrical charge that added to that warmth every time we came near each other. We knew it was there, and we played with it, but never touched it. Some days, the electrical charge ebbed, allowing us to revel in the warmth of our friendship. Other days, that electrical charge was unbearable and we wanted to rip each other's clothes off. On those days, we purposely played with it, daring to see which of the two of us would break first. We had yet to break.

After ten years, the electrical charge was mild if not completely muted. We did not discuss sex. We did not discuss our wants or dreams. We spoke like friends. There was no flirting, no indecent exchange. But there was something new. A lot of things new between us. Things that wouldn't come out until much later.

   The most noticeable change was that there was a constant fear of abandonment. An incessant insecurity, a belief that if we didn't cling desperately to each other, we would lose each other again. We knew why we had lost each other, but, in the end, after ten years, we understood how easy it is to lose someone and how hard it is to not be able to find them when you want them. Isaiah and I lived with the fear of losing each other for most of the rest of our lives.

   I clung to Isaiah with an obsessive need fueled by a severe fear of loss and abandonment. I'm sure Richard picked up on this. I'm sure, my own fears fueled Richard's insecurities. Isaiah and I knew if we met in person or spoke on the phone that the electrical charge would return. We both agreed not to exchange phone numbers or addresses because of this. It was a simple rule we lived by. And online, there simply was no sexual tension. Online, we were safe.

   I printed and handed every conversation exchanged between Isaiah and I to Richard. He not only read every conversation, but I made them readily available to him without his asking. I would not lie and had nothing to hide.

   Richard's hunting trips had given a financial hit that would threaten the last of my security. Bills were due and we had no money. The two thousand dollar hit from his hunting trip had taken its toll on us. Rent was overdue. We paid it at the expense of the cable and phone. Both services were shut off.

I worked two jobs at this point. I was back at the bookstore and the children's store and working only ten hours a week. But Richard was going mad. He was convinced I was leaving him and made it very clear how he felt. His worries erupted into frequent bouts of screaming, accusations, and petty nonsense. The abuse I experienced prior to finding Isaiah tripled.

I had nothing to think about, nothing to talk about. For me, there was nothing going on, nothing planned, nothing there between Isaiah and I, and Richard saw every exchange between us. There simple was nothing there to worry about. It all was in Richard's head.

Everything changed the morning I woke up to find the internet access gone.

The fear of loss and abandonment that sat in the background of my subconscious since November 21st awakened and I panicked. I was terrified, convinced if I did not speak to Isaiah, I would lose him all over again.

I scrounged up what jewelry I could find—the emerald earrings my father gave me for graduation, some diamond chipped necklaces, and gold rings I had—and, at eight A.M., I told Richard what I was doing and walked to the nearest pawn shop.

I needed sixty dollars to pay for the internet and get it turned back on. I made the exchange and walked out of the shop with sixty seven dollars. For that ten minute walk home, I was relieved until. . .

I got home to find the car gone and the house locked up. Richard and my children were gone.

There was no note, no message, no nothing. My children were simply gone. I had no phone, no internet, no car. I walked to the library. They weren't there. I walked home, confirmed they were still gone, and walked in the opposite direction to an electronics store. I used the sixty-seven dollars to buy a prepaid phone and I called Richard's mother.

"I haven't heard from him," she said.

"Can you call me please if you hear from him?"

I called my employer. I was supposed to work that afternoon.

"Hi, I can't make it in today because I don't know where my children are."

I called the police and was told I couldn't do anything for twenty-four hours. So I sat in my cold, empty house, and waited.

Nothing slows time like waiting. I held myself and rocked and watched the clock tick by while I waited for the twenty-four hours to end. How far can you get in twenty-four hours?

The silence was hell. Not knowing was worse. I thought of nothing else. Not Isaiah, not Richard, not my marriage. I only thought of my children. If they were safe, if Richard had truly flipped off the deep end and killed them. If they were healthy.

I rocked and waited. I was a mother who had no idea where her children were. I would lose my job for calling off. I knew this. I didn't care. I listened to the bathroom faucet drip, counting down every slow minute while I pulled my hair out.

I heard the car pull in. The car door slammed shut. I heard my children talking and all my fears vanished as hope flooded me and I toggled between shock, hope, and panic.

The door opened and my children poured in with the relief. Daniel, Anne, and Lynn.

I collected my children, gathering them into my arms. I took them up and I sobbed. I hugged and kissed each one as the life in me returned. I touched their faces, hugged their heads to me and cried into their hair. I gently herded them to their rooms, shaking as I released each one. I closed the bedroom door. The click queued my rage and I turned with the red of a leviathan. Richard had no idea I was off my meds. He had no idea what he was walking into.

"What the fuck do you think you're doing taking my children from me!" I shrieked.

"You were gone."

"I went to the pawn shop!"

"I thought you were running off with Isaiah," he said.

"I never said... I..." I screamed. "You took my children from me!"

"I did not," he said.

"No note! No message! I called your mother—"

"We went to your father's."

My brain exploded.

"My f-f-father's?"

"Yes," he said. "I needed someone to watch the kids so we could talk about this."

"Talk about... My father?"

"Yeah, I figured—"

"My father doesn't love me!" I screamed. "My father hates me! Why the fuck would you ever think my father would help me?"

"Well, I needed to talk to you and so I could find you—"

"I told you I was going to the pawn shop!"

"Yeah, you did," he said. "But I thought you lied and were leaving with Isaiah."

"I don't lie! I have never lied! Not to you! Not to anyone! You see every conversation we had! I am hiding nothing from you!"

"It doesn't matter. You're going to leave me!"

I screamed again. Dropped down to the couch and rocked while I held myself.

"Well?" he asked.

I looked up like a rabid dog. "What?"

"Aren't you going to get ready?"

"Where?" I asked.

"You have work."

"I called off!"

Now he was pissed. "You called off! We're hurting for money and you called off!"

"You took my children!" I said. "I didn't know where you were, when you would be back! If you'd be back!"

"You'll lose your job!"

"You don't take a mother's children! You don't do it!"

The argument continued well into the night and opened up an endless array of topics. Every argument and problem we ever had in seven years came in like someone had opened the flood gates. The screaming dissipated hours later, leaving behind a stale exhaustion that left us both worn and confused.

I lay in bed that night beside Richard, who slept soundly.

I still hadn't spoken to Isaiah.

Isaiah.

I walked to the kitchen and pulled out a piece of a paper. I drew a line down its center. At the top, I wrote pros and cons. In each column I wrote "Leaving Richard" and "Staying with Richard" and I began scribbling.

Thirty minutes later, I had exhausted all of my consequences.

I stared at my choices before me and took a long hard look at the lifestyle the children would live. I knew the life of a divorced child. I knew the very wrong way to proceed with a divorce. I knew the errors my mother made, when she went wrong and how. I examined what I, as a child of divorced parents, wanted and didn't want from a divorce. I knew what damaged me. What didn't. What should have happened between my parents. Above all else, the child must have stability. I also was raised in a screaming household. I knew what damage that does to a child. I knew the damage of a child being exposed to incessant fighting. Furthermore, I knew the character assassination between Richard and I was teaching my children all the wrong things about marriage.

I had just seen three months of life without Richard. I knew exactly what life would be like without him. No screaming, no fighting. There was peace. I was calm. I was cool. I was quiet. I was happy during those three months. The tension in the house vanished overnight.

With or without Isaiah, I was happiest without Richard. Is it more important for children to have their father or a happy home? That question was hard. Which was better for the children?

At the bottom of the page, I wrote one line.

To thine own self be true.

And all at once, I knew what I must do.

Isaiah or no, Richard had to go.

Chapter 35

I didn't dump Richard. I believe in formal argument, chances, and choices. If things didn't change between Richard and I, he would have to go. The lifestyle my children and I had been living was not healthy. It needed to change and either Richard and I needed to change the relationship or we needed to end the relationship.

Either way, the relationship we currently had was over. Richard made it clear that he would sooner get a divorce than seek marriage counseling, which meant marriage counseling was out of the question. I didn't have a problem with this. I had mastered formal argument and my years with Scott had trained me to shut down my emotions on a dime.

So that is what I did. I shelved my emotions, shut down, entered into a state of reasoning and formal argument, and proceeded with the longest three weeks of my life. Every night, Richard and I debated. I acted as referee while we argued and countered our arguments.

Broken

You shouldn't be your own referee, but I had a husband who refused counseling. My rules were simple. If he broke the rules, I terminated the conversation for the night and we would pick it up the next day.

Rule number one of formal argument: there can be no name calling. I would not condone the character assassination of which Richard was very fond of.

Rule number two: assumptions and accusations were banned. We were allowed to cite an incident and reflect on our feelings. We were not allowed to accuse and attack defensively.

And rule number three: we had to stay on topic. This was, by far, the hardest part of spousal arguing. Differentiating between a legitimate problem or a petty symptom and doing so objectively.

I made it clear to him what my intentions were, that I was considering ending the relationship. And that, even if we stayed together, there would be significant change to make us work. That what we had was unacceptable. He wanted to talk about Isaiah.

Isaiah was a grad student who lived in Boston where he was working on his master's degree and aimed to enter the PhD program for organic chemistry in six months. Isaiah had no idea what problems were going on in my marriage, nor had we ever discussed a relationship outside of confirming we weren't going to have one. My decision was based solely on how Richard had behaved over the last seven years. My final decision would be based solely on how Richard would behave over this argument.

For the next month, every night we argued formally, keeping to my rules best as we could. After one week, things went south. The debates began earlier and earlier in the day. And, in the fit of one of our fights, Richard grabbed my computer's tower and began pulling out the wires.

My book. My precious book. All one hundred and fifty thousand words were currently tucked away on that hard drive and he was walking out the door with the only copy.

"What are you doing?" I asked.

"I'm taking the computer. I'm going to smash it."

Everything in me shut down. Cold stark panic set in. I balled my fist and punched him in the face. I felt my thumb pop against his cheek bone, but he had dropped my computer and stumbled back.

I stood there, a little four-foot-eleven raging self and I seethed. The only thought on my mind was Ian and my precious book, and I would be damned if Richard took that from me. He grabbed his keys and ran out the door.

I inspected my thumb. I had clearly dislocated it. It swelled and hurt like a bitch. I didn't care. I had my book.

* * *

Richard came home a few hours later after we had cooled off.

He approached me right away with a new plan.

"I was doing some thinking and I want you to talk to your doctor about increasing the dosage on your medication."

"What?" I said.

"Something is off these past few weeks and—"

"I'm not taking my medication," I said.

He had a face like I had punched him again.

"What?" he growled.

"I stopped taking my meds."

"You— When? No wonder why you're acting like a psycho-bitch!"

"I am not a psycho-bitch!" I said. "I took myself off the meds months ago!"

"Yeah! And you've been acting like a crazy bitch since then!"

"You left! You weren't here for three months! And I was off the meds long before then!"

He didn't know what to say, so he stood dumbfounded for that moment.

"Off your fucking meds... no wonder you hit me," he grumbled.

"I hit you because you were trying to take my computer!" I shouted. "My book is on that computer! Why the frick did you think you could just take it?"

"Your father told me I should. It was his idea."

"Yeah, my father would," I said.

My father who never loved me a day in his life. My father who had no concept but to control others. My father who Richard believed was the best person to give advice on handling me. Handling me. I am a woman who is not handled. Of all people, my father wouldn't know this.

* * *

I remember the deterioration and one final moment later that week that changed everything. It was the moment I decided to give up on Richard... when I put my foot down and said, "I'm done."

For Scott, it was the day he slapped me.

For Richard, it was this day. We were arguing again. It was a calm argument and, I will be honest, I don't know what was said. I know I was giving him my views on marriage and relationships. I know I was not talking about Isaiah. Whatever I said enraged him.

He looked at me with such hate that he took me and threw me down on the bed. I felt him holding me there with his body, holding me by the wrists, and he shoved his face in mine and screamed, "Cunt! Cunt! Cunt!"

When he released me, I scrambled to the opposite side of the bed and yanked my wedding ring from my finger. I threw it at him. We were done. It was over. I will not keep a husband who has ever used that word on me. No husband of mine will ever call me that. Granted, I've called him names, he has called me names. But this...

A person is not defined by their choices when the world is right, but by their choices when the world goes wrong. We remember Hitler, Stalin, and Christopher Reeves all at the worst. And which of those men do you respect? This philosophy would go on to shape so much about me. I think this is what Richard taught me. Shaun taught me to fight. Piss-ant taught me standards. Joe taught me endurance. Scott taught me to persevere and keep a cool head. Richard taught me to own my choices, good or bad.

What I saw was a man who refused to take his children to the emergency room if needed because it inconvenienced him. What I saw was a man who refused to get his wife the medical attention she needed because it annoyed him. A man who scolded his wife for being sick. I saw a man who drove himself insane, mad with insecurity and jealousy, until he saw problems that weren't there. I would no longer involve myself with this man. I was done. I was tired. He severed the last of my love when he called me "cunt."

I let him know all of this. There were no lies, no secrets. I spelled out every emotion I had through every step of this process the moment that I had it. And he still insisted I lied. I told him the exact moment I was done with the marriage. I still didn't leave him. He asked to keep trying, I said, "Yes. We can still talk," and we did.

Two weeks before Christmas, Richard developed a strong belief that if he couldn't sleep, then I shouldn't sleep.

The first day, I was tired. The second day, I was beat. The third day I was beyond drugged and incoherent. The fourth day, I fell asleep in the middle of my sentence and it took him ten minutes to wake me up again.

"Elizabeth!"

"What?" I said as if nothing had happened.

"You fell asleep."

"No, I didn't."

"Yes, you did," he said. "You were in the middle of a sentence when you passed out."

I thought for a long moment and remembered and yes. I had literally been in the middle of a sentence.

"What were you saying?" he asked.

"What?" I had no idea what he was talking about.

"Finish the sentence!"

That is why he woke me? So I could finish my damn sentence?

I was so tired I couldn't even recall the topic. And he was oblivious to my exhaustion.

"Never mind," he said. He stood from the bed and sighed. "You know what. I think I'm going to move in with my mother."

"What?" I slurred and forced back a large smile. *I get to sleep!* "Okay," I said.

Inside I was smiling. I was finally going to be allowed sleep. I couldn't wait.

I slept for three days.

I woke up once to find Richard standing over me. He had covered my body with roses. I took the house key from him that day and told him not to come in while I was sleeping. He left and I went back to sleep. I slept for another two days.

When I woke up, I was refreshed, my head was clear, and I could think. I told him not to come back.

Chapter 36

"How did the children handle it?" William asked.

"The children didn't even know he was gone," I said. "In their minds, he left in September. In December, they never asked, not once, about their father. Amid the screaming and the debates, the fighting and name calling, Richard dished out his usual approach of locking me in the bedroom. I lost both my jobs due to stress that affected my attendance.

"Richard refused to drive me to work and would not allow me to take the bus. He would not take me to a clinic for my thumb, which had swollen and maintained a permanent state of agony. When I finally did get to the doctor, they confirmed it had been dislocated and healed in the wrong position. It forever hurt and my mobility was limited."

William glanced at my thumb.

I smiled.

"I reset it a year later," I said.

"You reset your thumb?" he asked.

"Yep. I pulled it straight until it popped and released a bubble from the joint that I watched travel up my thumb. That felt weird. It was excruciating. The joint tripled in size from the swelling as it had when I first dislocated it. But after it healed, it was like I had never injured it."

"Where was Isaiah in all this?" William asked.

"We spoke very little when we spoke at all during this time."

"And you never told him what was going on with your marriage?" he asked.

"I did near the end," I said. "I kept it vague. Told him there were complications and Richard and I were trying to work things out. I explained my absence and assured him I would be on the computer less and less through that time. I told Isaiah nothing more.

"I was raised listening to my mother bash my father. My mother is a gossip whore. I loathe, detest, despise a woman who gossips. I would not condone such behavior. The trials and tribulations between a husband and a wife should stay between a husband and a wife. Nor do I believe a spouse should ever speak poorly of their mate to others, no matter what. I also do not believe a marriage in trouble should ever be shared. It is private and is only between two people. My marriage was not news to share with anyone. And Isaiah and I still had not discussed a relationship."

"So... what about Isaiah?" William asked.

I furrowed my brow.

"What about him?"

William smiled.

"You can't tell me that after all those years, when you did eventually see him... You didn't..."

I smiled.

"Yes," I said. "Later, we would."

"How much later? How long did you wait?"

"How long did we wait?" I hid my grin behind my fist. "Fifteen years."

"That's not what I meant," William scolded me. "After you and Richard split up, how long did you wait?"

"We didn't. Life's too short."

"So..."

"I hate making plans," I evaded. "Detest them. Plans feel like a prison. What if I changed my mind? Changed my mood? Changed my heart? Don't get me wrong, I am not one of those women who can't make up her mind. I know what I want. I always know exactly what I want. I am very decisive. But I hate plans. I hate building expectations. Plans leave no room for freedom. We made no plans. But we didn't wait either. Whatever played out would play out. But yes, we both knew if we were together, we would invariably have sex."

* * *

A week after Richard moved out, Isaiah and I swapped phone numbers. I immediately went down to the courts and filed for custody, separation, and divorce, and by the end of December, I had court dates for everything.

The divorce was amiable and fast. Richard wanted nothing. I wanted nothing and invited him to take anything he wanted. He took only what he needed and left everything else. For the next five years, he would swing by and pick through his stuff. He didn't want to take from the children. He provided six hundred dollars every month up until a court agreement was made. The six hundred dollars kept the rent...

I can't say it was caught up, but it postponed the eviction notices and I began job hunting.

Christmas Day, Richard invited us to his mother's. We got there and within ten minutes, he and I were in a screaming match. He told me to get in the car. He would drive me home. The moment I was buckled in, he drove in the opposite direction.

"What are you doing?" I asked.

"Kidnapping you."

"What?" I shrieked.

"We need to talk and I'm not taking you home until you do."

"Let me out of the car!"

He refused.

He drove for an hour, insisting we talk while I screamed to let me out of the car. He countered saying that he was kidnapping me and that I would listen.

After an hour, he saw that I wouldn't talk under those conditions—or any conditions, for that matter. He took me home.

The day after Christmas, Isaiah drove up from Boston.

Ten years.

For ten years, I had suffocated. Yes. It feels like a long slow suffocation. The desperation, the loneliness, the feeling of complete helplessness, lack of control, inability to direct your own fate... all of it.

You kill everything inside of you, anything that makes you feel, you destroy it just so you can live without the pain. After a while, you forget that you feel nothing. You get used to the state of perpetual numb. You forget that you aren't feeling.

When Isaiah walked through my front door that night, I saw his hands.

His hands. Those hands that I had remembered. I never touched him. Not then. I had no idea what he would feel like or taste like. I only remembered his hands.

We were shaking. Like we had been chained to the sea floor for ten years and suddenly, we both were being forced to the surface and experiencing the bends. Our bodies shook, we gasped for air, unsure what to do with so much air. It breathed life into me again. It wasn't lust. It was need. Obsession? Perhaps.

Relief? So much relief. I didn't fall into his arms. I wasn't calm or content. It was a surge of relief so great that I felt my legs give out from under me and he caught me. I fell into him and we both broke. Our bodies trembled so violently, we felt brittle and were certain we would break with how much we shook.

Disbelief. Constant disbelief. That is what a separation like that feels like. It would take us another two years to look at one another and not say, 'I can't believe you're here.'

You asked me if we did. Yes. We did... during a December thunderstorm.

* * *

I should end the story here.

If this were a romance, the story would end here. Part of me wants to end the story here. To send you on your way and tell you that you have your biography, now get out. You'll hear no more from me. That is how I should end this. Right now, with Isaiah and I making love in December rain.

That is how it would have ended if...

Maybe I'll give you a choice. If you want your happy ending, close the book and stop reading right now. Consider the story over and we lived happily ever after in New York. And I never went to Ireland. I never had a problem that was too great that Isaiah couldn't fix.

Close the book here and pretend I was never broken.

Part Five: Breaking the Looking Glass

Chapter 37

In spring of 2009, I had no job, was five thousand dollars in debt, and owed three months in back rent. I had an eviction notice, a shut off notice for utilities, no driver's license, no car, a credit score of 347, and three children.

And the sun was shining.

In May, I found a job as a debt collector. It was the dirtiest job I have ever worked. It was a job that allowed my children to have a place to live. I contacted everyone who I owed money to and made arrangements to catch up.

On the second day of training, I fell on the steps going to my car and landed on my leg. I cracked my femur. The impact split my skin and within an hour I had one of the largest bruises...

Bruise is an understatement. My leg turned black. Eighteen inches by ten inches of black on my left thigh. Isaiah picked me up off the ground and told me to go to the hospital. Second day on a new job with rent and electric waiting on that first pay check? Screw the hospital. I went to work.

I iced the wound... eventually... and worked through it. Granted, I couldn't walk, but my job required I sit in a chair anyway, so I was fine. I welcomed pain, remember? That wound would take two years to heal, but not completely. To this day, it bothers me.

Four weeks later, I had a paycheck and began paying on the five thousand I owed plus the back payments. Two weeks after that, I went down to Social Services and was approved for a one thousand dollar loan. I threw it onto my electric bill and began making twenty-five dollar payments. Two weeks after that, Isaiah and I went to the bank and he co-signed on a personal loan of four thousand dollars. I paid off all my debt, used my paychecks to catch up, and, by August, I was keeping on top of my bills and was paying on my bank loan.

I was twenty-nine years old. Autumn was fast approaching. I was financially stable and in a loving, secure relationship.

The lifestyle was everything I needed for everything to go wrong.

* * *

"Why would it go wrong?" William asked. "You had it made?"

"Did I?" I asked. "Yes, I suppose I did."

"Why would there be a problem?" William asked.

"Because I had dragons sleeping within," I said. "Dragons I didn't know were there. And nothing awakens a sleeping dragon more like happiness and all things good."

* * *

The programming Scott had conditioned into me was still there. I hadn't accessed it in seven years. It was dormant. Richard and I had enabled my fear of men by secluding me. In turn, I also developed a fear of people, of leaving my home.

Richard was right to be worried. I can not be around men. He had called me heroin and he was right. He didn't know why. He didn't understand. Nor did I. He saw firsthand how men respond to me. They love me hard and fast. They go mad with desire and they're there, caught in my voodoo before they realize it's happened. Voodoo. That's what Penelope calls it.

Richard knew that if I were around men, I would break down. I still had a fear of men. And my fear still triggered a desire to soothe them, to sedate them by any means necessary so they don't hurt me. All of this lay in waiting for that spring of 2009 when I returned to the work force.

At first, I kept my distance and remained shy while I went through my training. I was a single mother of three children with food and shelter on the line. I busted my ass at that job. After the four weeks of training, I was moved out to the call center and was seated beside a man named Reggie.

Reggie was a six foot two black man, and I was convinced he was going to rape me right then and there. I didn't think that was an unusual thought to have. I was terrified. So I smiled. I flirted. I do what I do. He smiled back and fell for me hard and I relaxed knowing I was safe because he liked me.

I moved on to the next one. Toby.

Toby was wonderfully lively, ten years younger than me, kind of dim, sweet as heather in summer, and reminded me so much of a little boy. He was my height, was the happiest, jolliest—Toby was jolly—the friendliest. He posed the least threat and so I flirted with him the least.

Matt was Toby's counterpart. The Beavis to his Butthead. The Bill to his Ted. He was taller than me, flirtatious, and developed a sexual interest in me. We flirted, he smiled, and I tamed him. I was safe without having to put out.

Jason was a gentlemen. Mature, in a committed relationship with a wonderful woman, and was kind and intelligent. He posed no threat. Jason was the music giver! It was Jason who introduced me to music beyond Beethoven.

Through Jason, I learned of bands people like: Metallica, and Mumford and Sons. Jason spoke my language with a strange dialect. Music.

Music who I had long since abandoned. Music who I once made love to every day for hours while I played and composed. Music who loved me first, who knew me, who soothed me. And who I gave up and turned my heart off to when I lost my Isaiah.

"Where's the music?"

"What?" I asked Isaiah. He looked around the silent apartment.

"It's you," he said. "I've been visiting you for six months now and there's no music."

I remembered. I had thrown it away all those years ago when I closed the lid of my piano and walked away. Music had been the largest line that tethered me to my pain and the first of the lines I killed to ease the hurt.

I still had my boxes sealed away in the room with Angel. I never thought of that. She was still there, still screaming, but I could no longer hear. I still felt little to nothing. I didn't have that luxury. I needed to focus on work and my children. I didn't have time for music.

Love was the only emotion I permitted myself. All others were locked away. Forgotten where they belonged.

"I..." I tried to find the words to explain. "I gave it up."

He looked at me in horror.

"You... gave it up." He shook his head with a look of disgust. "Why would you do that?"

"Because..."

How do I explain the hurt I had? How do I explain how much music forced me to feel?

"It's you," he said.

I felt my locks on my boxes breaking. I couldn't let them out. I couldn't feel.

"I..."

"You need music," he said. "It's all you are. It is you. You gave up the thing that made you you."

You couldn't hold me, I wanted to say to him. *I had to turn my heart into stone. I had to become cold so that I could breathe. I couldn't do that when music reminded me.*

He wouldn't understand.

"I don't..." I tried to explain.

It was coming back. The boxes were breaking. The boxes were—

"I don't have a piano anymore," I argued as if that clinched it. And it was true. I didn't.

"So your compositions?" he asked. "Your singing? Your piano?"

The boxes were breaking. It was getting harder to focus. I was forcing down too much.

"I shut it all down," I said. "It hurt too much. I shut down the music so that I may live."

"But it's you!"

I shrugged. I could see Angel holding her head on the floor and rocking.

"I haven't listened to music," I said. "I haven't sung a note or played since you left."

He looked at me in disbelief.

I remembered that day. I remembered the music and oh how I ached to play. I missed music. I missed Erik. I missed it all. I missed Puccini and Beethoven.

The loneliness, the emptiness, the hurt. The emotions, the memories of that day, the nightmares... Angel's screams reached me and I fell to the floor screaming. He was right. My music had been my solace and I lived without it for ten years. It had kept me chained to the hurt.

Tribble was there within moments, purring and nudging my head with her velvet nose as I hugged myself on the floor. I scooped her into my arms and I held her. I sobbed into her fur while she purred and snuggled my face and I cried.

Over the purrs and my sobbing, Angel screamed. I heard Isaiah's keys rattle and the front door close as I sat on the floor crying into Tribble.

He left me.

I buried my face into Tribble's coat and wept.

Two hours later, Isaiah returned. He had an eighty-eight key, Steinway electric performance level portable piano with weighted keys. My piano. I named her Abigail.

Chapter 38

At work, I flourished. My fear of men directed my every decision. I smiled. I listened. I never judged. I put them at ease. Something I'm still unsure how I do. They adored me, they swarmed me. Something about me made them feel good, just like heroin. And I relished the approval they gave me.

Toby felt warm and delightfully stupid. The kind of stupid you wanted to be. Matt felt laid back and high. Who am I kidding? Matt was in a perpetual state of high. Reggie felt like a gentle giant and was the biggest nerd since Leonard Nimoy. He had a fantastic sense of humor. Reggie was a teddy bear and oh, so sweet. He had an anime character on his desk with a fourteen inch sword. I swiped that figurine more times than not.

Jason felt cool and laid back.

And then there was Nick.

Nick, I could not figure out. He was my age. No children. No girlfriend. No plans, no dreams, and no future. I couldn't read him. I couldn't predict him. I couldn't get close to feel him. There was a wall surrounding him. I could not figure out Nick. I still can't. Nick scared me the most.

Those boys became close to me. They became my pack. My brothers. My kin. We hung together on breaks and ate together on lunches. We started going to each other's houses. We went to the bars together. We played football together. Listened to music.

Very quickly, they learned I was laid back and open-minded. They learned that I didn't judge them. I understood them. Of course, they had to test the waters. Test my limits. See exactly how much I could tolerate.

How gross can I get before Elizabeth gets squeamish? Let's found out, shall we! That became the daily challenge of our group. Where were my limits? Where exactly did my masculine understanding break down?

Oh, the things they showed me. The things they told me. The conversations I got to hear.

We shared photos of hot women. Crass stories of sexual mishaps. Anything for a laugh. That seemed to be the goal. There were days when I took the football to the face. I had a pretty good arm at one point. On par with a few of them.

And they tested me... shock factor galore. It became the daily trial to see if they could break me. And I stepped up and dished it back, which only delighted them further... which only encouraged them.

Soon, they weren't challenging each other to find my breaking point. They teamed up against me in an effort to one up me. Who would break first: them or me? That became our game.

I learned so much about men. I studied them. Tested them. I played with them to learn just as much as they played with me. We pushed each other to our limits.

They showed me more ugly pussies...

They taught me how to drink. Oh my god, the Jäger bombs! I built up such a tolerance...

I came to learn so much from them. In trying to determine where that breaking point was, they actually toughened me up for anything they could dish out and I learned to loosen up and take it. I learned to ease up and laugh.

I have no breaking point. If I do, I haven't found it yet. They taught me to truly throw my head back, laugh, and enjoy life. No matter how grotesque a picture they showed, I smiled, said, "sweet" and quickly found one to one up them.

I learned how laid back and wonderful men truly are. They just want to have a good time. Truly. But unlike women, they really know how and aim to do that every second they get. They are always on the look out for a good time. And they hate having to do what they don't want to do. But when they do, they turn it into a game and find a way to enjoy it. Above all, men hate being miserable and usually find a way to not be.

Men are... amazing creatures. I studied them and defined their three basic needs: food, sex, sleep. In between those three needs, he seeks comfort and relaxation. Men enjoy a good time and wish for nothing more than to seek it out. This lifestyle has taught them to appreciate the simple, silly, and completely immature things in life that women tend to overlook. And I'm telling you, women are missing out. They really need to learn to relax, play, and laugh more.

This is where my father issues began kicking in. I was still trying to be a male to earn his approval. I figured, if I studied them, learned to be like them, then maybe my daddy would love me.

But my experiences had taught me to fear them. And I was not able to ignore that fear surrounded by so many of them. The more I learned, the more I hung out with my boys. The more I became their brother, the louder my fear became until the urge to sleep with Nick, to make him safe, to ensure I wouldn't get hurt, was something I couldn't ignore.

By October, a part of me ached to sleep with Nick. I didn't want to. I knew that in all good conscience. If I was given the choice to destroy the feeling, I would. Something else urged me to have sex with him. Like I had to. I didn't want it. I didn't even find him attractive. I didn't love him or desire a relationship. I didn't pine for him, think of him, or desire him, but when he was around me, I needed to fuck him. I felt threatened. Fear made me want to fuck him to guarantee my safety. It was a need. Not lust. No desire. It was fear and need. The same need to pick up a loaded gun and fire, all before he could fire first. Nothing more. Nothing less.

When I met the boys, I told Isaiah about each one. When they started letting me play football with them, I told him. I ran my findings past him and returned to work to reassess the next round of data. Every night, I would run it by Isaiah.

The music... Isaiah was familiar with the bands and after telling him of my latest discoveries, he would recommend his own collection of rock music, which I would take back to work with me the next day.

I told Isaiah. I did not lie nor did I hold anything back. Nor did I do anything with Nick while I battled the urges. I told Isaiah about those too. I held nothing back. I would not lie. I wasn't sure of my own will-power. I wasn't sure of my own limits. I wasn't sure of anything. I knew, if things proceeded, I would cave. And I hated it. I viewed myself as a threat to Isaiah. I was terrified I would hurt him. I told Isaiah that too.

That December, I left Isaiah.

Chapter 39

"You left Isaiah?" William asked.

"Yes." I felt the tears line my face. I hugged my legs into my chest.

"After ten years of waiting... and only ten months of dating... You left him," William repeated. "Why would you do that?"

"I hurt everyone who has ever loved me," I said. "I do it without wanting to or even knowing I do it. That time, I could feel this thing inside of me. Like building pressure fated to go off. I had no idea when, and all I wanted to do was get away as far from him as I could before it did."

"So you left him to not hurt him."

"Yes."

"But you hurt him by leaving him," William said.

"Not as much as if I had stayed," I argued. "I lessened his hurt."

"But why would you... why?"

"I don't know," I said and shook with a fresh wave of tears. "Perhaps I purposely sabotaged the relationship I had, to destroy the intimacy he and I were developing. Perhaps I was dangerously close to revealing my emotions. Perhaps it was all subconscious and I was sabotaging this all in such a way that I looked like a victim, or maybe I was simply running."

"Commitment issues," William proposed.

"A person with commitment issues can still be intimate," I argued. "I can't. I can be married. I just can't be close. When I feel vulnerable, I go cold. Painfully frigid. These aren't my words. This is how others have described me. I am formal. I shut down and my heart grows cold so that I can't hurt. But those who are close. Those who feel it, they are pushed away. They stand at the door screaming to come in. And I can't let them. They'll hurt me."

I felt William watch me as I cried into knees.

"Problem is. . . Isaiah didn't leave me."

* * *

My mind was dark. I had stopped mothering my children. I was spiraling out of control. I was shutting down. The music hit me. I felt everything and then nothing. Not guilt. Not love. Not lust. Not hate. I went cold and logical to attempt to quell and control the urge. But something inside of me still said I needed to sleep with Nick. I knew if I slept with Nick, I would hurt Isaiah. I couldn't hurt Isaiah. But I felt myself losing control. I felt like a bomb was strapped to my chest, counting down to my own demise and I couldn't get it off. I had to get away from Isaiah as quickly as possible to protect Isaiah.

Leaving Isaiah would hurt him a lot less than betraying Isaiah. And so I broke up with Isaiah.

It was like a black hole that sucked me dry of every emotion. It left me writhing in that door-less room, naked on the floor, surrounded once more by my Death Men. I wanted to die and I didn't know why.

The night I slept with Nick, Isaiah knew. I lied about nothing, but when he looked me in the eye and asked me if I had, I looked right at him and said, "I do not lie. But if you ask me about that night, I will."

Isaiah had only one response. He asked that I speak to a friend of his: David. I loved Isaiah. I would never tell him no. I agreed to speak to his friend.

David was a student of psychology. He had no license and it was made very clear to me that his friend was not giving me psychological advice. He came to me as a friend who I could confide in. And confide I did.

Isaiah spoke to David, then asked me if he could give David my email address. I agreed and that afternoon, I received an email. My first thought on David was that he was professional and smart. Within moments, he had me opening up to him. I broke everything down rather logically.

I explained how I felt about Isaiah. I loved him. I didn't love Nick, but I wanted to fuck Nick. I didn't think of Nick, pine for him, or want him. But when he was around me, I wanted to fuck him. I had to fuck him.

David asked me about the boys. I explained to him my need to be accepted by them. He asked me about Scott and I told him everything. I told him about Joe... about Piss-ant and my half-brother.

David wasted no time and made it very clear that I cheated on Isaiah. I argued with him and said that I left Isaiah first and I had. David insisted it didn't matter, that, because I dumped Isaiah with intent to sleep with Nick, it was still considered cheating. He asked if I had even apologized to Isaiah.

I was angry. I didn't feel I did anything wrong. I didn't lie. I made it very clear to Isaiah how I felt. What I wanted. What was wrong. I wasn't cruel. I didn't string Isaiah along nor did I try to toggle between two lovers. I didn't need to apologize to Isaiah about cheating on Isaiah because I didn't cheat on Isaiah. I made it very clear what I wanted. What I didn't want. That something inside of me was wrong. That I needed to sleep with Nick when I didn't want to. That I wasn't sure if I could help it. I told David about the bomb and how my only thought was to get away from Isaiah as fast as I could before it went off. I did not sleep with Nick until after I had left Isaiah. David said we never really broke up. In my mind, we had. David insisted I apologize and said accepting responsibility was part of the healing process. I agreed to apologize to Isaiah for something I didn't do.

The next few weeks, David and I talked. I ran through my experiences with Scott. I did not discuss 9/11. I talked about Joe and Piss-ant. We identified my fear of men. How terrified I was around them. David asked if I was afraid of Isaiah. I said no, but I was afraid of angry males and Isaiah was never angry so I was fine with Isaiah. David said he had an exercise for me.

I felt an unease come over me.

"You need to be around an angry male," David had written.

Panic hit me. I felt that emotion right away.

"No!" I wrote back.

"You need to be around an angry male," he insisted.

"I can't!"

"I will tell Isaiah something that will make him angry," David explained.

I wanted to scream. I hugged myself and started rocking.

"Please. No," I begged in that email.

"You need this."

"I can't... I'll do anything else. I can't be around angry males," I wrote.

"Why not?"

"They'll hurt me!" I wrote. "They always hurt me!"

"You need to be around them and note your body changes," David wrote back. "You need to note your state of arousal. You need to do this. It's Isaiah. You know he won't hurt you."

I agreed.

* * *

An hour later, I emerged from my room and called Isaiah into my bedroom per David's directions.

"David said he sent you an email," I said.

Isaiah followed me into my bedroom and sat at the computer.

Already I felt my blood pressure rising. I hugged and rocked myself on the bed and waited.

Isaiah logged on to his email and read. A moment later, he punched my desk and I ran for the door, but Isaiah intercepted me. He pulled me into his lap while he shook with rage. The results were immediate. I wanted to fuck him. I wanted to fuck him and run.

I braced for the beatings. My body responded and prepared for sex as his arms around me shook with rage. His body was like a cage and I couldn't escape. I wanted to mount him and claw at him and fuck him. I wanted him to cum so I could run, but Isaiah wouldn't let me go and so I shut down.

I slid back into my mind and slid once more to my worlds. The wind and the green of Ireland flooded back to me and the clouds moved in from the sea. I threw my head back to the skies and smiled. I could hear the stream nearby and wasted no time seeking it out.

She called to me and I listened. I found the stream and I followed through the wood. How I missed my forest, my cottage, my realm. How I wished for nothing else, but to stay there until I died.

* * *

It was January. I had pulled away from the boys at work and poured myself into my book again. I hadn't slept with Nick since I started speaking to David. Isaiah and I, not sure when or how, were back together. My boys didn't take the rejection well. The group split up and dwindled. Some of us quit the job and went on to other places. Those of us who were left, went our own way.

I had been speaking to David now for a month and we had become fast friends. A little part of me had grown attracted to him, which I shared with Isaiah as we dove into my subconscious. David walked me through the movies. How every time I watched a movie I associated it with rape and felt I was expected to perform.

We learned that I was able to watch the movies alone, but with another, my heightened sense of awareness and fear kicked in. With a male in the room, I braced for rape. We began exploring the avenues with Joe and Piss-ant and the damage they had inflicted. Isaiah was still living in Boston and drove the six hours almost every weekend. Those weekends were spent jumping between emails to David and repairing our relationship.

But most of all, I heard Angel. I couldn't see her, but I heard. Beneath the screams, she was trying to talk. Isaiah and David insisted I needed to listen, but I couldn't make out her words. She only ever screamed. A week of discussion and emails followed. They were adamant that I speak to her.

I couldn't listen. I couldn't...

The sessions would end before I could make out what she was saying.

David had started working with Isaiah as well. David would send off a response to me, then send off one to Isaiah.

We had identified my fear of men, which David determined was the center of all my issues. We had finally called my rapes for what they were: rapes, and we identified my daddy issues. David explained that my rapes had led to a fear of open spaces, fear of people and crowds, and a general fear of the unknown. Being locked in that room with Joe developed a strange fear of closed doors: caves, tunnels, cars... I almost want to say it was a fear of an inability to escape or a fear of a loss of freedom, which I wonder is part of my problem with marriage. I was still left with the conditioning Scott had programed into me with the movies.

David would talk to me and then I would leave the room and Isaiah would answer his emails from David. When Isaiah finished, I would return to my room and converse with David.

I was enjoying the process. I was starting to feel in control again. My head was clearing and I could identify my urges and triggers. I could call them what they were and begin to control them. The word rape still left a vile taste in my mouth, but I had grown by leaps and bounds. I was with my children again and was responsible again.

I truly can't tell you how long David and I wrote back and forth. Maybe a month, maybe two... I can't remember. I do remember the last day we spoke very well.

"Okay, get out," Isaiah said with a playful smile.

Things had been going great between Isaiah and I. I was understanding my problem and had learned to recognize the warning signs. I was learning to control my urges... or so I thought. I had learned to accept the word rape.

"No." I smiled. "I want to stay with you." I climbed up on my bed. "I promise I won't look."

"Okay," he said. "But no peeking."

I giggled and hugged the pillow then buried my face and waited.

I heard Isaiah's hesitation then the chorus of the clickety-clack of the keys. I was hopping. I was jumping. I was eager. I was in such a mood that day. I felt like I could soar and recalled the endless emails. The elation. I was finally free to open the boxes of emotions. I could handle them. I glanced over my shoulder and in a matter of moments, I slipped into the other world and this one vanished.

Chapter 40

I stood in my room. I shifted my feet on the white marble. Sunlight poured into the room like a golden waterfall. I looked behind me. The two cat statues of black onyx flanked the door. The bed was made up with a silk sheet. The water fall shower fell from the ceiling into the pool. It all was still here.

The white gauze curtain swayed in the window and I grinned. I could not help but grin. I entered the balcony and looked down at the river that fell into the ravine. As always, I could jump and I would land in the pool below. I could smell the earth and the green. I could feel the wind and the spray of mist carried on the breeze like never before. It was real. I could touch it.

And I knew, beyond the trees was my cottage and stream.

Elizabeth!

I turned and could see Isaiah in a faded screen in the mist.

Elizabeth! Oh god!

I saw him pace my bedroom on the other side. He was dialing a phone.

David! Please pick up!

I looked at my body, staring off into space, clutching the pillow and in a daze. It hurt. It felt unpleasant. I turned back to the balcony. I positioned myself to climb up on the banister and jump.

Yes! David! Hi! I don't know what to do! I don't know what happened. She just isn't moving.

I furrowed my brow. I felt irate.

Who is he talking to? I thought. I was so angry. I pulled myself up on the banister.

The wind swept through me. The falls thundered and the sun enveloped me like a warm blanket. I raised my hands to the sky and breathed deep. I was ready to jump and not come back. Not this time. I would be free and live in my wood with the stream.

There I would be. Forever more. Free and—

She won't wake up. I don't know.

I looked back to the room and at the image of Isaiah pacing my room. He was ruining my day. Who was he talking to? There was no David. He looked silly talking to no one on the phone.

I returned to the balcony, but Isaiah was being too loud.

I don't know! She isn't responding. She isn't moving! I don't know what to do! Okay. I'll try it!

I looked back to the image just as he picked up my body. My eyes stared, dead to him and the world around me. I watched him carry my body to the bathroom. He placed me in the tub.

A breeze grazed my legs and I was ready to turn and run back to my forest and trees when I watched him turn on the cold water.

"No—"

Broken

* * *

In the bath tub, I gasped as the cold water hit me. The balcony, the sunlight, my room was gone. I was back in my mind in this world. I didn't want to be. I wanted to go back. I wanted to go back. Maybe if I didn't speak or eat. Maybe if I just died. Then maybe it all would stop.

He's calling my name. I can hear him. He's calling me. I don't want to answer. I don't. He doesn't know what he did. He doesn't know that I saw. That there is no David. It was him all along.

Everything I wrote. Everything I did. Everything David had told me to do... All of it. It had all been Isaiah. Just Isaiah all along.

And what will you do, Elizabeth? Angel said. *I finally could hear her words. Stay in your mind, locked in that room with no doors where the Death Men will find us? Or will you get out? Accept that what he did was the best thing for us, for you right now?*

"I won't trust him," I said and she answered.

I know.

"I won't trust ever again."

No, Angel said. *You won't.*

"I can't forgive," I said.

You won't.

"I can't forget."

You won't, she agreed.

"I just want to go back to my Irish wood."

He did it for you, Elizabeth. Does that not matter?

"I don't care!" I shouted back. "He lied to me! I trusted him!"

He did it for you because right now, you needed this.

"I want to go back to the wood."

What he did, she said. *This... this is what you needed.*

"It doesn't matter."
He meant well. You're better because of it. You know now. He made you aware. Now what will you do?

* * *

I blinked and focused my eyes on Isaiah. He was crying. He gasped and held me. A cool calm hate enveloped me. He had lied to me. I had trusted him. I had opened up.

"You lied to me," I said.

"I know," he said. "I didn't know what else to do..."

He shook his head and I let the cold venom take me. My heart shut down and I welcomed the logic.

"I didn't know what else to do," he muttered over and over as if that mattered.

"You lied to me," I said.

"I'm so sorry... I'm sorry."

He was sorry. I didn't care.

He meant well, Angel argued. *You're better because of it. Now what will you do?*

Wasn't I better? Wasn't I functioning? Wasn't I feeling again?

Isaiah proceeded to implore. "I'm so sorry. So sorry."

I took a deep breath and passed my judgment.

"You did what you had to do," I said and listened to him cry with relief.

He muttered his thanks and apologies. I didn't hear what he said. I didn't care. I knew he didn't see the cold hate in my eyes. I knew he missed that completely.

* * *

"He pretended to be a psychiatrist," William said.

"No," I corrected. "He pretended to be a student studying psychiatry and it was made very clear to me that the emails exchanged were not psychological advice. That we were just friends and that it was to help David out with his studies. I understood that David was not a trained psychologist."

"Still. You thought you were talking to David."

"Yes."

"How... how did that... make you feel?"

"Betrayed," I said. "I had trusted Isaiah. I had trusted David. You grow fond of someone. You love them, and you think they're real, then you learn they're not. It's worse than if David had been real and died."

"What did you see when you looked up?" William asked. "What made you leave this world and not want to come back?"

I sighed.

"When I looked over Isaiah's shoulder, I didn't see an emailed response from Isaiah to David. I was looking at an email from Isaiah to myself doctored to look like it was coming from David.

"It wasn't real," I said, shaking my head. "That is what came to mind. It wasn't real. None of it. I couldn't handle it. I slipped back into the safest place I knew I had. That room when I was a child. I lived in a part of my mind that was very real to me at a time when I was constantly threatened."

"You said you wanted Nick or that you needed him," William started and I knew what he was asking.

* * *

Of all the emotions I've had to describe, this... verb has been the hardest to explain. I did not love Nick. I knew this. I had no emotional attachment to him at all. I looked at him and was disgusted. He was very unattractive to me. There was no lust. I hate to say that I was driven to sleep with him because I wasn't. Nor did I want to, but he didn't rape me. Did I have a choice? Most people would say yes. And yes... I had a choice. But that feels like a lie to me. I could have chosen to not be around him... I guess. I could have chosen to quit my job.

It is so hard to explain this to people who don't understand.

Most people think there are certain set emotions in a woman who has an affair. Selfishness, greed, lust, disregard for the victim—her spouse. No. None of these emotions existed in my head or heart. In fact, all I could think of was Isaiah and not hurting him. I did not want to feel or desire or want anything with Nick. If I could, I would have ripped the urge to sleep with Nick out of me. But I was afraid not to sleep with Nick. I didn't need to sleep with him. I had to do it. I had to in the same way you have to shoot your favorite dog because he has rabies. That is what it felt like. It was that kind of 'had.'

My only concern was Isaiah. Not hurting Isaiah. But I had this thing inside of me. Like a poison that was changing me. I felt it changing me and I hated it. The metaphor of a time bomb strapped to me... it is such a perfect metaphor for this. It felt just like that and my only focus was getting Isaiah away from ground zero. Problem is, Isaiah wouldn't go.

Learning that David had never been a psych student—or that he never existed—made me question everything we had covered. Suddenly the exercises, the lessons, the process, all of it was the advice of a jealous boyfriend and not a professional in training. Was David... Isaiah right? Only a psychologist can scrutinize the details and answer that.

Until that happens, I have to question everything that took place.

Isaiah is damn lucky I came back. I wasn't planning on it. I saw no reason to and was more than ready to make that final jump and never come back. I didn't care.

The results of the "David incident" left me with a deep rooted anger, betrayal, and distrust that I would never discuss. Furthermore, the issues I had unearthed... all of them, my fear of men, my fear of leaving the house... I turned my back on all of it and closed the door. I was aware of my rapes. I was aware of my conditioned response to movies. But any progress I had made came to a screeching halt, and Angel kept screaming. I ignored her. I got used to her. My emotions, most of them—the anger, the hate, jealousy, guilt, rage, most of the pain—they remained locked in the steel room.

The final unofficial diagnoses is that I was a rape victim suffering from a plethora of fears all stemming from my rapes. The diagnoses could not have been more fucking wrong. One thing I will say. David/Isaiah made me aware of my problems and triggers. Some of them. It was a start. That I could not deny.

We walked away from that experience and never spoke of it again. Little did either of us know that David/Isaiah had barely begun to scratch the surface.

Chapter 41

February of 2010, my debts were paid off in full and I started taking driving lessons. With my fear of escape identified, I could get into a car again without too much trouble. I still had a severe case of arachnophobia. I think I always will. When I see spiders, I can still feel them on me. During a panic attack, I can't get them off. The smallest image—a black circle with eight lines drawn into it—is enough to trigger a minor panic attack, which I can handle and calm myself out of. My worse attacks send me into full hysterics. Crying, rocking, hugging myself while I brush the spiders that aren't there off me. I am more afraid of baby spiders than the big ones. In fact, the smaller they are, the more scared I am.

Even in telling you this, I feel them on me and I'm brushing my arms to get them off.

My relationship with Isaiah was forever shaky after the incident with David. We had a severe lack of trust in the other. He had abandonment issues. I had everything else.

Broken

We both had separation anxiety. Naturally, the best cure for this was marriage and, in 2012, Isaiah proposed.

At that time, Tribble was fourteen years old and a bout of bad breath and excessive drool led me to think she had a bad tooth—

* * *

I stopped.

William furrowed his brow while I sat remembering.

Within seconds, two years of memories flashed from one image to the next... I felt my sanity slipping, I felt my mind pull away from me and just as I broke, the kitchen and William slipped away.

* * *

The Irish sky was blue today and the wind was unforgivable. It whipped my skirts about my legs. I walked along the edge of the Cliffs of Moher, and as I walked, Ian sang:

"Tip and tup the level plains.
Bring them up and o'er again
Sink them down, bring them up
Don't forget to raise your cup."

I followed the singing across the field and came to stand at the edge where dozens of buckets sat filled to the brim with a silver liquid. There at the edge of the cliff, Ian and Erik dropped a bucket suspended by a long rope over the cliff. As they fed the rope, Ian sang:

"Tip and tup the level plains.
Bring them up and o'er again
Sink them down, bring them up

Don't forget to raise your cup."

"What are you doing there, boys?" I asked, holding my hair back from the wind.

"We're gathering buckets of insanity," Ian heaved. "We're bringing it over to this side."

They hoisted the bucket brimming with the silver liquid and I watched them pour the insanity into one of the empty buckets on the ground.

"Some of the best stuff comes from this side," he said.

Once their bucket was empty, they lowered it over the side of the cliff again. Ian commenced with his song.

"Tip and tup the level plains.
Bring them up and o'er again
Sink them down, bring them up
Don't forget to raise your cup."
"*Elizabeth?*"

* * *

I looked at William seated in front of me at my kitchen table. I could still hear Ian's song.

"Hm?" I said.

"Elizabeth?" William asked again.

Tip and Tup the level plains.
Bring them up and o'er again.

I closed my eyes and shook my head.
"It's so hard," I whispered.
"What's hard?" William asked.

Sink them down, bring them up.
Don't forget to raise your cup.

Broken

"Staying on this side," I said.
"Which side, Elizabeth?" William asked.

Tip and tup the level plains.
Bring them up and o'er again.

"You don't see them?" I asked.
"See what?" William asked.
"You can't hear?"

Sink them down, bring them up.
Don't forget to raise your cup.

William shook his head.
"Ian and Erik," I said. "They're bailing buckets of insanity from the Cliffs of Moher. They say some of the best stuff comes from that side."
I saw the worry in William's eyes and wondered why.
"What side, Elizabeth?"

Tip and tup the level plains.
Bring them up and o'er again.

"The side of insanity. It's just over the cliff there," I said.

Sink them down, bring them up.
Don't forget to raise your cup.

"And Ian's singing," I whispered. "You can't hear it?"
"No, Elizabeth," William said. "I can't hear it."
"It's so hard staying in this realm." I pinched the bridge of my nose.
"Elizabeth?" William asked. "Do you have a doctor?"
"No," I said. "Doctors only want to sell you meds and besides... look at all the buckets of insanity that Ian and Erik just bailed up for me."

"Elizabeth," William said. "Where is Tribble?"
I whispered:

"Black and blood drips down the mind.
Where death should be, there's life.
Broken... cracked. It bleeds the psych'.
Like death, life feeds the lies."

"Elizabeth," William said patiently. "Where is Tribble?"

"Tribble." I gasped. "She had mouth cancer. I took her to the doctor and they told me she had mouth cancer. They gave her a shot of cortisone that shut down her immune system. She was allergic to her own immune system and the cancer was provoking her immune system. So the cortisone shut it down and increased her cancer. But she lived with it for two years. She was fine, but it came back and the cancer had spread. I watched it eat out her mouth. It ate her teeth and twisted her jaw. She purred for me. Every day, she sat with me when I ate. She sat beside me... she held on for me. She wouldn't let me go."

I looked at Ian, who stood by my side.

"She loved me with those eyes. And I couldn't tell... I couldn't tell if she was hurt because she always purred. I had to kill her. I took her to the vet and they gave her a shot. I held her as she died. And I cried. I cried and she wasn't there. She was always there. For seventeen years, she was there, always there."

She hasn't been right in the head since, boy, Ian said. *She's messed up. That cat kept her grounded. She used Tribble to pull her back and now that she's gone, there's no reason to come back now, is there?*

"Ian... Shut up, Ian. You talk too much," I growled.

That's when you started slipping, Ian said to me. *It's when I showed up. And Erik came back. Isn't that right?*

I gave Ian a dirty look he promptly ignored.

What she isn't telling you, is that was June of 2014, Ian continued. *That's when she shut everything off. But you won't write any of this in that book, will you. No, you can't hear me can you. Because I'm not real, Elizabeth. I'm only in your head. Not his.*

"Shut up, Ian! You fucking prick!"

When did you get Pat's book? Ian said. *How long after Tribble died? Four months? Was it four months? No... It was six months later. You launched your world of social media in October and found everyone, didn't you. You found Pat and Jacob. You found Raven.*

"Shut the fuck up about Raven."

"Who's Raven, Elizabeth?" William asked.

But already you were slipping, Ian said ignoring William. *You were slipping. You're still grieving her. Still holding out. You're still waiting for Tribble to pick you up off the floor. Where is she?*

"She's dead," I said. "Where the shadows whisper, 'Lies.'"

You could have handled Pat's book if Tribble were here. But without her, you can't. And now you're telling this story and talking to me and Tribble isn't here to pull you back. How are you going to get back this time? I'm not going to pull you back. Is William? You've thrown all others away. Everyone else is gone. You're still in that wood in Ireland.

"I don't want to go," I said.

Why should you? Where's Raven?

"Raven." A tear slipped from my eye. "I don't want him to see this."

Will he ground you?

"Raven can't."

Can't he? Ian asked. *Let him. At least wake up and tell the rest of your story.*

"I miss Tribble, Ian. And I miss Raven... so much."

"Elizabeth?" William said.

I looked across the table at the horrified look in William's eyes.

"I'm sorry, William..." I said. "Where were we?"

"We were..."

Not yet, William. Ian said. *She isn't ready.*

"I can't talk," I said. "I'm in the rabbit hole and it's dark in here. I'm going for a walk. I need to clear my head."

Don't let her alone, boy! Don't let her go! Don'— Argh! Fuck!

Chapter 42

I followed Elizabeth out the door, happy to leave the cottage and the fan boy behind for the moment. I never did well indoors and despite the situation, I was relieved to be outside again.

Elizabeth was moving, already she was wandering across the yard. I thought she would stomp right through the stream, but she was paying attention enough for that and stepped over it.

I followed her for a ways into the trees. The moon was full tonight, but the cloud cover was thick. The occasional streak of light found its way down to her for only a moment, blocked by the forest canopy. Once the trees cleared, she stopped where the rolling hills began and spanned as far as the eye could see. There it was that the moonlight touched down. An ancient stone wall, so old that the land had formed up and around it, cut through the land. So old it moved like a natural vein as if the Celtic gods had built it there themselves.

Elizabeth settled herself onto the stone. I watched her reach into her pocket and pull out her cell, giving me the time to catch up and stand beside her. To the right. Always to the right where she liked me to be.

I peered down at her email and saw her write.

Hey you.

I know you're not available right now and that's fine. I just need... you. Just you right now. Nothing more.

I miss you and I am not well. I'm tired and it's been so fucking hard remembering all of this. What I need right now is to hear your voice and lay in your arms, and I know you can't do that right now so...

I'm writing this all out instead because it's all I've got.

I really can't say any more than what's already been said, and I can't say anything you don't already know. I just wanted to write to feel a little bit closer to you after the day that I've had. I miss you.

Always.

Elizabeth

I watched her send the email.

"You know that's not what you want to say," I said.

"It doesn't matter what I want to say," she said, gazing out over the hills.

I smiled. She knew I wouldn't hold my tongue. She knew me too well.

"It matters to you," I said.

She sighed. "I'm tired, Ian. Go away."

"You don't just miss him."

What she needed was to make love to him. She would never admit that. Not to him or herself.

"It doesn't matter," she argued. Of course she argued.

"It matters," I said. "You won't tell him what you feel. What you think. You won't even tell yourself. You've got to tell someone. Tell me."

"You are me, you Uskit."

I ignored the insult.

"She isn't here so you turn to him. Is that it?"

She looked down at her hands.

"Say the words, Elizabeth. If you don't say them, the words will just eat you."

She dropped her hands to her lap and raised her face to the sky.

"I need him, alright?"

I watched her eyes fill with moonlight and tears.

"More than ever, I need him! And so what? He isn't here. He can't be here. I knew this going in. I accepted it."

"He'd be here if he could," I said.

"I don't want him here. He can't be here. He'd only get hurt."

"But you need him."

"He doesn't need to know about any of this."

I sighed and sat on the stone wall beside her.

"You know what he would do if he were here right now, don't you?"

She nodded and a tear spilled down her cheek.

"Come put your sweet head on my shoulder, lass," I said.

She smiled and sighed, relieving just a smidgeon of that strength she prized.

"Thank you, Ian."

I felt her relax into me, and I smiled.

"Ian."

She looked up at me, her head still on my shoulder.

"Kiss me."

If ever a lass looked more forlorn, I couldn't recall. I leaned down and brushed her lips with mine.

Chapter 43

The skies had begun to lighten with the first of morning riding over the mountains of Ireland. Ian brooded behind me as I pushed open the door and exchanged a look with William. In my absence, he had taken the liberty to clear off the table.

A fresh batch of coffee was brewing and it looked like he had straightened his notes. I was somewhat irate that there was nothing left for me to do and so seated myself at the table and recovered my blanket.

"What time is it?" I asked.

"Nearly dawn," he said. "Are you alright?"

The question surprised me. People don't ask. Then again, I usually do too good of a job hiding things.

Genuine concern blanketed his face while he studied mine and I nodded, not bothering with a fake smile.

"Yes," I said.

"You sound like you have something else on your mind?" he said.

"I do." I nodded. "One final part to all of this."

Broken

I smiled.

William said nothing, but watched and waited, taking his queues from me. I was ready for this day to be over and knew just how to proceed. I jumped back into it for the last time.

* * *

I love animals. I'm an incurable ailurophile, but I adore all animals. When Isaiah proposed, we had a number of pets in the house. In addition to Tribble, we had a lion head rabbit, Lily-Pippin, who had been with us for four years, and a tank full of Shubunkins and Ryunkins. Our fish count totaled more than forty, all of whom I had had more than three years.

Shortly after receiving Tribble's cancer diagnoses, Pippin suffered from a heartache. He died in my arms. I felt him go stiff while I was holding him. Two days later, our fish contracted red velvet disease. Red Velvet disease... I call it White Death. That is exactly what it is. Parasites breed and form a white cloud in the water. They attach themselves to the fish and burrow into them, making them bleed until the fish look like they're covered with red velvet. Any sensible fish owner would think to do a water change, but that in fact kills the fish faster. The parasites cling to the fish during a water change, breed to compensate for the die-off in population, and triple in numbers. The milky residue returns with a vengeance. Every day for three weeks, I woke to find another fish dead.

I was no stranger to grief, but this...

What slowly frayed my sanity was the quantity of death. I couldn't get away from it.

I know they're just fish. It wasn't about the fish. It wasn't how they were dying. Okay, maybe that was it in part. I spent weeks watching parasites burrow holes through the heads of my fish. I had just buried Pippin. Every morning for three weeks, I woke and Death greeted me with another dead fish, and Tribble was dying of cancer. It was in this condition that one of my friends at work killed herself.

If ever there was a day I can say I went mad, it was that day. I couldn't ground myself, I couldn't find myself. I couldn't go home to Tribble who was dying and where Death was there waiting for me. I had no doubt he dipped his hand into the fish tank and had claimed another victim. I drove up to my grandparents' house. I went to the only place I knew would give me solace. I went back to the woods.

I wandered the path and the gorge for hours. I screamed and cried. I can handle grief. But to lose so much in such a short time...

Was it me?

I must have asked that question aloud for an hour before I began screaming at Death. Didn't I have enough? I'd been burying people and pets my whole life. I'm pretty sure I had paid my dues.

Thinking back to that month...

Every time my half-brother beat me, I reflected on what I had done. Why the event occurred. What was it for? After every rape, every death, every trial in my life, I followed it up with one question: What am I being prepared for?

I couldn't believe this was it. I couldn't believe I had endured three years waiting for Piss-ant for nothing. No, that was training for something bigger coming my way. I couldn't believe the rapes with Joe, the rapes with Scott, and the ten years away from Isaiah had been for nothing. I was certain I was being prepared for something. That month with Pippin, my fish, and my friend dying, I was being prepared. I just couldn't see what.

It took me four months to recover from that month. I lost my job. It was two months before the wedding, but this time we were financially stable enough that Isaiah gave me the okay to dedicate all my time to writing.

The process returned me to my cave where I shut myself in with Ian, my book, and me.

Isaiah and I were hand-fasted in the summer of 2013 on the solstice, complete with a forty foot bonfire under the roundest full moon of the year. It was epic. Through all of this, I continued to write my first book. Eighteen months later, I finished. But eighteen months without men, medication, therapy, or counseling was two years too long. David/Isaiah had made me aware of my issues. But addressing them was something entirely different. I regressed.

Within that time, Tribble's cancer had taken a turn for the worse. She purred happily at my side right up to her final day when I made the call and drove her in.

I stayed with her for hours. I held her and cried. We put her in the box and Isaiah helped me bury her. I let her go... No. I didn't. I never let her go. I turned her body over to Isaiah, but hadn't begun to let go. I held myself together. I let the tears fall. But the moment I was inside the house, I broke. I fell to my knees and I screamed long and hard and long and, for the first time in seventeen years, Tribble wasn't there.

I could cry all day and let the grief eat me. She was no longer there to anchor me or bring me back. So, I did what I always do. I shut it down. I buried it. I killed my emotion, and I went cold.

With Tribble's death, time slipped by. The hand-fasting contract between Isaiah and I expired. We had discussed getting legally married, but the financial backlash in the state of New York was financial suicide and so, we did nothing.

Three months later, April of 2014, my book was finished. In October, I launched into the world of social media. I took to it like a fish to water and found that it complemented and enabled my mental state. I made connections, found my editor, and formed writing groups that developed into a strong comradeship. It filled part of the loneliness I had had my whole life.

* * *

By November, I had met Pat online, who offered to beta read my manuscript. Coming from someone of her caliber, the offer she made was a substantial one. One that I am eternally grateful for. Within a few short weeks, she asked if I would be willing to return the favor. I happily agreed.

Her book was about a rape victim.

I thought I could handle it. I thought I was ready. Maybe I wasn't ready. I was certain I was. I explained the situation to Isaiah and he asked if I could handle it. I assured him I could. I told Pat yes.

The next month, I underwent conversations that explored the psyche of a rape victim. By delving into my past, I helped Pat with her character. I was cold, systematic, and logical about the process. I was cold. That should have been my first clue.

Around the same time, I was tearing apart my own manuscript and subjecting it to edits one last time. The work I was doing forced me to contact one of my beta readers: Jacob. He and I had grown quite close and were writing via email nearly every day. The conversations were growing more in depth as we picked apart and analyzed my book.

I plugged away and he did his best to answer, but the emails were limiting us and the topic was delving into a complex area.

"Can I just call you?" Jacob asked.

And there was the panic.

"No! No, I can't!" I wrote.

"Well, how about I text you? I don't have email at the house and this is getting involved. I can just call you and we can get through this a lot faster."

"No! Never mind. Thanks!"

Before he could ask, I was gone.

But a few days later, I was right back to needing the answers I had asked for. I tried again and after several rounds of questions, the answers grew longer.

"Can't I just call you?" Jacob asked.

"No!"

"Text you? Can I text you?"

"I can't!" I wrote.

"Why not?"

"I just can't!"

Online, I was a social butterfly. Online, I was exactly who I wanted to be. Online, I could let my guard down without fear of losing control. And if I had an issue or a bad day, I could hide it so easily from everyone. Online, I was safe.

By the end of the second day, we were back to the same exchange.

"Look, if only for five minutes," Jacob said. "Not long."

"I can't."

"Why?"

I had to tell him.

"I'm a shut-in," I wrote.

"Whaaaaaaaaaaaaat!?"

"Yes. Very. I don't...I don't speak to people. I'm a recluse."

"Okay. Well, how about we text? Can we text? I promise I won't call. I'll just text."

I thought about it.

"Promise no calling?" I said.

"No calling."

I thought about it some more. Already, I felt the panic followed by the arousal. But if we were only texting...

"Okay," I wrote.

The texts lasted a day.

"This is really getting intense," he wrote. "You're really getting involved here. Can I call?"

Panic. I felt myself grow wet and my body responded to the trigger.

"No! No calling!"

"It's okay. I understand no people," he wrote. "But how about we try this out. I'll call and say one word. You don't even have to say anything. You just answer. I'll say, 'sup,' then hang up. You don't even have to say anything."

My body was shaking and the urge to fuck something was unbearable. "I...I can't..."

"Well, what if we just listen to each other breathe? Could you do that?"

He wouldn't back down. He had to understand.

"I'm terrified of men!" I wrote.

Silence.

It felt like forever.

"Whaaaaaaaaaaaaat!?"

Already my state of arousal was high. The panic waged while my body prepared for sex. I knew how bad I had gotten in the last two years. I knew exactly the mindset I was in. If I heard him now, I would throw myself at him. I would absolutely pursue him and beg him to fuck me.

But I liked him. I loved our friendship and I didn't want to change that. I loved writing with him and working with him.

"Please let me call you," he wrote.

I stared at the text.

Why do you care? Why can't you just go? Just go!

I grabbed one of my katanas from the display and clutched it for dear life while waiting for the panic to ease, waiting for my arousal to subside. All I wanted to do all over again was fuck and run, but the urge this time was so much worse than ever before. I couldn't even leave the house.

"I can't," I wrote.

"Why can't you?"

"Because I will fuck you," I wrote. "I will want to fuck you to be safe. But it isn't me. I will tell you things to make you fuck me. I will beg you. But I don't want it. And I would do this to make you love me, so you won't hurt me. But I don't want you to love me. Because you can't have me. And I would hurt you when I leave you. If you call, I will throw myself at you."

"Let me call you," he wrote.

It took me twenty minutes to calm down enough to talk to him. My body shook and I spent the conversation gripping my katana and biting my tongue. I wanted to fuck and run.

He seemed to know exactly what to say. He asked me about my characters and my book. I answered, quietly battling back a plethora of propositions. He asked about my writing and mundane things, things he already knew the questions to. Anything to keep me calm.

I thought knowing what it was inside of me, knowing exactly what I could expect, would make it far more manageable. It didn't. I knew what I wanted. Knew why I wanted and I thought that alone would be enough to control it. It didn't. I made it through three questions before I asked the one question at the forefront of my mind.

"What do you want with me?"

"I want to be your friend," he answered.

"But why?" I asked. "What do you get out of this?"

"What do I get out of it? Our friendship."

"But..." I couldn't understand. "Don't you want to have sex with me?"

"No."

This really confused me.

"I don't understand," I said. "Why would you waste your time with me if you don't want sex?"

"Because we're friends."

I didn't understand. No male had ever wanted to just be my friend. No male was ever just my friend.

"But what is your goal?" I asked. "What is your purpose? If not to sleep with me, then what?"

"I want to show you that you can have a male friend without having sex with them."

I rolled the answer around in my head. I had no idea what to make of it. I could see no error in his logic, no holes in his argument. Not ones I could logically pick apart, but something was still inherently wrong with his logic. I did find his reasoning highly suspicious. I accepted it... for now.

I spoke to Jacob for eight hours that day.

Broken

    I hung up the phone and hugged my legs to my chest. With him off the phone, I felt myself relax again as I eased back into my solitude.

    Aside from my family, it had been nearly two years since I had spoken to a male and that's when I realized, the sessions I had five years ago with David hadn't changed a thing. I was still afraid of men. I was still locked up in a room. I still wanted to fuck them if they came near me. I still had a raging amount of fear inside of me. I was still in the Asian jungles and Angel was screaming.

Chapter 44

I told Jacob about my past. About my rapists and how I had become what I was. A good portion of that day was spent with him calming me down and trying to get me to relax and lower my guard. Now and then he stopped to ask me if I was still afraid. If I still wanted to fuck him.

I told him the truth. That I did. Of course I did. I had made only one proposition the entire conversation. He handled it well. At the end of the day, we parted ways with the decision that he would talk to me the next day. We didn't even get into the writing or work that day. I had a male friend—for the longest time, that word felt weird to me—and he didn't want to sleep with me. I had never had such a thing. Not really. Not without there being some desire there. And if it wasn't there, it's because they weren't that close.

The next day, I spoke to Jacob. Again my panic was high, mirrored by a severe state of arousal. I calmed down faster that day, but was still quiet and on my guard. By the third day, I started opening up. By the end of the fourth day, there was no fear, I was unaroused, and by the fifth day, there was no panic at all. By the fifth day, Jacob and I were as close as two friends could be without being lovers. I think it's called romantic friendship. The kind of friendship where you could sleep in the same bed and not have sex.

Something else happened though, almost at once between us. Something I'm still trying to figure out. We learned that we were strangely comfortable saying anything to each. Anything at all. We could open up and pour our hearts out. I could tell him anything and did. Almost anything. A lot more than I had ever told anyone, even Isaiah. He had the same lack of reserve. We flirted, we played with each other and a good portion of our friendship felt like... nothing I had ever had before. I wanted to curl in his lap and go to sleep. I wanted his arms around me. I felt like a child around him. And he was some sort of sentinel. I was safe in his arms, with him.

* * *

Pat and I weren't done with each other. Far from it. She continued to analyze the mind of a rape survivor while I walked her through certain events, helping her hone the exact thoughts of a victim, based on my experiences anyway. The mental process, the thoughts, the feelings of guilt. She and I debated over her main character's mental profile and how it differed from mine.

I finally reached one point in Pat's book where I could relate to the circumstance perfectly. I was saying things that forced me to confess what I knew Pat already knew. I opened up and told her about my rapes and my views on men. Pat was wonderful. Very understanding and, of course, she had figured it out. It was in one of these conversations where I explained my views on women.

"I'm simply not comfortable with women," I said. "I never had been. I'm still trying to figure you out and a few other women who I have friended recently. I don't understand how we hit it off so well."

Pat's next email began:

"Uhm... Elizabeth. I'm a man."

I wanted to throw up.

Pat and I were close. Granted, not like Jacob and I. But he made it to my inner circle. The error was an honest mistake and Pat went on to explain that he meant no deceit and he didn't. He apologized profusely, and was sincere about the misunderstanding. If I had known he was male, I already would have been flirting and possibly attempted to proposition him. Like this—with him so close and me caught unaware—I didn't know what to do.

I thought back to everything I had said.

Everything was online. I assumed Pat was female. I simply assumed it. I had never asked. Pat certainly had no way of knowing what gender I thought he was. And he set me straight the moment I said, "You're female."

I started playing back through all my conversations with him. Fear, panic, arousal... But hadn't he already proven he was harmless? I had opened up to him. I had told him everything. And he was male.

I wanted Jacob. To crawl in his lap and vanish there.

I wasn't deceived. This I knew. Pat did not lie or try to trick me. It was a genuine mistake because I had assumed. It is still considered rude to ask one's gender online. Stupid propriety. Simply stupid.

I wrote back to Pat and told him it was okay. I wasn't mad or upset. It was my own fault for assuming. Inside, I was scared... unsure. I don't let men in... except Jacob... and here was Pat fully into my circle without the proper preparations.

I was slipping. I felt myself sliding back into the realms of my psyche, back to my rooms with no doors. Jacob was my comfort, my go-to, my answer when I felt scared or shaken up. He held my hand and carried me through the rooms with no doors while Pat and I ventured down the psychological make-up of a rape victim.

I had grown cold, methodical. I was shutting down emotionally. Again, I told everything to Isaiah, relayed everything back as it happened. But I felt myself slipping. I could get through this. I wasn't feeling any of it.

Writing my book was like sliding into one of my worlds. I required little prompting to slip into my tenth century Norway and Ireland. I don't know when it became harder to be in this world than the next. Maybe it was with Tribble's passing. Maybe it was with my rapes revisited. Maybe it was all the research I was doing in Ireland for my book that carried me back to my Irish realm. Maybe it was the online realm I had uncovered through social media. Maybe it was my ever-growing fondness for Jacob. Maybe it was a combination of all those things hitting me at once. Maybe it was Tribble's death, which I was still struggling with.

Somewhere, between all those realms, I turned and saw my Raven.

Chapter 45

All else ceased to be. It was as if he and I stood alone in the world and there was no one else. I climbed out of my mind and touched my bare feet down on Irish grass.

"Hello," I said across the hills. "You're from Eire's Land." I didn't ask.

"Yes," he said.

I came to stand beside him and in my mind, we gazed upon her hills side by side. There was a breeze I could not feel. And cool crisp air I wanted to touch. I could almost taste the wind.

"So, if I were to ask you what Irish air smells like, could you tell me?"

He inhaled and I watched him remember.

"It smells of morning dew on blades of grass and Alder tree, and the faint smell of fireplace..."

Grinning, I fell into his words that gave life to the wind.

"...and sheep poop."

I laughed and he smiled.

"Are you Irish, lass?"

He called me lass. It warmed my heart and my smile widened.

"On my mum's side. Also German and English. But Ireland..."

There was so much I wanted to say. And suddenly, all at once, here, with him, I was at ease like I had never been before.

Together we gazed at the rolling hills and I tried to imagine the scents he described. I inhaled and felt the longing I had known for so long. The secrets in my heart that I had harbored. I looked at him and knew, if anyone would understand, he would. I opened my mouth and said exactly what was in my heart. With him, how could I not?

"Have you ever felt like you belong somewhere else? Like a land calls to you and you hear it, but you can't get to it. So you spend your life trying to replicate it, but all you want to do is go home?"

I felt him slide into my words as I spoke them. He looked at me and I could see the same longing in his blue eyes.

"Yes," he said. I could hear the understanding in his voice. And I knew. He loved her and wanted her as much as I.

"So, I must ask," I said. "Do you like Guinness?"

He chuckled and I grinned. Already, I loved making him smile and every part of me wanted to spend my life making him smile.

"I'm Irish, lass. Guinness is in my blood. It flows with it."

I had been around music and writing enough to know musical prose when I heard it. Every word he spoke was with a rhythm that swept my heart to him and all I wanted was to hear him speak, to bathe in his words like music.

"I love Guinness," I said. "I don't care much for hops, though." I felt the lie and corrected it. "I hate hops. But I love Guinness."

"I hate hops too," he said.
"You write?" I asked.
"Of course," he said.
"And who do you read?"
"I love Poe," he said.
Poe.
"Annabel Lee." I breathed the name.
"Yes!" he said.
I exclaimed. "And the Raven!"
"I love ravens!"
"You remind me of a raven," I said. "Poe's raven." And he did. Something about him, his words, his eyes. Everything about him reminded me so much of Poe. A sweet sensual shadow that lingers over the pages of Poe. That is what he reminded me of.
"I live for macabre," he said.
And the Irish wind blew.
"Poe has a music that no other has mastered," I said.
"Yes!" he said.
"Oh, the music." I sighed.
"The music." He smiled.
"You play?"
"Of course," he said. "Music is my life."
"I breathe it."
"I drink it."
"Make love to it," I said.
We stopped and stared through the Irish air.
"Well," he said.
"For now."
"Sláinte," he said.
I saw my lips move on his.
Instead, I slipped away and returned to the life I had.

* * *

Broken

I lay awake staring at the clock. It was going on three A.M. Why couldn't I think? Why I couldn't I breathe? Why couldn't I move without there being a fire pulse through me? All I could think of was him. Isaiah lay beside me, asleep, unaware of the demons I battled. All other thoughts melted away. No other thought, but my Raven.

Looking at him was like looking into his soul and I saw me standing there. He stared back and I knew he saw himself standing there in me. In that silence, I could see the life I could have with him. I could see him sinking deep into me. Kissing me. Making love to me. We would embrace and lose ourselves in each other.

In that moment, I saw him and I knew, I could love him for the rest of my life.

Careful, Angel said.

Her voice came through loud and clear from her room despite being silent for years.

You could love him, she said. *Too easily, you could love him. And you know what happens to those who you love.*

I hurt them, I answered.

Be careful.

I had warned Jacob. I had told him not to fall in love with me. I checked with him often.

"Do you love me?" I'd ask, afraid of the answer.

"No," Jacob would say. "Don't worry."

I'd breathe a sigh of relief.

"I don't love you," Jacob often reaffirmed.

"Good," I always said. "Don't."

No one can have you, Elizabeth. You're a mistress they can not keep. A lover they can not wife and they'll want to. They always want to. You will know them and love them so deeply, but in the end, you will leave them. You are a woman who can not be had and that hurts them.

She was right. I had to be careful. For I could love him. Yes. If ever there was anyone in this world who I could love as deeply as I knew how, it would be my Raven.
Be careful.

* * *

Be careful.
I repeated the mantra. I could love him too easily. But I can't. Just be careful.
I wandered the hill-side and welcomed the wind that passed o'er me. He was there on the hill and I smiled.
"Dia duit, lass," he said and smiled.
I have loved deeply, passionately, completely, swiftly, and fondly. I have known soft love, gentle love, hard love, crazed love, obsessed love, and love brewed slowly. Love that faded, love that ended dead on a dime, and love I savored... but this... When they say it hits you like lightning, it really does hit you that hard, that sudden, and that strong, and you feel it in that instant.
It was instant... like he took up a sword glowing bright from the forge and thrust the blade hard right through me. He pierced my heart. It impaled me and poured an inferno down into me that spread from my chest to every fiber of my being.
I gasped and in that moment, just like that, I loved him long and deep and hard and for the rest of my life.
I stopped there and stared into his eyes.
He stared back and saw me too.
With but a word, you have the power to reach into the very heart of me and possess me, I wanted to say. Already you own me. I am yours. Command me. I will do as you bid, you only need but to ask. As simple as a smile, a whisper, a wish. I would fight to the ends of the Earth and bring you

back your deepest dreams. Command me. For only then am I whole.

I said none of this.

After a moment, I approached him.

"Beautiful morning," he said. "Almost as beautiful as you."

His words twisted the blade through my heart, but it felt good. Too good.

"It is and..." I made sure he looked into my eyes. "...you need to be careful." *For I could love you until I die and you can not have me, for I can not be had.*

"I'm sorry," he said and it pulled at my heart.

But if anyone were to have me, I'd want it to be you. "Please, no sorrys," I said instead. "You did nothing wrong."

"I'm Irish, lass," he said. "We only ever say sorry."

So like me. You are I, I thought. Again, I saw him in me.

In silence we stood, while I watched the world around me and let my mind wander.

Be careful. Angel's voice rang loud and clear. If he loves you, he can not have you.

But it was too late.

I loved him. I knew the look in his eye, the choices he made with words. He mirrored me. I had no doubt he loved me too. But things were complicated. To leave things unspoken... I may already love him, but that didn't mean...

No. He couldn't have me. He needed to know that.

I thought back to my conversations with Pat and I thought of Jacob. I thought of Isaiah and Nick three years ago. I thought of Joe and Piss-ant and Scott. I thought of everything and Ireland. And standing there, I thought of him.

To thine own self be true.

I never lie. I will never hold back again.

"Why can't I stop thinking of you?" I had but whispered the words, but he heard. He turned and looked at me.

"Forgive my forwardness," I said. "Life's too short. I tend to be blunt."

He was listening.

"I like you," I said. "A lot. Really a lot. So much more than I should. I can't even tell you everything about you that I like because then I would be in serious trouble.

"There are too many reasons why I can't "more than" like you. But I love talking to you. I love what you love and I love the way you speak. I love how much you remind me so much of everything I love, like Ireland, music, writing, Poe, and so... so much more. I love how easy it is to pour my heart out to you."

I watched my words reach down into him. I saw me slide into his mind and heart, just like he had slid into mine. If ever I was meant to love anyone, it was him and I think, at that moment, he knew this.

"So here's the deal," I said. "I tell you that I like you and that I can't ever be more than just your friend. And I won't tell you how much I can't stop thinking about you or how I replay our conversations over in mind a little bit more than I should, or how much I think about making love to you... how much you make my blood burn when I think of you. I won't say any of that. Instead, I will tell you that I like you. A lot more than I should and that we are just friends... good friends... because we can never be more than that."

There, I thought. Good. I said it. I will leave now.

I turned, but he caught my hand and with it, my breath.

"What do you want with me, Raven?"

"This," he said. "What we have. What we are right now. I want you to know that if ever I could, I would go to you so fast."

I could feel the fire. Every word we spoke rode on the heat from the blade he slid through me.

And just like that, I saw the same wants and dreams in me reflected in him, if just for that moment.

In my mind, right there I made love to him. I touched him to watch him move with me. I tasted him, I drank him. I took him into me. When I looked in his eyes, I lived and loved and died in his arms. I loved him as completely and as deeply as I was ever able to love. And all at once, I didn't care what would become of me, what my fate would bring, if I died never being known or remembered. If I died never being loved or accepted again, I didn't care. All that mattered was that I loved him and treasured his happiness far deeper than I could ever love my own.

Our time was up. I had to go back. I could hear the other worlds calling me. I brushed my lips over his and as I turned, I heard him call me, 'Wife.'

Chapter 46

Everything Raven and I had said, everything we had promised each other, simply suspended itself between us. Telling him was supposed to make it easier. So why didn't it? Why couldn't I think? When all I wanted to do was taste him, to know if he savored his kisses slow and sweet. Was he a hungry lover or a domineering lover who took control, delicious, strong control that assured me he would have me, drink me, devour me, with so much assertion I would meet in his arms. Or was he an aggressive partner who would pin me to the wall with his body while he dropped his guard trusting that I could take whatever he gave to me. That I would rise up and meet him.

No. What I wanted more than anything was to sink into his kiss and devour him. Maybe there I could clear my mind and forget the world, our commitments, our lives, if only for a short while. Maybe there I could forget what I was... that I was broken. What I wouldn't give to feel his fingers weave into my hair, while he held me in place and kissed me, drank his fill of me.

I had thought of nothing all week but Raven. I couldn't focus, couldn't think. I couldn't stay in this realm. I so desperately wanted to slip back.

I would moan into your mouth and arch my back, inviting you in. Encouraging you on with every breath I took, I wanted to say to him.

What are you doing? Angel asked.

Ian stood to the right of me, awaiting my answer.

It's Nick all over again, Angel said.

She wasn't wrong. Or was she? I wasn't sure. What was I doing? Was I just repeating behavior from three years ago? Were my feelings legitimate? Was I strapped to the bomb all over again?

I threw that out right away. I was in control. I was certain of that. I could control. This wasn't the same thing. But why was I pushing everything away—my children, Isaiah, this world?

"Elizabeth!"

I came to and looked across the table at the faces of my children while they ate dinner. I wasn't eating. I never ate. I looked at Isaiah, but Ireland came back to me, and I felt the wind wash over me. I breathed deep a—

"Elizabeth!"

I was seated again at the dinner table. Isaiah was there.

"Children, go to your room," he said.

I watched my babes obediently scramble away.

I gazed out the window. The lilacs were sleeping nestled beneath winter's blanket and cold. I missed the lilacs. I missed my roses. I missed my Raven.

"Elizabeth?"

"Hm?" I asked and looked at Isaiah.

"Elizabeth. Are you oka—"

I slipped away again. Back to the lake where Erik stood. I gazed down at the clear still water, but raised my eyes to the steel room. There, Angel lay curled up on the floor.

"It's just like three years ago," she said. "Three years ago, the same. You loved so hard, so completely. You loved Isaiah deeply. But you hurt him then and you will hurt him now."

"And then what, Beth?" Ian said. "Would you then hurt your Raven?"

"I won't hurt Raven," I said. "I won't—"

"If you leave Isaiah, and go with your Raven, you know just what would happen," Angel said.

"I would love him," I said, but Angel was shaking her head.

I looked to Erik standing in his silence and Ian with that hardened look that confirmed he too knew the truth.

"You'd leave Raven like you always do," Angel said. "Like the black widow you are who leaves behind a trail of broken hearts."

"I don't want to," I said. "I'm tired of hurting people. I hurt Isaiah already once before. I didn't want to hurt Isaiah. I didn't mean to. I can not hurt Raven."

"And yet you will," Angel said. "You always do."

"I don't want to hurt them," I said. "I don't ever want to hurt anyone ever again."

"But you will," Ian said.

"You will," Angel said. "You always will."

"You know what this means... Don't you?" I spun around to Erik's voice. Erik who never spoke.

I knew the answer before I spoke it.

"I can't be with anybody," I muttered.

"You are still alone," Angel said. "Trapped in this room with no doors... and the Death Men will find you. The Death Men are there. They will find you."

I threw my hands to my head and I fell to the cold steel floor.

"No matter how much you try," Angel said. "You are alone. It's what you are. Alone. Stop fighting it. Stop running. You were born alone, lived alone, loved alone, cried alone. Tribble is gone. You will die alone."

"I am," I said.

"Even now," Ian said.

"Alone," I whispered.

"Stop running," Angel said.

My hand fell to my lap and the tears stopped. A calm overcame me. Peace.

At least no one would get hurt. "I will leave Isaiah and go to Ireland. There, where no one can find me," I said. "There, I can't hurt those I love. If I can't have Isaiah or Raven or anyone..."

I stood from the floor and looked to each. My Erik, my Angel, and Ian.

"If I am to live the rest of my days alone... at least I can have Ireland. Maybe then the pain won't hurt so much—"

"Elizabeth!"

Isaiah's voice pulled me back and I returned to this world. I was sitting at the dinner table. Isaiah was there waiting as if for an answer.

"Yes?" I asked.

"Where were you just now, because you weren't here?"

Ireland.

He didn't know. Not of my worlds. Not of the voices in my head. No one knew. My future was clear to me. The constant screaming in my head was gone and for once, I knew where I must belong.

"I'm moving to Ireland," I said.

"Yeah. I know," he said.

I blinked with shock.

"How do you mean you know? I only just decided," I said.

He shrugged like I had simply repeated the same hum drum news I'd been spouting for thirty years.

"You've talked of nothing else your whole life and when you said, you'd go, you also said, you could never leave."

"Oh." I thought for a bit. "Well, I'm going."

I stood from the dining table to make my way back upstairs to my room.

"Are you sure this is what you want?" he asked.

I stopped at the kitchen door and turned back to him.

"Will this make you happy?" he asked.

Without a word, I went back to my room and did only what I knew how. I began to write. "Who am I?"

Chapter 47

My editor returned my book to me and the final revisions were coming along. I couldn't focus. I couldn't eat. I couldn't sleep. Every waking, conscious thought was of my Raven.

Every night I lay awake staring at the ceiling and allowing my thoughts to take me back to Ireland. I seemed to spend my days there a lot. There, we made love on the floor of my cottage before the fire. There, only he and I existed.

In this realm, I was cold again. I had fallen back into nothingness. And nothingness is what I had become for I felt nothing but my love for Raven. When I was in Ireland, I could smile, I could breathe, I could fly, if only in my mind. But when Ireland melted away and we parted ways, I dipped back into nothingness again where I lived and where I'd die.

* * *

"How many "slowlys" do you have?" I texted Jacob.

"Ugh! Too many," he replied.

"Such a stupid adverb," I wrote. "Slowly, I sat. Slowly, I turned. Slowly, I trudged... Really! Is there any other way to trudge but slowly? You try it! Trudge quickly then get back to me and report. Such a stupid adverb."

"I'm not trudging quickly," he wrote.

"Why not!?" I wrote. "It's for research!"

"Elizabeth?" I turned to Isaiah behind me. "Nell is here."

I gasped, dropped my phone to my desk, and flew down the stairs.

Penelope who I hadn't seen in months. Penelope who I loved. Penelope, my dearest friend.

I ran into her arms and held her, giggling. "Oh! Dear friend, I missed you so!"

"Have a seat," Isaiah said.

I looked at the table.

My swords were out, three coffee mugs, spoons, and Isaiah wasn't leaving the room.

"This is an intervention, isn't it?" I deduced.

Both looked surprised.

"Oh, damn!" Nell said. "I had a script written up! With lines! I had a power point planned with a flow chart and everything!"

I backed away from the table, putting as much space between them as I could.

Isaiah handed me my sword and I clutched it. I clutched it for dear life and descended into the jungle.

"Here's the thing," Nell began. "We're worried about you."

I'm fine.

"You don't eat. You don't sleep."

I'm in love.

"You don't talk to people.

I'm a writer.

"You never come out of your cave."

I'm a writer.

"Isaiah told me some of the things you were talking about with Pat and Jacob and we're worried, sweetie," Nell said. "That's all."

I wanted to run. I wanted to kill them and run. I wanted to stab them, burn the bodies, and run. Maybe shout something about napalm on my way out the door. One sword wasn't enough. I wanted my combat boots, my fatigues, my war paint, and guns. As far as I was concerned, this was war and I was lord of the jungle. I needed to fight.

"We think it would do you well to speak to a therapist," Nell said.

A therapist. A head doctor. I needed one. I know I needed one. But I couldn't be fixed. I knew this. I was fine with what I was. Why couldn't they be? Why couldn't they accept what I had already chosen? That I was destined to be alone.

"I don't have a problem seeing a doctor, but the ones I need aren't good enough in this area," I said. We lived in the ass of New York and it had the worst case of crotch rot imaginable. "I'll have to go to the City or Boston to find what I need."

"There may be something here," Isaiah said. "You need meds."

"I'm not taking meds." I took them once. I remembered too well.

"You have issues," Nell said. "You're not dealing with them."

"Aren't I?" I asked.

"No," Isaiah said. "You're not."

I thought I was. "I took on Pat's rape book. I'm dealing with it. I'm working through things with Jacob."

"We think you need more," Nell said.

"I'm getting more!" I said. "I'm planning on getting a group together to talk!" And I was too.

Silence.

"You are?" Nell asked.

"Yes!" I said. "I have four others who I am close to online. We started a group a few months ago with just the five of us. There is a male in the group. I was planning on talking to them."

"When?" Isaiah asked.

"Next week," I said. I wasn't lying. "I have to wait for one of the members to settle some personal problems she's having, but then, yes. I was planning on talking to them about my past."

"Damn it!" Nell said. "One week!" She looked at Isaiah. "I told you we should have waited!"

"I can handle this!" I said. "I don't need you. I don't need anybody! I will handle this as I have always handled everything. Alone!"

"But you're not alone," Isaiah said.

"I am!" I shouted. "And I want to be! I like alone! It's what I am. What I have been. What I always will be. I don't have a problem with my being alone. Why do you?"

"Because it isn't normal," Nell said. "It isn't healthy."

"It's normal for me," I said. "It's what I know and it's safe! I like it! What isn't okay for me is people. When they're around me, I'm scared. Like right now. I want to kill you both and run. I want to fight before you hurt me! I feel like I'm playing a game of Russian Roulette with every person I know and all I want to do is pull the trigger before they kill me!

"I know this! I know I can't be around people and I've accepted this." I was defensive, but calm. No anger. Frustration. Desperation. They had to hear. To understand. "I have finally come to terms with this. And I'm happy here!

For the first time in my life, I'm happy. Why can't you accept this?"

"And what about your friends?" Nell asked. "And Isaiah?"

"So long as you're not close, I know what to do with you," I said. "It's when you're close that I can't see you as friend or foe. Get too close, and I won't recognize you. I'll attack you and I'll hurt you. Just go away. I don't want to hurt anyone ever again."

Nell and Isaiah exchanged a wordless conversation filled with confusion.

They weren't understanding it at all. I could see that. They were looking at me blinded by shock and I knew. Neither could understand why anyone would ever consciously choose the life I had made. I wanted them to understand. I wanted them to know. I wanted them to be at ease and not to worry or hurt with my decision.

"I know three things," I said. "I am beautiful, I am smart, and I should have been a boy because my daddy told me so. I live every day wanting my father to love me and knowing he never will. I grew up under Shaun's fist while he threatened to kill me every damn day. I watched him stone animals to death and throw their mangled bodies at me. He tortured my cats to lure me out of my room, so that he could beat me. And when I cried to my parents, I was told that "boys will be boys" and that I "deserved" it. I have heard rabbits scream. I have held cats dying in my hands. I was the only one who loved them. It was the least I could do for them. I grieved for them alone.

"Every day of my life that I cried, I cried alone. Every cat of mine who I buried, I grieved alone. I grieved until I learned how to do it alone. I lay bleeding and broken on the floor of my room waiting for someone. . . anyone to pick me up, and no one ever came. I had no friends, no parents, no kin that cared or knew of the isolation I endured. When I tried to run away, I was scolded. When I slit my wrists, I was laughed at. I was forever screaming and no one ever heard me."

It all flowed out. It all poured out, and I couldn't hold it in any longer. I ripped the chains from Angel's hands. I broke the locks on the boxes that held my emotions and I released it all.

"The lack of a father's love drove me to seek it out in others. And those who I found were cruel monsters. They beat me, they raped me, they enslaved me. They reinforced that no one loved me. That I was worthless. And when I found the strength inside of me to leave my rapist after being locked in a room for six months where I lived as his sex slave, I was picked up by a pedophile who raped me for five more years.

"He made me watch movies to arouse me so he could queue my body to respond to his will. He taught my body to lust, depend, and need sex every time I felt fear or anger or watched television. He would reward me with books, the only luxury I had when I was a teenager. I was starved for them. And those books were all I had so that I could learn to escape the hell I was in.

"I taught myself logic and philosophy so that I could win my freedom.

"And when the New York towers fell that September, he raped me. Do you want to know how I spent my September 11th? I was raped. While New York screamed and bled and died, he raped me and the towers fell. And then he left me, crying and naked on my bed, while he ran back to New York.

"While the country screamed that day, I lay naked on my bed unable to go home, unable to be with my people, unable to pull their bodies from their hell. While I lay in mine, all I could think of was theirs. Smelling of the sex I said I didn't want, I lay there, where he left me alone to cry. I should have gone home! He should have died that day! Not them! Not my kin!"

I fell to the floor and I screamed. I listened to Nell cry between my own sobs. Neither Isaiah nor Nell moved.

"So, no," I said. "I do not believe in a god. I do not believe in love. I do not believe anyone should trust. I don't believe in chivalry, or a knight in shining armor who will save me. I do not believe in intimacy or gentleness. I believe in myself! I stood up on my own every time and I fought back! I took my beatings and I smiled because I refused to cry! I refused to cave! I survived! And now I can not live as if I belong in anything but a war! It's all I have ever known! I am broken.

"And now you want to tell me there is hope. There is love and help. Now you wish to tell me that everything I ever believed up to now has been a lie? Forgive me. But I don't see it. I have never seen anything, but the nightmare."

They let me rant. They let me talk. They watched me scream as I backed away, grasping my sword. As I calmed down, I drew nearer and lowered my weapon, only to raise it again and pace as they pressed me. The day wore on for hours. Six hours of them drilling me, putting my logic to the test. My reasoning. I was worn and beaten and exhausted.

It was with a weary head that I dropped, finally, into a chair at the table with them.

"I have lived my whole life on an island," I said. "And there, I am safe. There, I know who I am, what I am, and what I am to do. Fight and kill. There is a war on my island. I know the war I am fighting is against myself. I know the bullets and bombs in the air are my own. I have my swords, my machete, my fatigues. I'm in the jungles of Cambodia and I am there alone.

"If someone approaches, I will not see friend from foe. I will see only a threat, and I will kill. I will kill before you can kill me. No one can be on this island. No one can be with me. Get on your boats and stay at sea where I can recognize you as friend. I will venture out to visit you on occasion. But if you ever come to my shores, I won't ask who you are or what you are. I will kill you. That is how I have lived. That is how I will continue to live. And this is how I will die. This is how I have ever lived. It's what I am. I've just now accepted it. I'm not fighting it anymore."

"But you don't have to," Nell said.

"Doesn't matter," I said. "This is what I know. This is where I'm safe. War is comforting to me like mother's milk. Like a womb. I'm thirty-five. I've known nothing else. You're not going to change me now. You can't fix me. I'm too broken."

"Don't you want someone there with you?" Nell asked.

And then I thought of him, my Raven, and he was there with me.

I slipped back into that world. He was beside me seated in the grass while I sharpened my swords. And I knew, he had been there all along. He and he alone. He who I trusted. He who loved me. He who wanted me as much as I wanted him. And that, I did not doubt. Not for one moment. He who, in the depths of his fibers, there beat a man as gentle and quiet and honest as I had once been beneath my own armor and war.

I had forged myself a cocoon made out of dragon-skin. Forged a shell as hard as tungsten and in the tender center within me, there sat the child that I once was, barefoot with hair to my knees.

Broken

The battles scars couldn't touch me, not there. That child would forever play in the gardens and dance with the rain. The child who would bury her face into lilacs and roses and blooms of hyacinth, and breathe in their sweet perfumes. She could ride on the wind and bathe in the stars. She who danced beneath the moon hearing music of her own as she ran through the shadows of the forest. The same child who scaled barefoot the cliffs of her glen and stripped her clothes off to stand naked in the rain while she gazed out over the waterfalls.

That was who I was. Who I fought to protect. She was fragile and kind and gentle and bore not a single scar from the war I had fought for her. Forever protected in her dragon shell from my scars and my blood. She remained unscathed and pure.

She was the keeper of my smile and my laugh. She who housed my hopes, my dreams, my spirit. She was the center of my being, the bane of my existence, she was my be-all and end-all. She is who I gave to my Raven.

All others who knew me saw only snippets and parts of her. All others caught glimpses of a giggling girl who left a trail of sunlight in her wake. Zipping about them like a sprite on the currents of an Irish stream. No other ever got close enough to see more than just a glimpse. But my Raven, my beautiful gentle raven. He was strong enough and quiet enough to enter. Only he ever saw her, only he could possess her, only he I wanted inside.

I believe he too has a boy inside of him much like my girl. With the same deep seated joy. Pure and simple and perfect joy. Keepers of our smiles and laughter. I could see him with a bow he fashioned for himself, climbing trees barefoot paying no mind if the bark scraped his feet. I could see him running wild across the plains. I could see him playing with the goats and running alongside me in the forest barefoot enjoying the occasional prick of a fallen pine needle on our arches. I know because I did this too and I know he knows it.

"Elizabeth," Isaiah called.
I came to and focused on the kitchen.
"What?" I asked
"You blacked out again," he said. "Where did you go?"
"Uh... Ireland," I answered.
I watched Nell and Isaiah exchange a set of worried glances.
"You need help, Elizabeth," Isaiah said. "You need a doctor."
"You find me one who can handle this, and I'll go."

Chapter 48

Morning light poured in through the green room window as I gazed at William, awaiting his questions and response.

He cleared his throat, dry from not speaking for the last few hours.

"Your Raven," he asked. "Was he real?"

I smiled slyly.

"I can't tell if he was a real man you met," William said. "Or if he was another character you saw in your mind like Ian or Erik."

My cat mewed at the birds outside the bay window.

"Is Raven real?" he asked.

"That's the question now, isn't it?" I asked.

"Are you living in Ireland now to be with him, or are you living here to live out a fantasy you had?"

I sighed and gazed out the window to stare at the Irish morning light. The forest beckoned. Outside my door, I knew the stream rushed through the wood. Skies were clear. The evening's storm had passed.

"I do so love Ireland," I said. "I could just be living in Ireland because I love Eire and used Ireland as a metaphor for something completely unrelated. I may be here because it reminded me of my mother and those rare moments I could see her smile. Perhaps I am here because I truly do look to be alone from all others. I spent my life wishing to be a hermit. Or, my Raven could have been a deeper level of intimacy between Jacob and I. Or..." I grinned. "... I wrote the whole thing in to screw with you."

William pensively shifted his eyes.

"Is Raven real?"

"Everything I have told you, through my perspective, was real," I answered.

He nodded, but said nothing.

"There was more I needed to say," I said. "More I needed to tell him, but the words, they alluded me at that time. He needed to know so much more. He needed to know that I believed we would come together. Right there, at that moment, I could see us loving each other to the end of our days. With a silent love, the kind we never speak of, for why waste words on what can not be?"

"Because life is short and you refuse to live with regrets," William said.

I gazed at William. The boy had my attention.

"What would you say to him?" he asked. "If he were real, I mean... If he is real?"

"That, despite my belief—that love was passing and faded and grew and changed—that I did believe I would love him to the end of our days," I said. "I could see us, he and I, forever using the other as a source of comfort when all else failed us. Because, while neither of us could ever completely trust anyone, we could and did trust each other enough and somehow, we knew we would not fail the other to the best of our ability. That, if ever we did fail each other, we would know that the other tried their best and that was all that mattered.

"I would tell him that—although I can not marry ever again, and although I needed my space and my freedom to ebb and flow like the waves—that I truly, sincerely, wanted to try with him. That while I ran from door to door, or man to man, while I lived my life loving and smiling and laughing as much as I could, that my door, my heart, and my bed, forever had a place for him. And that if he ever wanted more, he had but to ask and I would do my best to let him break me in. If ever there was anyone who could break me, he could."

William listened, no longer interested in scribbling his notes. I continued.

"For the first time in my life, for him, I wanted to be fixed. I wanted to be normal. I wanted to be able to settle down, marry, grow old, and die with him. And that, even though I couldn't, I sure as hell wanted to try. And more than ever, I wanted all those things with him. That is how he made me feel."

"So Raven is your hope? Your future? Your potential?"

I grinned. "Perhaps."

William grimaced.

"I love him so completely that I would never take anything from him or cause him pain," I said. "I would sooner keep my silence, and bear my burden alone, than share my pain and hurt him. I love him so completely that, for the first time in my life, I truly valued someone's happiness above my own. No judgment. Pure freedom. Complete love. That is what I gave him. That is what I still wish for him. That is all I can ever do for him because I love him."

The sun rose, spilling its light into my cottage.

"When did you move to Ireland?" he asked.

"I made the decision in March of 2015. I realized how stupid it was to love something so completely and not do something about it. I loved Ireland. For as long as I could remember, I was called to the land of my kin. She is in my blood and everything that I am, everything that I loved, supported, and embraced came from Ireland.

"Like my kin, I loved, revered, and worshipped knowledge and the written word. Music, earth, the rains... It was time to go home. I wanted to go home. My children were young. My youngest was seven at the time and legally I was not allowed to move them out of the area without permission. On 7 March 2015, I made the decision to move as soon as my youngest turned eighteen.

"I began learning Irish-Gaelic and researching everything required to move there. I dedicated the next ten years to saving up and preparing for the move. In 2025, I moved. After a couple years living here, I found a place I could afford and settled in."

"Alone," William said.

"Always alone," I said.

"And you're happy here? Like this?"

"I am a wife that can not be had," I said. "From a distance, where my issues can not be seen, I am a laid back, gentle, kind, beautiful, intelligent woman with a sharp wit, thick skin, and the balls to drink you under the table or to try.

"I love easy, judge no one, laugh often, and smile always. I listen, I love, I joke, I support, I comfort. I keep my tears in check, my emotions in check, and my heart is forever open. I am not jealous, I give you freedom, speak my mind. I do not lie, and will never seek to change you or hold you down. And I hold all the passion of Ireland in my heart. To boot, I took the time to learn what a man wants and needs... in and out of bed. I don't cook. And I can not be had. If you're lucky, I'll love you. Don't ever love me back. I'm only worth a dollar."

I watched William slowly pack up his bags.
"Something is on your mind. Speak, William."
"Nah, it's nothing," he said.
I rolled my eyes and added an impatient sigh.
"If you've learned nothing from me, learn this," I said. "Life is short! Be brave! Be bold! Be blunt! No regrets!"
He threw down his files. I could see the angst boiling over.
"Speak your mind boldly, William," I said.
"You want bold?" he asked. "You wasted your life!"
"Did I?"
"You're here alone and dying... alone! And you don't have to be! You can have love. You have it waiting for you!"
"Perhaps," I agreed.
"Then why don't you take it?"
I shrugged. "It isn't worth the risk."
"Risk?"
"Where I stand, I am alone. Just alone. And I can handle alone. But if I do as you say, open up and let others in, if I take that chance then I risk disappointment. And not only will I be alone, I'll be disappointed as well and that, I can not bear."
"But you'll gain so much," he said.
"You say," I answered. "I may. But it's not worth the risk."
"So you choose this as an alternative?"
"I do."
"Loneliness is horrible!" he said. "Why? Why would you ever choose this when you had love? You had it! People spend their lives getting what you had! And you threw it

away! And for what? For Ireland? For someone who lives in your mind? A fantasy?"

"You presume too much, William."

"So he's real?" William asked.

"He could be."

He released a growl and bellowed. "You had it!"

"No!" I shouted. "I didn't. Loneliness is something I have battled my entire life. Or so I thought. One day I finally realized that I was fighting something I could not change. Loneliness is the state of isolation and no matter how many people I let in, no matter how many lovers, husbands, friends I had... my state of loneliness was a constant.

"I didn't choose loneliness. I simple chose to accept it! To stop fighting it. Once I did that, my war ended. What I chose was to no longer bring anyone down with me. I am a black widow. I am the worst kind. I am the widow who destroys lives, kills hearts, and shatters dreams and walks away, leaving the man a hollowed shell and a life that resembles mine. And I do this without wanting or meaning to. I do it without knowing I've done it at all!

"But I, unlike them, am broken. I'm fucked up so much that I can live quite comfortably with my lot. While others—normal people, unbroken people—can't. No one is scarred enough to live with me. Not Isaiah. Not even Raven. So, no, William. I am too broken to be loved."

I watched William rub his hands over his face with frustration. I felt sorry for him. But I couldn't let him leave here without understanding what I was.

"I am the other side of sane," I said, "if you think of sanity as a tunnel with one end bright and clear and happy. We all proceed down this tunnel. And the deeper into this tunnel we go, the darker, more insane you get. Some people, like Jacob, never even entered the tunnel. While others—Joe—entered and made it back out. Some went so deep that they went insane, lost the ability to cope, or killed themselves. Hemingway went there. Van Gogh. Others entered the darkest caverns into despair and made it out again, the worse for wear. That is where your murderers, rapists, and pedophiles go.

"I found the tunnel's end and the light that shines from the other side of sanity. Who others have done what I have done and have emerged unscarred, unscathed, and as kind as I? I am still smiling a warm and sincere smile. While others emerge cold and cruel and vile.

"I have simply come to terms with what I am and I know if I were to change this about me, I could not live as I do now, happy and content and alone. If I try to fix this mess I have become, I will not survive it. And will do more damage than good. No. There are no others like me. I am very much alone, as I will ever be."

"Where is Isaiah?" William asked. I thoughts this was his main concern.

"Isaiah spends his time in the States," I said. "Now and then he makes it to Ireland. We talk often and are still very close friends."

"What about sex?" he asked.

"We can if you want. Means no difference to me. How's the table sound?"

He looked at me in horror.

"Sorry," I quelled my chuckle. "That was a little bit of me coming out again."

He rolled his eyes, shook his head and wiped the sweat from his brow.

"My needs are met," I answered.

"What?" he asked with his face scrunched up.

"My needs are met," I assured him and smiled. "I am smiling with my head held high. I am smiling with my face to the sky. And although I am dying inside, I am crying with my head raised high. I only wish to love greater than I have hurt. And I will spend the rest of my days laughing and smiling to compensate for all the crying I have done."

His shoulders sagged and I saw the defeat.

"But you'll be alone," he said.

"Yes." I gave a nod.

"And you'll die alone."

"Alone," I said. "Yes. I shall die exactly as I have lived: alone."

William took up his files and his recorder. I watched him slip on his coat, and, after throwing his bag over his shoulder, he went to my door.

"For what's it's worth, Elizabeth, I'm sorry."

I smiled.

"Oh, dear friend. Do not pity me. It is I who pities all of you."

"You pity. . . " He shook his head.

"For I live in the world of fantasy quite easily. I can embrace everything that I love, that I want, that I am, and I do it freely, openly. . . bluntly. Adverbs really are a wonderful thing. I live with no guilt or regret. Ever. Every choice I make is mine and I'm free. While others are still in search for happiness, for their balance, I have finally found mine. And I didn't find it in money, success, or love. I found it in me."

"But it cost you," he said.

"Despite my trials, my beatings, my rapes, I had a very great life and it was all worth it," I said. "Every moment."

I watched him nod. He understood. He heard. And with a bit of a smile upturned on his lips, he closed my door behind him.

Epilogue

For the first time in decades I was free of the past, free of the screams, free of the room that bound me. I gasped and dropped my head to my hand. The elation, the pressure, the relief flooded through me and I permitted myself this moment to breath. I smiled as I cried. It was done.

I gazed at the ninety-six thousand word manuscript and punched in the words 'THE END.' I hit save and sat back in my chair for a moment and took up the warm Guinness sitting beside me. After chugging the last of the beer, I returned my hands to the keys.

"Control. Home," I said as I enter the command into my keyboard. Under the word 'Broken,' I typed 'by William D. Shaw' then sat back in my chair and relished the accomplishment just as the familiar plink of an email notification came through.

Heat filled my chest. I grinned wide and felt the haze invade my mind. I clicked on the message and slipped back into Ireland where I lay smiling in Raven's arms. Together we watched the fire from the piles of blankets, clothes, and pillows scattered about on the cottage floor.

I felt him kiss the top of head and I tightened my hold on him.

"You know none of this is real, right?" he whispered. "It's just a fantasy."

I buried my face in his chest and felt him breathe beneath me.

"I know that," I said. "But if I can't have you, then I'll settle for Ireland. Besides I've had a bad day today and I need this. I want to cry."

"Cry?" I heard the worry in his voice. "No, no, no. Don't cry."

He took my face in his hands and brushed my tears away. He kissed my bottom lip softly.

"What's wrong, dear?"

"Such a bad week," I said. I wanted to tell him about the intervention, about the book, about... everything.

"I'm sorry, lass," he said. "Lay your sweet head on my chest."

And I obeyed. A lot had been said that week. There was a lot he needed to know. There was too much he needed to know if this was to go any further. I couldn't have him come to me thinking I could be a wife. Thinking I would be okay as just a wife. He needed to know what I was. He needed to know what I am.

"There's a lot you need to know," I began.

He ran his fingers through my hair.

"I'm broken," I said. "I'm afraid of relationships. Fucking terrified of relationships. I can't be married. I can't have anyone close to me. That's how I live. I'm comfortable around war. With my swords and my war paint. And alone. Always alone. It's like I live on an island with my war and I'm alone and I love it."

His breathing had slowed as if all his attention went into listening to me. I felt fear and angst from him.

"But you. . ." I looked into his eyes. "You walked in and sat down beside me and it feels so right. I can't live without you. I love what we have, where we are. . . And if ever there is a chance for more, I would take it in a moment's breath. I love this. Whatever it is, I love it. I need it so much in my life. I need you. I need exactly what we are like this."

"So you just want a friendship from me?" he asked. I felt the worry like he was losing me. "Do you not like me anymore than just that?"

I hadn't been clear.

"Oh, no! No, no, no, no, no," I said and sat up.

"So all you really want from me is sex?" he asked.

I saw the fear in his eyes. Fear I understood. I smiled with relief. I knew at last the words to say.

"Absolutely not," I said. "I would want you to teach me. I would want you to teach me how to be intimate and how to let you in. I would show you all my cards, everything that I am and I would say please teach me to be gentle and sensual and romantic. Please teach me how to accept love because I don't know how."

I felt him relax again under me and I moved my mouth over his then pulled my fur hide blanket over us. He needed to hold onto me as much as I to him. We needed each other. I wasn't sure why. As we lay by the fire, I ran my fingers through his hair until he slept holding me. And still I lay listening to him breathe.

I had spoken to my group of friends. But it still left me without answers. Pat's book was finished, and my services on that project were no longer needed. Jacob and I had found a comfortable balance with our friendship. But the conversations, the reflections, the questions raised, there was simply too much still left unanswered.

"This isn't real," I heard him say and I lifted my head from his chest.

"What?" I asked. He was awake and watching me with such sadness in his eyes.

"None of this," he said, indicating the room. "It isn't real. Not I. Not this... not any of it."

I furrowed my brow. Had the last two months really meant nothing to him?

"Why would you say this to me?" I asked.

"Because it's true," he said. "You need to hear it."

The room was getting dark. It was harder to see him. Ireland was slipping and I was falling. "It's time to wake up from the lies, Elizabeth."

I sat staring at my computer. The sun in New York was shining. The window was open and a cold spring breeze blew in. I looked at the room around me. The air around me was real. I could smell the spring air. I could feel the chill. I could see the yellow paint on my bedroom walls. It was all surreal and I felt like I was standing in a Dali painting.

I saved "Broken," then opened a new window on my computer and did the only thing I knew to do. I wrote.

"*Pleasuring you has always been my greatest pleasure even when it meant your pleasure would equate to my pain. Regardless of whether I meant something to you or not, that doesn't matter. You meant the world to me right up to the end, even when you found a way to wake me from the lies. And for that, you will always be my dearest friend, my sweetest love, regardless of whether or not you were real.*"

I stood from my office chair and absorbed the numbness. The children were outside playing. Their laughter

Broken

sounded so strange, as if the worlds in my head were more real to me than this one... as if I had forgotten how to use my senses. I smelled the spices and beef from the stew cooking downstairs in the kitchen. I had no doubt Isaiah would have dinner ready soon. A trip to the kitchen was in order. I needed another Guinness anyway.

Did I really *need* a Guinness? Was I really that dependent on alcohol? When did that happen?

I slowly walked down the stairs, bracing myself on the walls as if I didn't trust my own feet to keep me upright. Downstairs, I scanned the living room as if seeing it for the first time. I couldn't assess the level of danger. But my guard was up and I desired my swords. I eyed Abigail resting against the living room wall and turned the corner into the kitchen as I replayed the question Isaiah had asked me twenty days ago on the seventh of March.

I'm moving to Ireland, I had said.

Are you sure this is what you want? he had asked. *Will this make you happy?*

Thirteen days had passed since I had sat down with the children to eat that day. I set to work on *Broken* that night. I had done little else since then. I had eaten almost nothing. I looked like a skeleton dripping with skin. My face was sallow and sunken in. A streak of silver now framed my face. How long was I gone? Had I really changed that much?

I found Isaiah beside the kitchen sink.

"It's done," I said.

Isaiah studied my face. Already I could feel my sanity slipping with my nerve. The emotions were heavy. There were too many.

"Your memoir?" he asked.

I nodded. "Yes."

He tossed the dish cloth into the sink. He was angry. I wanted to kill him, to attack and run.

"And?" he asked. "Have you made your decision?"

"Yes," I said. Already, I felt my mind slipping back to the worlds I now knew weren't real. I shifted my eyes around the kitchen. It felt foreign, dangerous. I couldn't determine one world from the next. It was so hard to stay in this realm. It hurt to stand there, to feel. It hurt to use my senses. The emotions were raw. I could feel them moving in. They would be here soon and so much more than I ever could handle on my own. I needed help.

I looked at Isaiah and found his eyes through my madness.

"I think it's time I see a doctor."

* * *

The individuals portrayed as Elizabeth's Father, Shaun, and Scott no longer exists.

Thank you for listening, and, as always, thank you for your support.

May the kindest of words always find you.

– Angela B. Chrysler

* * *

Congratulations! You have unlocked "The Looking Glass." Go to http://www.angelabchrysler.com, search "The Looking Glass," and enter the password "Don Quixote" to access the special features reserved just for you.

Acknowledgements

Deepest thanks goes to my husband, for his eternal love, patience, and endurance. You truly are the rock in my storm.

Thank you, my three wonderful children, for your endless love and the hundreds of hugs a day.

Thank you, Stanislava D. Kohut, for your understanding, encouragement, friendship, and on-going support.

Thank you to Mia Darien my beautiful editor. Without you, I would be lost. Thank you to Indigo Forest Designs for another gorgeous cover.

Thank you to my family, who have always done their best, even in our darkest times. Special love and thanks to my brother, Adm. You have no idea how much you mean to me.

And thanks to you, dearest reader, for taking the time to listen to my story. I can not begin to tell you how good it feels finally being heard.

I have no intent on shutting up.

To the lonely, abused, and unheard...

A very special note to you, who read this book because you saw similarities in your own life and could relate. I know you'll read this book. I know because I too read books like this to see if others are ever like me and to feel not so alone. Memoirs of trauma survivors are becoming one of my favorite things to read. It is as if we are speaking to each through our books and saying, I know and I understand. You are not alone. Through these pages I speak to you and say, I know, I understand, and you are not alone. There are many of us, just like you trapped in our own hell. We're looking for each other. I'm on the other side and I'm telling you, it gets better. Hang in there. You are enough. Be strong. You are enough. Your time will come. Trust that there are others out there willing to hear you. They will listen. They will help. Don't give up. You are enough.

About the Author

Angela B. Chrysler is a passionate writer, made logician out of need to escape a pedophile. She is also a die-hard nerd, who studies philosophy, theology, historical linguistics, music composition, and medieval European history

in New York with a dry sense of humor and an unusual sense of sarcasm.

Ms. Chrysler is a survivor. She lives in a quiet garden, far away from noise and abuse, with her husband and children, who love her and often ask for hugs. She also lives with three spoiled cats, who will never be hurt again. http://www.angelabchrysler.com

Read side notes, follow the author's healing progress, and learn about her diagnoses in her online therapy journal "Unbreaking Me"

http://www.angelabchrysler.com/category/unbreaking-me/

Manufactured by Amazon.ca
Bolton, ON